Journey to High Lonesome

Journey to High Lonesome

Men of the Outlaw Trail

ROSANNE BITTNER

Dedicated to fellow writers and dear friends, Lucy Kubash (Will O' The Wisp), and Diana Stout (Determined Hearts). Writers need what we call beta readers to help us be the best we can be, which means unselfishly sharing honest criticism and suggestions with each other. Lucy and Diana saw a problem with my original plot for this book, and their observations led to a re-write that made this a much better story than the first version.

Also, a big thank you to my new editor, author Laurie Kuna, (Some Practical Magic) who is also a retired English teacher and a beta reader for several other authors.

Lucy Kubash – www.lucynaylorkubash.com
Diana Stout – www.sharpenedpencilsproductions.com
Laurie C. Kuna – FaceBook: Author Laurie Carroll Kuna

All characters in this novel are fictitious. Any resemblance to those who might have lived during the time and locations in this story is purely coincidental.

Table of Contents

Prologue ...

November, 1862 ...

Ashley stood at the side of the livery barn, shivering with dread at the shouted accusations of the citizens' mob nearby. She could hear her father's pleas with men who'd been his friends most of his life, but the current mood in Texas had a way of ignoring friendships. A young man was dead, and someone should pay.

"Nick Calhoun saved my daughter from a fate worse than death!" Ashley's father bellowed. "Sid MacIntyre beat her and was trying to do worse when Nick stopped him. All of you know the kind of bully Sid was! At seventeen, he was bigger than most grown men! He should have gone with his brute of a father to fight for the Confederacy instead of staying home to prey on innocent young women. He *deserved* to die!"

The air filled with yelling and arguments, both for and against hanging Nick Calhoun. Gainesville itself was in a hanging mood. Just the previous month forty-one men had been hanged for suspicion of being Union sympathizers, most of them with no trial at all. Now Ashley feared Nick would suffer the same fate, just because he'd defended her.

A big, strong Irishman five years her senior, Nick had caught Sid MacIntyre attacking her in the barn at her father's farm. Nick's Irish temper and big fists took charge, and he'd beaten Sid to a bloody pulp—a beating that had led to death when Sid hit his head against a support post in the barn and cracked his skull.

Ashley covered her face with her hands. If they hanged Nick, she would want to die, too.

"Nick Calhoun came here from New York City," one of the men in the mob reminded others. "He's no Texian, and he's no *Confederate*. His parents were foreigners. If you're not *from* this country, you're not a citizen, and you're definitely no *Texian!*"

More shouts ensued, until Ashley's father was able to quiet most of them again.

"Nick has worked on my farm for six years now," Howard Vale retorted. "Long enough to *become* a Texian—*and* a Confederate! He's like a son to me, and he's my best farm hand. My *foreman*. I'd trust him not just with *my* life, but my wife and daughter's lives, too. Sid's death was an *accident*, and all of you damn well know it!"

The men quieted, mumbling among themselves. Ashley took hope in the fact that they seemed to be considering leniency for Nick. Howard Vale wasn't a big man, but he had an air of authority about him. He was a prosperous farmer and well respected in the community. Others usually listened to him, and that seemed to be happening here.

"Nick can be a great benefit to the Confederate cause," her father reminded the crowd. "Let him live and fight for *Texas!*"

Shouts filled the air again, this time in support of the war and Texas.

"Wait a minute! Wait a minute!"

Ashley recognized the voice of Till Brady, who owned a grocery store in town.

"Ask yourselves why Nick went into that barn in the first place."

More mumbling could be heard—raised voices again.

"Howard, how do you know he wasn't going there to abuse your daughter *himself*? He's of an age to be noticing her as a woman."

Ashley sucked in her breath at the ugly remark.

"You take that back," she heard Nick shout. "I would *never* hurt Ashley or take advantage of her!"

"She's a beautiful young woman now," Till yelled back. "Do you really expect us to believe you haven't noticed?"

"You filthy-minded sonofabitch," Nick growled. "Ashley Vale is like a *sister* to me, and she's an honorable young lady who doesn't deserve the insult you just suggested. You should apologize to her father for what you just insinuated!"

"Or what?" Till answered. "You'll *kill* me?"

Ashley heard scuffling sounds and shivered with dread.

"Get him off! Get him off!" men yelled.

Ashley peeked around the corner of the livery to see men pulling Nick and Till Brady apart.

"That's enough!" Ashley's father shouted. He faced Till, once men dragged Nick out of the way. "What you implied is an insult to my daughter. She would never invite such a thing, and Nick would never take advantage. She's been alone with him out there on the farm several different times. He's never even gone into the *house* when she's there alone."

"How would you know, if you're not there?" Till spit back.

Ashley moved out of sight again, covering her face at the awful remark, which felt even worse after what she'd just been through with Sid MacIntyre.

"I know because I know Nick Calhoun and I know my *daughter*!" Howard answered.

There came a pause.

"All of you need to stop this!" Howard added. "I never want to hear a suggestion again that my daughter is anything but honorable. And I have no doubt about how much Nick Calhoun respects my wife *and* my daughter!"

"Were you going to let him stay out there alone on the farm with them when you march off to war the day after tomorrow?" Till asked.

"Of course, I was," Ashley's father answered. "But if you men are going to think the worst if I do, I won't let that happen—not to Nick *or* to Patricia or Ashley! I'll take Nick with me when I go. He's strong and he's good with a rifle. He'll be a great benefit to the Confederacy! Make his service to Texas be his punishment—his *sentence,* if you want to call it that."

"I guess that wouldn't be so bad," another man spoke up. It sounded like Harvey True, the town blacksmith. "Heck, we all know Sid MacIntyre is the one we should be talking about when it comes to abusing women. He's always been a trouble-maker—him and his father both. The fact remains that he was attacking Howard's daughter, and Nick here was only trying to stop it. Sid hit his head and died, a plain accident the way I see it."

Ashley knew her father agreed about the MacIntyres being troublemakers. He'd never liked Sid's father, Abel MacIntyre, a big brute of a man and the town bully. Abel had tried to pretend reform when he'd joined Ashley's parents' church. But he'd begun hanging around Ashley's mother, boldly hinting at feelings for her and harassing her with constant attempts at being near her at church events. Howard finally arranged to get the man kicked out of church, and Abel, thankfully, had marched off to war in a huff, claiming he would return an honored Confederate and, "Show Patricia Vale what a brave and respectable man I am."

"Sid wasn't right in the head," Harvey added. "We all know it. That's why he stayed here to pick cotton for the other farmers when Abel left. He couldn't be trusted with a gun and would have been useless in the war. Why don't all of you admit that Gainesville is better off without either one of the MacIntyres?"

"All right. All right," another man spoke up. Ashley recognized the voice of the local judge, Roy Stem. "I agree this might not warrant a hanging. Nick has never shown anything but a desire to be a true Texian like the rest of us, and the fact remains we all know Sid MacIntyre was an addle-headed bully. I'd like to take a vote before I make my decision."

A vote! Ashley could only pray it would go the right way. She daringly peeked around the corner again, hoping no one would see. Her father had ordered her to stay home and rest since the horror of Sid MacIntyre's attack still burned in her soul. It had happened only yesterday, and this morning her father and Nick had taken Sid's dead body into town.

"We should be allowed to see the girl's bruises before we decide," Till Brady spoke up.

"I'll not put her through the humiliation," Ashley's father answered. "It's not necessary, and the fact remains that Nick should not be held liable for Sid's death. The boy brought it on himself by attacking my daughter!"

"Enough!" Judge Stem shouted. "It's time to vote. All who think Nicholas Calhoun should be hanged, raise your hands."

Ashley closed her eyes and moved out of sight again when she saw only a few hands go up.

"All who vote Nick goes free but that he should go off to war with Howard Vale to fight for Texas and the Confederacy, raise your hands!"

Mentioning fighting for the Confederacy brought supportive shouts from most of them. Ashley noted that the judge, a good friend of her father's, had worded the vote just right, mixing Nick's name with fighting for "the cause," as most men called it.

"It's settled then." Judge Stem told them. "Nick won't hang, but he's got to join the war along with Howard Vale."

"He should at least stay here in jail until he leaves," someone suggested. Ashley thought it sounded like the livery owner,

Larry Grant. "Howard, you bring his things here, and we'll see he gets a Confederate hat and jacket and weapons. We want to be sure he leaves with you and doesn't run off once you get him back to your farm."

"Nick would never run away from this, but if it means no hanging, then take him to the jail," Ashley's father answered.

"I will agree to that," Judge Stem told them. "Take him away."

But I love him! Ashley wanted to shout the words. How was she going to go on if Nick was taken away? No one knew that just hours before her attack, she and Nick had kissed … A secret, sweet, delicious kiss that had awakened a thousand womanly desires inside that she never knew existed. Until Nick folded her into his arms to tell her almost apologetically that he saw her now as more than a friend or a sister.

"I think I love you, Ash."

She would never forget those words. Nick had argued that his feelings were all wrong. She was too young. He wasn't good enough for her. And he'd said there were things she didn't know about him—things that meant they could never be together. He'd not told her what those things were before desire took over and Nick's mouth was on hers and she in turn had lost all reason.

She'd returned his kiss with needful, probably sinful enthusiasm, because she'd loved him since he came to their farm when she was only ten years old. She'd never told anyone, including Nick, in all the time since then, thinking such a strong, experienced, handsome young city boy like Nick Calhoun would laugh at her if she told him she loved him.

But early yesterday … after she'd blurted out that she loved him, too, he hadn't laughed. He hadn't laughed at all. He'd kissed her again, but then gently pushed her away.

We can't do this, Ash. I just wanted you to know how I feel about you, so you'll understand why I have to leave. I couldn't just go without explaining why.

No one needed to send Nick to war. He loved her enough that he'd already decided to leave anyway, for her own good. But he couldn't tell that to the men who held him now because he'd have to explain that he was going away because he loved her. In this situation, it would only mar her reputation if he told the truth. Those men out there might think worse of him and hang him after all. And for that very reason, she, too, could say nothing. She didn't dare try to defend Nick without her forbidden love for him showing. That would make Till Brady's ugly accusations seem true.

This was all so wrong, but there was nothing she could do. Nick would be taken away, and she had no hope of talking to him once more, no hope of convincing him to stay, that he *was* good enough for her... no chance to tell him once more that she loved him with all her heart. He would march off to war and could be killed, and all they would ever have was that one kiss behind the house... a kiss that had made her ache to belong to him in every way.

"I want a judge to sign a paper stating that Nick Calhoun is a free and innocent man," Howard Vale yelled above shouts from the remaining men.

"You'll get one before you leave," Judge Stem answered.

Ashley stood up and dared to peek around the corner once more, hoping for a last glance at the man she loved so dearly, and so secretly.

There it was—that look of complete, hopeless surrender—there in Nick Calhoun's eyes when his gaze met hers! One brief moment. One quick look that said *I love you, but it's over. Forget about me.* He didn't need to say the words. It was all there in that look, a look she knew she would never forget.

Before her attack—and before the kiss they'd shared—Nick had simply been a homeless young man who'd shown up at her father's farm looking for work. He'd worked faithfully and hard and had gained Howard Vale's complete trust and respect. Ashley had come to see him as a big brother who was always looking out for her, but there had always been a kind of mystery surrounding him. He'd told them only that his parents died back in New York, no other explanation about his life there or why he'd come to Texas. Now she wondered again about his remark that there were things she didn't know about him.

She hated this war and what it did to men. Things had become dark and frightening, and the "great hanging" in Gainesville was an ugly stain on the town's reputation. Members of the citizens' mob who'd hanged so many men went on about their business now as though they'd acted righteously, and most still sat in church on Sunday mornings.

She watched men drag Nick away, feeling her heart being ripped out over the way he'd looked at her. So alone. Yes, that was why she'd always felt a bit sorry for him, and probably why she loved him. He'd always seemed like such a lonely, lost soul.

She turned away and stumbled to her horse. She was supposed to stay home that morning, but she hadn't been able to. She'd had to know what would happen to Nick. Had to see him once more, and hoped against hope he could come back home.

She cried so hard it took all her strength to climb up on her horse, deciding she would never tell her father or her mother or anyone else about Nick's kiss. Everyone might think, like Till Brady, that Nick had gone to that barn for the wrong reasons—that he had killed Sid MacIntyre deliberately, out of jealousy.

She headed down a back road toward her father's farm—the place Nick had called home for six years, but now would probably never see again.

"I'll love you forever, Nick Calhoun," she vowed, "forever, and forever. And I will wait for you, because I know you'll come back. I know it in my heart."

Part I

Chapter One

Early August, 1868...

$\mathcal{A}$shley set down two pails of blackberries she'd picked from a wild patch a few hundred yards behind the neat, frame home she shared with her mother. She paused at the bottom of the porch steps, listening intently. Something didn't feel right. She heard only the tweets of birds hidden in an overgrown Oleander bush at the corner of the house, and the rhythmic chirping of crickets under the wooden steps, but nothing unusual or alarming.

You're imagining things, she told herself.

A soft breeze blew a few strands of her red hair across her face. She pushed it behind her ears, still feeling uneasy. An unwarranted sense of danger crept through her bloodstream because the front door stood open. Because of late-summer flies from the nearby horse barn, her mother *never* left the front door open this time of year. It had no screen door because, as her mother often said, "*That front door is too beautiful to spoil its appearance with a screen door.*"

A good friend from church had made the heavy oak door by hand, in memory of Ashley's father who'd come home from the war with an infected leg wound that eventually killed him...another casualty of the awful war that had destroyed too many lives in the worst way. It was through her father that she'd

3

learned Nick was also wounded... *"Too gravely to have lived,"* her father told them. *"After I was wounded, I lost track of Nick. He might have been captured by the Yankees, but even if he wasn't, he couldn't possibly still be alive."*

Ashley still cried at night over the thought of never seeing Nick again. She didn't believe the rumors that he'd lived and now led an outlaw life, helping gangs of men harass the Federals, robbing Federal banks in retribution for how the South had been ravaged during and after the war. She simply couldn't picture Nick doing those things. But Sheriff Matthews, the new law in Gainesville, claimed a sheriff in Illinois had told him there was a Five Thousand Dollar warrant on Nicholas Calhoun in that state, for murder, robbery and mayhem.

Ashley shook away the awful news and refused to believe it. It had to be some kind of mistake. She'd resigned herself to the reality that, whatever the reason, she'd never see Nick again. And right now, she had to find her mother and end this awful feeling of dread and fear.

"Mother?" she called, loudly enough for the woman to hear from inside the house.

There came no reply.

Ashley took a handkerchief from a pocket on her skirt and dabbed at the sweat on her face. It was hot. It seemed that in Texas the days were *always* hot, even when other parts of the country were beginning to cool down. She looked toward the front door again, thinking how proud Patricia Vale was of her tidy, lovely home and its manicured front lawn outlined with a white picket fence. All the shrubs and roses around the house were planted by her own hands, and since Ashley's father died, the woman had worked hard keeping up the property as best she could, with Ashley's help. She'd finally sold some of the farmland to others in order to have the money to pay carpetbaggers and tax collectors who'd been biting at her heels since the war ended.

Maybe mother is out in the barn. Still, why would she go through the front door instead of the back door off the kitchen? And if she'd gone out another way, why would she leave the front door open? She climbed the porch steps and slowly pushed the door wider. A familiar squeak in the middle hinge sounded especially spooky today. "Mother?" she called again. And again, no reply.

For some reason, even though nothing looked awry, dread overwhelmed Ashley. She took a deep breath and told herself to calm down. It might be nothing. She stepped inside and turned to a small table next to the front door, where they kept Ashley's father's army pistol in a drawer. Hatred and prejudice left over from the war still caused problems and hard feelings in Gainesville, and now that they were two women alone, Ashley shared her mother's decision to keep a gun handy, as well as a rifle propped behind the front door. Adding to peoples' fears was the fact that a gang of thieves had lately been raiding outlying farms and stealing livestock. So far, the culprits had not been caught.

Still, this morning had been quiet. While picking berries, Ashley had heard no shouting, no voices at all. Nor did she hear the pounding of horses' hooves indicating several men making off with livestock. The horses she'd turned out this morning were still grazing quietly behind the barn when she'd walked past with the berries.

Heart pounding, Ashley took her father's pistol from the drawer. With a deep breath she walked through the living room, which was as wide as the house, with a back door that led outside to her mother's rose garden. A large stone fireplace graced the end wall, where her mother liked to sit in her rocker with her knitting. To the right was an archway made of oak that led to a long hallway.

As she turned to the hallway, Ashley glanced inside the small library room on the left and saw nothing. Across the hall from the library was the dining room, and beyond that on the right of the hall was a large kitchen. She listened for the sound of rattling dishes and pots and pans, the sound of footsteps, but the house remained eerily silent.

"Mother?" she called again. She turned fully to walk down the hallway, and that was when her breath caught in her throat and a soaring pain shot through her chest.

"Mother!" she screamed. There at the end of the hall and directly below the second-floor balcony lay her mother's body in what appeared to be a lifeless heap. Still wearing the pale blue dress she'd put on that morning, the woman's body lay flat, facing up, but her legs were twisted to the side.

"Oh, my God!" Ashley gasped. She ran down the hall and went to her knees beside her mother's body. Tossing the gun aside, she grasped the woman's shoulders. "Mother!" she cried again. She shook the woman slightly, then realized her head didn't moved with her body. In horror and dread, Ashley reached out to grasp the woman's face and immediately realized that Patricia Vale's neck was broken. She groaned in horror as she drew back, afraid to pick her mother up in her arms.

"Oh, dear God! Dear God!" Ashley wailed. "Noooo!"

She took hold of one of her mother's hands and bent over, resting her head on the woman's chest and listening for a heartbeat as she felt for a pulse at her wrist. She heard and felt nothing.

"Mama," she wept, suddenly feeling like a little girl who was alone in the world. She sobbed, mourning the fact that her mother had died alone and violently. She would never tend her gardens again, never hear the birds again, never pick up her knitting again.

So much loss! Her father. Nick. Now her mother, too. How much more was she supposed to take? She fully collapsed beside her mother's body, weeping so hard she could barely catch her breath—tears for the awful, painful way her father had died—tears for Nick for never coming home—tears for her mother's lonely parting from this world. Tears for the many men from Gainesville who'd died in the war, and for the wives and children left behind. She begged God to make her mother whole again, but she knew it was a fruitless plea.

She paid no attention to time as morning moved past noon and she cried herself into an exhausted sleep, later stirring when a fly buzzed past her ear. The fly caused her to bolt awake, and she sat up to full alertness, remembering that she'd left the front door open. She managed to stand, then looked down at her mother's body, feeling sick at the reality that this was not just a bad dream. It was real. Two more flies landed on a deep cut at the side of her mother's head, and Ashley realized she needed to do something about the body, and quickly.

She bent down and picked up the pistol from the floor, then hurried into the kitchen to set it on the table. She grabbed a towel and blew her nose and wiped her eyes, then dipped one end of the towel into a pan of water and ran it over her face to help stop her crying and clear her thoughts.

She threw that towel into the porcelain sink and took a clean towel from a drawer, hurrying into the hallway and shuddering again at the sight of her mother's dead body and the odd position of her head. Blood had soaked her hair and dried, and her face looked blue. Ashley quickly shooed away flies and covered the woman's head and neck with the towel. She had to get help, report this, find the coroner, make burial arrangements. She needed to saddle a horse and ride into town and report this.

Think, Ashley! She needed to get help. It struck her then how truly alone she was.

God, help me.

She stepped over her mother's body and ran to close the front door, then hurried back to head upstairs. She needed to go to her bedroom and change into her riding skirt and boots, needed to wash her face better, needed to comb and tuck her hair. She took hold of the decorative wooden post at the bottom of the stairway and started up, then noticed the post knob was sticky. She removed her hand and looked at her palm.

Blood! She noticed then that more blood was smeared on the post. As she made her way up the stairs, she noticed even more blood on the railing. She glanced up at the landing far to the right over which her mother must have fallen and noticed everything was intact. She reasoned that the railing should be bowed or cracked in the area where her mother's body must have gone over—some indication that her mother had simply fallen—some kind of damage. Her mother was a stout woman and had been fretting about her weight. Ashley reasoned that even if she'd fallen over the railing without breaking it, she'd have fallen straight down, which was where her body lay.

But that did not explain blood on the hand railing off to the side where the stairs curved upward. It did not explain blood on the bottom post. How could there be blood clear over here if her mother had fallen from the landing higher and to the right? And why had the front door been standing open when she first got back with the berries? If her mother had been in the house long enough to go up the stairs to get something, she never would have left the front door open while doing so.

Someone *else* must have opened it! Maybe her mother fell when she came to the landing to see who it was. But that still did not explain the blood on the side railing and bottom post. A terrible, gut-wrenching thought came to mind then. Maybe someone had come through the front door and grabbed her mother, beaten her…maybe dragged her up the stairs and thrown her over the railing deliberately so it would look like an accident. Maybe…

No! She had to stop thinking that anyone could have been this cruel, or that her mother might have suffered first, or that this could happen again ... to *her!* She had to get to the bottom of this, or she would never sleep again. Who could have done this? And *why?* She studied the blood on her palm again. More and more she was sure her mother's fall was no accident. A mixture of hatred for whoever might have done this, and terror over the fact that it could happen to her, too, ran hot through her blood.

She rushed up the stairs and to her room, where she quickly washed her hands and face, then stuck combs into the sides of her hair to secure it better. There was no time to twist her auburn mane into a more appropriate up-do. None of that mattered now. She changed her blouse and pulled on a riding skirt, tucking the freshly-starched and pressed blouse inside the waist. She stood still then, listening. All was still silent. Whoever had done this had come and gone like a ghost.

If only she hadn't gone out to pick berries that morning, her mother might still be alive. She grabbed her riding gloves from a dresser and a wide-brimmed straw hat from a hook on the wall. She stuck the hat on her head and tied it under her chin, then ran to a window at the back of her bedroom and looked out to see that the few cattle they still owned were grazing calmly in tall grass south of the house, beyond the fenced horses. Whoever had done this was apparently not part of any gang out to steal livestock.

She walked out of the room, pausing to peer over the upper landing to look down at her mother's dead body, trying to put the pieces of what had happened together and still reaching the conclusion that her mother must have been murdered. Her stomach ached at the realization that she'd never even had the chance to tell the woman once more that she loved her. She'd never had the chance to say good-bye for one last time ... to hold her close. She'd never been able to say good-bye to Nick, either, and she hated the empty, helpless, chronic sorrow that lingered in her soul. But right now, she had to ignore that sorrow. There were things that needed taking care of.

She hurried down the stairs, back down the hallway and out through the front door. The beautiful front door her mother never left open. She closed it and started down the steps, then stopped in her tracks part way down the front path when she saw him...a man...riding up the long driveway from the road.

Was he the murderer? She realized she'd left her father's pistol in the house on the kitchen table. The man riding toward her wore a gun and rode a solid black horse—a big horse for a big man.

Ashley remained frozen in place, unable to make herself run to the stables, or run for the house. She argued inwardly that maybe this wasn't someone out to get her at all. He wasn't riding hard—just a gentle walk, like he had all day to reach her. Something about him looked familiar, and she hoped it was someone who could help her. When he came close enough that she could see his face, he pushed back his hat.

Instantly, Ashley's already-confused emotions exploded in a hundred directions as she gasped his name. "*Nick!*"

Chapter Two

$\mathcal{E}$ye contact brought a tumble of memories and emotions as Ashley stood dumbfounded, hardly able to think straight. Nicholas Calhoun had returned from the dead! He was sitting on a horse right in front of her, and he'd filled out into more of a man than when he left—a good six feet plus of muscle and power. He didn't need to dismount for her to realize he'd actually grown taller than the 21-year-old man who'd left for war. The rolled-up sleeves of his white shirt revealed solid, strong forearms—arms she desperately needed to feel around her right now. He dismounted and walked closer. "Ash, I couldn't get back until now. I—"

Ashley literally threw herself at him, wrapping her arms around his middle and bursting into tears from the overwhelming events of the day.

Nick folded her closer, leaning down to kiss her hair. "Ashley, I have so much to tell you. I'm so sorry I couldn't get here any sooner. I wasn't sure how you'd feel, or—"

"Nick, you don't understand." She struggled to get the words out between sobs. "Something has happened, and—my God, Nick—Father told us you were dead! *Dead!*" She leaned her head back and met his gaze. He looked so sad—different— harder. A stubble of a beard covered his square jaw, and his black hair was longer than she remembered, falling to his shoulders from beneath his black, wide-brimmed hat. He was changed, yet the same handsome Irishman who'd left six years ago. She clung to him, literally feeling faint. "Is it really you?"

"It's really me, and we need to talk. I'm sure your father *did* think I was dead, the way things were at Chickamauga, but so much happened after that. And when I first left here—" He looked toward the house. "We need to talk, Ash. And I need to get inside and out of sight."

"But my father *saw* you lying wounded and said he was sure you'd died. When we never heard from you again..."

Nick put his fingers to her lips. "Ash, it's a long story. I would have written, but I was in a Union prison. That mob that sent me off to war couldn't have picked a better punishment for me killing Sid MacIntyre." He turned, keeping an arm around her shoulders. "Let's go into the house where it's cooler. I have so much to tell you, and none of it is good. I just thought you deserved an explanation. I'm a wanted man now, Ash, and I'm taking a risk coming here."

Ashley struggled to keep her wobbly legs from giving out on her as she pulled aside and looked him over, noticing his gun again through eyes blurred with tears. *Wanted!* Yes, he had that look about him—the look of an outlaw. That's what had changed. She shook her head. "Nick, I don't understand."

"I know you don't. That's why I'm here. If I'd known coming back here would upset you this much, I would have sent a letter first to warn you, but letters can be traced, and I can't afford that right now. Besides, I thought it would be better to come in person and explain."

"It's not that, Nick. We *can't* talk right now. There isn't time." Why did she feel so safe with him? He wore a gun, she hadn't seen him in years, and he was running from the law. From the time she'd met him as a ten-year-old, Nick Calhoun had been a bit of a loner, a troubled man. He'd been in his share of fist fights, mainly over teasing and name-calling from others who considered him a "foreigner," not a true Texian. It was the reason he'd spent most of his time working hard on the farm, avoiding town and living alone in the barn.

Ashley wiped at her eyes, hardly able to believe this was real. Absolutely *nothing* about today's events seemed real. "Nick, it's not just the surprise of you returning from the dead that has me so upset. It's just that—your timing couldn't be worse. Yet for my sake, it couldn't be better. I need someone to hold me right now—more than you know." She watched his dark eyes... kind, loving eyes... not the eyes of an outlaw. "Nick, my mother is *dead*! She's in the house this very moment with a broken neck, and there's blood all over the stair railing and support post. I couldn't move her because her head..." *Dear God!* Her legs started to go out from under her again, but Nick reached out and grabbed her.

"What the hell are you talking about?"

"I found her an hour or two ago," Ashley told him. "I just sat with her all that time, crying—until I realized I had to get help. That's what I was doing when I ran out of the house just now." She clung to his powerful arms. "Nick, I think... I think she's been murdered!"

"My God!" Nick picked her up in his arms and carried her to the old iron bench in the front yard. He set her on it. "You stay here. I'll go check things out."

His familiar voice was comforting—a little lower now, a man older than the one who'd left. Ashley met his gaze, seeing nothing but love and concern in his eyes. "Nick, I don't know what to do."

"Right now, just sit still." He leaned closer and kissed her cheek, then rose and headed for the house, his boots making a crunching sound against the gravel.

The sound of his footsteps seemed unusually sharp, perhaps because there was no wind today, and Ashley realized that, strangely, the birds had stopped singing. Even the animals had stopped making any sound. She glanced at Nick's horse, a sleek, black animal that perfectly fit the big man who rode him.

She put a hand to where her cheek still tingled from Nick's kiss. She reminded herself that she had no idea how he might have changed over the years. Some men had come back from the war behaving like complete strangers. Bessie Streeter's husband had shot himself only a couple of weeks ago, after being back for three years. And Martha Lewis's husband drank himself to death. Rita Stark had to divorce her husband because he'd returned an angry man who sometimes beat her and their children.

Right now, Nick certainly looked like the outlaw he'd apparently become, with that gun on his hip and that air of danger about him. A hundred different feelings pounded at Ashley's heart and rushed through her blood, causing an odd numbness through her whole body.

Nick was alive! For six years she'd mourned the fact that she'd never had the chance to say thank-you, or good-bye, or most important of all, tell him again that she loved him. Had he only come back just to say a permanent good-bye? If so, she would be completely alone now. And if Nick left again, it would be harder to take than the first time, because she'd finally come to accept the fact that he was dead. Now here he was, alive and well, and a full, handsome man twenty-seven years old. But she would likely have to forget him all over again.

She breathed deeply for self-control and took a fresh handkerchief from the pocket of her tan riding skirt, using it to wipe at the tears on her face. She removed her hat and smoothed back the sides of her hair, re-securing the combs there before putting her hat back on.

How did she look to Nick now? She'd been sixteen when he left for war. Six years had gone by—six years of sun and dust and hard work helping her mother keep things going. After all she'd been through, she felt much older than twenty-two, and she was sure her auburn hair no longer held the shining luster it once had. So much loss. So much death.

Nick had apparently risked jail and maybe even a hanging by coming here just for her. She heard the front door open and close, and she glanced back to see him coming down the porch steps. She'd regained at least some of her composure, and she wiped at her eyes again and drew a deep breath before hurrying toward the house to meet him half-way.

"My God," he said when he reached her. "You were right that her neck is broken." He removed his hat and ran a hand through his hair, then paced for a few seconds. "Seeing her like that—it reminded me of my own mother." He stopped and faced her again. "Ash, that's just one more thing I came here to tell you—about my mother and something that happened back in New York before I arrived here in Gainesville. But right now, my problems are beside the point."

"Nick, you have no idea how glad I am you showed up right when I needed someone to help. I'm so sorry about how things were when you had to leave so long ago. I never got the chance to thank you for what you did that day in the barn, or even to tell you good-bye."

"You don't need to explain." Nick looked her over with the same love in his eyes she'd seen there before he was sent off to war. Maybe he hadn't changed after all. "God, Ash, you've turned into such a beautiful woman. Seeing you so full-grown, but seeing the hardship and sorrow in those pretty green eyes— I'm so sorry for so many things, things I never told you about me, feelings for you I never should have shown or admitted because you were so young that day we kissed." He looked around. "This place became home for me." He met her eyes again. "Do you still own it?"

"Only a few acres, the house and some livestock and a little of the farm wagons and equipment. Elton Presley bought most of the land, and he farms it now." If only they could talk longer! "Nick, I'm so sorry you've come back to this. Everything is so awful and mixed-up and wrong, and if you're in danger, you should go."

He shook his head. "I can't leave you in this mess—not with your mother lying murdered in the house. Besides, you might be in danger, too. Where were you when it happened?"

Ashley struggled to find her voice. "I was picking wild blackberries way out back, over that big hill behind the house. You probably saw them still sitting in front of the house."

Nick nodded. "I remember that hill where they grew. We picked them together sometimes. That's probably why you never heard anything. Hills make a good sound barrier."

Did you learn that in finding ways to hide from the law? Ashley kept the question to herself.

Nick sighed deeply. "It's a damn good thing you weren't in the house when whoever did this was there. You could be dead, too." Nick led her back to the bench and sat down with her. "Did you have any enemies? Maybe a neighbor or a tax collector? Someone from that damn mob that almost hanged me? Did Abel MacIntyre ever come back here?"

"No." Ashley felt nauseous, not sure she could handle this sudden slam to her normal, everyday life. "He was listed as dead, too, and no one has seen hide nor hair of him since he left for the war. If he was alive, he surely would have come back here for his son's sake, but he never did."

"So, he never knew I killed Sid."

"No. I'd all but forgotten about Abel. Besides, why would he kill my mother for something you did to his son? He was always making advances toward her. He'd have no reason to hurt her."

"Maybe not. It's just that—the way your mother died—it takes a brutally strong man to do that."

Ashley put a hand to her stomach. "My God," she whispered. She met Nick's gaze. "There's so much you don't know. Father died from his wound only a year or so after you and he left together. He told us you were both at Chickamauga, and that you were killed there."

"I might as well have been. I was captured and taken to Elmira Prison in New York. It was a living hell, and I didn't get proper treatment for a bayonet wound to my left side. It got infected, and the pain was god-awful. They gave me nothing for it. It's a miracle I lived." He turned away. "War does things to a man, Ash. I'm not the same person as before that mob in town threatened to hang me. I'll never forget that, or some of the things that happened in the war and in prison. It creates a hate inside that's hard to deal with." He shook his head. "There's no time to talk about it now. You need to go into town and report your mother's murder."

Ashley reached out and touched his arm. "Please don't go away yet, Nick. Maybe you can find a place to hide until all this is over—a way to come back so we can talk. For a while the sheriff and his deputies will be milling around here, and others who'll want to help. I'll have to plan a funeral and decide what I'm going to do next, but I can't stand the thought of not talking to you again. There's too much left unresolved, and knowing you're alive—you have no idea what this means to me. Please promise you'll find a way to come back when things settle down."

Nick put a big hand over hers. "I promise."

Ashley wanted him to hold her again. She felt so alone and scared, and here was a man she *should* be afraid of, considering his reputation, but she felt no fear at all.

Nick sighed and shook his head. "You aren't married, or seeing someone else after all this time?"

Ashley shook her head. "No. I waited for you, Nick. I couldn't bring myself to believe you were really dead."

Pain filled his gaze. "God, Ash, you shouldn't have waited. You should have gone on with your life without me. You're beautiful and desirable and loyal and loving—all the things a man would want. I wasn't expecting to come back and find you so alone."

Ashley studied him longingly. "I *love* you, Nick. I've *always* loved you. And things got so busy after you left, what with the farm and my mother standing against carpetbaggers and bill collectors, and trying to hang on to the house and at least some of the land, let alone both of us taking care of Father those several weeks and struggling to farm enough corn and cotton to make some money." She took strength in Nick's strong grip on her hand. "Poor mother! She didn't deserve such an awful death."

"Tell me something," Nick said, frowning. "Has there been anyone new around town who wore a patch over his eye?"

Ashley frowned. "No. I don't understand."

Nick let go of her hand and stood up to reach into his pants pocket. He held out a black eye patch, the ends still tied in a knot. "This was on the floor inside the house, partly under a side table near your mother's body. She must have torn it off the killer in her struggle."

Ashley's eyes widened at the sight of the patch and the realization she might have just missed being murdered herself. She cringed away from touching the it. "I don't know anyone around here or in town who wears one of those things, except old Alfred Coons. Maybe you remember him."

"I remember a *lot* of things, most of them things I'd rather forget."

Ashley's heart ached at his remark. "Mr. Coons was decrepit back then, and he's even more decrepit now. He isn't capable of committing such violence. He needs help just to dress and get out of the house to go to church. A child could push him over."

Nick sighed again. "Well, the eye patch is a good clue. There's somebody out there with an ugly or missing eye. He ought to be easy to find." He hung the black patch over the arm of the bench and paced. Ashley noticed his wide, leather gun belt was fully packed with cartridges, as though he might get in a gun battle at any moment.

"My God, your mother's murderer could have still been in the house when you first got back. I'm just damn sorry I didn't come along sooner. I might have seen or heard something, maybe even stopped what was happening." He rubbed at the back of his neck. "You'd better get going. Take that eye patch with you into town. It will help the sheriff know what kind of man they're looking for—big and strong, and with one bad eye. I'll follow you for safety's sake, but I'll stay out of sight. At least there are plenty of woods between here and town. I don't want the sheriff or anyone else to know I've been here, so don't mention me. When you get back, I'll be gone."

Ashley took the eye patch from the bench and shivered as she shoved it into a pocket on her riding skirt. She walked closer to Nick. "But you'll keep your promise to come back?"

He nodded. "I'll come back soon enough. Right now, you have no more time to waste." He put a hand to the side of her face. "A lot of things have changed me, Ash, and not for the better. There are things I need to tell you, but for now I hope they catch the guy who did this. And if I were you, I'd get someone to stay with you for a while. And keep things locked, understand?"

Ashley put a hand to her eyes. "But how will we be able to talk again if someone is staying with me? I don't want you to get into any more trouble than you already are."

Nick took hold of her arms. "Don't worry about me. I'll find a way to see you again. Just do what needs doing. I'll go saddle a horse for you."

Ashley nodded as he urged her to sit back down. "Saddle Patsy, the brown and white paint in the pasture behind the barn. She's my favorite."

Nick untied his horse. "I remember that, too. I'll get her, but I need to get Satan out of sight for now. I'll take him to the barn." He headed that way, leading his horse by the reins. "Come on, boy."

Ashley watched him, wondering how she was supposed to handle all this emotion. "Nick!"

He stopped and turned.

"Thank you. I'm not sure what I'd have done if you hadn't shown up." She wiped at more tears.

Nick smiled sadly. "I'm just sorry I can't stay with you through all of this. I'm sorry about a *lot* of things." He turned and kept walking.

Ashley waited, watching shrubs and trees sway in a soft wind, noticing the birds had started singing again. After twenty minutes or so, Nick came out of the barn leading his own horse and Patsy. The Paint looked small walking beside Nick's big, black gelding.

"Here you go," he said when he reached her, handing over Patsy's reins.

Ashley stood up and took the reins, looking up at Nick. "You *will* come back?" she asked yet again.

He leaned down and kissed her cheek again, then moved his lips to brush the corner of her mouth. "I'll come back," he said softly. He stepped aside to let her mount up. "Get going. You won't see me, but I'll be watching."

Ashley climbed onto Patsy and adjusted her riding skirt, then paused. "I can't believe you're really here and alive. I never thought in a million years I'd see you again."

Nick looked her over in a way that the woman in her knew was more than friendship. "I always cared about you, Ash. Your family became *my* family. I thought about you night and day after I left." He stepped away. "You'd better get going. It will be dark soon."

There was no arguing the matter. Her beloved mother lay dead inside the house, so Ashley had no choice but to leave. She fought tears as she turned Patsy and rode down the driveway toward town a mile away.

She looked back once to see Nick riding into the nearby trees. *Still looking out for me.* He seemed so alone, just like the day men had dragged him off to jail. Would he keep his promise to see her again before riding out of her life? Even if he did come back, she knew it would only be to say a final good-bye. She had to face that truth—or fall to pieces.

Chapter Three

Gainesville bustled with normal daily life as Ashley rode into town. Little did anyone know about the horrific incident that had brought her there, and she dreaded the chaos that would follow.

Her mind swirled with indecision. Would Nick even come back once more like he'd promised? People would be all over the farm investigating her mother's murder. In the meantime, she had a funeral to plan. After all that was over, what should she do about the house and livestock? It was all too much to take care of on her own, and now the house would hold the awful memory of her mother's violent death. Selling it all would mean she could get out of Gainesville and maybe start life over someplace new. She was tired of the questions and doubts in peoples' minds over what had really happened when Nick killed Sid MacIntyre. No one needed to say anything. It was there in their eyes and attitudes.

Rumors. Maybe she'd either invited Sid MacIntyre into the barn, or maybe there had been something going on all along between her and Nick Calhoun. Maybe Nick had killed Sid out of jealousy. Now, if people knew Nick had come back to see her, the stories about them would start circulating again, let alone Nick might risk a hanging. He was, after all, a wanted man. She would gladly go away with him, but she had no doubt that wasn't what he wanted. It was too late for the sweet, innocent love they'd shared in that one kiss so long ago. Nick was leading a life on the run, and he'd already told her he'd only come back to explain and for one last good-bye.

Her confusion and depression were made worse at the moment by the fact that she had to report her mother's murder to Sheriff Clay Becker, a man she dreaded running into, even under normal circumstances. Clay had that patronizing attitude that all women needed a man to take care of them, and she had become his primary target. He'd often asked her to accompany him to church, picnics and dances. He'd even asked her to marry him several weeks back, but she'd turned him down. She considered him no more than a concerned friend, more of a father figure than a man she'd want to marry.

Clay was a solid man with soft blue eyes, a nice smile, and a good heart, but he was sixteen years older than she. She didn't doubt that as soon as he learned her mother was dead, his attitude would be even more condescending when it came to her living alone on the farm.

"Ashley, dear! How's your mother?"

The question came from Clara Peele, who was crossing the street as Ashley rode by. Clara was one of her mother's good friends from church. She would be truly devastated to learn about Patricia Vale's death.

"I'm afraid something terrible has happened, Clara," Ashley answered. She halted Patsy near the sheriff's office and dismounted, tying the horse to a hitching post. "Would you do me a favor and wait for me on the bench there in front of the dry goods store? I have to talk to the sheriff."

"Oh, my dear, what is wrong?" Clara asked. "Is it Patricia? Is she all right?"

"Just give me a few minutes," Ashley answered, taking some packages from Clara's arms and setting them on the bench for her. Without further explanation, she walked two buildings down to the sheriff's office and took a deep breath before stepping inside. She had to be strong now and not fall apart in front of Clay. She entered his office to find him cleaning a rifle at his desk.

Clay looked up and grinned, always happy to see her, always hopeful she would come into town just to see him and perhaps accept his proposal. "Well!" he said, as he rose. "To what do I owe the pleasure of your company, young lady?"

Ashley brushed at her riding skirt. "It has nothing to do with pleasure, Clay. I'm here because—" The words stuck in her throat for a moment, while reality finally began to set in. Nick's surprising return from the dead had only added to her distress. She felt like she was living both a dream and a nightmare. "Have you seen a stranger around town? Maybe one with a bad eye? Wearing an eye patch?"

Clay looked her over appreciatively. "Now why in the world would you ask a question like that?"

Ashley felt light-headed. She stumbled a little when she turned to find a chair. The sheriff was quickly at her side, grasping one arm and helping her sit down. "Sorry if I seemed to joke a little too much, Ashley. I can see you're truly upset." Clay quickly dragged over a second chair from a deputy's desk and sat down facing her. He grasped her hand, and Ashley let him. "What's happened?" he asked in his "I'm the concerned sheriff" attitude. His voice always seemed to grow deeper when he moved into actual police work.

"My mother..." Ashley wiped at a tear with shaky fingers. "She's dead, and I think it was murder."

Clay took a quick breath. "*What?*" He squeezed her hand tighter. "When? How? What does a man with a bad eye have to do with it? Are you all right? Did you see who did it? You aren't hurt, are you?"

Ashley had to appreciate the man's genuine concern as he rattled off the questions. "I'm fine, Clay." She took a deep breath in an effort to speak without sobbing. "I went out early this morning to pick blackberries. Things were fine when I left. When I came back, I noticed the front door was standing open. My mother never leaves the door open this time of year because the flies are so bad, so right away I suspected something was wrong. I went inside...and the house was...so quiet. I walked down the hallway—and there she was." She pulled her hand away and covered her face as she broke into tears. "All beat up...her neck broken so badly that when I started to move her—" She couldn't finish the ugly details.

"Good God!" Clay said, rising.

Ashley heard his heavy footsteps as he went to the door and looked outside. He pulled the rope on a bell he kept just outside the door to alert his deputies and any other men who might want to join a posse when he needed quick help. He turned back and sat down near her again, touching her arm. "What's this about a man with a bad eye?"

"I...I found blood on the stair railing in places it shouldn't be if she'd simply fallen. And Mother's face was all bruised, a deep cut on her head...things that indicated someone must have beaten her and broken her neck and then tried to make it *look* like a fall. Or maybe the fall broke her neck. I don't know which. I looked around, and I spotted an eye patch lying nearby on the floor." She lied to leave Nick out of the conversation. She wiped at her eyes and straightened, reaching into a pocket of her riding skirt and pulling out the patch. She handed it out.

"I'll be!" Clay took the patch. "This should be a big help in finding the man who did this."

"Yes." Ashley took a handkerchief from her other pocket and wiped at her eyes and nose. Just then George Stout came barging into the office. One of Clay's deputies, George was a big, burly man in every way—tall, overweight, mean looking, and always in need of a shave. Women joked about how he was just a big stuffed bear whose bite didn't match his appearance. He was actually a kind man with a wife and six children.

"What is it, Sheriff?" he asked in his deep voice.

"Something terrible has happened out at Patricia Vale's farm. Stay outside a few more minutes and gather up any men who volunteer for a posse. Keep them outside until I can explain."

"Sure." George walked out, and Ashley heard him order someone to get his horse. "Trouble at the Vale farm," he told whoever it was.

"What's happened?" Ashley recognized Clara's voice. "I saw Ashley a few minutes ago, and she wouldn't tell me anything. Said to wait out here for her."

"Don't know yet," George answered.

Inside, Clay gently squeezed Ashley's arm. "Do you have any other details before we ride out there?"

Ashley drew a deep breath and leaned back in the chair. "Just—" The horror of her mother's condition overwhelmed her. "Clay, I want her body treated with respect. Because of her broken neck, they'll have to be careful when they pick her up."

Clay nodded. "Of course. I'll ride out there with the men and have a look around. We'll bring your mother back here to the undertaker's. You stay here and make the proper arrangements. If you don't feel like doing that right now, go with Clara or someone and lie down for a while first. Your mother will be fine at the undertaker's. We'll spread the word about a man with a bad eye, so the whole town will be looking for someone like that. I'll see if I can find any other clues at the house." He shook his head. "I'm so sorry, Ashley. What a horrible morning you've suffered. It sounds like you were very lucky that whoever did this was gone when you got there."

Ashley nodded. Nick had said the same thing. Hearing Clay say the same thing Nick had gave her the shivers. "I took a gun from a stand next to the door. Mother and I kept it there for protection. When I found her body, I dropped it and I don't remember what I did with it after that. It might be on the kitchen table. If you find a Civil War pistol lying around somewhere, it's mine. It doesn't belong to whoever did this."

"Sure." Clay frowned. "Ashley, could you tell if your mother was... well, violated?"

"I don't know, but I don't think so. I don't think whoever killed her had time for much else. I realize now that I didn't check to see if anything valuable was missing. I was too concerned about what to do about my mother."

"I understand. You can check for things like that when you're able to go back there. If anything belonging to your mother or you was stolen and we find it on some stranger, we'll have even more proof he's the killer." Clay rose. "I'll get Clara. Promise me you'll go to her house and lie down until we get back. Don't go back home just yet, all right?"

Ashley nodded.

"And we need to talk about whether you should go back at all. After what happened to your mother, you have no business living out there in the sticks all alone in that big house so far from town. I'm not about to let you do that. Whoever's been doing the raiding around here hasn't been caught yet. You absolutely should not be out there alone."

Ashley understood the man's concern, but she resented his thinking he had a right to tell her what to do. And how would she be able to talk to Nick again if she wasn't at the house? Still, she knew Clay was right, and that irritated her.

In minutes all was chaos, just as Ashley had suspected. Shouting. Men gathering on horseback, checking their weapons. Clara nearly fainted from the news. She and other women herded Ashley to Clara's small frame house at the end of the street, where they peppered her with questions, forced hot tea down her throat, fussed over her, insisted she lie down while they got the doctor to give her something for her nerves and her grief—something to help her sleep.

Ashley had no idea how much time passed, what the posse was doing at her house, what had happened to Nick. She knew only the deep, shocking reality that her mother was really dead and that Nick had come back and wanted to talk to her. About what? She had arrangements to take care of, decisions to make. She took something the doctor gave her, and she floated into that mystic semi-conscious area between awake and sleep, where she saw a misty vision of Nick Calhoun. He was holding her mother in his arms... or was it her own body he held? He smiled at her, and that was her last thought before falling into a much-needed sleep.

Chapter Four

Life became a tumble of constant questions, funeral planning, people offering to let Ashley live with them, warnings not to stay alone at the farm, deputies taking turns camping outside Ashley's house for her protection, more deputies returning to look for more clues, women friends coming over to wash away blood stains after investigations were through. Those same women took turns staying in the house, doing Ashley's chores, cooking and cleaning. She couldn't help being impressed and touched by all they did. She knew it was mostly for her mother. Patricia had a host of friends and had been very active in church, often volunteering her time to help with fund-raising projects for the church and for the poor.

The hunt for her murderer was on, and everyone kept watch for a man with a bad eye. For days a posse searched for tracks, but a heavy rainstorm the night of the incident obliterated what tracks might have been left around the house. No stranger with a bad eye was found, not in Gainesville, and not in the surrounding outlying area.

Ashley went through the ordeal of choosing a burial dress for her mother and decided on a lovely pink frock Patricia had often worn to church. The undertaker did a good job of making the body presentable, with no sign of a broken neck. Her mother's hair was nicely coifed, and a touch of face paint helped her color and hid the bruises. Visitation was at the farmhouse, and again, townswomen provided all the food and did all the work.

Now, men lowered Patricia Vale's casket into a grave dug in the back yard beside Howard's burial plot. Ashley took comfort in knowing her mother's personal Bible was in the casket with her, along with roses cut from Patricia's own garden. Also in the coffin was the last bit of knitting she'd been working on before she died. Ashley envisioned her mother sitting in front of the fireplace in the great room, talking about the coming winter and whom they might invite to the house for Christmas holidays.

"We certainly need to invite Sheriff Becker," she'd said not long ago. Her mother had been adamant that Ashley should accept the man's offer of marriage, but Ashley simply had no such feelings for him.

Now she stood at the grave wearing the same black funeral dress she'd worn for her father's funeral. When would all the losses end? Too many Gainesville citizens had been lost to the war. And if Nick should be caught, she'd probably be attending his funeral, too, and his death would be just as violent as her father's and mother's had been.

She glanced at her father's tombstone beside the gaping hole that would soon swallow up her mother. *Here lies Howard Vale,* it read. *Born July 1, 1818 – Died June 28, 1863. A good husband and father. A loyal Confederate.*

So much ugliness. So much killing. So many hard feelings. All the awful hangings. She felt worn out from sheer grief and realized Nick must feel the same way. She wanted to scream at the men lowering her mother's casket to please stop, but no. Down, down into the earth it went, like all the others.

Where was Nick? He said he would come back to talk, but she was constantly surrounded by friends and the law, so he'd stayed away. For all she knew, he'd ridden off again and wouldn't come back at all. And while most of Gainesville's able men were gone hunting for a man with one bad eye, there had been more raids on farms and ranches in the area, with more cattle and horses stolen. Was it Nick and some gang he rode with doing the raiding? She had no doubt that he hated Gainesville and everyone in it.

A few fences had been broken down in the recent raids, and crops were partially trampled, but no barns burned, and no one hurt or killed. That would be like Nick. Outlaw that he was, she could not bring herself to believe he would kill innocent people who had nothing to do with his situation. And whether it was Nick or not, no one could ever find where the stolen livestock had been taken. The closest anyone had come to catching those who'd done the raiding was when tracks were discovered that led west toward wild, unsettled country, places where none of the members of Gainesville's posse cared to go. Trying to track all of them was impossible. Some led west, some north, some south toward Mexico. Whoever it was, they were clever at confusing those who searched for them.

"We have no authority in Mexico," Clay had complained about the possibility of cattle being taken there. He'd pressed Ashley to let some of the men in town herd her own livestock to Grant's Stables in town, where they could be tended for the winter. Members of Patricia's church had agreed to combine what money they could raise to pay stable owner, Larry Grant, for winter care.

Ashley appreciated their kind gesture, but she hated feeling so obligated to everyone. For now, she wondered why she was even thinking about such things in the middle of her mother's funeral. Maybe it was because she was trying *not* to think about today's realities. She'd never see her mother again. And maybe she'd never see Nick again.

Now, here she was, totally alone. If she gave the word, Clay Becker would marry her on a moment's notice, and her and her mother's friends were kind and dependable. She still had the house and some livestock, but she had some big decisions to make. She couldn't make those decisions until she found out why Nick had ridden into her life again, what it was he needed to tell her, but she was never alone now. She *needed* to be alone. She could think things out better if people would just stay away for a while. And Nick truly *would* never come back if she was always surrounded this way.

The preacher gave his eulogy. He led everyone in the hymn *Shall We Gather at the River.* It seemed the whole town had attended. Luckily, the weather was not so hot and humid today. It was cool but sunny, the kind of day her mother would have loved.

Prayers. More hymns. The service was over. Good wishes came to her from those who remained around the gravesite. Many of her own women friends hugged her. They were all married and had children—and all of them probably wondered why she didn't accept the sheriff's offer of marriage. They didn't understand that deep inside she'd been totally in love with Nick Calhoun and had mourned his death. She'd never told them, fearing it would only verify the rumors left from when he'd defended her. And her father's long, drawn-out struggle with his own death, followed by helping her mother hang on to what was left of the farm and doing laundry for others to help bring in extra money meant she'd had no time to think about other men. She'd been through struggles most of her friends wouldn't understand.

She accepted more good wishes as they left the grave—offers of help and words of concern. A few men suggested she should sell the house and move into town. Now that Elton Presley had been farming the land, he wanted to buy the house and move his family there.

Ashley felt strongly she should sell it. The house was sturdy and lovely. The barn and stables were in good shape. The livestock was worth decent money, and she still owned a supply wagon, a plow and other tools, and a buggy. Everything she had was thanks to money left to her and her mother by her thrifty and hard-working father and to the extra work she and her mother had done to hang on to what they had left.

Through all the good wishes, Ashley hardly remembered one word that was said. People would fill their bellies now on chicken and corn and pies. Children would go back to their playing. Men and women would clean up after eating and everyone would go back to their daily lives. She would be left with a lot of decisions to make—decisions that might be easier if she saw Nick again and knew all the reasons he'd come back.

Then there was Clay Becker to think about. He would likely come around more often. Even now he approached her with a look of genuine sorrow in his eyes. He moved an arm around her waist and walked with her.

"After this, if there's anything you need, young lady, you just holler," he told her.

She knew the man meant well. "Thank you, Clay." She looked around, checking for people in the distance. *Nick, where are you?* She sensed his presence. In fact, she had the eerie feeling he'd been somewhere close this whole time ... watching and waiting.

"And I know you're hurting right now and undecided about a lot of things, Ashley, honey, but you remember I'm here for you and that I still want to marry you."

"I know that, Clay, but I can't think about that right now, and I've told you several times—"

"I know. You don't love me that way. But the offer is always there, my dear."

"I just need some time alone. I need to think."

"I don't think that's wise, Ashley."

"It's my life, Clay. I'm a grown woman, and I've been basically alone since Father left for war and I had to put up with all the gossip about me and Nick Calhoun. You weren't here then, but you came not long after. You know about the awful hangings. Now my mother has been murdered. There are too many bad memories here, Clay. I'm seriously thinking of leaving. I'm tired of all of it—and tired of the ugly reputation of this town."

Clay stopped walking and touched her arm. "Ashley, don't leave. I'm sorry if I hit a raw nerve. I just worry about you—*care* about you. You can't just go running off on your own."

Ashley pulled down her veil again and turned away. "Yes, I can. I'm sorry to be short with you, but it's just been a horrible week and a day of devastating sorrow. I'd better get to the house and see to the guests. Everyone has been so kind and helpful." She started walking again. "And I *do* need some time alone, Clay. I'll be fine."

Clay frowned as he kept pace with her. "Well, I suppose you can send all the ladies home who've been staying with you, but I intend to leave men outside to guard things for a while yet. Let me do that much."

"If you insist." *Maybe Nick can find a way to avoid them.* She was anxious now to talk to him again.

Clay walked Ashley to the house, where women busily served food to the mourners. Ashley paused at the front door as Clay went inside. She studied the surrounding countryside. *Nick, where are you?* She had so many questions for him, but she also didn't want to be responsible for him being caught and probably hanged. She could never handle that. Not on top of all that had already happened.

Nick Calhoun was her last connection to a time when she was young and happy, a little girl with a silly crush on one of the help. A time when both her parents were still alive, the farm active and prosperous. Before the awful hangings. Before the ugly war, her father's death and thinking Nick was dead, too. Before her mother's shocking death.

Chapter Five

Early September...

Ashley peered down from her bedroom window when she heard several horses and men's shouts at the front of the house. Sheriff Becker and his posse were back after nearly three weeks of searching both for her mother's killer and for the local livestock thief. The sheriff thought the two crimes might be connected, even though Ashley had told him none of her own livestock had been stolen the day of the murder. She didn't doubt that part of Clay's reason for finding the culprit was not just the danger she might be in, but also because he wanted to be her hero, which might convince her to marry him. She watched as he shouted orders.

"George, you and Ken stay the night here and keep watch. Blake and Harvey can go on home with the others."

Lately Ashley felt even more irritated at the constant presence of two men camped outside her house every night. Volunteers rotated themselves for the job. She was used to the peace and quiet of the farm this time of year, with most crops in, most of the canning done, and quiet evening talks by the fire with her mother. She felt obligated to feed the men who watched over her, and though they could be trusted, was uncomfortable knowing they were right outside her door.

Her life had been turned so upside-down that she'd finally made the decision to sell everything and leave. Where she would go depended on what Nick might tell her. The last thing she wanted to do was leave without seeing him again. That would be the hardest thing she'd ever do, but she'd still not heard from him.

George Stout and the man named Ken dismounted and untied their bed rolls, while the two men who'd stayed the previous two nights headed for the stables to load their gear and go home. The rest of the posse left, yipping and shouting, anxious to get back to their families. Sheriff Becker looked up and caught Ashley looking out from the bedroom window. He waved, and she waved back.

"Mind if I come inside for a few minutes?" Clay shouted.

"That's fine. I have coffee." Ashley left the window and looked in the mirror to tuck some stray hairs into a bun at the nape of her neck and smooth her dress. She'd really wanted to tell Clay no—that she wished he'd leave and take all the men with him—but she couldn't bring herself to be so rude. She hurried down the stairs, grasping only the right railing on her way and wincing when a small cut on her right index finger scraped across a rough spot in the wood. She'd cut her finger on a thorn when trimming her mother's roses that morning, and the cut brought back bad memories of the blood stains on the railing and the landing post. Even though they'd been washed away, she could still see them every time she passed the spot.

Shivering, she hurried on down, forcing herself to not even look at the landing post. She again smoothed the skirt of her deep blue, polished cotton dress. It was presentable for company, yet plain and simple enough for farm chores.

Clay came inside just as she reached the bottom of the stairs, and she called to him to come into the kitchen. She took two coffee mugs from a cabinet and set them on the table. She reached for the coffee pot. "Did you learn anything?"

Clay sighed as he removed leather gloves and laid them on the table. He took off his wide-brimmed hat and hung it on the corner of a chair. "Nothing," he answered. "It was another dead end." He ran his hands through his hair to smooth out the dents left by his hat, then pulled out the chair to sit down. "By the way, I brushed off the trail dust as best I could before coming inside."

"That's fine. Thank you." Ashley poured his coffee and then a cup for herself. She came to the table and sat down. "It's too bad you haven't been able to find any more clues."

Clay sipped some of his coffee. "It wasn't so much a dead end as it was deliberately confusing. Whoever is raiding the livestock around here splits up later every time, making it difficult to decide which trail to follow." He shook his head. "I really want to find the man who killed your mother, Ashley. I'm doing my best, but by now he could be clear to California for all we know. Especially now that the Union Pacific goes nearly to Utah. With no major mountain snows yet, he could easily have gone on from there. They say by next year trains will be able to go all the way from New York through to California in a matter of days. Hard to believe."

"Yes, it is."

"The tracks led us every which way. We could see we were on a wild goose chase, so we gave it up. I'm sorry we haven't been able to do more. This thing just has me baffled. The cattle thieves, *and* that one-eyed man, should have been easy to find."

Ashley drank some coffee. "He was probably some transient looking for work. Maybe he was drunk and was going to try to have his way with my mother and she fought him. Then he saw or heard me coming and ran off. Who knows? Like you said, he could have made it to the railroad farther north and is hundreds of miles from here by now, never to be heard from again."

Clay nodded. "I wondered a bit about Abel MacIntyre, but he's dead, so it couldn't be him. Besides, we'd have seen him come back to town. He'd have ranted and raved about Nick Calhoun killing his son. We would have had all kinds of warnings—at least that's what others tell me. I never knew Abel *or* Nick —or even your father."

Ashley struggled not to show her surprise that he, too, mentioned Abel MacIntyre. She almost said *Nick thought the same thing,* but caught herself. "It wouldn't have been Abel anyway. He liked my mother. With my father gone, he'd have tried to court her, but she would have had nothing to do with him."

"Well, whoever it was, I have to hope you're right about him being gone for good. It's just so upsetting for other women in the area to not know for sure. It makes them afraid."

Ashley sighed. "Mother used to say that all things come out in the wash. Some day we might know the answers." She met Clay's kind eyes. "But if the man who killed her decides to come back, I won't be here. I'm selling the house to Elton Presley and leaving Gainesville."

Clay frowned and leaned closer. "*Leaving?* You've really made up your mind to go?"

"You said I should sell this place, and I agree. But I'm not moving into town like you suggested."

"But where would you go?"

Was she crazy for doing what she'd decided to do? "I've read fliers and a couple of newspaper articles about how some women are going farther west to settle under the Homestead Act. Here in Texas that would, of course, be north, not west, to places like Oklahoma or Nebraska. The war has left a lot of women widowed and without property. What better way to start over and leave bad memories behind than to settle someplace new? Claim free land?"

The air hung silent for a few minutes. Ashley stared at her coffee cup, deliberately avoiding Clay's eyes.

"But...you *can't* go off alone, Ashley! These are still very dangerous times. You should know that, just by what happened to your mother. Heading north means going through Indian Country. And even without that danger, there are outlaws all over the place, especially now since the war. Desperate men who've lost everything. Don't forget that Nick Calhoun might still be alive, and he's a wanted man now."

Fighting for composure, Ashley looked away. "Father said Nick was killed at Chickamauga. I don't believe he's alive and living the life of an outlaw."

Clay shook his head. "Well, I *do* believe it's true, Ashley. A man in one town we stopped in somewhere outside of Dallas said he'd been in a Union prison with Nick. He heard us talking about Gainesville and remembered Nick had mentioned he was from there. He said Nick escaped, killed two prison guards in the process. Said Nick was in such bad shape at the time he wasn't sure how he managed to overtake them. Wasn't even sure if Nick killed both of them or if one of the other men who escaped with him killed one. Either way, Nick escaped, and later this guy saw a wanted poster on Nick, not just for killing the guards, but for helping rob a bank. A teller got shot, and Nick got blamed for it. The guy also heard the Federal government wanted Nick for gun running."

"But even if that's true, wasn't everything he did just part of war?"

Clay shook his head. "The bank robbery and gun running were after the war was over. In fact, the prison escape was also right after the war, but I don't think the men at that prison knew it yet. Even so, the Federal government doesn't care. It's my belief they want to make all Confederates pay for what they see as treason." He looked at Ashley with true concern. "You don't think he'd hurt your mother, do you?"

Ashley's eyes widened in shock at the remark. "Of *course* not! Nick was like part of our family. He always treated my mother with concern and respect, and he sometimes talked about how he missed his own mother, who died back in New York. He never told us the details, but he cared a lot about my mother And he was like a big brother to me. You know that, Clay. You weren't here then, but you've heard it all. Nick saved me from that awful attack by Abel MacIntyre's son. You didn't know them, either, but Abel and Sid were awful people. Brutal men. Bullies. And people have told you how much my father cared about Nick, almost like a son. He's the one who saved Nick from a hanging."

"And that near hanging was because Nick killed a young man with his bare fists for hurting *you*. Is it true, Ashley, that there was never anything more between the two of you back then? You were a beautiful sixteen-year-old, and Nick was four or five years older. How could he not—"

"Don't say another word! I was ten when Nick came to work here. He always saw me as that ten-year-old. He defended me like any brother would, and don't forget that Sid MacIntyre's death was an *accident*. Nick never meant to kill him. I'm just..." She wiped at sudden tears. "I'm sorry. Nick Calhoun was a good friend. I hate hearing what you just told me about him." She couldn't tell him the real reason for her tears. If the Federal government wanted Nick, there was no hope of him ever being a free man. And maybe, since having to wait so long to meet with her, he'd already left for parts unknown, never to return. She'd never felt so alone.

"I'm damn sorry, Ashley. I didn't think about how such news might affect you." Clay frowned with deep concern. "So much has happened to you, young lady. It's all the more reason you shouldn't go off alone. Even if you make it to wherever you go, it takes hard work to settle new land. You'll need a man to help you. That could be me, if you'd let me."

Ashley finally met his gaze. "Clay, my mother and I farmed this place alone after Father went off to war. We managed our money well and kept the livestock and worked hard after he died. I know how to grow corn and squash and potatoes, and how to tend livestock, work a plow, hoe a garden. I can cook and sew and drive a team and stack wood and store feed. I know how to hunt for my own food. Father taught me. And I know how to can vegetables, churn my own butter and bake my own bread. I have a decent amount of money saved, and once I sell this place and all the furniture, farm equipment and livestock, I'll have plenty more to start over someplace new. Enough to hire someone to help at first, if I have to. I deeply appreciate your offer, but not all women are completely helpless without a man."

"And you're still young and lovely and don't have that prairie-woman look about you. If you go running off to unsettled country to start over, you'll end up an old woman before your time, if you even live to see such a thing. Tornadoes, draughts, outlaws, hostiles of all kinds, hot sun, wild animals, and all kinds of accidents that could happen...You out there alone with no help. Please don't do something so foolish!"

Ashley held his gaze, feeling sorry for him because she knew how sincere his worry was for her. But in her eyes, he was looking at her like a father, not like a lover. She straightened in her chair and wiped at remaining tears. "Clay, I've been told by others my whole life what I should do and how I should behave. When I was little I had to be a good girl and go to church several times a week. I had to dress just so and speak well and mind my manners. I worked hard, yet there was always someone to look after me, including Nick, who almost got hanged for being *too* protective. I'm not going to marry just for provisions and protection. I'll be fine on my own. You're a good man, Clay Becker, but I don't love you."

"But *I* love *you*, Ashley. You could *learn* to love me."

She shook her head. "It doesn't work that way."

Clay rose, pacing. "I'm asking you once more to marry me, Ashley. Please don't go into an unknown land alone. You've already been through too much."

"And it only made me stronger." Ashley rose and reached out to take his hand. "I can't marry you, Clay. I wouldn't be happy." She studied the hard lines of experience and loneliness in his face. "There are several single women in town who'd love your attention, and you know it."

Clay smiled, a sadness in his eyes. "But they aren't *you*. Everything about you is beautiful—your hair—your eyes—your shape—your personality and kindness. You've had a bad time of it. It's time you relaxed and enjoyed life."

Ashley squeezed his hand. "And that's what I intend to do. No one can *make* someone love them, Clay, not the way you want. I love you as a friend, but that's all."

"Is that how you loved Nick Calhoun?"

Ashley blinked in confusion. "Why would you ask that?"

"Because I saw it in your eyes when I mentioned he's still alive. I saw how you turned away to hide your feelings. Have you seen him?"

"No!" Ashley let go of his hand. "How could I? You said he's a wanted man now. God only knows where he is, and considering what he's done and that he's running from the law, he would never come here and complicate my life that way. It's been six years since he left, and everything is changed now."

"You aren't leaving with *him*, are you?"

Ashley folded her arms. "Of course not! I'm not some fainting flower who needs to fall into some man's arms, Clay Matthews. And I'm not the only woman alone who's decided to settle under the Homestead Act." She raised her chin. "It just so happens I'll be traveling with Isaac Stone and his wife and son. You already know Isaac wants to expand his supply business now that the war's over. He's planning to haul freight north, to make a new pathway from northern Texas through Oklahoma and Kansas to the Union Pacific near North Platte, Nebraska. Isaac wants to set up a store there. I can work for him until I decide to claim land of my own. Isaac feels that once a supply route is established, the railroad will start expanding north and south, not just east and west. It all sounds exciting to me, and Rachael Stone wants some woman company along the way. They agreed to let me come along. Isaac and all his men will provide plenty of protection. I'll be fine."

Clay ran a hand through his hair again. "I can see you're determined. Your mother always said you could be stubborn, and now I see it." He stepped closer. "Ashley, if this doesn't turn out like you expected and you find out you *do* need a man, you come running right back here, understand? If for some reason Isaac turns back, you turn back with him. And if you can't, you get word to me, and I'll come to wherever you are and make sure you get back safely. Will you promise me that?"

Ashley forced a smile. "I promise. But you'll probably be married to someone else by then."

Their gazes held in a mutual understanding. Ashley hated hurting the man, but she knew by his attitude that she'd soon learn to resent his belief that a wife should dutifully depend on her husband in every respect. Marrying a man like Clay Becker would never make her happy. "Thank you for all your help, Clay, and for trying so hard to find out who killed my mother."

"I'm sorry that didn't happen, but I'm going to keep trying. You just promise to come to me when all your plans are made and let me see you off. And be sure to let me know where you land so I can stay in touch if we find your mother's killer. But first, promise me you'll still give this more thought."

"I promise."

Clay held her gaze a moment longer. "I love you, Ashley." He leaned in to kiss her cheek, then turned and took his hat from the chair and picked up his gloves. "I'd better get back to town. I'll have paperwork to catch up on." He put his hat on. "I'm leaving two men here again. I just don't feel right leaving you out here alone after what happened to your mother."

"If you insist. Thank you. I'll see that they get fed."

Clay tipped his hat. Looking sad and concerned, he sighed again before turning to walk out the front door. Ashley followed him, standing at the door and waving as he rode off.

Was she crazy to be selling everything and going alone into new country? She only knew she couldn't stay in Gainesville any longer. She ached for her mother's company, wished the woman was here to talk to, but she was truly on her own now. Rachael Stone had been one of her mother's best friends, so she knew her well and would enjoy traveling with her.

Besides, Nick had never come back, so she'd probably never know what he'd wanted. After all that had happened between them, and because of the life he led now, it was probably best this way. After all, she'd thought him dead and had learned to live with that. Perhaps she should think of him that way again. He was a wanted outlaw, a man she could never share a normal life with, even if that's what he'd come to ask her.

Still, it broke her heart to have seen him again for that short moment. Seen the love in his eyes, the loneliness. And it hurt that she'd likely never know what he'd come to tell her.

Chapter Six

*A*shley took the combs from her hair and brushed out the tangles, then looked at herself in the mirror. Was she really brave enough to head to Nebraska on her own? She'd already signed the papers to sell the house and livestock, so there was no turning back unless she wanted to move into town, where she'd have to find a job or marry Clay Becker, neither of which she cared to do. Living in town would only mean a constant reminder of the ugly hanging mobs and the screaming protests of all the men who'd hanged. Every time she passed those hanging trees, she could see those bodies dangling there, some still kicking. The victims weren't even afforded proper hanging platforms and protocol so they would die instantly.

And the nasty gossip about her and Nick Calhoun, now a wanted outlaw, would not go away, either. When Clay brought that up, it only verified her suspicion that the gossip had not subsided or been forgotten. No matter who might want to marry and settle with her here, he would have to deal with what others might say about her.

And living close to home would mean seeing the old house and farm and being forced to remember it all too vividly—Father and Mother—how Mother had died. Ashley's happy childhood, Nick's friendship … the kiss. If she ever did marry, it would have to be to a man who knew nothing about Nick's near hanging or the story behind it.

There was nothing left here for her now, and she couldn't sit around waiting for Nick to return. She doubted he would. Isaac Stone would be leaving soon. It was time for her to go. She'd be with people she knew, and she had a promised job once they arrived in Nebraska. She could settle first near Isaac and Rachael then look for her own land. The thought of trying something new and different lightened her heart and gave her hope for escaping the ugliness that had started with the war between the States and all the hatred and misunderstandings that came with it.

But there would always be Nick... and that kiss. When he'd come to see her the day her mother died, he'd looked more lost and lonely than ever. Seeing him again had brought back so many nostalgic but painful memories. And now she was left with never knowing what he wanted to tell her.

Maybe her vision of him was distorted because she'd been so much younger when she knew him. She'd thought she could help or change him, a young girl who'd also thought she loved him but felt too young and shy to even suggest such a thing. Nick in turn saw her more as a little sister, until his lips had covered her mouth with such care and passion, making her want to let him do sinful things.

She blinked back tears. "I loved you, Nick. I *still* love you." She wished there was a way they could still be together, but maybe that wasn't what he wanted after all.

She straightened, determined to put all the bad memories away. She was alone now. It was time to move on. She turned from the mirror, concentrating on what was still left unpacked. She had to decide if she could eliminate some of it to keep her wagon light. Isaac had insisted that was important because his own wagons would be heavy with supplies, and he didn't want to have to worry about extra wagons breaking down.

She stood up and took her robe from a hook near the bedroom door. She pulled it on over her flannel gown and tied it.

With so much to think about, sleep was impossible. She decided to go down to the kitchen and make herself some tea. For once the house was dead quiet. Two men kept guard outside, one at the front door and one near the barn, but inside she was alone. Things had calmed, and she was enjoying the peace.

Everything was settled. Papers had been signed. All her most important things had been packed and stored with her wagon in town. Tomorrow she would finish packing what little was left and go stay with Rachael Stone until the supply wagons left Gainesville. She personally knew all the drivers, and one other driver was taking his wife along, so she felt perfectly safe traveling with them. They were all experienced at this type of travel, and they all knew how to use rifles for protection.

She paused to go back to her dressing table and pull her hair back at the sides, replacing the combs she'd removed for bed. There was always a chance one of the guards outside would want to come in and make sure she was all right. It would be bad enough being caught in her robe, worse for her hair to be completely undone. She headed down the stairs, still struggling against the vision of her mother being beaten and thrown against the railing. That memory was another reason she had to leave this house for good.

She hurried past the bottom post and walked into the kitchen, lighting an oil lamp in the middle of the kitchen table. She walked to the stove and added a few small pieces of wood under the burner grate that she always kept warm for water or coffee. She replaced the grate and set a kettle of water on it, then folded her arms and stepped back to wait for the water to heat.

Suddenly the oil lamp behind her went out and the kitchen went dark. Someone very big and very strong grabbed her around the arms in a grip that made it impossible to fight. At the same time a big hand covered her mouth tightly. She gasped and tried to get away, her first thought being that the one-eyed man who'd killed her mother had come back to kill her, too. She wiggled and kicked as someone dragged her out of the kitchen and into the dark hallway.

"Don't scream," a man said softly close to Ashley's ear. "It's just me, Nick. I know there are men outside. You know I'd never hurt you, Ash, but I had to sneak in. I was afraid you'd scream if I startled you."

Ashley relaxed into his grip.

"We need to have that talk. Nod your head if you're okay with this."

Ashley nodded her head vigorously.

Nick slowly moved his hand from over her mouth. "I'm sorry, but I don't want those men outside to know I'm here. Take the kettle off the burner plate so it won't steam and whistle."

By moonlight, Ashley did as she was told, then let out a soft gasp when Nick picked her up in his arms as though she weighed no more than a child.

"Someone might see or hear us down here," he whispered.

He turned and carried her out of the kitchen and up the stairs, which were dimly visible by an oil lamp Ashley kept lit at night to see her way if necessary. He paused in front of her bedroom door.

"This still your room?"

"Yes."

Nick knew the house well, had practically lived in it with them the last two years he'd worked for the family. The only reason her father had decided against Nick having a room in the house was it would look bad for Ashley. Nick shoved her bedroom door open with his foot and carried her inside, then set her on her feet and softly closed the door. He walked to her dressing table and killed the flame of her oil lamp.

"I can't risk someone seeing our shadows."

The room seemed too dark now, but Ashley could see Nick by a bright ray of moonlight that gleamed through a window where the curtains were still open. An aura of strength and power permeated the dark room, confusing Ashley with whether she should still trust this man or not. Was she wrong to think he was still just the old Nick who'd risked a hanging to defend her? Apparently, he was changed. And whether it was because of the war or not, he was a wanted man now.

Chapter Seven

"How did you get in?" Ashley asked softly.

"Through an unlocked back window. There are only two men outside, one in front and one near the barn. The fools never thought to guard the back of the house. I've been watching this place for the past three days."

"Watching from where? How did you manage to elude all the men who've been swarming around here?"

"A man *learns* how to stay out of sight when he sees his face on wanted posters."

Ashley took another deep breath, studying his tall silhouette in the darkness, no features but a dark shadow—broad shoulders—a full man who could knock her out with one blow. He stepped closer, and Ashley could see him in a shaft of bright moonlight. She backed away.

"Ash, don't be afraid of me." He kept his voice to a near whisper. "You know I'd never bring you harm. I haven't changed in that respect, no matter what you've heard about me."

"What I've heard is bank robbery and *murder*. And are you and whatever men you ride with the ones stealing all the cattle and horses around here? Are you that angry at the people of Gainesville?" Ashley caught a flash of outlaw in his dark eyes, a mixture of his terrible loneliness and hatred.

"If they hadn't tried to hang me when all I did was help you, and if I hadn't been sent off to a war I didn't give a damn about, I wouldn't have ended up suffering a hell I can't even describe," he answered in a low growl. "And I wouldn't have lost *you!*"

"But you *haven't* lost me, Nick."

"We can't be together now. It's the same thing. As far as the stolen cattle, those cattle bring good money in South Texas and northern Mexico. I need money for where I'm going, and rustling and herding a few head of cattle is a lot easier than robbing banks and trains and getting into gun battles with lawmen and bank guards. There aren't exactly a lot of jobs out there a wanted man can get, Ashley!"

She shook her head. "Nick, this is all wrong. It isn't like you to do these things."

"Well, it is now. It's too late for anything else. All I can do now is get out of here and head for places where lawmen aren't allowed. I just couldn't bring myself to leave without letting you know I'm alive and that I...I haven't stopped thinking about you in all these years. I loved you when I left, and I *still* love you. I just didn't think it was fair to ride off to Outlaw Country without explaining a few things, or without a real good-bye."

"Outlaw Country? What are you talking about?"

"I'm going away, Ash. For good. I'm headed to South Texas with the stolen livestock. Then I'll head west, to high country in the Rockies. I met some men who've been there and are going back. Men who lost whole families, farms and businesses in the war, men who ended up doing things they would've never normally done. Things that landed them in trouble with the law, like dealing with carpetbaggers and tax collectors in their own way."

"Like *killing* them? Are they the same men who rob banks and murder innocent tellers?"

"It's not like that with me, Ash."

"Sheriff Becker said—"

"Are you going to marry him?" Nick interrupted.

"What?"

"I have a source here in Gainesville. He said Clay Becker wants to marry you. I actually thought you'd be married by now. He's the kind of man you *should* marry, Ash. Not a man like me."

"But I'm *not* going to marry him. In fact, I'm leaving Gainesville. I was afraid you wouldn't show up in time for us to talk before I go. I'm traveling with Isaac Stone and his wife."

"I heard that, too, but I thought you'd take the easier way and marry Becker, even though I was sure you didn't love him. Your first man should be—" He sighed deeply. "Promise me that when you marry, it will be for love, Ash. *Real* love, and no other reason. I want you to be happy."

Ashley blinked in surprise at the words. "Nick, *you're* the man I love. I wanted to tell you before they marched you off to war, but I never got the chance. When Father told me you'd been killed, I was devastated. I hated that I never got to tell you my true feelings."

Nick stepped a little closer again. "You *can't* love me, Ash. There's no future in it."

"But we could—"

"No." Nick took hold of her arms. "Look, I was afraid to tell you or your father how I felt back then because I was just farm help, and there was something you didn't know about me, something that happened back in New York. Besides, I was afraid that if I spoke my true feelings you wouldn't feel the same and you'd be upset, and your father might have fired me."

"Nick, he wouldn't have done that. He cared a lot about you."

"Maybe as a young man needing a home, and as a good worker. But I *wasn't* honest about the reason I came to Gainesville." He let go of her and paced. "Besides, I highly doubt he saw me as son-in-law material. I felt guilty that day they almost hanged me, when your father said he totally trusted me around you. Little did he know I'd already kissed you and wanted you. If he'd known the truth then, I'd have been hanged."

"I don't believe that. You should have told him, Nick. We hadn't done one thing wrong. He might have accepted you."

He stopped pacing and stood closer again, his hands on his hips. "That doesn't matter now. It's water over the damn. And things I did before I came here, things I've done since then ... I'm no husband material for a beautiful, well-bred young woman like you. It's too late to even *think* about loving each other. There is no way in hell I'd ask you to live the kind of life I'll lead from here on, but I just, I wanted to explain everything that happened and why I have no hope of getting out of the charges against me. If I'm going to stop running, I have to go where lawmen *don't* go. They have their own code of living out in the mountains. Some men take their whole family with them, but it's no place for a woman like you. Living out there is bound to be hard and dangerous."

"But I'd have *you*. You'd take care of me. You'd protect me. I don't want you to ride off alone, Nick. You've lived alone most of your life."

Nick moved to sit down on the edge of the bed, shaking his head. "I'm just here to set you straight so you can go on with your life. I half hoped I'd come back to find you married and maybe even with a kid."

Ashley sat down on the chair at her dressing table. "Nick, I hardly dated. I helped my mother with the house and farm while she nursed my father, and through all that and beyond I mourned your death. And during the rest of the war and even afterward, most of the available young men in Gainesville had also gone off to war, too many of them killed, so between that and helping my mother keep the farm going, there wasn't the time or even the opportunity to see other young men. And some of the few left here wouldn't date me anyway because of the rumors."

Nick straightened and frowned. "*What* rumors?"

"Rumors about you and me. That we—"

Nick leaned forward. "That we *what*? That you were messing with the hired help? That I killed Sid MacIntyre because I was jealous?" He removed his hat and tossed it onto the bed, then rose and paced again. "For God's sake, that is so unfair to you!"

Ashley could feel his anger. She suspected it was that quick anger, like what she'd seen in him when he'd beaten Sid MacIntyre, that kept getting him in trouble. "Nick, it's all right."

"No, it isn't!" he snapped. "My God, how I hate this town. I'm *glad* you're getting out, too. I hope you believe me when I tell you I hope you find a good man and marry and be happy, Ash." He came over and sat down on the bed again. "I'm sorry for all of this. I probably shouldn't have come back at all. I should have let you go on thinking I was dead, but I just, I thought you had a right to know I'm alive and that you're almost all I thought about when I was in that prison. I didn't want you to think I just left and forgot about you, not after that kiss and telling you I loved you."

"Nick, maybe you've done some bad things, but you're good in your heart. I *know* you are." Ashley felt him watching her in the dark. She felt a heavy dread moving through her. This wasn't a *come with me* visit. This was *good-bye*. "Please reconsider what you're doing. I don't need to know whatever you came to tell me about your past. It's okay. I loved you when you left, and I *still* love you. You're telling me to get married and be happy, but how am I supposed to forget you now that I know you're still alive and that you love me? Take me with you, Nick!"

He ran his hands through his hair, then rested his elbows on his knees, looking straight at her in the moonlight. "I've killed men, Ash. Even before I came to Gainesville. That's *why* I came to Gainesville. Because it was far, far away from New York. I was *running* and *hiding,* even back then. That's why I stayed here on the farm and minded my own business most of the time. I'm big and strong, and I'm good with my fists. That, combined with my Irish temper, is dangerous. It gets me in trouble. Back in New York my Irish immigrant parents weren't treated very well. I grew up defending them and myself. I got into a lot of fights. It got worse after my father died from pneumonia. My mother worked so hard it wore her out. When I was twelve, she got too sick to work, so I went to work myself hawking newspapers and hauling big crates of fruit at a warehouse. When I was fifteen, I—"

He hesitated, and Ashley noticed a little catch in his words. "What happened, Nick?"

"I, uh…" He paused again and cleared his throat. "I came home to find my mother beaten to death and…abused in the way no woman wants to be abused." He took a deep breath and cleared his throat again.

"Oh, Nick, I'm so sorry! And here I sent you into the house to find my own mother murdered the same way. I never should have let you see that."

"Oh, I've seen worse—much worse—in the war and in that prison." He rose and paced again. "At any rate, I was pretty street-wise back then. I knew how to ask around, how to get information. I had to use my fists a few times to get it, but I damn well found out who raped and killed my mother. I found him and I beat him to a pulp. He was still alive when I picked up an iron pipe and landed it on his skull. Someone had called the police by then, and a policeman saw me. He almost caught me, but I managed to out-run him."

He went to a window and looked out, but Ashley could tell he was just avoiding letting her see his tears. He breathed heavily for several long seconds before clearing his throat and coming over to sit on the bed again. "I knew that policeman, Ash, so I was done for. I ran. Hopped on a train and took it as far west as it would go. Luckily, I had a little money on me and was able to buy some clean clothes and a horse. I got a job loading steamboats on the Mississippi but felt like I wasn't far enough away yet. And a lot of people travel by steamboat, so I was scared I'd still somehow be caught. I left that job and kept going west, landed here in Gainesville and found the job here on your farm, where I could hide in the country and keep to myself."

"Nick, you couldn't help what you did back in New York, not after finding your mother that way."

"I could have left him there, alive but unconscious and bleeding. But all I could see was what he'd done to my mother, so I picked up that iron pipe."

He stood up again and wiped at his eyes, his constant movement telling Ashley he was truly nervous about being caught. At the same time, she felt the little boy in him wanting to cry over his mother, the lost and scared boy who'd had no one to turn to with his loss and his problems.

"Now you know why I beat Sid like I did. I saw him trying to force himself on you, and I saw my mother all over again. I couldn't control my rage. That made *two* men I'd killed. And God knows how many I killed in the war. People think that's forgivable, and maybe it is, but not for someone who'd already killed two men. I'm damn lucky I've avoided being hanged or imprisoned all these years. If those men who sent me to war six years ago had known I'd killed a man back in New York by bashing his head in with an iron pipe, they'd have executed me for sure."

"Oh, Nick, you had *reason*. I know your *heart*. I wouldn't be afraid to leave with you."

Nick shook his head. "That's not all of it, Ash. I went to that god-awful Union prison, where I suffered horrible sickness and pain from my wound, a wound they did nothing about." He sat down on the bed again. "A guard who hated me for being Irish and for fighting for the South deliberately kicked my wound when it was finally beginning to heal. The blow re-opened it and led to even more agony. When I got better, I killed that guard. They were going to hang me for it, so there's a third hanging I barely missed. A couple of men imprisoned with me plotted to help me escape. By some miracle, we all got out of there. But I killed another guard while escaping." He ran a hand through his hair again. "Is this getting ugly enough for you?"

"Nick, it was *war.*"

"It was *me!* My anger. My *temper.*" Again he rose and nervously paced. "My God, Ash, I weighed all of maybe a hundred and ten pounds when I got out of that prison. Do you know how awful that is for a man my size and height? I was a skeleton! It took me and the others nearly six *months* to get back into shape, and we had nothing—no food—no home. We just *ran.* And to eat we robbed a bank and stole cattle and did whatever we had to do to survive. It's true that in one bank robbery a teller got shot, but it wasn't me who killed him. One of the others shot him, but the teller had pulled a gun on him. Still, I got blamed for it and ended up on a wanted poster. And the Federal government wants me for killing those two guards in that prison because it was deliberate killing, not part of a battle. And I don't doubt I'm still wanted in New York, so I have no choice now but to head west. With no promise of exactly how or where I'll settle."

Ashley stood up to face him. "Nick, I'm so sorry. So much has changed since that day you kissed me. I never, ever once saw the anger in you. All I saw was loneliness, and that's all that's wrong now. I can *help* you, Nick. Take me with you. Let me love you!"

"Just *knowing* you love me is all I need. I can't take you with me because I'm going to a place that's dangerous and lawless, but it's not just because of that. I *won't* take you with me, because I'll likely kill again once I'm out there."

Ashley hung her head. "I don't know what to say. This is a side of you I never saw, Nick, but I know you weren't like this when you left. The thing in New York I can understand."

"Yeah, well, the war changed all of that. The thing with Sid, that truly was an accident. I didn't want to deliberately kill again like I killed the man who attacked my mother. Even after they sent me off with your father, I dreamed of coming back – for you. But after what this town tried to do to me— and now the Federal government wanting me—it's just... It's all gone too far. I would take you with me, but I'm afraid the kind of life *I'd* have to live in lawless country would be too hard on you. I won't let you try to build a life around a wanted man."

"We could try."

Nick shook his head. "It wouldn't be enough, not for somebody like you. I just felt like I had to settle that for once and for all. I was afraid you'd find out I was still alive and you'd wonder why I never told you or came to see you. We were damn good friends when I left, if nothing more. But the *way* I left—things just seemed so unfinished. So here I am. I just wanted to tell you a real good-bye and explain the reasons why."

Ashley wiped at tears. "I hate good-byes. It seems like that's all I've faced for six years. Now I'll have to say good-bye again. To you, and to my mother and this farm."

Nick came closer and knelt in front of her chair. "I'm so sorry, Ash. As far as protecting you, I want you to know I'll be watching for a big, strong man with a bad eye, anyone who could be the man who killed your mother. If he has any sense, he'll head for Outlaw Country, too, and if he does, I'll damn well find him and make sure he can never abuse another woman like that again."

"You mean, you'd *kill* him?"

"If I have to. Why not? It would mean you're safe, and the man would apparently be no loss to society. I'm already wanted for murder and bank robbery. What's one more killing?"

Ashley closed her eyes and shook her head. "You will never convince me that's the real you, Nick Calhoun. I've known the good side, the softer side. I've known the hard-working man who was a good and loyal friend to my father. The man who risked his life and reputation to save me from a fate worse than death. The man who kissed me and dreamed of settling."

Nick took hold of her hands. "I lived here with your family for six years, and they were the best six years of my life. I served with your father in the war. And I never forgot you or our friendship and how good you always were to me." He kissed the back of her hand. "I just...I wanted you to know how special you are to me. How special you will *always* be to me. And I want you to be safe when you leave for Nebraska."

He squeezed her hands, and Ashley could see his faint, reassuring smile in the moonlight. "You're traveling with some pretty good men, and I heard one of the others is taking his wife with him, too, so with a couple of women along, you'll be even safer."

"How do you know so much about me and this trip, Nick Calhoun?"

"One of my men moved to Gainesville recently. He's not wanted, so he agreed to come here and let me know what's going on, so I'd be prepared when I came to find you. He's been here since before I showed up, and he's going on that trip north with Isaac Strong."

"Nick!" Ashley drew in her breath but couldn't help her own smile. "You've been *spying* on me?"

He shrugged. "Sort of."

"*Sort* of? Who is it?"

"His name is Cliff Albertson."

"Cliff?" Ashley rose, and Nick stood up with her. They still held hands. "I know him! He came to town a couple of months ago and he works for Isaac. He's been in touch with you this whole time?"

"He was with me in prison and was one of those who escaped. He's a good man. I'd bet my life on him, Ash. You can trust him. He's going with Isaac to keep an eye on you, but Isaac doesn't know the real reason he volunteered to go."

Ashley frowned, still clinging to his hands—strong hands—hands that made her feel safe. "I don't know whether to thank you or be angry with you for having someone watch me without my knowledge."

"I just couldn't let you make that trip alone. I trust Cliff completely, and I'll feel a lot better knowing he's along. He'll make sure you're safe. When it's over, he'll stay on to help you more if you need it. Eventually he'll catch up to us out west, and I'll know how things went." Nick let go of one hand and touched the side of Ashley's face. "I've got to go, Ash. Every minute I stay is a risk."

"Nick, I'd still rather go west with you. I *love* you. I don't want you to be alone."

"You have no idea how tempting it is to take you with me, but this is for your own good."

Ashley closed her eyes and rested her forehead against his chest, breathing in the scent of him and never wanting to forget it. "Please don't leave me behind, Nick."

He let go of her other hand and pulled her closer, twisting his fingers into her hair.

"*Hair as red as the autumn blaze in the maple trees.*" Ashley wondered if he remember saying that to her once?

"We don't have any choice, Ash. I'm doing this because I love you. I'm just sorry it all turned out like this, but believe me when I tell you you're better off without me."

Ashley leaned back to look up at him, and he leaned down to kiss her lightly. Why did she let him? It was beautiful. It was warm. It was delicious. She knew it would only make their parting more painful, yet she didn't want the kiss to end. In one quick moment of passion and desire Nick moved his arms around her and lifted her off her feet while the kiss lingered.

Deeper. Sinfully deeper. Ashley wrapped her arms around his neck, recklessly returning his hungry kiss with open lips, hating the thought of him doing this with some other woman in lawless country. It should only be with her. Nick Calhoun should be her first man. The only man allowed to break her into a full woman.

Isn't that how it should have been? He'd be so good to her. So patient. And though she'd never been bedded, she knew this was the only man she'd enjoy taking inside her.

He groaned with the want of her, finally leaving her lips and nuzzling her neck. "You smell so damn good." With one hand he kept a grip on her hair while he kissed her again.

Ashley thought how easy it would be to fall into her bed with him. She wore only a night gown and robe. "Make love to me, Nick. Please. I want it to be you, even if we can't stay together."

"Don't say that. You don't know what you are asking, Ash, or what it does to me to hear you say it!"

"I don't care how it all turns out," she answered as he nuzzled her neck again.

He kept a strong arm behind her back. She put her head back and let his lips wander down her neck as he moved his other hand under one breast, lifting it, running a thumb over it, feeling its taut nipple through her robe. He groaned, moving his mouth back to hers, kissing her hungrily. Ashley could feel his hardness against her thigh. Virgin though she was, she knew what she was feeling, and she wanted him inside her, but he suddenly pulled away.

"We can't do this," he protested. "God, Ash, I didn't mean for that to happen. I'm sorry! Doing what we want to do right now would be the worst mistake of our lives, especially for you. I could get you pregnant. I love you, but everything is changed now."

He stepped farther back.

"Nick, *please!*" Ashley stepped closer.

"No." He gently pushed her away. "I'm so damn sorry I kissed you like that. Touched you like that. I shouldn't have."

"But we—"

"Hey! Whose horse is that?"

"Jesus, they found my horse," Nick exclaimed. He grasped Ashley's face and gave her a last quick kiss. "Good-bye, Ash. Be happy. Be happy with someone else." He grabbed his hat from the bed, then shoved something into his pocket. "Always remember that I love you." He put on his hat and tossed something onto the bed, then ran to a window at the back of her bedroom.

"Nick, don't let this be forever!"

"It *is* forever. Be the proper woman you were meant to be, Ash."

"Nick, I love you!"

He was already out the window. Ashley leaned out to see him climb down a trellis and disappear into the darkness.

"There he is!" Someone fired a shot.

"Oh, my God! Nick!" she called out the window.

"Get him!"

"Get away from that horse or die!"

She recognized Nick's voice.

"I know both you men, and I don't want to shoot either one of you."

"My God, it's Nick Calhoun!"

"I just came to say good-bye to a friend. Don't make any more of it. You boys don't want to have to admit I got inside the house without you even knowing it, do you? Don't make me shoot. Remember that I let you live."

"Shit," someone answered. "Let him go."

Moments later Ashley heard a horse gallop off. She wilted to the floor. If this got out, the stories about her letting an outlaw into her bedroom would certainly add plenty to her reasons for leaving Gainesville. She could still taste Nick's kiss. She still ached for much more and felt literal pain at knowing she would never know him that way. Never see him again.

She sobbed his name, feeling sick and alone. Someone shouted up to her then.

"You okay, Miss Vale?"

Ashley clung to the window sill and pulled herself up. "I'm fine. He was only here a couple of minutes to say good-bye when you spotted his horse," she lied, hoping to ward off the worst of the gossip. "Nick was like a brother to me at one time. He didn't mean any harm."

Suddenly weary, she stumbled to her bed and ran her hand along the quilt to find whatever Nick had thrown there. She felt something foreign. Wiping at her eyes and forcing back more tears, she picked up whatever it was and walked over to the oil lamp to re-light it so she could study what she'd found. She raised it to the light, realizing then that it was a black leather hat band, Nick's hat band, she was sure. He had pulled it off and left it there so she'd have something of his. She glanced at the bed then and saw a roll of money.

"Oh, Nick." She walked to the bed and picked it up. "Oh, my God." It was made up of hundred-dollar bills. She unrolled it and counted. There were ten of them. "Nick, I'd rather be poor and have you."

She reached up to remove the combs from her hair, partly undone when he ran his fingers into it.

The combs were gone! He'd taken them with him without her even knowing it. She realized that was what he'd shoved into his pocket. The realization that he wanted something of her with him broke her heart.

She hurried back to the window and could no longer hear his horse. He was gone, and she knew this time truly was forever. He loved her enough to leave her, but she would have put up with anything to go with him. How was she ever going to love someone else? How could she ever forget him?

"God go with you, too, Nick Calhoun," she said softly.

She couldn't help more tears. Had one of those men wounded him? He could easily have shot back, but he hadn't.

"You're *not* bad, Nick. You're just looking for love and acceptance in all the wrong ways. I could have given you those things."

She was more relieved than ever that she was leaving Gainesville. She could never stay here now. Maybe going away would help her broken heart.

Part II

Chapter Eight

"Are you real sure about this, Ashley?"

Ashley climbed down from her covered farm wagon to face Isaac Stone.

"Yes, and I'm all packed," she told the man with confidence, thinking how she'd rather be heading west with Nick, but there was no way to change things now. "My wagon is light-weight, easy for horses like Max and Brutus to pull." She patted the rump of one of her three huge draft horses. "I have my father's hunting rifle and his army pistol with me, and I have all the supplies I need to do my own camping and cooking along the way." It irritated her that she had to repeat all the reasons why she could make this trip, but she didn't want to anger Isaac by showing her aggravation.

Stone, a bearded man with weathered skin and missing most of his front teeth, shook his head and stuck his thumbs into his wide gun belt. "Ma'am, this will be a hard trip. But I have to say, my wife will appreciate the company of another woman. So will Spence Lamar's wife. She's young like you, and she and Spence haven't been married long, so she's nervous about this trip. But they hope to stay wherever we land and help open a new store there."

"And I'm very relieved to know there will be two other women along," Ashley answered.

"Well, it won't be easy, mind you. There's no good pathway north, so we'll be covering some rough ground. I intend to be one of those who creates a new trail. We'll run into wind, dust, outlaws, hostiles, and maybe a few things we don't even know about. It's bad enough havin' lots of supplies with us, but havin' a pretty, young, unattached woman along – that's gonna' make things even rougher. Even the two married ones will be in danger. But you—I mean—I heard the rumor about Nick Calhoun sneaking back here to see you. I don't want any trouble from his kind."

His unjust remark made Ashley bristle, and hearing Nick's name brought a catch to her heart. "Nick only came by to tell me he's alive and on his way west, never to come back." She struggled not to show her anger. "He was like family, and he had a right to see me. Don't forget that he risked a hanging just to help me against Sid MacIntyre. But he's gone now, for good. And if you're worried about me and those rumors – " She raised her chin confidently and pulled back the wool jacket she wore to reveal the butt of her father's gun sticking out from the belt of her riding skirt. "I'm ready to defend myself *and* my reputation. I'll mind my own business and will appreciate it if you and your men do the same."

Stone shook his head. "I just want you to be extra sure about this, Ashley. You're young and maybe too trusting, but the wife and your ma were good friends, and we both know you're respectable. It's just that rumors can cause a lot of trouble sometimes, but most of the men with us know you good enough."

"And I paid you the required fifty dollars to go along, Isaac, even though I know the dangers. I want to leave Gainesville, and I'm willing to take the risks involved."

Isaac put his hands on his hips and leaned closer. "Look, girl, I don't want any trouble from Nick Calhoun either. Is he for sure gone?"

Ashley resisted a sudden urge to cry. Instead, she answered firmly, "Yes. I wouldn't lie about that. He's gone west and doesn't plan on ever coming back. And with the awful way my mother died, I can't stay in that house any longer. So, I'm headed north to start life over. That's all there is to it."

Stone adjusted his hat. "All right, then. You've been duly warned." The man turned to address his wife while Ashley climbed into her wagon seat. Stone's son, Bobby, waved to her and climbed into the Stone wagon seat beside his mother. He was fifteen now and able to handle a team and a rifle. The young man was proud and excited about staying in Nebraska when this trip was over and helping his parents set up a new store there.

Ashley glanced past her wagon at a line of six wagons full of flour and sugar, canned goods, guns and ammunition, corn, potatoes, oil for lamps, bolts of cloth, farming tools, some furniture and a host of other supplies headed north instead of west. She did not miss the fact that every wagon driver was turned around looking at her, all of them probably doubting that she could do this on her own. It gave her the resolve she needed to prove them wrong.

"You're so brave, Ashley," Clara Peele told her. The woman was one of several who'd come to the freight depot to see Ashley off. "But your mother would be so upset if she knew about this."

"I'd like to think she'd wish me well," Ashley called to Clara. "She knew I wasn't totally happy here, Clara."

Clara, yet another Gainesville war widow, dabbed at her eyes with a handkerchief. She was a tall, rather spindly woman who always wore a shawl, whether it was cold out or ninety degrees. "Your mother was a good friend."

Several other women from church who'd gathered to see Ashley off nodded, a few also wiping at their eyes. Little did they know that her own regrets were that she wouldn't really miss any of them all that much. It was the fact that she'd likely never see Nick again that made her sad.

Where was he now? Would he make it to Outlaw Country and find a way to survive there? Her other regret was that she'd never be able to visit her parents' graves again, never work in her mother's rose garden or help with cooking and canning in their big kitchen again. The farmhouse was the only home she'd ever known, but now it belonged to someone else.

She waved to the men and women who'd been kind enough to have another good-bye get-together for her at the church the previous night. They'd served cake and coffee and asked a lot of questions. Many expressed their concern for her safety, and others asked about the Homestead Act.

One other widowed woman, Sara Lane, who'd lost both a husband and a son in the war, had planned to travel with the wagon train and settle under the Homestead Act, but she'd backed out at the last minute, too afraid of what could happen on such a trip. Now Sara held a handkerchief under her nose, weeping and smiling at the same time as she waved to Ashley, who wished she hadn't changed her mind. It would have been so much easier and more comforting if yet another woman had come along. But she had Rachael Stone and Sandra Lamar to talk with. Rachael was more the motherly type, and Sandra was Ashley's age. Having their company would be a big help.

But Sandra has a husband along.

If things could have been different, she might be making this trip as Nick Calhoun's wife. She looked around again. She didn't see Cliff Albertson. In the past, she'd seen him stocking shelves in Isaac's supply store and knew who he was, but she'd never actually talked him. Now she had a thousand questions to ask him about Nick. It warmed her heart to know Nick had thought to send someone along to secretly watch out for her.

"Head 'em up!" Isaac Stone shouted as he climbed into the lead wagon.

Ashley picked up the reins. "I will write you as soon as I get settled," she told Clara who nodded and turned away, crying. Ashley felt sorry for her mother's best friend.

The lead wagon, a big, heavy Conestoga packed with supplies and driven by Isaac, got under way, followed by Rachael Stone and their son Billy, in a covered prairie schooner. Stone's son let out a war whoop, waving to some of his friends. Ashley had to smile at his energy and joy. This would be a big adventure for him. Behind Rachael was another heavy Conestoga with the sign STONE FREIGHTING painted on the side and driven by old Hoot Stowers, a widower who'd worked for Isaac for years. Bill Sanders, a middle-aged man of average build and looks followed Hoot in another packed Conestoga. He was leaving his wife and four children behind.

Each of the Conestogas was pulled by six oxen, with two relief oxen tied to the backs. Rachael's wagon was pulled by four oxen, another two tied to the back. Hoot Stowers's and Bill Sanders's wagons were each covered with burlap and led by six oxen, with an extra ox tied to the back of each wagon.

The fifth wagon, a smaller cook wagon pulled by six mules, was driven by Morgan Peters, a widower with grown children. Beside him sat a black man named Will, who had once been Morgan's slave. He'd actually always been more friend than slave, and since the end of the war, Morgan had given Will his emancipation papers and now paid him a wage. Will was the designated cook for the freighters, and the cook wagon was filled with firewood, pots and pans, and food for the journey. Ashley, though, also intended to do some of the cooking, as would the other two women. Two extra mules were tied to the back of Morgan's wagon.

Spence Lamar drove the sixth wagon in front of Ashley's. Spence was younger, and he and Sandra would stay behind in Nebraska with Billy and Rachael Stone once they reached their final destination. He had some schooling and would help with the new store and take care of the books. The Lamar wagon, and Ashley's, were prairie schooners, smaller farm wagons with arched canvas covers. Spence's was pulled by six mules rather than by draft horses, and he was hauling lighter goods for Isaac, things like dress material and ribbon, buttons, socks and such. He snapped the reins and whistled, getting his mules in motion. Two oxen tied to the back of his wagon reluctantly began walking behind.

Ashley drove the seventh wagon. She adjusted her leather gloves before picking up the reins and calling "Git up!" to Max and Brutus, her two best draft horses. She'd kept them just for this trip. Tied to the back of her wagon was Patsy, the mare she favored for riding, and one extra draft horse she called Lexington.

She looked around again for Cliff, finally noticing him herding a remuda of six more mules and eight riding horses, all extra animals that might be needed. She wondered if he'd managed to make sure her wagon was last in line so he'd be closer to her as they traveled and could see everything going on around her.

So, Cliff will serve as wrangler. Ashley wondered if he'd done that type of work for a living before the war. No one knew much about him, other than he was a single man who'd simply ridden into Gainesville one day. She realized she was the only one who knew the real reason, but since they'd left, she'd still not talked to him. She took comfort in knowing he was a good enough friend to Nick to agree to do this. It made her feel a little bit like Nick himself was riding with her.

She looked back again, and Cliff waved his hat to her. The few times she'd seen him in Isaac's store, she'd not paid much attention and remembered only that he was a nice-looking man of perhaps thirty, but she hardly remembered the details of his looks. Others had commented once or twice that the "new man in town" always kept to himself and lived alone.

Ashley waved to him and turned back around, realizing she could never tell the others why Cliff had really come along. If they knew he was Nick's friend, Isaac might fire him and tell him he couldn't come with them. He might even get into trouble, and so would she. If Isaac knew who Cliff really was, he'd fear Nick Calhoun had plans to raid their wagons, and he'd think Ashley had lied about Nick heading west.

"Let's head out!" Isaac yelled.

Ashley thought what an odd and unexpected turn her life had taken. It was all she could do not to break into tears. Not because she was leaving Gainesville, but because this meant truly and forever leaving Nick Calhoun, her family, everything she'd known and loved up to now. She had no idea where she would finally land, and wherever that was, she would be alone. Nick could never come back to civilized country again.

She sat straighter, more resolved than ever to make this work. She couldn't change anything, so she had to buck up and survive. There was no time left for tears. The families and friends of the drivers ran alongside the wagons for a short distance, calling out more good-byes and wishing them good luck and God speed. Before they managed to get all the way out of town, they passed Clay, who sat on his horse watching. He pushed back his hat and nodded to Ashley.

"God speed," he told her, sadness in his eyes. "Remember that I'll be here if you change your mind."

Ashley felt a stab of unnecessary guilt for not agreeing to marry Clay. She prayed inwardly that he'd find a woman who could end his loneliness, and for a brief moment wondered if not staying and marrying him was a foolish mistake. She held the reins in one hand and gave Clay a short wave.

"Good-bye, Clay. Thank you for everything." She realized his men had probably told him about Nick visiting her two nights prior. Surely, he wondered what had really happened, but he'd never asked.

Finally, those running beside the wagons fell away. Ashley didn't look back anymore. She was headed for a new life. Gone forever would be Gainesville. Her mother and father's graves. Clay Becker. Clara. The old farm. Her old life…and Nick Calhoun. Her only memory of him would be the hatband he'd left on her bed. And he'd have her combs to remember her by.

She forced away the memory of that last kiss, the pleasure of his mouth searching hers, the desperate needs he'd ignited when his thumb moved over her breast. She'd wanted him to reach inside her gown and feel her breasts, taste them. She'd wanted desperately to let Nick take her virginity so that he would own it like no other man ever would.

She refused to be ashamed of her bold offer to let him bed her, and she loved him even more for refusing out of respect for her future happiness. But she knew she'd never want another man the way she'd wanted him.

"Nick," she groaned, tears blurring her vision. She suddenly couldn't think of the right words to describe how alone she felt at that moment.

Chapter Nine

There were seven of them, including Nick, who wasn't sure how he'd fallen into the role of leader, but it had been that way since escaping from Elmira prison, where he and four of the men who rode with him had spent time in a hell that had changed them forever. He appreciated all of them for their loyalty and friendship, but he also knew any one of them could decide to ride off on his own at any time.

They all suffered the pain of personal loss—a pain they hoped they could one day overcome and somehow be able to live a normal life. For now, they rode together for companionship and survival, once good men, now lost and lonely and struggling to pick up the pieces from the war.

Trace Belle, a slim, blond-haired, blue-eyed rough-and-tumble whom they all called "Ringer," joined the Confederate Army at fifteen and was still only twenty-two. He lay sleeping next to thirty-year-old Bob Calloway, who preferred being called Cal. He'd lost a wife, a son and his farm to the war. Cal was husky and good-looking, but not the best with a gun. He was better with a rifle and liked to joke a lot. Wherever they went, Cal was more interested in picking up women than anything else, and the others suspected it was just a pretense at avoiding the deep pain of his loss. Cal, Trace, and Nick had their faces on wanted posters.

Buck Davis was a freed black man who, ironically, had fought for the Confederacy. Older than the rest of them, he'd quickly made friends in prison because he was handy at conning guards out of food and tobacco. Buck had saved Nick's life through his in-born ability to treat wounds, even though he'd never been educated in doctoring. After their escape, Buck stayed with them and learned how to handle a handgun with speed and accuracy. He didn't know his true age, but he had white hair and a white beard, and his muscles were beginning to wither a little. None of that seemed to slow him down.

Sam Brady had never spent time at Elmira. Nick and the others met him deep in the Adirondacks after their escape. He was a tall, gangly man with dark hair that hung past his shoulders. He seldom spoke or smiled, and the men knew little about him, but when it came to quick action and defending the others, he was dependable and sure. Nick guessed Sam to be around thirty-five or forty. He'd been living the life of a hermit when they met him, but realizing their need to rest and hide and fatten themselves up, he'd helped them with food and shelter. Sam remained a bit of a recluse and didn't talk much about his past, but he'd decided to ride with them when they left northern New York and headed south. He carried a big knife and was good with it. Asking him about his past seemed to anger him, so no one asked anymore.

Cliff Albertson, also a prison escapee, was with Ashley now, and that helped ease Nick's worry over the trip she was making. Cliff had mentioned only once that he'd lost a wife to an attack by Union soldiers and had joined the war "just to kill Bluecoats." He was the kind of man anyone could tell was good inside and probably longed to live a normal life again, but he'd admitted that would be hard without the woman he'd loved.

Cliff and Nick had talked a lot about how Nick's feelings for Ashley, and Cliff seemed to understand how much Nick hated being unable to be with her. Once Nick learned Ashley was leaving Gainesville, he'd asked Cliff to make the trip with Isaac Stone, since he already worked for Isaac. Being the good friend he'd become, Cliff readily agreed to make the trip and keep an eye on Ashley until she was settled, after which he'd join Nick and the others in Outlaw Country.

Their seventh man was Renaldo Cortez, a single man they'd found breaking horses in southern Texas. Renaldo and Nick had formed an instant friendship that made little sense considering their cultural differences, but Nick felt closer to Renaldo than to any of the others besides Cliff. Renaldo's easy-going and usually light-hearted personality was a comfort. He was non-judgmental and didn't have Nick's quick temper, and the man was slow to anger. He seemed to have a genuine interest in being a sounding board for a man and his troubles, and Nick and the others often found themselves spilling out their feelings and their sad stories to the man.

Renaldo was Nick's age and good looking but humble man who seemed genuinely concerned about others. His part in their oddly-mixed group was to care for the remuda of spare horses, and he'd agreed to help break mustangs and help herd cattle once Nick settled in Outlaw Country, where he hoped to start his own ranch.

Thinking of settling brought Ashley to mind, and how nice it would be to have her with him, especially once he found a way to settle. He ached at the thought of her waiting for him in their bed at night, loving him, giving him children, all the things they would never know. He had no one but himself to blame for his situation, and it sickened him to think how it had affected Ashley's life, too.

He lit a cheroot, the end glowing red in the dark night. He and Renaldo sat on a low hill listening to the soft singing of Buck Davis, whose turn it was to ride among the cattle to keep an eye on them. Most of the herd had been purchased from ranchers, some were wandering mavericks, and some were stolen from Gainesville, which gave Nick great satisfaction. Now they were headed for south Texas to sell their herd before heading west. Disease among cattle there had devastated some ranchers, so there was good money in taking healthy beef there.

"So, we will still go to the mountains without the woman, *me amigo?*" Renaldo asked Nick quietly.

The question brought a sharp pain to Nick's heart. "Yes, without the woman." *The woman* was the term the men had begun using when referring to Ashley. Just the word "woman" disturbed Nick with thoughts of Ashley's beauty, her smile, her womanly softness, the breasts he wanted to touch again. "Soon as we deliver these cattle to that buyer in south Texas, we'll leave for Outlaw Country," he added.

"I think it is a good plan. I hope we can keep the cattle healthy until we reach Brownsville."

A horse shuddered somewhere amid the livestock, and a steer let out a deep bellow.

"I just wish it wasn't so far," Nick answered. "It'll be a hard trip, and I need to get back north and find a way to check on that supply train Ashley's traveling with before we head for the mountains."

Renaldo shook his head. "Cliff will take care of her."

"I know, but he's only one man. I'll still feel better if I can find a way to check on her myself."

Renaldo removed his sombrero and laid it beside him, then watched the crackling fire. "It will take us a good two weeks or more to reach south Texas and sell the cattle, *mi amigo,* then another two weeks getting back. That means a month to six weeks making it all the way north to try to find your woman. She will probably have reached wherever she is going by then."

Nick smiled sadly. "She's not *my* woman, Renaldo. I'd like it if she was, but that can't be now." He thought about her kiss the night he left. He'd wanted nothing more than to lie down in that bed with her, be the one to make a full woman of her, even if they couldn't stay together. He hated the thought of some other man being her first, but even if he'd given in to his own desire, it would have been foolish and wrong. It would've destroyed Ashley's reputation, and he would've been caught and hanged once the guards downstairs found his horse. If he couldn't marry Ashley, he didn't have a right to do anything else.

"It is sad how life turns out for us," Renaldo told him.

Nick reached into his jacket and touched his shirt pocket, where he'd placed two of Ashley's hair combs. "Yes, it is. Ashley's too gentle and too smart and too much of a lady to marry the likes of a wanted man. I could never give her the life she deserves, especially not now. We talked about it that last night I was with her. She wanted to come with me, but I just couldn't do that to her."

God, he could still taste that kiss. The young girl who'd seemed more like a sister to him had turned into a beautiful woman, and if things had turned out differently, he might have been able to marry her. "Now all I can do is make sure she makes it north safely."

"And you still want to find the one-eyed man who killed her mother?" Renaldo asked.

"I sure as hell do. Personally, I think he's left for parts unknown and she doesn't need to worry about him, but I'd rest easier if I could find him."

"Maybe he will head for Outlaw Country, too, like us. Maybe you will find him there, *mi amigo*." Renaldo settled farther down into his bedroll. "Maybe he, too, was in the war and has a grudge of some kind. You say that the woman's father was an officer. Maybe he had something to do with the killer losing his eye."

Nick frowned, watching the flames dance in colors of red, yellow and blue. "Yes." He looked at Renaldo. "You're pretty clever, Renaldo. I never thought of connecting any of it to Ashley's father or the war, but I *did* think the same as you—that he headed for Outlaw Country."

Renaldo stretched. "It just seems to me that this one-eyed man picked out that woman on purpose, you know? You said nothing was stolen. And there were no other attacks in the area. Just hers."

Nick took the cheroot from his lips and tapped off some ashes. "I've thought about that, but I can't imagine why anyone in town would've wanted to kill Patricia Vale. She was a nice woman. Kind. It's more likely her killer was some drifter who thought he'd get under her skirts and then steal her money. I think she fell in the struggle and when he realized she was dead, he ran without taking anything. Maybe he saw Ashley coming and thought someone might be with her. Who knows? I'm just grateful he was gone when Ashley got there."

Renaldo nodded. "Who knows what drives a man to do what he does? War destroys lives, even if it does not physically kill you."

Nick tossed the stub of his smoke into the fire. "Renaldo, you keep surprising me with your insightfulness."

"What is insightfulness?"

Nick smiled. "Never mind. You just have a way with words." An owl hooted somewhere in the distance, and a cloud moved over the moon, making the night darker for a moment. Nick pulled his lambskin coat tighter around his neck. September brought chilly nights, even when the days were still hot. The farther south they went, the warmer it got. Chilly nights would soon end.

Nick laid back and rested his head against his saddle. He pulled a blanket over himself and thought about Ashley...that kiss...how pretty she was. He probably should have let her continue thinking he was dead, but then she never would have known the truth. She never would have known all the reasons why she *shouldn't* love him. Still, the thought of her marrying some other man made him ache to be the one in her bed. He hated the possibility that some other man wouldn't treat her right.

Either way, he had to accept that she could never belong to him, and he had no right hating whoever she finally took for a husband. He stretched and pulled his hat down over his eyes. "We'd better get some shuteye, Renaldo. We have a lot of riding to do tomorrow."

"*Si, señor.*" Renaldo made a grunting sound as he settled into his bedroll.

Nick wondered, if he'd find wherever Ashley had settled farther north, if he should go see her once more. He sighed with disgust at himself for even thinking such a thing. Saying good-bye yet again would be much too hard for both of them, and that's what they would have to do. He couldn't go through that again, and he suspected it would be just as hard on Ashley. He'd have to check on her through someone else, and then he would leave without her knowing he was ever there.

Chapter Ten

Early October...

Ashley shivered into her wool coat, hoping the sudden sleet storm that swept across the wide-open plains of the Texas-Oklahoma border would last only the day. She was well aware that this time of year no one could predict the weather from one day to the next, but she'd hoped for the mostly summer temperatures that still prevailed in September and October. She could only pray Isaac would make it to Kansas before truly inclement weather hit them. If worse came to worse, she could winter there in some small town.

She winced when the wagon hit yet another rough patch in the uneven landscape, and she prayed nothing would break. She hated the thought of having to ask for help fixing a wheel or hub, even though it wouldn't be the first time such problems had plagued them. The cook wagon had lost a wheel two days back, when it literally fell apart after hitting a hole Morgan Peters didn't notice until it was too late. And the second wagon, heavy with corn and potatoes, had almost caught fire when the grease on one of the wheel hubs wore down to nearly dry and began smoking from rubbing on the axle.

Both accidents brought a barrage of cussing from the men for having to stop for repairs. They later apologized to the women for their language, but Isaac was worried now that he'd loaded the three big freight wagons too heavily. He ordered everyone to slow down and keep a better eye out for holes and ruts, and to check wheels, hubs and axles more closely. They lost another full day when some of the animals showed signs of excessive weariness.

All the problems they'd experienced so far meant the trip would take longer than planned, and men were getting ornery. They'd been in a better mood this morning until the sleet storm swept down on them unexpectedly.

"Lessons learned, boys, lessons learned," Isaac told them more than once. "That's the reason for this trip—to find out what it takes."

Most days were spent in quiet thought, the only sound being an almost-constant wind and the creak of the wagons and occasional shudder and snort of one of the oxen, the whinny of horses, or a driver calling out to the animals pulling his wagon, shouting "gee" and "haw" or cussing them out for something.

Cliff Albertson had a loud sneeze they all swore could be heard for miles, and it happened often from the dust he breathed at the back of the line of wagons as he herded the remuda. Everyone joked about it, and he wasn't allowed to watch the animals at night for fear the sudden loud noise of his sneeze on a quiet night would start a stampede. Rachael Stone gave him a pillow to use to muffle himself at night.

So far Cliff had not even talked to Ashley, but she felt him watching, and it helped ease her worry over heading into country bound to be more active with renegades and outlaws. All men had rifles ready and kept a constant eye out for both dangerous men and dangerous animals. This part of Oklahoma had the well-earned name of "no man's land" because of its lawlessness. If they could get through there unscathed, they would make it to Kansas, where they would be a little safer. Still, according to

Isaac, southern Kansas had also become a refuge for displaced natives and for outlaws.

In both Oklahoma and Kansas, more and more people were settling under the Homestead Act, which infuriated the Indians and attracted outlaws. Ashley took hope in the fact that several growing farm towns along the way would give them refuge. Isaac hoped they might even be able to find a soldier escort at the Wichita Agency, which made her feel more confident, though Cliff was along.

Although they had a cook wagon with them, she and the other women did some of the cooking, using mostly the cook wagon supplies. Ashley enjoyed the company of the other women, and so far, the men treated her with respect. But she felt their underlying suspicions over what had happened with Nick. Because of that, she kept to herself as much as possible and refused to show any weakness. She managed to handle the heavy yokes and hitches for her draft horses by herself, sometimes wishing a man would help, but she refused to ask.

In spite of the hardships, each extra day made it easier to leave Gainesville and all her memories behind. She'd even been able to ease her mind and heart over Nick, although she couldn't help wondering where he was … what he was doing … if he was already on his way west to Outlaw Country. Did he think about her anymore? Was he still looking for the man who'd killed her mother?

Isaac interrupted her thoughts when he drew his wagon to a halt and stood up, shouting something back to the rest of them. His words were blown away with the cold, stiff wind.

" … stop for the night," Ashley thought she heard, and something about "shelter … cliffs."

She squinted and tried to see ahead through the sleet that blew past them sideways. The icy rain had grown so heavy that it was building into slush on the ground. Isaac got his wagon underway again, and they all followed, trusting that the man knew what he was doing.

After roughly thirty minutes they came upon an area where a wall-like rock rose out of the ground with no logic as to why it should be there. It looked as though the huge freak of nature ran on for a good half-mile, its top flat as a pancake. Now Ashley understood Isaac's shouts. He guided the wagon train right up against the cliff, and a wonderful relief from the wind seemed to make the temperature rise by a good ten degrees. Ashley was no longer cold, and she was glad the animals would also be out of the wind.

"Well, now, if we'd all been praying for a break, God couldn't have done a better job of bringin' it," Morgan Peters yelled from the cook wagon.

"Yahoo!" Spence Lamar shouted.

Men climbed down from their wagons and began unhitching teams, and women started setting up camps. Ashley did the same, but she hesitated when a man spoke up behind her.

"Can I help you?"

Ashley turned to see the quiet Cliff Albertson standing close by.

"The remuda is fine, and I only have my own horse to tend to," he told her. "I've been watching you handle those big, heavy yokes every day, and I feel sorry for you, and a little guilty for not helping. I was just waiting 'til everybody got used to each other so helping out wouldn't start rumors."

Ashley wasn't sure what to make of the man's offer. "I—I'm fine," she answered. "I promised Isaac I could handle everything myself. That I wouldn't be a bother to anyone." She reached up to unbuckle one of the straps on Max.

"It's no bother, Ma'am. Nick would want me to help. Besides, I expect we should talk. Let me help with your horses for the next couple of days. Act interested in my friendship. Nobody will think anything of it because we're both single, and we'll just pretend a casual attraction but not do anything to stir up any trouble. I promise. It's just that I know Nick wouldn't want you doing so much heavy work, and the other men—they'd understand. Some of them have been wanting to help, too, but they're worried about gossip."

Ashley frowned, facing Cliff and thinking how unreadable his eyes were. "I worry about gossip, too."

Cliff shrugged. "Just act like you're tired and appreciate the help. Let me take care of those harnesses for you. Go get some things out of your wagon and start your campfire."

Ashley blinked and looked past him at the others who were all busy doing their own unloading. No one seemed to notice her talking to Cliff, at least not at the moment. She put her hands on her hips. "Just remember that I promised Isaac Stone I wouldn't cause any problems on this trip, including associating with any of the men in the wrong way."

Cliff nodded. "Sure." He grinned, a soft smile that spoke of a good man. "Besides, in spite of the able, fine looking woman you are, I wouldn't be interested. I've been watching you handle yourself, and a woman like you is too independent for a man like me. I've always preferred the meek and bashful sort. Nick, on the other hand, has strong feelings for you, and he's a good friend. So, let me keep my promise to him and go on about your business. Let me take care of those horses."

Ashley couldn't help a chuckle. She tried to tuck some loose strands of hair that had fallen from the combs in her hair, and she thought how she needed a bath and certainly wasn't exactly "fine looking" at the moment. "I appreciate the initial compliment, and the fact that you're doing this for Nick. If it weren't for that, I wouldn't be so inclined to take orders from you." She turned to walk to the back of her wagon, then looked at him again. "Thank you for going out of your way like this."

Cliff tipped his hat. "I don't mind. You're for sure easy to look at, and Nick saved my life in the war, so I owe him. We escaped Elmira together."

Ashley lowered the rear wagon gate to get out some firewood. Cliff's remark about Nick's strong feelings for her reawakened thoughts of the man she loved but would never see again. She blinked back tears, angry at herself for allowing them. She only loved him more for learning he'd saved Cliff's life.

"Always the defender," she said softly.

It was one of the main reasons she loved him.

Chapter Eleven

Ashley sat on an overturned wash tub and used a long fork to flip over one of two pieces of pork Cliff had given her. He'd dug it out from its packing in a barrel of lard and brought it to her from his supplies.

"I talked to Isaac about this," he'd told her earlier. "I told him I asked if you'd be kind enough to cook some of my pork for me and that you agreed. I made sure he didn't think something was going on between us."

Apparently, Isaac believed Cliff. He'd come to see her and let her know it was fine if she wanted to cook Cliff's meat for him. She was growing tired of the subtle insinuation that she was open prey for single men, and that because she was single, too, it might cause trouble for even the married men.

Cliff walked into the light of her fire. The days were shorter now, and although they hadn't eaten yet, it was already dark.

"That smells good. I thank you for cooking it."

"It's no problem. As long as I get to eat some of it, too."

Cliff sat down on a blanket across from her and smiled, a rare sight for the taciturn man few knew much about. Ashley realized she'd only seen him smile twice, and both times were today. She surmised he felt more relaxed because she was letting him help more.

"Of course, you can have some of it," he told her.

A medium-built, solid man, Ashley thought him nice looking, but in a rugged, middle-aged way. He had the look of a
man who'd seen too much of hard times and maybe personal
loss. She guessed his age at late thirties, but sometimes hard living made a man look older than he really was. Age and weather
had formed lines around his blue eyes. His sandy hair needed to
be washed and cut, but most men on this trip needed the same
thing.

"You should smile more often," she told him. "Most people
say you always seem angry with the world."

He quickly sobered again. "Maybe I am."

Ashley turned to a gunny sack and pulled out a biscuit. "Too
many of us feel that way because of what the war did to us." She
placed the biscuit on a tin plate and set it near the fire. "I'll warm
this a little and you can eat it with your pork. Would you like
coffee?"

"I'd like that just fine."

Ashley poured some coffee into a tin cup. Most of her uten-
sils were tin, better for travel over hard, bumpy ground. Her
china had been carefully packed into straw in nailed crates. "I'm
sure you heard about the hangings in Gainesville."

"Yes, Ma'am."

"That's what I mean about war. It brings out the animal in
men—sometimes even in women."

Cliff nodded and took the cup of coffee Ashley handed him.

"It changed Nick, too," Ashley added.

"It changed *all* of us," Cliff answered. "Nick's a good man
inside. He didn't want any of this."

"*No one* did." Ashley kept her voice down, worried someone might hear them talking about Nick and wonder why. She
leaned a little closer to Cliff. "Tell me about Nick—what prison
was like—why he did some of the things he did—stealing and
killing. That's not the Nick I knew."

Cliff sipped a little more coffee. "He *still* isn't that man. I won't tell you about prison because what went on there isn't for the ears of a nice lady like you. I'm sure he gave you a pretty good idea when he talked with you. Suffice it to say we were skeletons when we got out of there. How we found the strength to kill a couple of guards and get their guns and get past more guards, I'll never know. But once we were out, for those first few months it was a matter of survival, and, Ma'am, you don't want to know what a man will do for that. We lived off the land and what we could steal, then made our way down to Tennessee, all hungry and wore out again. If it weren't for a trapper we met in the Adirondacks, we'd probably all be dead from starvation and neglect. His name is Sam Brady, and he followed us on down to Tennessee. He's still with us. He fed us—let us rest and fatten up in those mountains in New York, then helped keep us in food all the way south. We were full of need and hate, Ma'am, hate for the Union, for that prison, all of it. That's what led to some of the raiding and robbing we did."

He drank more coffee. Ashley said nothing, suspecting that if she said too much, he'd stop talking. She poured herself a cup and drank some.

"I lost a wife in the war. So, I had nothing to go home to because my parents are dead, too."

"I'm sorry."

Cliff sighed. "Most of the others didn't have anything to go back to either. We all stayed together—raided Union supplies and trains—stole from Yankee banks. Took guns from places that sold them, then turned around and smuggled them to Confederates who wanted to keep fighting even after the war ended. We learned how to handle guns real good ourselves. Nick is a natural leader, with that Irish temper and all. He fell into the role without anybody even questioning it."

Ashley turned the meat again, waiting to be sure Cliff was finished.

"He talked about you a lot in prison. Always felt he wasn't good enough for you, but even so, it was pretty obvious to the rest of us that he loves you."

Ashley felt the color coming into her cheeks. "I love him, too. I want to go with him to Outlaw Country, but he refused to take me. Are *you* going there when this trip is over?"

"Yes, Ma'am."

Ashley turned the pork again. "I'm glad. You seem like a good friend. Nick has always seemed so lonely."

"We're *all* lonely in our own way, even when we're surrounded by people."

Ashley set her cup aside and put a piece of pork on the plate that already held the warmed biscuit. She handed the plate to Cliff, then gave him a knife and fork. "You're right."

Cliff stirred the biscuit around. "I took the job in Gainesville because Nick wanted me to see if you were still there. What had happened to you and all of that. I didn't mind because I wanted to quit what we were doing for a while and see if I could live like a normal man ought to. My mug isn't on any wanted posters, so I had that freedom. Driving wagons for Isaac helped feed my wandering needs, so I'm happy enough for now." He bit off a piece of biscuit. "Nick couldn't handle not seeing you at least once more, so he took the chance. He wanted you to know he was alive and why he didn't come back sooner...and why he has to head west." Cliff stabbed the pork with his fork and took a bite off the end of the meat.

Ashley poked at her own food. After taking another bite, she said, "I'd often wondered if Nick ever even thought about me...before he died, I mean. My father told me he'd been killed at Chickamauga. I cried for three days. Actually, I cried inside every day until I found out he's still alive. He never knew just how much I loved him. I was only sixteen when he left."

"He thought about you more than you know, Ma'am. Sometimes he'd talk about you so much that the men would get kind of tired hearing it."

Ashley stuck her fork into another piece of pork and reached over to put it on Cliff's plate. "You can have this. I'm not all that hungry. I'll just eat a biscuit."

She reached into the burlap bag and pulled out another biscuit, then put it into the pan of hot pork grease and stirred it around a little to soften it up and give it some flavor. She could hardly believe she was talking to this near stranger about her personal feelings or the fact that Nick Calhoun loved her. She pulled the pan from the fire and cut into the now-soft biscuit with a fork.

"Do you know where Nick is now?"

Cliff swallowed another piece of meat. "By now he's down in south Texas. He'll come back this way after he unloads some livestock. I expect he'll check on you again before he goes on west."

"I almost wish he wouldn't. I don't think I could stand saying good-bye again."

Cliff nodded. "I can understand that. It's hard for Nick because he loves you, but now that he's a wanted man, he just feels he has to stay out of your life. I have a feeling that if he checks on you again, it'll just be by finding me and learning from me that you made it safely to wherever you land. I don't think he'll put you through the hurt of seeing him again. Meantime, I just want you to know I'll be keeping an eye on you, and once in a while I'll help you with those draft horses and such. Once I know you've found where you want to be and that you're safely settled, I'll find Nick and we'll head west. Nick wants to build himself a ranch in Outlaw Country and figure out a way to settle."

Ashley stirred her biscuit again and cut off another piece. Settling meant that Nick would likely find some other woman to marry. The thought of it brought a burning jealousy.

"We've lived in the Adirondacks and the Smoky Mountains, so we know mountain life," Cliff added, "and believe it or not, there are actually families in Outlaw Country. Men who took their families with them, or started families after they got there. At least that's what we're told. Some have businesses. Some have ranches. It's true they deal with other outlaws, and there's pretty much no law of any kind, but the men there live by a code of their own. Most women are well respected, even the—well—you know what I mean."

Ashley closed her eyes against the painful thought of Nick turning to such women. "I'm afraid I do."

Cliff set his plate aside and sighed. "I'm sorry, Ma'am. I had no right mentioning that. What I'm getting at is that Nick will end up settling, just like he says he wants to do."

"And start a ranch with stolen livestock?"

Cliff took a stick from the fire and lit a pre-rolled cigarette. "Maybe not. We ought to all have enough money along to buy a starter herd. We can round up strays. In country like that a man has to be careful about stealing cattle. He might end up stirring up the wrong man and find himself hanging by the neck from a tree. Like I said, men out there set their own laws, and there's no such thing as a fair trial."

"Well, it's not all that much better in civilized country. Look what happened in Gainesville. It's shameful." Ashley bit into another piece of her biscuit.

"Yes, Ma'am, that's a fact." Cliff smoked quietly for a moment, then rose and stretched. "I reckon I'd better leave before this looks like more than it is."

Ashley set her plate aside. "Yes, I suppose so." She rose. "Thank you, Cliff. For helping. And for telling me more about

Nick. Please tell him…I mean…when you see him again, which you obviously will, that I wish him all good things, and that I'll never forget him. Not ever. And if he changes his mind about taking me west with him—"

"He won't, Ma'am. I know him. He's determined you'll end up happier and safer and live a better life without him. He loves you too much to risk you having a miserable life on the run or in dangerous country."

Ashley struggled to speak without breaking into tears. "He's chosen a life I don't agree with, but I understand why."

Cliff pulled his hat a little farther down on his forehead. "I won't come around much after this, but I'll be right by your side if anything goes wrong."

"Thank you, Cliff. You're a good friend. And thank you for taking care of my horses."

Cliff nodded, then turned and disappeared into the darkness. Ashley watched after him, her emotions deeply disturbed from talking about Nick. She was supposed to forget about him, but how in God's name was she going to do that? Every place she went, it seemed like he was there.

Chapter Twelve

Mid–October...

Bob Calloway reached over and pulled Katie Justice off her horse and onto his, scooting back and plopping her in front of him. "Now, that's better," he told her, nuzzling her neck. He secured her with one arm and moved that hand just under one of her breasts.

"You'll slow us down with two on a horse," Nick told the man they all called Cal. "You shouldn't have brought Katie along. She'll end up making trouble."

"Hell, *look* at her, Nick. Would *you* have left this behind?"

Nick studied the buxom woman Cal had picked up in a saloon in Brownsville. She had long, dark hair and brown eyes and was slim of figure. She claimed to be eighteen, but Nick wondered if she was even that. It was an unusually warm day, and she'd pulled her shawl off her shoulders, revealing heavy breasts that bounced rhythmically with the gait of Cal's horse. The low-cut, white lacy top she wore hid little, and Nick had no doubt she didn't *want* to hide anything. She was pretty in the face but only in a youthful, fresh way.

Katie looked back at Nick with eyes that flickered in a flirting gesture. She smiled and giggled. "I'm excited and not afraid," she told him. "You don't have to worry about me, Mister Calhoun."

"Believe me, little girl, I *do* have to worry. You aren't old enough to understand men."

"I understand plenty," Katie answered with a haughty air. She turned a little and kissed Cal on the throat. "Besides, Cal will take good care of me."

Nick glanced at Cal. "We're headed for Outlaw Country. You're putting her in danger."

Katie tossed her hair. "Maybe it's the kind of danger I *like.*"

"No, you *won't* like it," Nick told her flatly. He scowled at Cal. "She'd better not make trouble with the other men."

Cal chuckled. "They all know she's mine."

"Maybe so, but does *she* know it?"

"She knows it, all right," Cal answered.

Katie laughed and glanced at Nick again, looking him over with obvious appreciation. "Look, Mister Calhoun, my mother's dead, and my pa beats me and does bad things to me. I had to get out of Brownsville, and this is my chance. I'll put up with whatever I have to in order be away from that hell-hole where I was living. Don't you worry about me. I can take care of myself."

Nick pulled a cheroot from his pocket. "Call me Nick. And don't say you weren't warned."

"You should've brought along a woman for yourself," Katie told him slyly.

"I *could* have." He scowled at Cal again. "But I had better sense, and I respect her too much to take her where we're going, even though she offered to come with me."

"Come on, Nick. It won't be that bad," Cal insisted.

"Won't it? We'll be on the trail for weeks, and a lot colder days are coming." Nick turned his attention back to Katie. "I hope you brought along something to cover those breasts with to keep them warm."

Katie threw her head back against Cal's chest and laughed. "I have Cal to keep them warm. He can cover my breasts any way he wants, and don't tell me *you* wouldn't like to help."

Cal chuckled and kicked his horse's sides to ride ahead at a faster trot, pulling Katie's horse with him.

"Don't go more than a mile without putting her back on her own horse," Nick called out to him. "The extra weight is too much for a horse going as far as we are!" He sighed with frustration and lit his cheroot as he waited for Renaldo to catch up with the spare horses.

"That girl will make trouble," Renaldo called out to him. He rode up beside Nick, frowning.

"You think I don't know that? She's un-lit dynamite."

"*Si, señor,* that is true. But Cal, he has never been happy since losing his wife and son to raids back in that place called Kentucky. He does foolish things just to have something to do and to try to be happy."

"Like a lot of us."

"You are thinking about the woman again?"

"I think about her all the time."

"Did you decide if you will go and see her again?"

Nick smoked quietly and readjusted his hat. "It's a big country, Renaldo. I might never find her, but I want to try, if only to make sure she's safe and happy. I just think I'll find a way to do that without actually seeing her. We'll be riding through Kansas and Nebraska before heading west. Maybe we'll find Cliff along the way. He can let me know about Ashley. Then we'll head into Wyoming Territory. The new railroad goes right through Outlaw Country up there, and you can bet they'll be hauling gold and payroll to and from the mining camps. You know what that means."

Renaldo laughed. "*Si, señor.* Much money for us, no?"

Nick nodded. "Much money for us, yes. But not from robbing trains. I want to try staying away from that life from now on. It's *other* men out there who'll be robbing trains. I'm thinking more about ranching, raising horses for men who'll be on the run, or just passing through. And with the railroad coming there, I'd like to be close enough to ship cattle by train to slaughterhouses back east or up to San Francisco. Even the mining camps probably need horses, and they keep cattle for food. Maybe we'll even raise a few mules. Mining camps use mules."

"Mules?" Renaldo grinned.

"Sure. Why not? I want to build a legitimate ranch in the foothills. You'll be a big help. You have more experience in ranching than I do." Nick puffed on the cheroot and watched the rest of the men, some behind him, some ahead. "Either way, I don't want to live like this forever."

"I will be glad to stay and work with you, *mi amigo*."

"Thanks. Ever since I met you in Brownsville, you've been a good friend, Renaldo."

Renaldo grinned. "As you have been to me."

Nick watched the endless horizon of Texas high country as both men kept their horses at a walk. Saddles squeaked, horses shuddered, a couple of men talked, their words indistinguishable from a distance. Katie laughed again.

Nick thought about the direction his life had taken since his mother had been killed back in New York. He'd never gotten over how she died. Killing the man who'd abused and murdered her hadn't changed the fact that she was gone, and if he'd been home that day, he might have saved her. Maybe that was why he felt so responsible for Ashley. If something bad happened to her now, he'd feel guilty about that, too. If not for all the things he'd done wrong in his life, they might be together.

"Ah, you are thinking about the woman again," Renaldo told him, as though he'd read Nick's mind. "I can see it in your eyes."

Nick shook his head. "It shows that much?"

"*Sí.* Sometimes we cannot control our lives or our feelings like we think we can." He made the sign of the cross. "It is God who controls our lives, *mi amigo,* not us."

Nick scowled. "When in hell did you become a preacher, Renaldo?"

Renaldo laughed and shook his head. "Since all you do is talk about the woman. You can go to Outlaw Country and make for yourself the biggest, richest ranch a man could want, but I think always you will yearn for her, so you will never be truly happy. It is the love that matters, *señor,* not the money."

"Yeah, well, I don't see a woman in *your* life, my friend."

"Ah, but I love *all* women! Someday the right one will come along, and she will drive me crazy with want until I marry her. I think that is how it is for you with this woman you talk about more often than you realize."

"And I think you talk too much."

Renaldo shrugged and charged his horse farther ahead. Nick kept Satan at a slower pace, wishing Renaldo wasn't always so damn right in everything. Thoughts of Ashley were going to drive him crazy no matter what else he did with his life, or how successful he might be. He had to find her once more—just once more.

Chapter Thirteen

"*I* killed a woman. What do you think of that?"

The big man who plunked himself down at Seth Cunningham's table slugged down a shot of whiskey and grinned through yellowing teeth. He reached over and poured some whiskey into Seth's now-empty shot glass and poured himself another shot, then slammed the whiskey bottle onto the table.

"Name's Abel MacIntyre. What's yours?" he asked.

Seth figured any man who'd brag about killing a woman had to be just plain crazy. This lunatic seemed proud of his so-called accomplishment. Seth had come into the Big Hat Saloon in South Pass City to rest mid-journey from California to Texas, and he'd intended to mind his own business, especially in this lawless country. Now here was a man who'd bring trouble, whether he wanted it or not.

Worried he might offend MacIntyre and suffer for it, he answered the man's inquiry about his name. "Seth Cunningham. And thanks for the shot of whiskey." He only sipped a little, while Abel slugged down his own second shot and poured himself yet another.

"Broke her neck," Abel told Seth. "See these hands?" The man held up paws as big as a grizzly's. "You'd be surprised what I can do with these hands," he said proudly.

"I doubt that," Seth answered warily, wondering if the man was looking for a fight. "Looks to me like you could split a log without an axe."

Abel roared with laughter, and Seth decided he'd better choose his words carefully around the unwelcome, uninvited maniac. Macintyre was big all over, tall, broad and full-chested, with a big belly, thick legs, full lips, puffy cheeks...Just plain *big,* and ugly to boot.

Seth leaned back in his chair, deciding it might not be wise to get too close to the Scotsman, or so MacIntyre claimed to be as he continued bragging. He looked a good fifty years old and claimed his parents came to America from Scotland and settled in Texas, where they'd farmed before they died. He obviously liked to talk about himself, explaining he'd lived the last fifteen years in Gainesville, Texas, where he'd "tried religion" to help tame his temper and to make friends, something that was hard for him to do.

Seth could understand why making friends was difficult. Besides being big and threatening, he wore an eye patch, which only made him seem even more intimidating. He reminded Seth of a wild, dangerous pirate. He could just picture MacIntyre wielding a sword and cutting someone's head off with it.

Being a rather small-built man himself who'd killed men in the war, but never killed anyone deliberately, Seth wasn't sure how to answer Abel's declaration of murder, especially when it was a woman he'd killed. The last thing he wanted to do was to make the man angry.

"Why'd you kill her?" he asked.

Abel downed his fourth shot of whiskey and poured yet another. "She deserved it. She was always the snooty type, know what I mean? I was trying real hard to be a good person. Everybody in Gainesville liked me, in spite of my size, and I worked with the woman more than once on church projects."

Church? Seth found that hard to believe as he watched Abel drink another shot then pour himself still another, all while he was himself finishing the first shot. He contemplated ways to get away from MacIntyre without offending him, but Abel immediately filled his shot glass again.

"Have another!" he bellowed then put out his hand. "Can I call you friend?"

Being around a drunk Abel's size, and listening to him brag about murder made Seth wonder if he might be next. Worried Abel would take it wrong if he didn't shake his hand, he put out his own.

"Just don't break my hand."

With another loud guffaw, Able shook his hand, squeezing just hard enough to show he could pound Seth right into the floor and likely kill him if he chose. Seth gladly withdrew his hand after the handshake and had to rub it a little to get the feeling back. He wondered about the woman Abel claimed to have killed. If they'd gone to church together, what possible reason could justify her murder?

"Sounds like you were friends with the woman you killed. What happened?" He sipped a little of his second shot of whiskey.

Abel let out a grunt, staring at his shot glass. "She just *pretended* to be friends. She always treated me like I was beneath her, like I was *lucky* to be her friend. *That's* what happened! She was married. That makes no difference to me, but it did to her. I tried wooing her more than once, but she wouldn't budge on her morals." He leaned closer to Seth. "I used to be not bad looking. I didn't have a face all cut up and a bad eye like I do now, which is another reason I killed her. It's her *husband's* fault I look like this. In fact, I went to her house looking for *him*. I was going to beat the fucker into a bloody pulp!"

He raised the patch over his eye, and Seth struggled not to look too shocked at the ugly hole there. Abel had other scars, one on his forehead above his eye and one down across his cheek and through his lips. He also had a deep crease along the left side of his head. Part of his left ear was missing. That last one looked like a gunshot wound.

"I'm real sorry for you, Abel, but what does the woman's husband have to do with your injury? Did *he* do that to you?"

"He sure did! His name was Colonel Howard Vale, Confederate Army. Me and him ended up fighting together at Chattanooga. The sonofabitch always had it in for me for messing around with his wife, so he shot me during the battle. Figured he'd use that to claim I was shot by the Blue Coats. He slashed his sword across my face then and left me for dead. Them Blue devil Yankees picked me up and dragged me off as a prisoner. Seems Howard Vale figured me dead because he'd shot me in the chest *and* in the head, but it takes a lot to kill a man like me!" Abel leaned back and pounded his chest proudly.

"Oh, that's pretty obvious." Seth sipped a little more of his whiskey while Abel slugged down his own. Seth realized he'd lost count of just how many shots the man had guzzled, but then he figured it took quite a bit of alcohol to make him really drunk. At least he *hoped* it did since he didn't want to be around a totally drunk Abel MacIntyre.

"I heard later from new prisoners coming into the hell-hole of a prison where the Yankees kept me that Howard Vale ended up shot in another battle—Chickamauga, I think—got sent home to heal. After the war I was going to go to Gainesville and kill him, but I got in a fight somewhere in Mississippi and hit the man so hard he went unconscious and never woke up. I was sent back to jail for it. Didn't get out 'til around six months ago."

Seth reminded himself to keep a friendly attitude. Here in Outlaw Country, no man could be trusted. Most of those who came here were already in trouble back East for every-thing from rape and robbery to treason against the Federals to murder. He glanced sidelong at another big man who sat at the next table playing cards. He wore buckskins, and a heavy beard hid most of his face, but his dark eyes were sharp and clear, the eyes of a man who hadn't had much to drink yet. Seth wondered if he was maybe a guide or a mountain man, a hunter. Like most out here, he was likely some kind of law-breaker and probably wanted.

Either way, Seth didn't like the way he was scowling, and all senses came alert. The arrival of Abel MacIntyre, a stranger in a saloon full of men and women who probably came here often and knew each other, was not going to end well. Everyone in there could hear Abel's bragging, and he sensed they didn't like what they were hearing any more than Seth did. He'd heard there was an unspoken code in Outlaw Country about hurting women, even the whores. After all, women in places like this were pretty scarce, and the men treasured them.

Seth hated being stuck in the middle like this. He'd just been getting ready to leave when Abel sat down at his table. Now Seth wondered what the hell the bearded man sitting at the next table was thinking. He felt caught between a grizzly bear and a lion, and he squirmed a little in his chair, not wanting to get involved in any way with either one. Each looked strong and ruthless. Since coming to Outlaw Country, he'd seen men shot and then dumped into the street just to get them out of the way. He didn't care to be one of them.

Pretending interest, he turned his attention back to Abel, hoping to find an opening for an excuse to get the hell out of the saloon.

"Sounds like you had a long string of bad luck, what with going to jail after being let out of prison. Apparently, you finally made it back to Gainesville. Did you kill the woman's husband, too, since he was the one who shot you?"

Abel shook his head. "Didn't get the chance. The fucker had already died years before. From infection to his leg wound. I knew the house where the woman lived. I'd been in it back before the war. I walked in to confront her and the man both, but she told me he'd died."

Abel chuckled and slugged down another shot. "Boy, you should have seen the look in Patricia Vale's eyes when she saw me standin' in the hallway. She was goddamned surprised. She started backin' up as she told me about her husband, who'd told her I was dead. And there I was, *alive,* and standin' right in front of her, eye patch and all." He gave Seth's leg a nudge with his boot. "A head wound can make you a little crazy, you know? I ain't been right since Howard Vale did this to me. And after the way his wife was always so snooty to me, it felt good to see her standin' there wide-eyed, all alone and vulnerable. I told her what her husband did to me and that I sorely needed some kind of revenge. I figured I'd finally get a poke at the woman—pay her back for snubbin' me all them years earlier, and pay Vale back by fuckin' his woman. She turned and ran upstairs, but I grabbed her and clobbered her good—threw her around a little—banged her head on the stair railings."

Seth noticed the buckskin-clad man shift in his chair, the way a man moved when he was trying to control his anger.

"Somehow, she got away from me," Abel continued, "so I chased her all the way upstairs and grabbed her from behind. Got a good feel of one tit before I took hold of the front of her forehead and yanked her head backward hard as I could and broke her neck. I threw her over the railing to the floor below so's it would look like an accident. My only regret is that I never got the chance to poke her. Sometimes things just don't work out the way you plan it, know what I mean?"

Seth struggled with nausea. He put a hand to his stomach and swallowed. He couldn't begin to imagine killing a woman, let alone in the way Abel MacIntyre had. He drank the rest of his whiskey in one gulp, then glanced at the bearded man. The look in the man's eyes put fear in Seth's heart.

"I, uh, I guess I know what you mean."

A thick tension began to fill the air, and he contemplated the best way to make a fast exit if Abel and their nearest neighbor had a disagreement.

Abel put the whiskey bottle to his mouth and slugged down even more liquor. "I guess I was just so angry I didn't know my own strength. I get like that sometimes. Head wounds can do that to you. I was kind of hoping the woman's daughter might be around there somewhere. She'd be—I don't know—twenty or so by now, and right pretty I expect. If she'd been there, I could have taken out my revenge on her. I looked around a little but didn't see her, so I lit out.

"Never did tell anybody I was ever in town on account of I intended all along to go out to that farm and kill Howard Vale and get a piece of his wife. If nobody ever saw me, they wouldn't know who to suspect because they all thought me dead. So, I just lit out and headed west. I heard there were places out here where men could live without being bothered by the law. I landed here in South Pass City. I reckon' this'll have to be home for a time. Out here a man can hide forever."

Seth nodded. "I see." He straightened in his seat and shoved his shot glass toward Abel. "I have to get going, Abel. You came here from Texas, but Texas is where I'm headed. I came through here from the California gold hills. I never had any luck. Figured I'd look for work in Texas, where the cattle business is booming now."

Abel wiped his hand across the bottom of his nose, then spit tobacco juice onto the saloon's straw-covered floor. "Where are you from originally?"

Seth shrugged. "All over. Mostly Kansas." He scooted back his chair, feeling an air of strong animosity from the bearded man beside them. He figured it was time to get the hell out of the saloon. He stood up. "My wife died before the war, and her folks took in my daughter before I left for the war. They live in west Texas. The girl hardly knows me now, but I figured I'd go back to Texas and at least visit her one more time." He nodded in a friendly manner, hoping to end the conversation on Abel MacIntyre's good side. "Thanks for the whiskey."

Abel grinned. "Well, now, maybe we'll run into each other again."

I hope not, Seth thought. "Maybe. But I don't expect it will be in Texas, since you'd be best to never go back there."

Abel let out another huge guffaw at the remark as Seth turned to walk out, but a loud crash forced him to look back. In that one quick moment, the bearded man had pounced and knocked Abel MacIntyre to the floor. Seth ducked out of the way when he picked Abel up as though he were a child and threw him through the saloon's swinging doors and out into the street.

Seth couldn't believe his eyes, considering Abel's size, but the bearded man wasn't all that much smaller. Every man in the saloon immediately leapt to his feet and ran out the door to watch the fight, most of them picking sides and rooting for their choice. Glad to not be a part of any of it, Seth walked out behind them and watched from the boardwalk, where he could stand a little higher and see better. He was amazed at the attacker's strength. He beat on Abel furiously amid angry shouts of "woman-beater," "bastard," "coward," "fucking sonofabitch," "no man treats a woman that way," and several other expletives. A very few of them actually rooted for Abel, who got in a few punches, but by the time the fight was over, Abel MacIntyre lay in a bloody heap in the street.

"I'd *kill* you, you piece of shit," the bearded man declared, "except I'd rather see you lay there and suffer, knowin' how it feels to be beat on by somebody stronger. Get the hell out of South Pass City! I don't know you, and I don't know the woman you killed, but if I ever see your face again, I'll put my gun in your mouth and blow your brains out."

Abel's attacker straightened. He brushed off his buckskins and ran his hands through his long, wavy hair before picking up his hat from where it lay in the street. He plopped it on his head and flexed his hands, licking at the blood on his knuckles before heading back up the steps to the boardwalk. He stopped in front of Seth and glared at him.

"You mentioned a daughter. I have one, too, and I ain't seen her in years. I'm gonna' go see her. It's good you're doin' the same, even if you can't take care of her yourself. I can't either, but I aim to see my girl anyway."

Frozen in place and surprised by the strange comment from the seemingly ruthless man, Seth just nodded. "Yes, sir."

"You weren't friends with that bastard, were you?"

Seth shook his head vigorously. "No, sir. He just decided to sit down at my table."

The bearded man nodded. "That's what I figured. You'd best be on your way then. Just don't be helpin' that man."

"I have no intention of helping him. I'd have done the same thing you did, Mister, if I was big enough to do it."

The bearded man turned to the crowd. "I'll kill anybody that helps that sonofabitch!" he yelled before going back inside the saloon.

Seth breathed a sigh of relief and turned to a man who stood beside him shaking his head. "Who the hell was that?"

The man grinned. "That there was Moses Tucker. I don't know what that man out there in the street did, but it sure made Moses mad." He walked inside and Seth glanced at Abel.

Abel lay completely still, and Seth wondered if he was dead. He walked around the hitching post, untied his horse and mounted up, deciding maybe the man named Moses Tucker was right. He should get the hell out of South Pass City and go see his daughter.

Turning up the collar of his sheepskin coat against a chilly wind, he turned his horse and headed south, wondering if he should go to Gainesville and tell the law there about Abel MacIntyre murdering that woman named Patricia Vale. The problem was, he'd heard how easily a man could get himself hanged in Gainesville. He feared being accused of having something to do with Mrs. Vale's death if he went there with information about how it happened. Besides, he didn't know her. Her husband was apparently dead, and her daughter probably married and living in town and doing just fine.

He decided it was best to leave it all alone and avoid Gainesville when he went to see his daughter. After all, Abel had received proper punishment at the hands of Moses Tucker and might even be dead, which was just fine with Seth Cunningham.

Chapter Fourteen

Late October...

Sleet storms turned into hot days, then rain and, luckily, a good share of sunny days that were sometimes warm, sometimes very cold. Ashley had never seen such unusual and unpredictable weather as in western Oklahoma. Everyone was on pins and needles most of the time, on the watch for outlaws and hostiles. Isaac had explained that this was the most dangerous part of the trip. He figured if they got through it, he would prove this was a viable route to reaching the Union Pacific in Nebraska. It should also be a good way to pick up supplies from the East... things people in northern Texas seldom enjoyed, like furniture and paintings and designer clothing from Europe to New York City to St. Louis and on west.

Ashley smiled at the thought of paintings and designer clothing. She'd never be able to afford such things, nor would she have the need. She'd work for Isaac at first, and if she settled on her own, all she'd require was sturdy homespun dresses and men's boots. Her hands and fingernails would likely be dirty for quite a while, and her face would be plain, her hair wrapped into a bun most of the time. There would be no room for lovely dresses or for coloring her cheeks and putting flowers in her hair.

She supposed those things should matter to a young woman, but besides working for Isaac and then farming, she had no interest in attracting a man. Not unless that man was Nick Calhoun. It would be a long time before she could get Nick out of her heart and her blood, if ever. She didn't quite know what to think about the fact that he was paying Cliff to keep an eye on her. She wished he hadn't done that, mainly because having Cliff around kept reminding her of Nick and how much he cared about her.

Her thoughts were interrupted when she hit a deep rut that nearly bounced her right off the wagon seat. Up ahead Isaac Stone was turning his wagon. "Circle!" she thought she heard him shout. Her heart beat a little faster. He'd told them that if outlaws or hostiles appeared, they should circle the wagons for better protection and try to get the livestock inside the circle. She straightened in her seat and looked around.

It was then she saw them, a band of men headed their way and already shooting. Cliff went charging past her, herding horses, oxen and mules into the middle of the wagons as Isaac came back around toward Ashley's wagon, followed by the others.

"Close up the circle!" he shouted.

Ashley snapped the reins against Max and Brutus and followed behind Spence Lamar, her left front wagon wheel breaking off just as she got into place. Ashley let out a scream as she went tumbling off the seat. She landed in thick prairie grass, and a moment later Cliff was helping her up.

"You all right, Ma'am?"

"I think so. I hurt my shoulder a little."

"Get under your wagon," Cliff told her. "Grab your rifle first. We'll worry about fixing that wheel when this is over. I'll be close by!"

Cliff left, and Ashley quickly brushed herself off and rubbed at her sore shoulder. She could hear yips and shouts and thundering hooves as she yanked her father's rifle from under the wagon seat and then got to her knees, wincing with pain. She obeyed

Cliff's orders and crawled under the back end of her wagon, forced to ignore her pain for the more important need to defend herself.

"Stay under the wagon!" she heard Cliff yell from somewhere.

Her heart pounding, Ashley positioned herself and put the butt of her rifle to her shoulder. She pulled back the hammer and watched as the attackers drew closer, a grand mix of slovenly white men, a couple wearing tattered uniforms, both blue and gray, and one hostile wielding a bow and arrow. Men inside the circle of wagons were shouting orders at each other, and the air, once still and cold, was now permeated with the sound of panicked shouts, whooping outlaws, stampeding horses... and gunfire.

Would this be the end of all of them? Her dream of a new life suddenly seemed ridiculous. Maybe she should have stayed in Gainesville and married Clay. Or maybe she should have flung herself at Nick and begged harder to make him take her with him when he left her for places unknown.

As soon as the attackers came even closer, the gunfire grew almost constant. She heard someone cry out. She took aim at one man who was very close and fired. To her surprise, she hit her target, and the man fell from his horse, his body skidding within ten feet of her wagon, a bloody hole in his side. He looked dead but she couldn't be sure and just then it only mattered that he wasn't moving.

Some of the horses were whinnying in more of a scream than normal nervousness, all of them terrified by the gunfire. Ashley took aim again, but this time she missed.

"Hoot Stowers is down!" someone yelled.

Ashley watched more marauders fall and tried to determine how many there were all together. It appeared not so many that their own large group couldn't fight and hopefully chase off. She guessed there were only ten or twelve attackers and hoped there weren't more waiting somewhere behind a hill to ride in and slaughter all of them and then burn everything they couldn't take with them. Of the ten or twelve, four were down, as far as she could count.

Within about ten minutes, what was left of their attackers rode off. A couple of them managed to pick up bodies, but the one Ashley had shot was left behind. She waited for a few minutes until Isaac finally shouted, "I think they're gone!"

Ashley wiggled from under the wagon then to see Bill Sanders and Morgan Peters carrying old Hoot Stowers to the open area inside the wagons. They laid him on the ground.

"Damn!" Isaac swore, kneeling beside the man. "Hoot's been with me since before I started this business."

"He's dead, Isaac," Bill told him. "We'd better bury him and get the wagons moving. We'll have to fix the wheel on Ashley's wagon fast as we can."

Isaac hung his head and rubbed at his eyes. "Goddamn it," he swore again. "I never should have tried this."

"We all knew the risk, Mr. Stone," Will said gently in his deep voice. "Be glad your wife and son are okay."

"Yes, but this trip is too much risk for the women," Spence Lamar said.

"I knew the risk and took it willingly," Ashley spoke up, walking closer. "So did Rachael and Sandra." She shivered. "I got one of them myself. He's over near my wagon. You'll have to bury him, too."

Isaac rose and looked around. "Where's Cliff?"

Ashley felt a sudden pain in her gut at the realization Cliff had not made an appearance.

"Cliff! You all right?" Isaac shouted.

There came no answer. Ashley turned and hurried to look on the other side of the wagons. She saw him then, lying facedown on the ground near the end of her wagon, the Indian lying next to him. A huge ox stood nearby, positioned in a way that Ashley hadn't noticed Cliff's body when she first crawled out from under the wagon.

"Cliff!" She ran to his side, followed by Spence and Bill. Ashley groaned at the sight of a bloody wound in Cliff's chest. It didn't look like a bullet wound. She glanced at the dead Indian, who still held a tomahawk in his hand. "My God! Cliff!"

"Shit!" Bill Sanders swore when he walked up behind her. "That's one hell of a bloody wound. Is he dead, sweetheart?"

Ashley leaned closer, and Cliff's eyes fluttered open. "Oh, dear God," she wept. "Cliff, tell us what to do." She put a hand to the side of his face.

He stared at her a moment. "Nothing." He grimaced as he moved one leg. "Tell Nick...I tried...I meant...to stick with you...all the way." His words came in a near whisper, and the others couldn't hear him.

"What's he saying?" Isaac asked.

"I'm damn sorry. Ma'am. I...failed you."

Ashley couldn't help the tears then. "It's all right, Cliff. I'll be okay. I'm so sorry this happened to you! You didn't have to be here."

"No...I'm...so sorry. Don't forget...how much Nick... loves you." Cliff's eyes suddenly looked cold and lifeless.

"Cliff!" Ashley wept as she closed his eyelids before they would become too stiff. "Oh, dear Jesus, take him to Your arms."

Cliff had made a promise to watch out for her. He'd kept that promise, and it had cost him his life.

Isaac grasped Ashley's arms and pulled her to her feet. "Let him go," he told her.

"But he...he became a good friend." Ashley looked up at Isaac. "He was watching out for me."

"We all are, Ma'am. Come on away from him. We've got to get him and Hoot buried and fix your wagon and get the hell out of here."

"What about the other dead ones?"

"They aren't our responsibility, and those they rode with are bound to come back, if for nothing more than to get them."

Ashley watched the others carry Cliff's body over beside Hoot's.

"You and the other women had best get inside your wagons for now," Isaac told Ashley. "Some of those renegades might still be lurking. If they get a look at you, it's hard telling what they'll do to get their hands on you. Morgan and I will put a new wheel on your wagon. I guess I'll have to have Morgan tend the remuda now that Cliff is dead."

Ashley blindly obeyed and climbed into her wagon. She heard the men shouting orders again, heard the sound of shovels grating against dirt and gravel, felt her wagon being lifted as men put a spare wheel on it. She wasn't sure how much time had passed before she heard Isaac saying, "Ashes to ashes, dust to dust."

So far, she'd been too stunned for any more crying, and now that she felt the tears coming, she fought the urge to sob, not wanting to appear weak in front of the remaining men. She'd said she could do this, and she would. After all, she'd managed to kill one of the outlaws herself, hadn't she? She fought the desire to scream over that very fact. Yes. She'd killed a man, not an easy thing to accept, enemy or not. And she felt responsible for the death of another. *Cliff, I'm so sorry!* Why did she blame herself?

Another hour or so went by as men got things in order and finished fixing and greasing her wheel. Ashley took a few minutes to weep quietly into a quilt, telling herself she couldn't completely break down. Not now. They wanted to be on their way. She had to do her part. She climbed into the wagon seat and picked up the reins, glad her draft horses had not been hurt in the wild gunfire. One of the mules had been killed and had been unharnessed to be left behind. Another was hitched, and Morgan Peters mounted Cliff's horse and whistled at the remuda of horses, mules and oxen as the wagons got under way.

No one talked. They passed a large mound of dirt. Two wooden crosses made from spare firewood were planted at one end of the grave that held two men. Old Hoot Stowers, and Cliff Albertson.

I'm a loner. Always have been. Always will be. Cliff had told her once. Ashley realized she knew almost nothing more about him. Nick probably didn't know much about him either. He'd only known him from prison. Now he was dead, and who was there to care?

I care, Ashley thought. *I will pray for you, Cliff Albertson.* She looked away, feeling removed from her body. What in hell was she doing? So many left behind … Clay … Clara … old Alfred Coons … her father and mother … and now Hoot Stowers and Cliff. Nick had ridden off to who-knew-where, and she had no idea where he was right then.

He'll find you, Cliff had told her in one of their conversations.

Why, Nick? When? Where? She didn't even *want* him back in her life … or so she'd thought. Seeing him again would only make it harder for a second good-bye.

Chapter Fifteen

Nick sat on a flat rock on the banks of the Trinity River, enjoying the peace and quiet away from the now-busy cow town of Fort Worth. Since the Chisolm Trail had been cut through Texas, the once-small army fort was now one of the many watering stops for cowboys herding their cattle to the railroad in Kansas. The odor of cow dung penetrated the air everywhere within miles, and Fort Worth was now a busy center of supply stores, restaurants, law offices, booteries, tack stores, liveries, rooming houses, land offices, banks, doctors' offices, millineries, and, most important, saloons.

The dirt streets were busy with horses and wagons and young boys paid to continuously scoop up horse manure. Gamblers and cowboys roamed the streets and boardwalks, while prostitutes hung outside the saloons and on balconies advertising their voluptuous offerings to a host of lonely men.

He'd taken one of those offers himself the previous night, after doing too much drinking and gambling. He couldn't even remember her name now, but she had red hair and green eyes, and while he invaded her very pleasing body to release pent-up needs, his drunked-up brain saw Ashley lying there, opening those beautiful legs invitingly, smiling with pleasure as she took him in her own need.

Guilty as it made him feel, he found himself wishing that was all true. He'd like nothing better than to have awoken this morning to see Ashley lying beside him, but instead it was the woman he'd paid for his pleasure, and in the morning light she wasn't nearly as pretty as she'd seemed the night before, when he was drunk and the light was dim. She was young but already looked old, although in country where men outnumbered women probably ten to one, looks didn't seem to matter much. Practically any woman could get rich quick in places like this.

What bothered him most was that some such women ended up selling themselves to men out of desperation and hunger, and it could happen practically overnight once mines played out or once other reasons a town was born suddenly changed, let alone a husband or other family being killed. In places here and farther west, dangers and lawlessness prevailed, and Ashley had left Gainesville completely oblivious to how bad things could get. The pure and chaste young woman he'd left behind could find herself in a lot of trouble. If someone robbed her of her little fortune and her dignity, how would she get by? She'd never go back to Gainesville. She'd be too proud and stubborn to admit defeat.

There was no arguing about it. He had to find her. Had to know she was all right. If things had gone well, she should be in northern Oklahoma by now. She might even have made it to Kansas, or even to Nebraska and the Union Pacific, but that didn't mean she'd be safe. The brand-new railroad was vulnerable to outlaw and hostile attacks, too, and the towns where it stopped were mostly new and lawless. If Ashley found a piece of land, she'd have to hire men to help her build a cabin and break ground. Strange men she knew nothing about.

"Shit!" He got up and paced. He told himself that at least Cliff was with her, but he wasn't the kind of man to hang around long in one place. Cliff was a wanderer. He'd eventually move on, and Ashley would be alone.

He sat down on the rock again. He'd promised Ashley he'd stay away, but the fact remained that the man who'd killed her mother was still out there somewhere. Did he know her habits? Was he following her? Not only that, but desperate, lonely men did a lot of things out here they'd never do in tamer country. The damn woman should know she couldn't trust anyone.

He paused to light a pre-rolled cigarette, then breathed deeply of the soothing tobacco smoke and watched the dancing ripples of the river, thinking how soft and pleasant the splashing sound was compared to the loud piano music and screeching laughter inside the saloons. He took another drag on his cigarette, not sure why he felt so restless and uneasy that morning. He'd hoped coming out here where it was quieter would help, but it hadn't worked.

He wanted Ashley, in his life and in his bed. Now he wished he'd gone north with her. Sure, he was wanted, but once on the trail, what would Isaac Stone or anybody else have done about it? His biggest problem would have been watching Ashley every day and wanting her.

He stood up and paced again. If anything happened to her on that trip, he'd shoot himself. He felt like he'd let her down. If he'd known seeing her again would make him this miserable, he wouldn't have gone to see her at all. He wouldn't have known she was in danger from a murderer. Wouldn't have known she was out there traveling in lawless country all alone.

His thoughts were interrupted when he saw a rider coming. He recognized Renaldo's sombrero. The man was riding hard, as though something was wrong. Nick smashed out his partially-smoked cigarette on the flat rock and put the unused portion of the smoke back into his pocket as Renaldo reached him.

"What's wrong?" he asked, as Renaldo's roan mare shuddered and tossed her head.

"Cal is dead, *mi amigo*." Renaldo shook his head. "It is because of that girl he brought with us from Brownsville."

Nick hurried over to Satan, his big black gelding, and mounted up. "No surprise there. That girl's worse than a prostitute. She likes to make trouble where there shouldn't *be* any trouble." He rode up beside Renaldo. "What happened?"

Renaldo sighed. "Cal and I, we were having breakfast at that saloon, the *Silver Saddle*. They serve food there in the morning for all the drunks, you know?"

"I know."

"Well, after he spent the night in a room upstairs with Katie, Cal came down and drank more whiskey this morning. I noticed those two cowboys who tried to make trouble last night went upstairs then, but I did not say anything to Cal because it is morning, you know? I mean, I did not think anything of it because everything is quiet, you know? Those men, they tried to say Cal was cheating at cards last night, but you chased them out, remember?"

Nick was getting impatient at how long it sometimes took Renaldo to tell a story. "Of course, I remember. What *happened*, Renaldo?"

"Well, I remembered those two went upstairs last night with two of the saloon women, so I thought that was where they were going, but they came down about a half-hour later with Katie. She was wearing just a robe. She had both her arms hooked into those men's arms, one on each side, you know? And she was smiling."

Renaldo moved his body back and forth in his saddle, as though to mimic Katie's sexy walk.

"She walks up to Cal with those men and she says, *"There's nothing more satisfying for a woman than having two men make love to her at the same time."*

Nick rubbed at his eyes. "Jesus," he muttered. "And Cal went crazy?"

"*Si, senor.* He called Katie a slut and a bitch, and he pushed her. Those two men, they defended her, but they do it with smiles on their faces, like they enjoyed making Cal mad. One says, "*This is what you deserve for cheating us at cards last night.*" They started calling Cal names, and he called them names and says he will kill them for, you know, for doing what they did to Katie. He say "*Katie is my girl,*" and then one of the men, he draws his gun. Cal draws his and fires. But as Cal shoots at the first man, the second wings Cal in the arm, so Cal's shot only grazes the first across the shoulder. Then the other man shoots Cal again, many times over, until Cal falls dead. The killer looks at me and says, '*Tell your friend who threatened us last night that we are waiting for him. He should die, too.*' I think he meant you."

Nick drew his .44 and checked it, spinning the cartridge chamber to be sure it was full. "I'm sure they did, *amigo.*"

"The first man, he is okay. They are both waiting for you, *señor.* I would have helped Cal, but it is morning, and I had left my gun in a room upstairs. The woman there, she say she will watch it for me, so I had no gun with me."

"And it was two against one on Cal."

"*Si, señor.*"

"Cal isn't fast enough to take on two cowboys who are likely pretty handy with their pistols." Nick put his gun back in its holster. "What about the law? The sheriff might have already arrested the two men involved. And I can't risk being caught, but I won't let this go."

"The man who served our food, he says those killers run with a bunch of cowboys who are troublemakers when they come to town. The law stays away from them, he says. And the sheriff, he is off chasing others who robbed a bank three days ago. There is just a deputy in town, and he is afraid of the cowboys because they gang up together. The man who tells me this, he says the deputy will do nothing. He says the deputy knew you were in town, too, but he knows you have men behind you, so he will not give you trouble."

"You'd better get the boys together then. Those two that shot Cal are probably doing the same. They might figure they can take me for a reward, so we'll all ride in together, but let me handle the two we're after. I don't want a big shootout of some kind. Innocent people could get hurt."

"You are going to face *both* of them alone?"

"Renaldo, the mood I'm in, I think I could face *five* men and do just fine. I woke up angry, so I might as well take that anger out on something—or some*one*. Tell the rest of the men to stay out of it unless those cowboys decide to make it a free-for-all. And once this is over, we'll get the hell out of here and leave Katie Justice behind. She'll either get rich plying her trade, or mess with the wrong man some day and end up dead. I knew she was trouble the minute Cal picked her up down in Brownsville."

"*Si, señor.* I think the rest of the men will be glad to be rid of her, too. She flirted with *all* of them. That is the surest way of getting men to fight each other."

Nick's horse whinnied and turned in a circle as though sensing its rider's anger. "She's the type of woman who enjoys that. But I'm fighting for the way Cal died, not for that trouble-making she-devil." Nick removed his hat and smoothed back his tangled hair before putting it back on. "Go on, Renaldo. I'll give you an hour to get the rest of the men here."

"*Si, señor.*" Renaldo rode off and Nick watched after him, actually glad for the distraction. Now he could concentrate on going after Cal's killers instead of aching for Ashley.

Chapter Sixteen

$\mathcal{S}$eth Cunningham stood outside the *Silver Saddle Saloon*, wondering if he was destined to be followed by trouble every place he went. He'd seen many a brawl while in Outlaw Country, and the memory of Moses Tucker beating on Abel MacIntyre outside the *Big Hat Saloon* in Brown's Park remained vivid. Now here he stood on another boardwalk amid a crowd of men who'd gathered to watch yet another fight, this one most likely with guns.

He'd made it to Fort Worth, Texas, which reminded him of the outlaw country he'd left up in Wyoming. Since Fort Worth had become a destination for cowboys during cattle drives, the wild life of men hungry for whiskey, cards and women had turned the place into one of lawless free-for-all activity. Even now, when the cattle drives were over for the year, life remained dangerous and unruly because of those cowboys who'd chosen to stay there for the winter.

A crowd of men, some of them already drunk even though it was only noon, milled around the *Silver Saddle* in anticipation of a showdown between a bunch of cowboys who all worked for the same rancher, and some outlaw by the name of Nick Calhoun and the men who followed him.

And it's all over a woman who's not worth dying for, Seth thought. One man was already dead, and the woman involved, whom he'd heard was named Katie, was hardly more than in her teens.

She stood in the street, laughing with two of the cowhands, as excited as if she were about to be highly entertained. Seth had seen the shooting inside the saloon, and the man killed was supposedly Katie's lover but she didn't seem the least bit upset by his death. He glanced across the street at a sheriff's deputy, who stood in front of the town jail, looking as excited about what was coming as the rest of the crowd. The man apparently was not going to do a thing about this.

"Here they come!" someone shouted.

Everyone moved onto boardwalks on either side of the street, some going inside buildings to watch through windows. A few prostitutes stood on saloon balconies or hung out upstairs windows to watch, and Katie was shoved aside by the two men with her.

"Get out of the way," one of them told her. "You could get shot."

Seth thought how that wouldn't be much of a loss, but part of him thought it was too bad how young the woman was—a girl really, not a woman. The stupid kid had no idea the kind of life her behavior was going to lead her into. She grabbed a bottle of whiskey from a man beside her and drank some down. The man grinned and threw an arm around her.

"Come on, honey. Let's get you out of the way." He led her up the steps in front of the *Silver Saddle*, where they watched as five men rode in from around a side street and halted in front of six cowboys who'd spread themselves out to block the way, two of them those who'd killed the man called Cal inside the saloon.

Seth stood aside and folded his arms, studying the obvious leader of those who'd come to challenge the killers. He had no doubt the man in front was Nick Calhoun, supposedly wanted for robbery and murder. The deputy across the street stood near the jail door, making no move to arrest Calhoun.

Seth could understand why the deputy had chosen to stay out of this. Even some of the cowboys appeared suddenly nervous and wary when Calhoun rode closer. Danger, experience, leadership and authority emanated from him He was tall and well-built, with dark, wavy hair that sprouted in a wild array from under his black, wide-brimmed hat. He had a dangerous, threatening air about him, and somehow his arresting good looks only added to a hint of explosive violence about him—a violence that could be unleashed at any moment.

The gathered on-lookers, who moments ago had been shouting and laughing and placing bets on what was about to happen, grew suddenly and surprisingly quiet as they watched the confrontation. Calhoun sat on a big, black gelding as he spoke while the four men with him dismounted.

"Which ones of you killed Bob Calloway this morning?" Calhoun demanded.

The six cowboys all shifted a little, one of them already looking ready to run.

"You mean that lovesick coward who cheated us at cards last night?" one asked.

Seth recognized him as one of the shooters. A tall, decent-looking man named Hal Sloan. He looked as though he knew how to fare well in a fist fight, and Seth had already seen he was fast and able with a gun.

"Only men who gamble stupid accuse someone of cheating," Calhoun told Sloan. "It helps cover up the fact that they don't know what the hell they're doing. Is that what *you* are, mister? A stupid gambler?"

"I'm smart enough to know *you're* stupid for thinking you can face down six men on your own," Sloan answered.

"I'm *not* here to face six men," Calhoun answered. "I'm here to face you, and whichever of these men helped you kill Cal this morning. I'll face you both at once, but it has to be just you, your friend and me. Tell everyone else to stand down. You forced Cal's hand by fucking his woman, and that woman isn't worth men dying over, so let's keep this simple."

Seth glanced at Katie. She jerked away from the man she stood with and straightened her shoulders in a way that displayed her breasts more fully. She pouted her lips and threw her head back. "*Cal* thought I was worth dying for!" she shouted to Calhoun. "Admit it, Nick! *You* wanted me, too.*"

Nick Calhoun didn't take his eyes off Sloan as he answered Katie. "Like a man wants a venomous snake in his bed."

The whole crowd laughed, and Katie gasped and pressed her lips tightly together. Calhoun didn't crack a smile. He just kept staring at Sloan as the crowd quieted again. Nick climbed down from his horse and faced Sloan.

"Who's the second man that shot Cal this morning?"

A short, stocky man in a red checkered shirt stepped forward.

"*I* was. Name's Booner. Kevin Booner. And this here man beside me is Hal Sloan. We're both damn good with a sidearm, and if you're crazy enough to face us alone like your friend Cal did, then let's get this over with. You'll end up just as dead as *he* is, Mister." He spit tobacco juice into the dirt street, and some of it landed on the stubble of his beard. He wiped at it with his shirtsleeve.

"Fine," Calhoun answered. "Have your men back off, and mine will, too."

The other four with Sloan and Booner moved to the side of the street, and Nick Calhoun's <u>men</u> backed up another several feet, pulling their horses with them.

Seth and the whole crowd waited with anticipation. He figured Calhoun would die the same way his friend had. The woman called Katie quickly shuffled herself to the front of the crowd, watching defiantly.

"I hope you *die* today, Nick Calhoun," she declared. "I'll make a name for myself because of it!"

Again, Calhoun never took his eyes off of the men facing him as he spoke. "You already *have* a name, and it isn't Katie. Your first name is Troublemaking, and your last name is Slut. You aren't worth the spit of the other saloon women in this town, and it likely won't be long before they run you out."

The crowd broke into more laughter.

"Hey, Troublemaking Slut, you don't know the first thing about how to treat a man," one woman shouted from a balcony, creating another round of laughter.

Katie's lips moved into another pout, and she folded her arms and glared at Calhoun. "Get this over with, Nick, so I can dance on your grave."

Nick pushed his hat back and lowered his right hand to his side as again the crowd quieted. "I want it understood that I consider both of you rotten cowards for the way you shot Cal down,' he told Sloan and Booner. "And this is for him, not for that worthless man-eater over there."

"Fine with us." Booner stepped to the side, a few feet away from Sloan.

Things happened fast then. Booner and Sloan both went for their guns. Seth wasn't even sure when Calhoun drew his, because somehow his six-gun was out and blazing before either opponent could get off a shot. Seth watched the man fan his gun faster than he thought any man could, and Booner and Sloan went down. Sloan managed to get off a shot as he fell, and Calhoun jerked and stumbled, but didn't fall. Seth noticed blood was fast staining the left front of his white shirt, near his ribs, but Calhoun hardly blinked at the wound. He just stood a moment, gun still out and aimed, making sure both his opponents stayed down.

The crowd remained quiet as one man ran up, waving defensively at Calhoun. "I'm a doctor! I'm just gonna' check to see if they're dead."

Calhoun stood watching as the man examined Sloan and Booner. He rose then and scanned the crowd. "They're dead."

"Any of you thinking about revenge?" Calhoun asked the other four men. "I only have two bullets left in this gun, but whoever comes at me first is sure to die."

The others shifted and looked at each other, then shook their heads and walked away. It was only then that Seth noticed Nick Calhoun acknowledging he'd been wounded. He put his gun back in its holster and put his left hand to his side. His men ran up to him.

"How bad are you hurt, *señor*?" a Mexican man asked him.

"Just a flesh wound, Renaldo." Calhoun turned. "Anybody here hurt by the bullet that slid past me?"

Men shook their heads.

"I think it went into that barrel over there," one man spoke up.

Heads turned to a water barrel that had sprung a leak. Some of them laughed nervously.

"Let's go," Calhoun told the man called Renaldo.

"Don't you want to see that doctor, *amigo*?"

"No. I know when there's a bullet in me and when there isn't. You can wrap this once we get back to camp. The longer we stay here, the more likely there will be more trouble."

"*Si, Señor.*"

Another man brought up Calhoun's horse, and the wounded leader of what Seth figured were all outlaws in one form or another grimaced as he climbed into his saddle.

Not even sure why, Seth hurried over to Calhoun. "Mister, I'd like to ride with you if it's okay."

Calhoun looked down at him. "Why?"

"Because I've got nothing to do and no place to go. I saw your friend killed this morning, and I have to say I'm right glad to see those two die. I like the way you handled this, leaving your men out of it. Either way, you've lost a man. I figure maybe you need another."

The four others with Nick mounted up and rode closer, as though ready to defend him if they had to.

"I can always use one more. Gather your goods and meet us about a mile south, on the Trinity. We'll talk then. I need to get this lost slice of flesh bandaged."

Seth noticed blood starting to flow over Calhoun's fingers as he held his side. "Sure. Thanks."

Calhoun turned his horse and rode off, followed by the others. Seth hurriedly walked back inside the *Silver Saddle* to get his things from upstairs. One man stopped him.

"Why in hell do you want to ride with Nick Calhoun?"

Seth shrugged. "I've got nothing better to do, and there's something about the man that I like."

"But he's an outlaw. A wanted man, they say. And once an outlaw, *always* an outlaw. You'll end up in trouble and either in prison or livin' out your life in Outlaw Country," the stranger argued.

"Mister, my life has had no direction since the war. I have a daughter I visited recently, and she didn't even know me. And I've been to Outlaw Country. It's not all that bad if a man minds his own business."

The stranger shook his head. "Luck be with you, friend."

Seth walked inside the saloon, excited about riding with Nick Calhoun for a while. Hell, why not? At least for now, life held actual purpose.

Chapter Seventeen

Early November...

Surrounded by a section of twelve soldiers, Ashley headed Max and Brutus along a trail north to Kansas. To her grief and great disappointment, Isaac Stone had become very ill when they'd stopped at the Wichita Indian Agency in northern Oklahoma. He couldn't go on, so he'd sold most of his supplies to the agency and decided he'd made a bad decision leaving so late. The trip was mostly a straight shot north, and he'd been sure he could make it, but more breakdowns, the outlaw attack, and being held up by worse weather than he'd counted on had slowed them more than expected. The risk of heavier snowstorms made finishing the trip too dangerous, but Isaac might have tried if not for a terrible cough that had turned into pneumonia and killed him.

Rachael Stone's grief was pitiful. She wanted to take Isaac's body back home to Gainesville, so it was wrapped in gauze and burlap and loaded into a light-weight wagon. The heavier wagons were left at the Agency to be picked up in the spring, which meant they could travel faster going back. Rachael and the others left, everyone disillusioned, but Ashley couldn't bring herself to join them. She'd come too far, and she'd geared her thoughts and desires to looking toward the future. Going back would mean marrying Clay, and she'd never be happy in that situation. Her home was gone, and old gossip would make life there miserable, especially with her distress over knowing that even though Nick was alive after all, he was still out of her life.

She'd made up her mind to keep heading north. The others didn't need to, as their only purpose had been to get the supplies to Kansas and the forts there and on north into Nebraska. Isaac's son grieved deeply for his father, but he missed his friends in Gainesville. His excitement over the trip had vanished, and he wept bitterly when his father's body was loaded into a wagon to take home for burial.

Ashley missed all of them, as well as Hoot Stowers and Cliff Albertson. After spending nearly two weeks at the Wichita Agency hoping Isaac would live, she'd ended up losing valuable travel time. She was determined to keep going, maybe all the way to western Nebraska. She might even travel farther west once she reached the railroad.

When she was told a section of soldiers was headed north to help with construction work at Fort Larned in Kansas, she'd asked the Indian agent, Henry Shanklin, if she could go with them. Shanklin turned her down at first, but she'd been persistent until he finally gave in with a stern warning that he had strong reservations about his decision.

"I don't like you traveling alone with my men," he'd told her. "But I also don't like the idea of having to watch over you here all winter. I have enough problems looking after rag-tag soldiers and keeping order among the hostiles, as well as keeping up with constantly-changing government orders.

Ashley was relieved to finally be on her way. She wanted nothing more now than to get this trip over with. Rachael Stone had told her about a sister who lived in Abilene, Kansas, who would be glad to take her in for a while, but Ashley's excitement waned when she realized that traveling alone with men who didn't know her was far different from traveling with people from her hometown who knew her well.

She could see that some of the soldiers wondered if a woman traveling alone was just helpless enough that she might need to turn to one of them for help. And for the kind of attention she didn't want. When she first agreed to keep going, she thought a couple of Isaac's men also wanted to go on north, but they'd changed their minds, and now she was completely alone. She felt let down by the men she'd considered friends, men whom she thought cared what happened to her.

The leader of the Section, a Sergeant Rand Oglethorpe, insisted she park her wagon next to his tent at night so that if there was trouble from any of the other men, he'd know about it. Oglethorpe was a middle-aged widower who'd been in the army most of his life. He was hefty but surprisingly agile for his age and weight. He'd been through the war, like almost every man she'd known the last several years. It seemed every man had stories to tell, most more horror stories than interesting ones, but at times, stories with a bit of humor.

Oglethorpe preferred the humorous kind, but his jovial attitude seemed fake at times, and he often had to stop telling a story because he was headed into subjects not fit to talk about in front of a woman. Some of the others seemed to want to play on her emotions when they told sadder tales. Perhaps they thought they could win her affection, that she would throw her arms around them and offer a shoulder to cry on. Or more.

She'd hoped she could trust uniformed men, but soon learned that most soldiers at western posts were left-over rabble from the war who'd only joined for free food and shelter and because they'd lost everything and had nothing better to do with their lives. Western posts were some of the least desirable, according to Agent Shanklin. He'd warned her that most soldiers in these parts were disgruntled Confederates forced into serving the Union but no more trustworthy than common outlaws. Besides that, inclement weather, hostiles and loneliness only added to the restlessness in such men, who had to put up with inconveniences that spoiled a man's mood.

Ashley had foolishly thought that if they were Southern men, then she should be able to trust them because she was a Texian herself and her father had served in the war. There were even a couple of men along who were actually from Texas. She told herself they didn't have all that far to go to reach more civilized places in Kansas, so she shouldn't worry. Once they arrived, she could find Rachael's sister, and later find a safe way to travel on north, perhaps by stagecoach.

She told herself to be strong and aware and patient. Soon they would make it at least to Fort Larned. She just had to manage the rest of this trip on her own. But two men in particular made that difficult. The most annoying and useless of those on this journey was Private Daniel Drum, a small-built, common-looking man with mousy brown hair and a tooth missing in front. He rode at the right side of her wagon now, trying to strike up a conversation, as he did almost every day. He was a former Confederate, but he bore none of the gentlemanly manners a woman would expect from a fellow Southerner.

Ashley had not complained to Oglethorpe about Private Drum—yet—hoping to get to Kansas with no trouble, but her patience with the man was growing short, as it was with a Private Paul Brown, a Union man who seemed to be competing with Drum for her attention. Brown rode on the left side of her wagon, and both men always seemed to be sparring with each other as they insisted on finding ways to win her hand.

"We should reach Fort Dodge in three or four more days," Drum told her now, raising his voice above the squeaks and jingles and creaks of harness and wagons and army gear.

Ashley stared straight ahead and just nodded, trying to drop the hint that she did not want to talk.

"I'll bet you'll be glad to get some place safe and maybe get to sleep in a real bed," Private Brown added.

Ashley sensed his deliberate attempt to keep her attention away from Private Drum, as well as the hint that maybe she wouldn't want to be alone in her bed. "Will you bide the winter there, or go on to Fort Larned?" he asked.

I've mentioned more than once that I intend to go on to Nebraska, Ashley thought, hating their small talk. She wanted to scream her answer to both men. *Please stop bothering me! I'm not interested!* It irritated her no end how obvious it was that Drum and Brown were grasping at anything they could to pretend an innocent interest in her.

"You already know my answer to that, Private Brown," she said aloud, finding it difficult to be as rude as she would like to be. It wasn't her nature to be so unfriendly, and she knew she should appreciate the fact that she had an escort, but Daniel Drum and Paul Brown were both exasperatingly persistent in their attention to her. Cliff had been respectful and courteous. These two men didn't seem to know the meaning of either word.

"Well, I just thought you would give it some extra thought," Brown said. "A blizzard could hit this area any time, enough snow to stop a wagon or even a train. You could end up stranded out on the plains."

"There are forts and small towns all along the way now, even more building up because of ranchers herding their cattle to the railroad," she argued. "I'm sure I'll be fine." *Please go away.*

"Maybe you could get some kind of job for the winter." Private Drum spoke up. "You could build up some money—be safe 'til spring—make some friends, maybe. If you stayed at Fort Dodge or Fort Larned, you could meet a lot of men. I'll be out of this army by spring. I'd like to court you, seeing as how you're not spoken for."

"I'm not interested in meeting men, Private Drum, including you." She nodded toward Brown. "You either." Part of her felt bad about being so blunt, but her patience was wearing thin. "I appreciate the escort, but I'm tired, and all this talking wears me out, so please, both of you, leave me to myself a while."

Brown and Drum continued riding on either side of her for a few minutes until Drum spoke up again. "You'd change your tune if that no-good on the other side of you would stop butting in."

"*You're* the one who needs to stop bothering her," Private Brown shot back. "You ain't nothin' to look at, and you don't have a thing to offer a woman. Me, I keep clean and I shave, and more than one woman considers me good-looking."

Drum let out a guttural laugh. "With that missing tooth? You look ridiculous. No woman would think that's attractive, except for the whores, who'll sleep with any man for money."

Brown sat straighter in his saddle. "You shouldn't talk that way in front of this pretty woman. It's *you* who's upsetting this lady, Drum. And she ought to know you're a cheat who stole money from me in that last card game."

"You still think that?" Drum growled.

"I *know* it."

"And you're a no-good sonofabitch!" Drum answered.

"Please! Stop!" Ashley insisted. "I have no interest in what either of you has to say about the other. I insist you *both* leave me alone, or I'll complain to Sergeant Oglethorpe and have you reprimanded." She felt their anger at the remark, and for the next few minutes they rode on in silence again. Ashley wished both men would drop back and away from her.

Private Drum suddenly kicked his horse into a faster lope and rode around the front of Ashley's draft horses, stopping a few feet in front of them.

"You're quite the *bitch*, aren't you?" he called out.

Ashley stiffened and refused to acknowledge the remark. She urged her horses to keep going, forcing Drum to move out of the way. He joined Brown on the left side of her wagon.

Private Brown laughed. "Drum, I don't like you one bit, but I have to agree with you on the woman bein' a bitch. She thinks she's better than *both* of us."

Ashley's heart beat faster. This was building into something she didn't want. "Please, both of you, leave!" she repeated. "I don't appreciate your insulting words."

"And I'll remind you, lady, that you're the only woman among twelve men," Private Brown told her.

"And Sergeant Oglethorpe sleeps real hard," Private Drum added with a sly smile. "We're both getting a little fed up with your uppity attitude. A sock shoved halfway down your throat would muffle your screams real good. You remember that."

"Yeah," Brown said. "You ought to be a little more grateful for all the free protection you're getting, lady, and I might remind you that you chose to travel with us instead of staying at the Agency. That's as much as saying you're a woman alone looking for a man's help. Maybe there's something more than protection you're needing."

Ashley quickly grabbed her whip and lashed out at both men, snapping the whip against Brown's right cheek. He cried out and put a gloved hand to blood that instantly appeared at the cut. Drum rode closer, and Ashley pulled her wagon to a halt and lashed out again. Drum grabbed the whip and yanked it out of her hand.

Ashley heard Sergeant Oglethorpe shout for the whole section to stop. To her great relief, he rode up and faced his soldiers.

"What's going on here?" he demanded.

Ashley struggled to stay calm and look brave, but both men's words had shaken her because of the intimation that all the men had thought about how easy it would be to attack her while the sergeant slept.

"These two men threatened me in the worst way a woman can be threatened," she told the sergeant. "They spoke filthy words that you can imagine without me having to repeat them."

Oglethorpe turned to Privates Drum and Brown. "Is that true?"

"No, Sir!" Drum lied. "Miss Vale just likes attention. All I did was warn her how the *other* men talked, and that I'd keep an eye out for her because of it."

"I told her the same," Private Brown added.

"They're both lying," Ashley shot back. "They threatened me, and said all the other men were thinking about attacking me while you slept." She fought tears, not wanting to show any weakness. "I expected more from the United States Army, Sergeant Oglethorpe. I thought soldiers would be my safest escort, but apparently, I was mistaken. I never would have left the Wichita Agency if I'd known this was going to happen."

Sergeant Oglethorpe looked from Ashley to the two privates. "I'll get to the bottom of this when we reach Fort Larned," he told them, speaking loud enough for most of the other men to hear. "Until then, I'm leaning toward Miss Vale's explanation. Privates Drum and Brown, you will both ride at the back of the troops from here on and stay away from this woman. I'll listen to your stories separately, but Miss Vale doesn't strike me as the type who would lash out at a man with a whip if he didn't deeply offend her." He grabbed the whip from Drum and handed it back up to Ashley.

Ashley took he whip. "Thank you, Sergeant."

Oglethorpe tipped his hat, then rode farther around the line of wagons to make sure all the men heard him. "I'll not have any man among you insult Miss Vale in any way. If you do, you'll be court-martialed! Is that clear?"

They all nodded and answered "Yes, Sir."

"Some of you have questionable backgrounds back East, and others were once Confederates, so I'm aware that some among you don't have the proper respect for serving in the United States Cavalry. However, you chose to join this army, perhaps with ulterior motives, but you're now a part of it, and you will obey my orders and behave with honor. Is *that* understood?"

More "Yes, Sirs" were spoken throughout.

Oglethorpe turned to Drum and Brown. "Head to the back of the line!"

Both men cast a contemptuous glare toward Ashley, throwing her a threat without speaking a word.

Ashley glared right back. "I'll remind you that I carry a hand gun and know how to use it."

They didn't need to know she was not all that experienced in using her father's old Army pistol. Knowing she had one should be warning enough, or so she hoped.

Drum only smiled, making sure she knew she didn't scare him at all. He turned to Sergeant Oglethorpe. "Yes, Ma'am," he said curtly before riding to the back of the line.

Brown started to follow.

Oglethorpe grabbed the bridle of Brown's horse. "I don't want to hear about any fighting between you two back there. I know you don't get along, and I know the reason. Just don't let a woman make matters worse. Army men can hang on the gallows just as easily as common men. Remember that!"

"You know Drum's a liar and a cheat," Brown reminded him. "Don't make me ride with him, Sergeant."

Oglethorpe let go of Brown's bridle. "I'll take care of things, Private. For now, keep your nose clean. And stay away from the woman."

Ashley noticed the two men exchange a knowing look and wondered what it meant. Was Oglethorpe also not trustworthy?

"Yes, *sir!*" Brown kicked his horse's sides and rode to the back of the short line of soldiers. Ashley turned to watch, but because of her covered wagon, she couldn't see the greater share of the troops behind her. Were they quietly laughing at her? Did they believe Private Drum, or did they believe her? Was it true there were others who'd thought of ways to abuse her and get away with it?

"Miss Vale, from now on you'll have full privacy on this trip," Oglethorpe promised. "You never should have chosen to travel with a bunch of lonely men with questionable backgrounds, but since you have, I'll do my best to keep you safe."

"I promised I'd take care of myself and be no trouble, Sergeant. "I've done just that. I can't help the bad manners of the men in this Section, but I truly did believe U. S. soldiers would be far more honorable."

"And I apologize for the inconvenience and for any insults you've suffered."

"Thank you."

The sergeant turned his horse and rode to the front of the procession, then shouted an order to proceed. Ashley snapped the reins to Max and Brutus. "Get up there!"

Having Drum and Brown at the back of the line was a great relief, but their words were not. She felt no safer. And somehow, Sergeant Oglethorpe was far from reassuring. She'd felt just as uncomfortable around him for most of the trip as she had the others, and she didn't care for the look he'd shared with Private Brown. Thank God they were only about three days from Fort Dodge.

Chapter Eighteen

*A*gent Henry Shanklin greeted Nick with a nod and a rather skeptic grin. Nick knew that by all rights, Shanklin could try to arrest him and his men, but he also knew that in such remote places as the Wichita Agency, visitors who posed no real threat to soldiers or area settlers were welcome. They broke the monotony of the day. Nick figured the risk was worth it if he could learn something about Ashley and the freighting company she was traveling with.

Agent Shanklin knew him. Nick had stopped here for supplies months earlier when he his men were herding stolen cattle south from Kansas. Shanklin knew they were well armed and that trying to arrest them would end up in a gun battle no one wanted. The few soldiers here were needed for more important government duty, especially with a rise in hostile uprisings since the war ended.

Nick scanned the fort grounds and saw a few wagons that belonged to Isaac Stone. They were empty, which caused deep alarm and added to his taking the risk of stopping here. What the hell had happened? Isaac obviously hadn't gone on north, but where was Ashley? Was she headed back to Gainesville? He and the men had ridden in from the southwest, so they wouldn't have had the chance to run into the supply train.

Gray clouds spit snow as he dismounted and shook hands with Agent Shanklin. Soldiers stared as the rest of Nick's men gathered at the supply post to stock up on a few things before heading out again.

"I take it you and your men mean no trouble," Shanklin told Nick.

"None at all. I'm just here looking for information."

Shanklin shrugged. "Come inside then." He led Nick into his quarters and took a seat behind his desk. He offered Nick a chair across from him, then held out a box of cigars.

"It's been a while since I was last here." Nick took a cigar and sat down. He removed his hat and hung it on the corner of the chair. "I wasn't sure you'd remember me." He lit the cigar while Shanklin lit his own and puffed on it several times to get the end burning.

"Of course, I remember you. You're not the average man, Nick Calhoun. You just kind of bluster in on people with an air about you that says 'Don't mess with me.'"

Nick took the cigar from his lips. "Does that mean you won't arrest me this time either?"

"And face the rest of those men out there? Hell, no. I have too many other things to worry about than who might be wanted somewhere for something he might have done as a result of the war. I'd have to arrest half my men if that was the case."

Both men chuckled at the reality of the remark.

"You're right there," Nick told the agent.

Shanklin puffed on his cigar a few more times. "Besides, a visit from someone outside these fort walls is always welcome in this hell hole. And I sent a good share of my men north not long ago, so I'm short. I don't have enough here to try to arrest and escort six gunmen to wherever the hell I'd have to take you, while leaving others here to watch the agency and keep things under control." He puffed on the cigar again, then laid it in an ashtray. "Nick, I'm stuck here with a bunch of hostiles and a few inexperienced soldiers in no-man's land, and I'm beginning to wonder when someone'll come along to replace me so I can get back to civilization. Meantime, you said you weren't here just for supplies. What can I help you with?"

Nick studied the medium-built man whose hair was thinning. "I'm looking for someone, Henry. She might have come through here with a bunch of freighters two or three weeks back."

Shanklin leaned back in his chair. "Might *she* be a pretty little redhead with big green eyes and a complexion like milk?"

Nick nodded, but he already felt inner alarm. "That's her. Ashley Vale, from Gainesville, Texas."

"Sounds like you know her well."

"I know her *very* well. And I know she headed north. I saw empty supply wagons outside that belong to the freighting company she was traveling with. Is she here somewhere?"

Shanklin sighed. "I'm afraid not."

Nick felt a sick premonition at what might have happened. "Do you know where she is?"

Shanklin studied him a moment, a look in his eyes that told Nick he was a little bit afraid to tell him the truth. "Well, Nick, Isaac Stone got sick after they arrived, and he died of pneumonia, right here at the agency. We bought most of his supplies, and Stone's wife and son, along with every last one of his men headed back south with Stone's body. All except Miss Vale. Another young woman was with them, but she and her husband decided to go back to Gainesville, too. Miss Vale refused I told her she could winter here, but she wanted to keep going. I decided that was best because a pretty young woman stuck here alone with a bunch of lonely men would only bring trouble. I had a section of soldiers headed for Fort Larned to help with some construction there, so I figured they could take her with them and see her safely to Kansas. She said something about looking up some woman in Abilene—Mrs. Stone's sister, I think. She was going to stay with her if she could get that far. She agreed to go with my men."

"*Alone?*"

Shanklin nodded.

"There wasn't another man with her named Cliff Albertson? He worked for Isaac and was supposed to stay with her and watch out for her."

Shanklin shook his head. "Sorry, but she went alone." He pulled open a drawer and took out a slip of paper. "The freight wagons were attacked on their way here, and two men were killed." He handed the paper over to Nick. "I wrote their names down in case I might need them for something. One was Robert Stowers, who I guess was called Hoot. The other was Cliff Albertson, both from Gainesville. Then they waited here for two weeks hoping Stone would get well. If things had gone right, they'd have made it to Kansas two or three weeks ago, maybe even to Nebraska."

Nick read the names written on the paper, then closed his eyes and handed it back to Shanklin. "*Damn* it!" He rose, deep worry surging through his blood. "Cliff was a good man and a good friend. I hired him to go along and keep an eye on Ashley. Now she's completely alone and vulnerable."

"She'll be okay, Nick. A sergeant Rand Oglethorpe is in charge of the men. He's a good man. He'll watch out for her."

Nick set his cigar in an ashtray on the agent's desk and walked over to look out a window. "I don't like it. A bunch of lonely soldiers from a place this remote probably haven't seen something as pretty as Ashley in a long time. A soldier escort for the freighters would have been good, but a young woman alone is another story. You know better than most what kind of rabble the Army sends out here."

"Well, your Miss Vale is very independent and determined. She told me she carries her father's army pistol and knows how to use it. And like I told you, Oglethorpe will watch out for her."

Nick rubbed at the back of his neck. "She's independent and determined, all right, but I think she stretched the truth about being handy with that pistol," he grumbled. "And I'm sure she thinks she can trust men in uniform. If I know Ashley, she thinks any of those along who might have fought for the South and consider themselves Confederates at heart will respect her because she's from Texas, but men are men, and the war is over."

Nick walked back to his chair and sat down again. "It's not just her being a woman alone with a bunch of strange men that bothers me. Before Ashley left Texas, her mother was murdered, and no one knows who did it. For all I know, whoever it was could be following her." He leaned forward and rested his elbows on his knees. "How long ago did they leave?"

"You in love with her?"

"I asked how long ago they left," Nick answered with obvious irritation at the question.

Shanklin chuckled. "Couple of weeks. They might even be there by now —Fort Dodge, I mean. They were supposed to stop there first."

Nick ran a hand through his hair. "Something doesn't feel right. You shouldn't have let her go."

"I'm not her keeper, Nick. And once that woman decides on something, there's no arguing... as with most women, I guess. She running from *you*?"

Nick smiled sadly. "In a way."

"And you're running from the law."

"Once I make sure Ashley's safe and sound and settled, the men and I are heading west to Outlaw Country. I'll probably live out my life there. Who knows?"

"There a bounty on you?"

Nick stood and rested his hand on the butt of his gun. "You figure on collecting it?"

Shanklin put up his hand defensively. "Hell no! I still have a few brains left, in spite of living in this hellish place so long any man would be crazy by now. I was just wondering." He leaned back in his chair again. "Were you hoping to take that woman with you to Outlaw Country?"

Nick waved him off. "That's no place for a woman like Ashley. I just want to be sure she's settled before I go. I won't likely ever come back, and I'd go insane out there wondering if she ever landed where she wanted and got safely settled." He took his hat from the corner of the chair and put it back on. "That damn war destroyed a lot of lives, Henry, and not always through death or injury. It left me unfit for the civilized world, and Ashley knows it."

"And maybe you underestimate yourself. I see a good man in you, Nick. And yes, the war did that to a *lot* of men. Half the soldiers here were in that war, too, and the rest joined the Army because they didn't know what else to do with their lives."

"Yeah. I can understand that." Nick picked up his cigar. "Look, I'd like to camp here at the agency tonight, if that's okay with you. We also need some supplies."

"No problem, as long as you pay for the supplies and don't try to steal them."

"We'll pay." Nick scowled. "Just don't ask me how we got the money."

"You going after the woman?"

"I don't have any choice." Nick put the cigar back between his lips and puffed on it again to keep it lit. "We'll head out in the morning. Thanks for your hospitality. And do me a favor. Draw a map as best you can of the route those troops will take to Kansas."

"I'll do that, but it's a pretty straight shot, with a stop at Fort Dodge and then on east to Fort Larned. Stop back in an hour or so, and I'll have a map for you."

"Thanks." Nick turned and walked out. He untied his horse and walked it toward the supply store, where his men waited.

"Is she here, *señor?*" Renaldo asked as soon as he reached them.

"She was." Nick took the cigar from his lips. "The guy who owned the freighting company got sick and died here. The rest of them sold most of the supplies to the agency and headed back south."

"So, she's headed to Gainesville, too?" Ringer asked him.

"I wish she was." Nick felt even sicker inside. He'd failed her. He'd been so sure sending Cliff with her was all the protection she'd need, considering how many other men were going along. And women. He faced the others. "The wagon train was attacked before they got here. Cliff was killed. Then when the rest decided to head home after Isaac died, Ashley chose to keep going north with a section of soldiers."

"*Alone?*" Buck Davis asked, showing the same reaction Nick had when Shanklin told him the news.

"Yeah, *alone.* She's young and trusting and stubborn, and now she's the only woman with a bunch of rabble they call the Army. There are only ten or twelve of them, but it only takes one man with wrong ideas to turn the trip into a nightmare for her." He adjusted his hat as he studied them. "We'll buy some supplies here and camp outside the compound tonight, then head north as soon as it's light. I don't like any of this. If some of you don't want to go along, you have a right to head your own way come morning. I won't blame you. As for me, I'm not giving up until I know Ashley's all right."

They all replied that they intended to stick with Nick and help him find "the woman."

"I'm along for the ride, wherever you head," new man Seth Cunningham spoke up.

"Thanks," Nick told them all. "Go get whatever supplies you need. I'll be along."

All but Renaldo went inside. He watched as Nick tied Satan to a hitching post. "You are very worried," he stated rather than asked.

"I am." Nick smashed out his cigar against the hitching post. "If Cliff was with her, I wouldn't be so concerned. I just feel I have a responsibility to make sure she's okay, Renaldo."

"*Si*, I understand."

Nick sighed resignedly as he looked around. "I don't like any of this. Cliff's dead, and she's out there alone." He was anxious for morning. "I hope the rest of the men are willing to put up with hours in the saddle. Come sunup, I intend to push man and horse as hard as I can without killing either one. We need to reach Ashley as fast as possible. I have a bad feeling about this."

"*Si, señor.* We will be ready." Renaldo turned to go inside. "She will be okay, *mi amigo.* God is looking out for her."

Nick wished he could be as confident. "I hope you're right."

The thought of any of those men abusing the woman he loved, the woman who was once a little girl he'd always felt responsible for and thought of as a sister, tore at his insides.

It struck him that his concern wasn't just that she could be hurt, but that if some man forced himself on her, he'd be taking what belonged to Nick Calhoun! The thought made him feel crazy. If he found her, maybe he'd take her up on her offer to go with him to Outlaw Country. If she still wanted to go. The thought of never claiming her for himself, of never seeing her again, was much harder to handle than he thought it would be.

If he hadn't gone to see her in the first place, he wouldn't be going through this hell. He should have left well enough alone. *You're a goddamn fool, Nick Calhoun!*

Chapter Nineteen

$\mathcal{P}$rivate Paul Brown started awake when he felt a nudge. He quickly sat up, at first confused and frightened because of the hostile country where they were camped only three days from Fort Dodge. He started for his handgun, but someone grabbed his wrist.

"Shhhh," came a voice in near whisper. "Brownie, it's me. Oglethorpe."

Private Brown frowned and faced the man in the moonlight. "Something wrong?"

"Hell no. Come away from camp with me. We need to talk."

Frowning, Brownie threw off his blanket and pulled on his boots. Once on his feet, he grabbed his wool Army jacket to pull on over his long johns, then hurriedly followed the sergeant by moonlight into a stand of trees not far from where they were camped.

"What the hell's going on?"

"Keep your voice down," Oglethorpe answered. "I have a proposition for you."

Brownie ran a hand through sandy, unwashed hair and scratched at a scruffy beard. "In the middle of the night?"

"It has to be kept between us. I've figured out a way to get your money back from Private Drum. Didn't you lose a lot to him in a poker game before we left the agency to come up here?"

Brownie folded his arms against the chilly air, grasping the neck of his jacket to pull it closer around himself. "Yeah. So?"

"How much did you lose?"

"Two months' pay plus money I'd been savin'. And the sono-fabitch *cheated*! Ain't no doubt in my mind. I even lost my pa's pocket watch, and Drum just sat there grinnin'. He knew damn well he'd cheated, and that I couldn't prove it."

"Yeah? Well, how'd you like to get all that money back, and then-some, plus the watch? On top of that, I figured a way to get rid of Drum himself."

"What the hell are you talkin' about?"

"We'll use the woman."

"The *woman?*"

Oglthorpe slapped a hand over Brown's mouth. "Damn it, I said keep you voice down. And don't forget who's in charge here!"

Brownie shoved at him. "All right! All right!" he answered in a rough whisper. "Just tell me what the hell you're talking about."

"I'm talking about killing Private Drum and blaming it on the woman. We take his money, and when it's over we claim she must have killed him out of anger and retaliation for how he kept bothering her. We can even claim she took his money because she was getting desperate for a way to support herself, seeing as how she's alone now and has no escort. I could search her wagon for whatever valuables she might have and take those, too. If I find some cash, I'll say some of it must be Drum's, plus we can take whatever Drum has in his supplies. The woman has no way of proving one way or the other how much she had with her, or if some of it came from Drum. We take her to Fort Dodge and turn her over to the man in charge there. They'll have to put her behind bars while they figure out what to do with her. That's when we can go through her things and take what we can find.

And her getting in trouble that way is proper punishment for being so snooty to you."

Brownie frowned in thought. An owl hooted somewhere, and coyotes yipped and barked in the distance as he considered Oglthorpe's idea. "You're talkin' about killin' Drum outright?"

"Don't tell me the idea doesn't sit with you. The sonofabitch took you for every dime you have, and *everybody* thinks he was cheating. And he's been a thorn in your side ever since, especially over the woman. I'm telling you, this could work. The men already know how upset Miss High and Mighty is with Drum, and a female traveling alone always presents a picture of desperation." Oglethorpe stepped closer. "I can pretend to defend her, and you can stir up the rest of the men to think otherwise. You know, look around and hint at *who's next*? Make them suspect her. She can protest all she wants, but the more she protests, the guiltier she'll look, know what I mean?"

Brownie sighed. "I guess I wouldn't mind putting a bullet in Drum, but how in hell do we shoot him without bein' found out? How do we make it look like it was her?"

"Because it *will* be her that kills him."

"How in hell can you make that happen?"

"Easy. All we do is tell Drum she was asking about him—told us she was scared he might be right about all of us plotting against her and thought maybe, since he was interested in her, she needed somebody she could trust to watch over her. That since he flat-out told her she was in danger from the rest of us, she felt like maybe he was the only one she could trust. Drum wants her bad. If he thinks she'd welcome him inside her wagon, he'd go over there in a minute. "

Brown grinned. "You bet he would."

"Soon as he climbs inside that wagon, that woman will be so scared and surprised, she'll shoot him on the spot. We can say she must have seduced him. Men will wonder who's telling the truth, enough that they'll want to turn her over to the law and let them take care of it. Once Drum's dead, I'll go through his things. We could accuse Ashley Vale of conning Drum out of his dough before she shot him. We'll get the men all confused so they won't know *what* to believe. We end up dumping her at Fort Dodge because we have to stop there anyway before going on to Fort Larned. You and I can split what valuables we find plus Drum's money and be on our way."

Brownie nodded. "I reckon' it could work."

"I *know* it could work. And besides getting back your money, I wouldn't mind seeing that uppity bitch put in her place. She'll have a fine time explaining herself to those in charge at Fort Dodge. Most independent women like her are thought of as a little bit crazy anyway, and usually a little bit loose."

Brownie stifled a chuckle.

Oglethorpe nodded and patted Brownie's shoulder reassuringly. "One of those freighter men at the agency told me Ashley Vale has a reputation back in Gainesville. Some young man killed another man in a fight over her a few years back. Stories got passed around—that she'd been carrying on with both men and the fight was over jealousy. Some said one was just threatening her and the other defended her, but he said nobody was ever sure what really happened. The man involved is an outlaw now, wanted for murder and robbery, and he visited Miss Vale alone in her bedroom before she left to come north. What does that say about her? And now she's traveling alone. Any man would wonder about her reputation."

"That she's not all lady?" Brownie answered with a grin. "And that would make our story even more believable."

"Now you're understanding how this could work."

"Damn!" Brownie grinned. "We'd better work on Drum tomorrow. This has to happen quick. We'll be at Fort Dodge just a couple more nights from now."

"And the law is a lot more likely to believe soldiers than a crazy, man-hungry woman they don't know. No decent woman travels by herself."

Brownie nodded. "I wouldn't mind a poke at her myself."

"No. None of that," Oglethorpe warned. "If we take her to the fort all beat up and forced into something like that, the law will feel sorry for her and will be less likely to believe us. You leave her alone, understand? This has to look like something she brought on herself by seducing Drum."

Brownie rubbed the back of his neck. "If you say so."

"I *do* say so. Don't be messing with her that way. Just work on Drum tomorrow and make him believe she talked like she wanted to see him. I'll warn her that I've heard men talking, and that she'd better be extra aware at night. I'll tell her I'll be watching out for her, but I can't be everywhere at once. I'll warn her to keep her pistol ready."

"Good idea."

Oglethorpe looked over at the dwindling campfire. "You'd better get back to your bedroll. If anybody noticed you were gone, tell them you left to take a pee or you just couldn't sleep."

"I'll do that." Brownie grabbed the sergeant's hand and shook it. "Thanks. I need that money. And if this works out, it ought to be quite a show. She's gonna' be real shook up—maybe so shook up she'll look like the crazy, vengeful woman we'll make her out to be."

"That's right. Go on with you now." Oglethorpe disappeared into the surrounding darkness, and Brownie snuck back to his bedroll.

Oglethorpe stayed in the trees, grinning at his ingenious idea. He suspected Ashley Vale had plenty of money, and he wondered if she kept some of it in her corset. He'd enjoy finding out.

Chapter Twenty

"You're working the horses pretty hard, Nick." Seth wiped at foamy sweat that hit his pants from his horse's neck. "I know I'm new to this bunch, but I didn't figure on having to ride my horse to death if I joined up."

"It was your choice, and we're all pacing the horses the best we can," Nick answered. "We'll make camp in another twenty minutes or so and let the horses rest. I don't like this, either, but I don't have a lot of choice. I have this gut feeling we need to catch up with Ashley quickly, and it's not just because I don't trust those soldiers."

"What else is bothering you?"

Nick slowed Satan to a gentle lope. "Someone else might be after her with no good intentions. Not long before she left Gainesville, her mother was murdered. They never caught who did it. If it was somebody with a grudge against the family, he could be after Ashley, too." Satan snorted and shook his head. Sweat went flying, and Nick patted the horse's neck. "Stay calm, boy. We'll stop soon."

Seth kept his mare at an even pace and remained beside Nick.

"I know it had to have been a pretty big man who killed Ashley's mother because of how violently the woman died," Nick said. "Her neck was broken, and I have a feeling it wasn't just from being thrown over an upstairs railing. I think whoever killed her broke it before she went over."

Seth reined his horse to a halt. Nick slowed Satan and turned. "I said we weren't stopping yet. If you can't keep up, maybe you should quit us right now."

Seth shook his head and turned away. "Shit!"

"What's wrong?"

Seth momentarily stared silently at the distant horizon before finally facing Nick again. "My God! I think I know who killed that woman!"

Nick rode Satan closer, his eyes blazing with a burning need for revenge. "*What?*"

The other men caught up and circled them.

"What is going on, Boss?" Renaldo asked.

"I'm not sure yet," Nick answered, his eyes still on Seth. "You men go on ahead and find a place to make camp. Seth and I'll catch up."

The others frowned curiously at the way Nick was watching the new man.

"Whatever you say," Ringer told Nick. "Let's go boys." He headed his horse north again, and the others followed.

"Explain what you just told me," Nick told Seth. "And I hope the man you're talking about is no friend of yours."

Seth frowned, almost as though in pain. "He's *nobody's* friend, at least not to any ordinary man. He might even be dead by now. He's good at making enemies." His mare turned in a nervous circle, as though sensing Seth's upset. He took a moment to calm her before explaining more. "This woman you're looking for, is her first name Ashley?"

"Yes!" Nick took a cheroot from a pocket inside his jacket. "How in hell do you know that?"

"Because I've heard it, from the very lips of the man who killed her mother."

"And you're just now telling me?" Nick struck a large match and lit the cheroot.

"I'm just now telling you because I never made the connection 'til you mentioned how Miss Vale's mother died. A lot of people have the same last name. And nobody mentioned Gainesville or Ashley's mother at all. You and your men have a pact about not talking about your pasts, and not asking too many questions, so all I knew after I joined up was that before you headed west, you wanted to find some woman you needed to check on first. I know her name is Ashley, but when I asked one of the other men for details, he said that was for you to decide. I figured since I'm new, I'd best not sound too nosey, so I never asked. I thought your only concern was over the soldiers Ashley's traveling with."

Nick took the cheroot from his lips. "I don't believe this." He looked toward the other men who'd ridden ahead, then back at Seth. "Yes, that's her name. What else do you know about this?"

"I met a man in South Pass City. I was coming back from looking for gold in California and had no special place to go. I stopped there to rest up before coming to Texas. I went to a saloon for a few drinks and this man came to my table with a bottle of whiskey. He plopped down like he'd known me all his life. He was drunk and getting drunker. Big guy—biggest I've ever met. The sonofabitch's first words to me were, '*I killed a woman.*'"

"Jesus, I've been scratching my head over Patricia Vale's murder for weeks now, and here comes a perfect stranger who knows something about it." Satan sidestepped nervously and Nick reined him in, then dismounted. "Get off your horse. We'll walk our mounts while you tell me more. Have you ever been to Gainesville?"

"Never, but that's where this man was from." Seth dismounted and grabbed a towel from his gear. He used it to wipe some of the sweat from his horse's neck, then moved around to walk next to Nick. "Are *you* from Gainesville, too?"

"Yes. It's a long story."

"Well, from things I've heard about that town, I don't *want* to go there." He removed his hat and raised his arm to rub at his forehead, then put his hat back on. "Is it true about all the hangings?"

"It's true, all right. They almost hanged *me*, for killing a man who'd attacked Ashley in her family's barn. I worked for her father then. The name of the man who attacked Ashley was Sid MacIntyre."

"*What?*"

They both stopped walking.

"The man who killed Patricia Vale said his name was *Abel* MacIntyre."

Nick's eyes grew wide in surprise. "It *couldn't* have been! Abel was killed in the war."

"According to him, a man called Howard Vale only *thought* he was dead. This Howard Vale—he shot MacIntyre during a battle—some kind of argument over Vale's wife. He not only shot MacIntyre, but slashed a sword halfway through the man's face. Took out an eye."

The eye patch! "The man who killed Patricia left an eye patch behind!" Nick shook his head. "My God. That big, blustery sonofabitch could be after Ashley!"

"I don't think so, Nick. He's living in Outlaw Country, and he's afraid to go back to Gainesville. He has no idea Ashley left there. I really don't think he'll come back this way. Like I said, he might even be dead for sure this time."

"How's that?"

"Some man in the saloon heard him bragging about killing a woman. The men out there, they don't like women being abused. Women out in those parts are like gold to the men.

Anyway, some big mountain man type landed into MacIntyre. Threw him into the street and beat him near to death. He wasn't moving when I left. If he did live, I think he'll try to stay out there in the mountains, if he can still walk. He mentioned not daring to go back to Gainesville because they might figure out it was him that killed that woman."

Nick rubbed at the back of his neck, trying to think. "When MacIntyre talked to you at first, did he say anything about his son being dead?"

Seth shook his head. "No. I got the impression he never even went into town or saw anybody in Gainesville. He might not even have known about his son. Never even mentioned having one. I got the impression all he did was go straight to the house where he thought Howard and Patricia Vale lived. He was really out to kill Howard, but he found out Vale was dead, so he went after the wife. He was pretty bad off mentally. Maybe he forgot about his son. Something was real wrong with his brain from being shot in the head. Vale shot him there and in the chest. I expect he never dreamed MacIntyre could live through that, but he did."

Nick looked away, remembering. "I'll be damned. MacIntyre was the biggest man in Gainesville, and he had an interest in Ashley's mother. He left for war—left his son behind because Sid was kind of backward – messed up in the head. All he knew was how to pick cotton, but he was damn well aware of women. I got to know Ashley from working for her father. I caught Sid MacIntyre attacking her in the barn when she was only sixteen I went kind of crazy and dived into him. He hit his head on a post and died, and that's how I almost got myself hanged. They sent me off to war instead, and things that happened after that landed me in this fix I'm in now."

Seth rubbed at his eyes. "Jesus, Nick, I'm sorry I never put all this together before now, but like I said, I never knew all the details. Nobody said anything about the woman's mother being murdered back in Gainesville. Nobody even gave me any names."

Nick started walking his horse again. "It's not your fault. In fact, the best thing I ever did was let you join us. I never would've known any of this otherwise, or to be on the lookout for Abel MacIntyre." He shook his head in wonder. "Before the war and everything that happened because of it, Ashley had a nice family. They became *my* family, but my life and Ashley's changed almost overnight because of me accidentally killing Sid MacInture, and then being ordered to go with Ashley's father when he left for that damn war. I was already in love with Ashley when I left, but now I can't give her the life she deserves. All I want now is to find out if she's okay. I sure do thank you for telling me what you know. It's almost like God sent you into my pathway."

Seth grinned a little. "You believe in God?"

Nick kept walking. "Sure, I do. I was raised Catholic— communion, confession, the whole thing. I was even an altar boy when I was ten."

"I don't believe it." Seth shook his head.

"Believe it. I was born in New York City, but my parents were Irish immigrants. Still in all, even Ashley doesn't know I was raised Catholic. I never even gave thought to maybe it could make a difference."

Seth chuckled. "Something tells me it wouldn't."

Nick shrugged. "Either way, I quit going to church when my own mother was murdered back in New York. That was after my father died from pneumonia. I found the man who killed her and I beat him to death. I'm wanted in New York, too. I was only fifteen then. That's when I ran off and ended up in Gainesville. I figure killing that man and then Sid MacIntyre, and all the things I've done since then, means that the Man Upstairs won't want anything to do with helping me."

Their horse's hooves made squishing sounds as they continued on silently for a few minutes, plodding through sloppy mud and melting snow. When they reached camp, they tied their horses and faced each other.

"Strange how life turns out, Nick. I have a daughter I'll probably never see again."

"That's too bad."

Seth shrugged then sighed. "She's better off. I sure didn't know meeting up with you would lead to all this."

Nick thought about Renaldo's statement that God was watching out for Ashley. "Well, I said God led you to me, but if He did, it was for Ashley's sake, not mine."

They began unsaddling the horses and untying their gear. Nick suddenly stopped and turned to Seth, who could have sworn there were tears in his eyes. "I let her down, Seth. I let her down in the worst way a man can. If she's hurt or suffering, I'll never forgive myself." He walked past. "Take care of my things, will you?"

"Sure." Seth watched Nick walk away and sit down on a log near the campfire, then take off his hat and put his head in his hands. Seth was surprised at Nick telling him about being an altar boy. That sure was a contrast to the man he was now, but maybe, deep inside, he wasn't all that different after all. Life had just gotten in the way.

Chapter Twenty-One

Mid-November...

Ashley stirred awake, listening, sure something had alerted her deeper senses. Outside the wagon someone snored loudly. That would be Sergeant Oglethorpe, who'd told her to park her wagon next to his tent at night again for more safety. Was it his snoring that had caused her to wake up? How in heck was he supposed to watch over her when he slept so hard? Everything else seemed quiet, but ever since her words with privates Brown and Drum, she'd slept lightly and kept her father's old Army pistol nearby on top of a crate.

She lay there a while, hearing only the light wind that snuck through small openings when her wagon canvas blew away from the sides of the wagon in a few places. She'd almost fallen asleep again when she heard it, a rustling in the tall grass where they'd made camp. She sat up and pushed her hair behind her ears to listen more closely.

"Who's there?" she asked, her voice more whisper than clear.

"It's me," a man said softly.

Ashley reached for her pistol. "Me who? Show yourself!"

"Private Drum." Now his voice was right beside her wagon.

Ashley's heart beat harder. She held the gun out, pointed toward the back of the wagon. "Go away!"

"Brownie told me you wanted to hire someone to guard you from the rest of the men. I'll do it."

"I don't need a guard. I only need this gun I'm holding. Now go away before I scream!"

"Look, I don't mean you any harm, Miss Vale. I mean that. I'll sleep right nearby and keep watch until we make it to Fort Dodge."

"Sergeant Oglethorpe is watching out for me."

"He is?" Now Drum's voice was at the back of the wagon. "Seems to me he's snoring away and doesn't even know we're talking. And the rest of the men are far off. It doesn't look to me like Oglethorpe's doing a very good job of watching out for you."

Ashley gasped when Drum suddenly climbed inside. "Let me do the job, Ma'am."

"Get out!" Ashley said, louder now. She wondered why Oglethorpe was still snoring. Surely, he could hear her now.

"Look, lady, I only mean to help. Brownie said you were asking about me. I figured—"

"You figured wrong! Brownie lied to you. I don't know what's going on, but you need to get out of this wagon. If you touch me, I'll *shoot* you!" What did he have in mind? He was alone with her, and everybody else slept. She had no desire to shoot Drum, but terror engulfed her when he crawled even closer. What would the men think if he got close enough to try something and she hesitated and was raped? They'd think the worst! They'd think she'd invited him, and that's what he would tell them. Women were almost never believed in such situations. "I'm going to tell you once more to leave or I'll shoot you!" she repeated.

"Honey, if you wanted to shoot me, you'd have done it by now." Drum put a hand on her ankle.

By the light of a very dimly-lit lantern Ashley always kept close, she could see Drum's eyes. They were glazed over, and he was practically licking his lips, like a wolf who'd just found fresh meat. And she smelled liquor on his breath.

"Get out!" she growled once more. "I don't want to shoot you, but I *will* if you don't get out of here right now!"

Drum grinned and reached out. "Come on, honey. You want a man's protection, and you know it. And you'll feel a lot safer with a man's arms around you. Give me the pistol, sweetheart."

The alternative to shooting the man rushed over Ashley like a stiff, hot wind. Without the ability or the time to reason her situation any more deeply, she pulled the trigger. A little flame burst from the barrel of her father's pistol, and the gun jerked so hard it hurt her hand. The noise of the firing was so unexpectedly loud that it left her completely deaf for the next several seconds.

She watched Drum open his mouth. Was he screaming? His pale brown eyes were wide with surprise and horror, and blood gushed from his throat. Had the bullet gone all the way through his neck, or was it stuck in his throat? She couldn't tell, and, strangely, she didn't care. She just sat there staring at Private Drum. His eyes rolled upward so that she could only see their whites for a moment before he fell backward, still inside, his legs oddly bent underneath his body.

Ashley was sure she was screaming herself now, but she couldn't hear her own voice. She tossed the gun aside and crawled away from Drum, then climbed over the seat and out of the wagon. Someone reached up. Who was it? He grasped her about the waist and lifted her down. She screamed again and fought him, but he kept a grip on her arms and shook her slightly.

"Miss Vale! It's all right. It's me—Oglethorpe! What's going on?"

She could hear him now, but just barely. It was as though he was calling from a distance. *What happened? ... all right? ... here. Stay right here!*

Ashley clung to a wagon wheel while Oglethorpe climbed inside. Men began to gather around her then, all of them staring. Ashley realized she was wearing only her flannel nightgown and no robe. The frigid cold began to penetrate the thin material. She began shivering and rubbing the backs of her arms, more from shock than from the cold. Her mind swirled with what had just taken place. Had this been only a nightmare? Would she wake up now to learn this whole thing was just an awful dream?

... *"Blood all over the front of her nightgown..."*

Who said that? She looked down, but in the darkness she wasn't sure what she saw. She put her hands to the bodice of her gown. It was wet.

"My God!" she screamed. "My God! My God!" She looked pleadingly at the strange, shadowed faces that surrounded her. No one offered any help. Finally, she could hear the other men's voices, including Oglethorpe's, from inside the wagon.

"It's Drum!" he called out. "He's dead!"

One of the men who stood near Ashley finally took his blanket from around his shoulders and put it around her. She jerked away in terror, grasping the blanket close and imagining all of them attacking her, taking turns with her. She noticed Brownie then. He ran to the back of the wagon and handed something to Oglethorpe.

"Here's my gun, sir. Soon as I heard that shot, I grabbed it, just in case it would be needed."

Ashley frowned, wondering why he thought the sergeant would need a gun. Did they think she was dangerous?

The other men started asking questions, but Ashley just kept backing away.

"Private Drum is missing from his bedroll!" Brownie told the men. "He said the woman here had changed her mind about him. Said she wanted his protection! She must have tried to seduce him. Look at her! Why would she ask a man to come over here at night and then not even put on a robe!"

"Because she wanted his money," Sergeant Oglethorpe announced from somewhere at the back of the wagon.

Ashley could hardly believe what he was saying.

"Drum had a lot of money on him," Oglethorpe told the others. "I expect he'd offered to help her out financially, her being a woman alone and all. The man was fond of her. We all know that. But she shot him!"

Feeling returned to Ashley's legs enough that she walked on bare feet through the high grass to where Oglethorpe was speaking.

"You're lying!" she told Oglethorpe. She found herself wishing she could yell the words, but somehow her voice didn't' seem to work right. She felt totally removed from her words. From her entire body. "He...he *attacked* me! Why are you making up these lies?"

"Somebody hold a lantern on her," the sergeant ordered. "See if she has any bruises!"

"I don't." Ashley answered. "He grabbed my ankle, but he...he intended to do much more. I could see it in his eyes!"

"You *invited* him here, didn't you?" Brownie accused. "He *told* me you invited him!"

"I did no such thing!"

"Are you sure Drum is dead?" one of the other men asked.

"Of course, I'm sure," Oglethorpe told them. "He's been shot right in the throat."

The men all quieted for a moment.

"Jesus," one of them muttered.

"She's a damn seductress, and a thief!" Brownie suggested.

Ashley felt all eyes on her. She shrunk back against the wagon gate. "That's not true!" She wished she could say it in a stronger, more affirmative voice, but she was too full of terror and confusion.

"I don't know *what* the truth is," Oglethorpe told the men. "Something more happened here than the woman thinking Drum was going to attack her. He must have offered her money first. Maybe he thought if he was kind enough to offer his support in guarding her and keeping her well supplied, she'd like him better. Looks to me like he didn't deserve to get shot."

"Yeah!" various men answered, one man raising his fist.

"We never should've brought her along," another spoke up. "Having a woman along is bad luck. You can't let a pretty young thing like that one travel alone with a bunch of men who ain't seen a pretty young female in months. She ought to have known better."

"I expected United States soldiers to have manners and respect!" Ashley's voice was a little stronger now. "I should have known better than to think Union soldiers would be gentlemen."

Brownie stepped closer. "You'd better watch your attitude, Missy! You're in a lot of trouble. Remindin' these men that your heart is Confederate won't help your cause."

"*What* cause? Why are you saying I am in trouble, Private?" Ashley looked up at Sergeant Oglethorpe. "What's going on here? Can't you see what happened? You *know* Drum had been bothering me!"

Oglethorpe looked down at her from the wagon gate. "We all know that, but what I found in here makes me wonder. You don't look harmed, and you apparently let Private Drum into your wagon, in spite of the fact that you wore only your nightgown and no robe!"

"I did *not* invite him! He climbed in of his own accord, before I had a chance to react. He grabbed my ankle, and he was drunk and had a wild look in his eyes!"

"So, you *shot* him, without giving him a chance to explain?" Brownie asked. "I think he offered you money, and when you saw that, you decided to shoot him and claim he'd attacked you! Did the sergeant get to you too soon? Maybe you were going to hurry up and hide the money before anybody saw it."

"No!" Ashley answered. "I never even saw any money. Why are you trying to make me look bad? Is it because I turned you away? Because I put that cut on your face?"

"I don't give a damn what you did, lady. And I wouldn't have this mark if you hadn't led me and private Drum on all this time, flaunting yourself like you did, sittin' up there on your wagon seat all straight and pretty, stickin' your chest out and all!"

Ashley gasped at the filthy suggestion. "How *dare* you! I've kept to myself and fended for myself this whole trip! I never once asked for your *or* Private Drum's attention! I was parked beside the sergeant's tent for protection from the both of you." She looked up at Oglethorpe again. "And what kind of a soldier are you, snoring away while I was being attacked? You were no protection at all!"

"Miss Vale, you apparently talked so softly with Private Drum that it didn't even wake me up."

"I told him to get out of my wagon!" Ashley shot back. "I nearly screamed it! I *wasn't* talking softly!"

"You *had* to be. I never heard a thing," Oglethorpe insisted. "What was going on in here that you didn't want me to hear? How long was Drum in there with you? If you were really scared and had screamed, I would have waked up."

A desperate fear crept into Ashley's blood. Something felt very wrong, more wrong than Drum coming to her wagon. Sergeant Oglethorpe and Private Brown both seemed intent on making her look guilty of something. And where was the money Oglethorpe claimed he'd found? Drum wouldn't have had money on him in the middle of the night. "Where is the gun Brownie handed you?"

"What?"

"The gun! I saw him hand you a gun. Where is it?"

Oglethorpe scowled. "It's inside. I dropped it somewhere. I'll find it as soon as I get you situated."

Situated? What did Oglethorpe mean by that? And what did Brownie *really* hand him? Money? Something he could use to claim she took it from Drum?

"I might add that Drum had no weapon on him," the sergeant told her loudly enough for the others to hear. "You shot an unarmed man!" He ordered two other men to take Ashley into his tent and tie her wrists and ankles until he could decide what to do about the situation.

"You can't do this," Ashley argued.

"I'm leading this section, and I can do whatever I want, especially with a civilian who has no business traveling with us in the first place."

The man's earlier kindness had completely disappeared. Ashley struggled not to break down sobbing, hating to behave like a weak, frightened woman in front of all these men. She told herself to be strong. Somehow this would get straightened out. Thank God they weren't far from Fort Dodge.

The two men who'd received Oglethorpe's orders to take her away and tie her walked up.

"Come on, lady," one of them told her.

"Don't touch me!" Ashley demanded.

"Got no choice, lady. Don't make us hurt you. It's only for one more day and night, and then we'll be at Fort Dodge."

Ashley looked over at the sergeant. "And then what?"

"Then we turn you over to whoever is in charge and move on," Oglethorpe told her. "They can hold you there at the fort and wait for a judge or whoever to come along, and you can hand him your story. Right now I'm going to get Drum's body out of here and look things over. See if I can find any evidence you might be telling the truth, but it doesn't look good for you."

"You can't possibly believe I deliberately invited a man I couldn't stand to come visit me in the night and then tried to take his money! And why would he even have money on him in the middle of the night?"

"To offer it to *you*," the sergeant answered with emphasis. "And right now, it doesn't matter. You can argue your case with a judge. If Brownie and I need to testify, we'll do our best to make it look good for you, but right now I need to take care of a dead man who has a big hole in his throat." He turned his attention to the two men who'd taken Ashley's arms. "Get her away from here."

Ashley started to resist, then decided to cooperate. Fighting any of these men might get them excited in the wrong ways. And her money! What about her money? Men would be rummaging her things. If they found her money, she had no doubt they would keep it and she'd be left with nothing even if she did get out of this. She fought hard to hide her tears and desperation as they took her to Oglethorpe's tent and pushed her down in a corner. They grabbed some rope from the saddle and supplies Oglethorpe had stored in another corner of the tent and began tying her wrists and ankles. One of them found another blanket and they bunched it up to use like a pillow.

"Lay down there, Ma'am. We'll cover you better with that blanket around your shoulders."

Ashley swallowed back an urge to vomit. "Bring me another blanket from my wagon," she asked. "For God's sake, it's November! I'm cold, and I don't even have my robe! You could have let me put it on before bringing me in here."

"Yes, Ma'am."

Ashley knew the second man was a Private Ashton Riley. He unwrapped the blanket from her shoulders and tucked it tightly around her.

"I'll get a couple more blankets from your wagon," he told her.

"Thank you. Just make sure they don't have Private Drum's blood on them."

"Yes, Ma'am."

The first man left, and Riley started to follow. Ashley called to him. He turned to look back at her.

"You don't believe that awful story the sergeant told, do you?"

"I don't know *what* to believe, Ma'am."

"It's not true! Please, please believe me. And please protect me from the rest of those men, especially Brownie."

Riley sighed. "I'll do my best, Ma'am."

He left, and Ashley let the tears come. If Cliff had lived, this wouldn't be happening. Nick had tried to protect her, but that protection was gone. She wondered where Nick was now. She could only pray Cliff had been right that Nick might try to find her before going west, but he might be too late even if he did. She wept into the bunched-up blanket.

"Oh, Nick, I'm so sorry about Cliff," she sobbed.

Nick might not even look for her. Why should he, when he'd hired Cliff to look out for her, and when they'd agreed that a second good-bye would be too hard for both of them?

Even if he did come, she could be in a jail someplace where he would never find her. He'd likely never go to Fort Dodge first. He'd go straight north to Nebraska and the Union Pacific, probably to North Platte. Only then would he learn she'd never made it. And by then it would be too late.

Chapter Twenty-Two

*N*ick finished a cigarette and paced.

"He is coming, *mi amigo*," Renaldo yelled from a rocky slope above.

Nick quickly stepped out the cigarette and hurried up the hill from the camp he'd made below, out of sight of Fort Larned. The men had taken turns watching the open prairie between them and the fort, waiting for Seth Cunningham to return with news of Ashley, who Nick could only hope was still being held at Larned. After learning back at Fort Dodge that she'd been arrested for murdering a soldier, he'd felt crazy with a need to find and rescue her from a horrible fate based on what he was sure were lies.

He'd tracked the section of soldiers Ashley had traveled with all the way from the Wichita Agency in Oklahoma north to the Santa Fe Trail and Fort Dodge. Not wanting to draw too much attention to himself or those who rode with him, he'd sent Seth into Fort Dodge to ask about Ashley. As a ruse to learn Ashley's fate, Seth claimed to be her fiancé. He told the fort commander that she was running away from him, and he was determined to track her down.

Nick had trouble not exploding in a rage when Seth reported that the section of men had indeed stopped at Fort Dodge on their way to Fort Larned. At Fort Dodge they'd turned Ashley over for murder and theft.

"*Murder!*" Nick muttered. If Ashley *had* killed someone, it had to have been self-defense. What in God's name was going on? The commander at Fort Dodge told Seth he wanted nothing to do with Ashley's case and that he had sent her on to Fort Larned, the section's originally-intended destination.

"Let them take care of that crazy woman," the commander told Seth.

Crazy! That only told Nick that Ashley was in a bad state, probably so panicked and confused and frightened she was half out of her mind. He climbed over a boulder and made his way up to where Renaldo kept watch while the others waited below, weary from the hard ride to Fort Larned. Nick was touched and grateful for the way the men were sticking with him, risking the horses and the chance of being caught in order to help him find Ashley.

There was no time to waste now. Anything could happen, including putting Ashley in jail, let alone possible abuse by the soldiers. He had no doubt that, for some reason, she had somehow been falsely accused by someone. She'd never kill a man for no good reason, and definitely not steal from *anyone*.

His biggest concern was learning that the commander at Fort Dodge had sent Ashley's accusers along with her to Fort Larned, but at least he'd also sent a recently-widowed woman along with her. The woman wanted to go back home to family in Tennessee and had to catch a stagecoach at Fort Larned. There were also extra soldiers along, so at least Ashley wouldn't be traveling with only the soldiers who'd accused her of murder. She'd have some little bit of safety. And the widowed woman might afford Ashley companionship and more privacy.

Now came the matter of getting her out of this. He'd already managed to save her belongings. Seth had told the officer in charge at Fort Dodge that he owned Ashley's wagon and everything in it. He was allowed to claim it and drive it out of Fort

Dodge. Nick had asked Buck Davis to take it on north and west to the Union Pacific. He gave Buck enough money to ship himself and the wagon by train from wherever he caught it in Nebraska to Cheyenne in Wyoming Territory, where he was to wait for Nick and the others.

Thank God the Union Pacific tracks reached all the way to the mountains. Someone told Seth at the fort that they expected the tracks to be completed by next summer, when the U. P. would be met by the Central Pacific out of San Francisco. The joining of the two railroads was to take place somewhere in Utah.

Nick reached the top of the hill and moved to stand beside Renaldo, both men watching Seth heading their way below. Man and horse were a mere dot against the expanse of prairie that was coated with two or three inches of snow. Even from this distance, Seth's horse left a dark line of hoof prints as he rode hard toward their camp.

"He looks like he is in an extra hurry, *señor,*" Renaldo told Nick.

"Yeah, and that worries me. The commander at Fort Dodge sent her on to Fort Larned, but something must have gone wrong. She either isn't there, or something happened that requires us to move fast. Seth is about to ride that horse into food for buzzards."

"*Si,*" Renaldo answered softly, still watching Seth. "If the woman is not at that fort, where could she be? She must be so afraid by now. Maybe they turned her over to the real law, you think? Fort soldiers are not used to handling something like this, no?"

"No, they sure aren't." Nick thought how he would dearly love to get his hands on whoever was responsible for Ashley's predicament. He ached at the thought of how scared she must be. She should have waited until next spring to make the trip north in the first place, but she wasn't just running from bad memories and loss. She was probably also running from *him*, a wanted man who could never bring her the kind of life and happiness she wanted. She'd offered to stay with him, but he'd been so sure that was the wrong thing to do, for her own sake. Now he wished he'd let her come with him. He felt responsible for what she was going through now.

The figures of horse and man took more shape. Even from there, Nick could see white sweat on the horse's neck and rump.

"Jesus, Seth, take it easy." He turned to Renaldo. "Go down there and tell the men to saddle their horses. We might have to leave right away. And have someone saddle one of the spare horses for Seth. The one he's riding now will have to be left behind. We won't have time to let it rest first."

"*Sí.*" Renaldo left to carefully make his way down over the scattering of boulders that didn't seem to belong there any more than the high hill in the middle of an otherwise endless stretch of flat prairie did. Nick turned away from watching Seth and just sat there a moment, buttoning his sheepskin jacket higher around his neck.

Was Ashley warm? Was she hungry? Had she been ravaged by any of those soldiers? Was she feeling hopeless and lost? He told himself to stay calm so he could think straight.

"Shit!"

He'd been so sure that sending Cliff with her would mean she was safe. Now he couldn't help his feelings of guilt, and there was the continued worry and danger over Abel MacIntyre. Where in hell was the man?

He scrambled down after Renaldo and reached the bottom of the hill just as Seth rode in, panting from using extra energy just to stay in the saddle at such a hard run. He dismounted before his horse even came to a full stop.

"Get this horse unsaddled fast," he told the others. "And saddle a new one for me."

"Already done," Ringer told him. He made off with Seth's horse to unsaddle it while Seth removed his hat and pushed some of his shoulder-length hair behind his ears. He replaced his hat and faced Nick, taking a deep breath before speaking.

"They've shipped her even farther east," he told Nick.

"*What? Where?*" Nick asked in succession.

"Junction City."

"*Why?*"

"Same as at Fort Dodge. The Army doesn't want anything to do with her case. And they sent the two men who accused her as her escorts, so's they can testify against her."

"She's *alone* with those two?"

Seth nodded. "That's what the commander said."

"What about the woman who was traveling with her?"

"Her name was Dorothy Hemming. Some relatives who knew her husband had died were waiting at Fort Larned to pick her up and take her east by stagecoach. Ashley was held a couple of extra days while they figured out what to do with her. They finally put her on another stagecoach with the two men who've accompanied her all along. I got back here fast as I could because the commander told me that once Ashley Vale reaches Junction City, she'll be taken by train to Independence to stand trial by a jury of regular folks instead of Army personnel."

Nick turned and walked a few feet away, feeling like he'd explode. "*Damn* it!" He looked back at Seth. "So, she's even farther away from anyone who knows anything about what happened, except for the two who are accusing her and who are probably the same ones who planned all this. And for what reason? It makes no sense."

Every man remained quiet as Nick paced, seething with anger.

"Did you get the name of the men with her? Are they the same names the commander at Fort Dodge gave us?"

"Yes, sir. A private Paul Brown and Sergeant Rand Oglethorpe. The man killed was a Private Daniel Drum. The accusers are still saying Miss Vale seduced Drum into her wagon—talked him into bringing her some money to help her on account of she was traveling alone and would need money once she reached Nebraska. They said she'd told Drum to stay away from her earlier, but she'd changed her mind, wanted his protection. I guess there were a couple of men who said they'd swear she hated Drum, but the commander at Fort Larned thought they just felt sorry for her and were lying to get her favors, so he didn't' let them go along to testify. He needed them at the fort for construction work."

"Which means Ashley has no one to speak on her behalf at a trial." Nick's hands moved into fists. "Whatever their reason, I have a feeling Brown and Oglethorpe will make Ashley out to be a harlot who cheats men out of their money." He glanced around at Renaldo, Ringer, Sam and Seth. With Cal and Cliff dead, and Buck on his way to Wyoming, these four were all he had left. "None of you has to go on with me if you choose not to. Just be sure to ride on to Wyoming and find Buck before you go your own way. Tell him to keep waiting there because I'll *damn* well be along, and with Ashley Vale. You're all welcome to quit, or go on with me now, because I'm going to catch up with that train before it reaches Independence."

"*Señor*, I would not leave you to this alone," Renaldo told him. "And from what you tell us about the woman, she does not deserve this."

"The farther east you go, the more the danger builds that you'll be caught and arrested," Ringer told Nick. "You'll need our help."

"I've never ridden with outlaws before, Nick, but I've learned enough about this woman Ashley that I feel responsible to help," Seth said. "I trust your decisions."

"Thanks." Nick looked around "To *all* of you."

Seth grinned. "Hell, now the Army thinks she's my *fiancée*," he teased Nick. "And from your description of her, I guess I wouldn't mind if she *was*."

The others grinned and snickered. The humor of the remark helped ease Nick's fury.

"We've already cleaned up camp," Ringer said. "And saddled a fresh horse for Seth. There's still daylight left. We can put some miles on yet today."

Nick headed for Satan. "Let's go then. We might have to stop and buy or trade horses along the way, but we have to keep moving fast. We can't let Ashley get all the way to Independence. It's too big a city for us to be able to get her away from there without being caught."

Ringer nodded. "Come on, boys. We have a train to catch."

Nick rode off before the others even had a chance to mount up. They whistled and shouted and charged away behind him.

Chapter Twenty-Three

Early December...

Ashley's humiliation was matched only by her terror. Both were close to unbearable. At Fort Larned she'd been held in a tiny sod building that was the fort's poor excuse for a jail. It had a dirt floor, and the only furnishing was a chamber pot. She'd been left to sleep on a thin, filthy mattress on the floor.

Never did she dream that the Army could treat a woman that way. She'd already been tried and judged in the minds of the men, and surely the only thing keeping her from being ravaged by those who thought her a wanton woman was her own prayers. When she'd learned Dorothy Hemming was not going on with her to Junction City, she'd been unable to eat or sleep, knowing that only Sergeant Oglethorpe and Private Brown were accompanying her to her next stop.

Thank God she'd been allowed to put on one of her own dresses after she was first arrested so she didn't have to go through this hell still wearing only her bloody nightgown. And they'd traveled here to Junction City by stagecoach. At least there'd always been others around, so Oglethorpe and Brown couldn't abuse her on the way. But the humiliation she'd suffered at having her wrists cuffed and being unable to clean up and put on a different, cleaner dress after staying in that horrible, smelly hole of a jail cell for three days was literally painful. Two other women were along for part of the stagecoach journey, and they looked at her as though she were a saloon woman, both of them gasping in shock when Brownie gladly told them they were taking her to Independence to stand trial for murder.

Ashley felt hopeless and sick, sure she was coming down with something from the cold dampness of the prison cell at Fort Larned and from the filthy conditions inside. Not being able to eat only added to her weakening physical condition, and right then she preferred to die from whatever was wrong with her than to go on to Independence and stand trial for murder.

She sat in jail now in Junction City, shivering, her head aching. She had none of her things with her and couldn't wash or change. In two days, she'd been fed two bowls of oatmeal and had only water to drink. The cells were cold, and she had just two thin blankets and no pillow. She'd heard men talking about her being "crazy," and she supposed that by now she did appear that way, her hair a mess, the shock of her treatment leaving her so despondent and hopeless that she no longer answered any questions or spoke to anyone. She'd even heard the sheriff of Junction City suggest maybe she should be sent to a women's insane asylum.

"These women today think they can survive on their own," she'd heard the sheriff tell someone the previous night. "I hear they're even considering giving women the right to vote out in Wyoming. Can you believe that? Ain't no woman smart enough to be voting for our president."

Ashley's dream of working for Isaac and Rachael Stone and later claiming her own land and settling in Nebraska was gone. She longed to be back home with her mother and the life they'd led before the awful day she'd picked those berries and had come home to find Patricia Vale dead. She couldn't remember now what had happened to those berries. *What a silly, useless thought,* she decided.

Nick had come back that same day, and the thought of the safety of his arms felt wonderful right now. Going with him to Outlaw Country would have been far better than this, even though he was headed for a place far from civilization—a place where the law dared not go—a place where there couldn't possibly be any decent women, and where men were rough and mean and lawless and surely had no respect for women. After all, if men in civilized places could be this cruel, what would a bunch of outlaws be like?

But Nick was an outlaw, and if she was with him, she'd be safe and loved. What a strange contrast—the cruelty of men who were supposed to be civilized, and the gentleness of a wanted man. Apparently, the line between good and evil, law and lawlessness was so thin that things like what had happened to her were still possible. She remembered her father telling her once that there were no guarantees in life, no matter how hard a person tried to live religiously and according to the law.

He'd been right. Now she understood how some of those men back in Gainesville must have felt before they were hanged. Nearly all of them had been completely innocent, but they were given no chance to defend themselves. Now the same thing was happening to her.

Did they hang women in Missouri? Maybe there was still enough hatred left over from the border wars between Kansas and Missouri that a jury would have no trouble sentencing her to hang. Though she was from Texas, the supposed "killing" had taken place in Kansas, and a Missouri jury would see it that way. She feared her only hope of anything other than hanging was years in an awful prison, or being thrown into an asylum for insane women who dared to think independently or who were loose with men and needed treatment for their mental condition. She'd heard about women being confined for "sinful sexual conduct." God only knew what such places were like, or how the "sinfully sexual" ones were treated by men who worked in such places.

They came for her then. Sergeant Rand Oglethorpe and
Private Paul Brown, clean and shaved, their uniforms freshly
brushed, grins on their faces. Junction City's sheriff was with them.

"Time to board the train, honey," Brownie told her with a
grin. He stepped back as the sheriff unlocked her cell door.

Ashley looked pleadingly at the sheriff. "Please allow me to
clean up first. Surely there is a woman in this town who would
be willing to give me a clean dress to wear and let me brush my
hair and put some combs in it."

"You got money for those things?"

Ashley glanced at Oglethorpe. "No. I *had* money, but these
men stole every dime of it."

"Shut up, you snooty bitch," Private Brown told her.

Ashley held her chin high. "I've done nothing wrong,
Sheriff. It's these two men who urged the man I shot to attack
me. They took all his money *and* all of mine. All you have to
do is wire the law in Gainesville, Texas. The sheriff there, Clay
Becker, will tell you I'm a respectable woman and that this is all
a farce. Let Sheriff Becker come and get me. I can stand trial in
Gainesville instead of in a town where no one knows me and the
only witnesses are these two *liars!*"

"I'm just following orders, Ma'am," Junction City's sheriff
told her. "I have papers from Fort Dodge and Fort Larned that
you're to go on to Independence with these two men and stand
trial there. Maybe when you reach Independence, they'll let you
clean up and give you clean clothes and even wire Gainesville for
you. And they'll find a lawyer there to represent you."

Ashley took hope in his words. Yes, Independence was quite
a big city now because of the railroad. Surely the lawyers and
judges and others there would understand her situation better
and allow her some privileges, especially if she could find a lawyer who believed her story.

The sheriff unlocked her cell door and threw her wool coat at her. "Put that on."

Ashley gladly obeyed, shivering, her very bones aching. As soon as she pulled on her coat, Oglethorpe slapped cuffs on her again.

"Let's go." He took her by the arm, squeezing a little too tight. "Even if you could clean up here, there isn't time. We have a train to catch."

"But I'm sick." She looked pleadingly at the sheriff again. "Sheriff, I'm sick. I'm having chills, and I think I have a fever. I might even have something all of you could catch. Do you really want to be so close to me? Please let me see a doctor."

"You can see one in Independence," Oglethorpe told her. "And you're right. We *don't* want to be close to you, but not because you claim you're sick. We don't want to be close to you because you're starting to smell bad."

Both men laughed as they led her outside. A cold wind whipped at her face and blew her hair around.

"I need a hat," she complained. "Please find a hat for me."

"You'll be on the train and out of the wind soon enough," Brownie told her. "Maybe now you'll think twice about usin' your whip on a man. Not that you'll get the chance again. A woman ought not to be so uppity when she's the only one around a bunch of men. All you had to do was be nice to us, and none of this would be happenin'."

"And that right there is an admission that you're only doing this for spite," Ashley declared. "Both of you are the lowest form of life I've ever known."

Dizziness began to overwhelm her and she stumbled. Both men held her up.

"Maybe she really is sick," Brownie told Oglethorpe.

"She's faking. Trying to make others feel sorry for her."

Ashley felt people staring as she stumbled up the steps to the train station's platform.

"Oh, my," a woman said, shaking her head.

"She looks crazy," another spoke up.

"Stay back from her," came a man's voice.

Ashley was beginning to feel so ill and confused that she hardly noticed the faces of the people around her. Oglethorpe and Brownie forced her up the steps into a passenger car and half dragged her down the aisle to two seats at the back.

"Please," Ashley begged. "I'm sick. Everything hurts, and I have a fever and chills," she repeated. "And my head is pounding."

"It's just a few hours to Independence," Oglethorpe told her from somewhere.

"Yeah, you'll get help there, while me and the sergeant have a good ole' time eating steaks and gambling and sleeping in nice clean, warm beds," Brown added. "We get to stay in Independence and enjoy the good life while we wait for your trial."

Ashley was shoved into a window seat, and Oglethorpe plunked himself into the seat beside her. Private Brown sat down just behind her. Ashley noticed it was snowing outside. She wondered what the date was. Was Christmas coming soon? She remembered some wonderful Christmases back home, helping her mother bake cookies and decorate a tree, having company for dinner. She remembered Christmases when she was a little girl, when her father was home and they were a family. She would never know that now, and the way she felt, she might not even live long enough for a trial.

She watched wagons go by, watched other people who were gathered on the train platform. They were all blurry, but one face looked familiar. The man she watched was tall. He wore a black hat and a long, black duster. He looked up, searching the train windows. Then is gaze fell on her, and their eyes locked.

Nick!

Chapter Twenty-Four

Ashley almost shouted Nick's name, but in spite of her confused and sick condition, a little voice told her she didn't dare. Nick was a wanted man, and this train car held more soldiers than regular citizens. And he'd seen her. Had he actually tracked her here? If he did, she couldn't imagine how he'd managed it, but she'd prayed so hard for some kind of help.

She thanked God silently for answering those prayers, but her hope dwindled when Nick suddenly seemed to disappear. Her heart dived to hopelessness. She was so sick, she must have been hallucinating. She searched the crowd frantically but couldn't see him anymore.

Dear God, let it be real! She couldn't help the tears then, realizing she must have imagined seeing him. God wasn't with her after all.

"Stop your cryin'," Brown told her from his seat behind her.

Ashley paid no attention. The quick hope she'd taken in thinking she'd seen Nick Calhoun, followed by the disappointment of knowing her mind was just playing tricks on her, brought forth a desolation she couldn't control. She sobbed uncontrollably.

"Shut the hell up!" Oglethorpe told her, squeezing her arm painfully. "Everybody's staring at you! You should be embarrassed."

Ashley forced back tears as best she could. She wiped at her eyes with cold, bare fingers and huddled into her coat, longing for warmth and blankets and peace, opening her eyes occasionally to watch more people board the train.

It was then she saw him again. Nick Calhoun had just climbed aboard and was headed down the aisle toward where she sat! Junction City station was a busy landing spot for people traveling east and west. Ashley had noticed there were only two passenger cars on this particular train, which meant most of the seats were taken. In spite of a few still empty, Nick walked to the back of the car, watching her the whole way.

Ashley said nothing, and she struggled not to react to an urge to jump up and throw her arms around him. He surely had some kind of plan, and she didn't want to risk spoiling it all. And since he was a wanted man and several more soldiers had boarded the train, he was taking a huge risk at being caught. Her heart pounded harder when he took a seat next to Brown, right behind her and Sergeant Oglethorpe!

Ashley looked over at the sergeant and saw a worried look on his face when he turned to glance back at Brownie. A few more soldiers piled into the car, along with men and women of all ages and walks of life. One of them was a big Irishman who couldn't help drawing attention just by his size and the gun he wore on his hip, noticed, she was sure, by several people when the canvas duster he wore moved open a couple of times as he came down the aisle. Whatever Nick had in mind, it had to happen soon, before one or more of these soldiers put two and two together, especially when Nick sat down behind her.

The train whistle blew, and the car jerked when the engine's wheels spun on the tracks with their first rotation. The long wail of the whistle cried into the air several more times as the train began moving, heading even farther east. Ashley watched the train platform from her window. People waved. Children pointed. A couple of horses reared when the train whistle blew yet again.

They were underway—a woman headed to trial for murder, soldiers likely headed back home after serving at Western forts, passengers from all walks of life, and a wanted outlaw named Nick Calhoun, who was risking his neck being there. Ashley had never loved him more. He'd promised to find her before heading into Outlaw Country, and he'd kept his promise. She couldn't imagine how, but she trusted he knew what he was doing. She straightened in her seat and dared to turn her head to look back at Nick.

"Look back this way, you whore," Oglethorpe ordered. "Don't be gettin' any ideas about earnin' some stranger's pity." He grabbed her chin and forced her to turn back around, but the look Nick gave her in that quick moment she'd turned to him was all Ashley needed to boost her spirits. He'd not cracked a smile, but he'd nodded ever so slightly.

"Mind your business, Mister," she heard Brown tell Nick. "That filthy slut ahead of you is handcuffed because she's wanted for murder. We're takin' her to Independence for trial. Besides that, this train is full of soldiers, so don't be doing something stupid cuz you feel sorry for that harlot."

Ashley looked out the window again, her heart soaring at the sound of Nick's familiar deep voice.

"A man can't help being curious when he sees a woman in handcuffs. Who'd the bitch kill?"

"One of our own," Brown told him, sounding eager to talk. "Friend of mine, in fact. She lured him into her covered wagon for reasons you can imagine —the reason any man would gladly enter a single woman's wagon in the middle of the night, know what I mean?" He chuckled.

"I know what you mean, all right," Nick answered.

An ache to be in Nick's arms was almost more than Ashley could bear. Inwardly she prayed that whatever he had in mind would work without him getting caught or hurt.

"Did you hear that?" Oglethorpe told her, squeezing her arm again. "There's not a man on this train who gives a shit about a woman like you, so if you think you can get pity out of any of them, think again. Besides, most of them are soldiers, and they won't go against government orders."

Ashley shook with silent chills, her head still throbbing and sobs still wanting to come. Nick could be killed today, in which case she was doomed to death or prison. Right now, she ached so badly and was so full of fever that she wouldn't care if she did die. It would be better than going through the horror and humiliation of a trial and then being abandoned in prison or a home for insane women. She couldn't help jerking in another sob. What if Nick wasn't able to get her out of this mess?

"I told you to stop your goddamn crying," Oglethorpe ordered again.

"Maybe she thinks crying will win her some sympathy," Brownie spoke up with a chuckle. "How about it, Mister?" he asked Nick. "She grabbing your heart?"

"Doesn't mean a thing to me," Nick answered. "It just seems strange that she'd kill a soldier when there are others around. It sounds like that's what happened. Was she traveling with them or something?"

Oglethorpe gave a deep-throated laugh. "She sure was. She'd been flaunting herself in front of *all* the men, getting favors from them and such. She figured she could take one of them for his money, then kill him and make it look like self-defense. Me and Brownie back there, we saw right through it all."

"She was traveling with us up to Fort Dodge," Brown said. "Ain't no decent woman who'd travel alone with a bunch of men she don't know."

"Maybe she was just looking for safe travel," Nick suggested. "I hear several war widows have gone off to settle on their own under the Homestead Act. A woman alone needs watching after."

"Only crazy women think about settling on their own," Brown told him. "Too many women today think they can be independent, get along without a man. They learn the hard way they can't. And this one was damn snooty, acting high and mighty, like she had the right to pick and choose which ones of us she slept with and stole from. She's one of them women who uses her looks to seduce men."

"Well, she can't use her looks now," Oglethorpe spoke up. "She's a mess. I can hardly stand the smell of her. She's not so high and mighty now."

A few soldiers and a couple of civilians who'd heard the conversation turned to stare at Ashley. She sank deeper into her coat collar and looked out the window again.

"Why take her to Indpendence?" Nick asked.

"The Army doesn't want anything to do with her," Oglethorpe answered. "We got orders at Fort Larned to take her there for a citizen's trial. Brownie and I got to come along as witnesses."

"You witnessed the supposed murder?"

"We heard the gunshot and was there on the spot," Brown answered. "We knew she'd been messing with the man she shot, messing with *all* of us. But she treated me like shit. She even put this damn scar on my cheek with a whip." He turned to show Nick the still-healing cut on his right cheek. "See what I mean? She had a way of putting the men against each other."

"Sounds like a real she-devil."

"You bet," Oglethorpe spoke up. "She's not one to mess with, but she's learned her lesson."

The train was already out of town and racing across open prairie toward Independence. Ashley thought she heard somewhere that there was nothing between there and Junction City. They would be traveling through wide-open land where there were no forts or towns. The train whistle wailed into treeless country, voicing the cry in Ashley's own heart over her fate if Nick wasn't able to help her. The train car was, after all, full of soldiers with guns, and they were going too fast for anyone on a horse to catch up.

How on earth was Nick going to stop this train and get her off, if, indeed, that was his plan? She studied the horizon through tear-filled eyes as he asked more questions.

Are the other soldiers on this train all with you, or are they going their separate ways?

Will the law be meeting you in Independence?

Are you the only ones assigned to accompany the woman?

She looks sick. Have you gotten her any medical help?

All his questions were asked as casual conversation, until finally Brown seemed to get suspicious.

"You're askin' too many questions, Mister. She's our prisoner, and that's all you need to know."

Oglethorpe leaned around to glance at Nick. "Say, you look like some kind of gunman. Who the hell are you, anyway?"

"None of your fucking business," Nick answered.

Oglethorpe faced forward again. "And neither is this pitiful excuse of a woman any of *your* business. You don't like questions, and neither do we."

Ashley saw them then...riders several hundred yards outside the window. They seemed to be following the train, which now was starting to slow. The engineer blew the whistle several times. The train slowed even more.

"What's going on?" one of the soldiers sitting farther in front asked.

"I'll go see," another answered. He stood and headed for the front of the car and opened the door to walk out onto the car's platform.

"Must be something on the tracks," another man spoke up.

"Cattle," another soldier said as he looked out his window. "There are cowboys out there moving cattle right toward the tracks."

"What the hell?" Brown spoke up. "They ought to know better than that."

"How many are there?" Oglethorpe asked.

"Looks like six or eight cowboys."

"This is bullshit," Oglethorpe grumbled.

"No. There are several cowboys out there being paid to herd those cattle onto the tracks, and another four outside waiting to rescue someone."

Nick spoke the words.

Ashley heard the click of his gun as he cocked it. She turned to see him standing in the aisle and waving a six-gun at Oglethorpe and Brownie.

"That woman with you *is* my business," he told Oglethorpe. "Get her up and hand her over!"

Nick's eyes were no longer kind and loving. His voice was no longer soft and soothing. Death shone in his almost-black eyes, and his voice spoke commands, not simple requests.

Brown rose from his seat. "You can't—"

Nick shot him. Women screamed, including Ashley. Brown stood still a moment, looking from Nick to the bleeding wound in his chest, then slumped, falling to the floor behind Ashley's seat.

Nick waved his gun at a shocked Sergeant Oglethorpe. "I told you to turn the woman over!"

Several of the soldiers on the train had stood up, but they all looked at Nick nervously, none of them showing a desire to pull a gun on him. He backed up a little as Oglethorpe reached for Ashley.

"Any man who goes for a weapon dies!" Nick roared.

189

The train came to a complete halt as Oglethorpe grabbed Ashley's arm painfully and jerked her out of her seat, then shoved her into the aisle. "You know this murderess?"

Nick reached out with his free hand and pulled Ashley to his side. "Get behind me."

Ashley obeyed. Everyone could hear cattle bellowing now, heard the yips and shouts of cowboys. A Mexican man suddenly threw open the door at the back of the car.

"We are ready, *mi amigo*," he told Nick.

"Get her out of here and onto my horse," Nick ordered.

"That woman belongs to the Army!" Oglethorpe roared.

He went for his sidearm, and Ashley gasped when Nick shot him point-blank in the face. Women screamed again when Oglethorpe's body flew backward and landed in the aisle. Even some of the soldiers gasped and cussed.

"The woman belongs to *me* now," Nick answered, still waving his gun. He kept backing up as the Mexican man grabbed Ashley around the middle and pulled her out of the car. "You have to get on Nick's horse quick," he told her once they were outside. "Do not be afraid. We have come to help you."

Between her shock over what had just happened, her fevered condition and the trauma of being rescued, Ashley said nothing. She blindly obeyed as she tried to stay on her feet. The Mexican man led her to Nick's horse, the big, black gelding she remembered from the day Nick had ridden up her driveway—the day her mother died—the day her life had changed forever. Another man took her. He was bigger and taller, and he lifted her onto Nick's horse.

"Hang on," he told her. "They call me Ringer, and that other man is Renaldo. We ride with Nick. We have to get under way fast."

Ashley couldn't think straight. She hung on to the big horse's mane as best she could while the other two men mounted their own horses. She noticed a third man. He pulled a few extra horses with him. In the next moment Nick was there, mounting up fast.

"Thanks for the help!" Nick shouted to someone. "Keep those cattle on the tracks as long as you can!"

Ashley was sure she heard gunfire. Were the soldiers in the train car shooting at them?

Nick settled in behind her and his arms came around her as he grabbed the reins. "Sorry, Ash, but we have to ride hard and cover some ground between here and the posse they're bound to send looking for us. We'll pick up your things in Wyoming. We should be damn safe by then."

My things? Wyoming? How on earth will we get to Wyoming? Where are we going now? Is this real?

Ashley only knew she was finally away from Oglethorpe and Brown and strange soldiers and prison cells, away from abuse and hunger and cold and terror. She was in Nick Calhoun's arms, and right now she didn't care where they were headed. A blanket came around her head and shoulders, and a strong arm moved around her from behind, holding her so tightly that she didn't even need to hang on to Satan's mane.

"I've got you, Ash."

He suddenly made a grunting sound, and Ashley felt him jerk slightly. At the same time, something whistled past her ear. "Nick! Are you hit?"

"I'm okay."

Ashley ducked her head as Satan charged away.

Chapter Twenty-Five

Ashley was so sick that she barely remembered the hard ride, men shouting back and forth to each other—*Nick, you're bleeding!*

Had Nick been shot?

…Just a flesh wound—split up—keep to the creeks and rivers—lose our tracks—that farmer's house—fresh horses. She remembered a man speaking with a heavy Mexican accent. Sometimes when they stopped, he held her instead of Nick.

Mostly, she remembered Nick's voice, constantly telling her she was safe and that he'd get her someplace warm soon. She remembered being wrapped in many blankets. Remembered one night in what seemed an abandoned shack. She drank something hot, lay beside a warm fire. Remembered watching a mouse skitter up to the hearth and just sit there, the poor little thing probably also trying to keep warm. And she remembered someone strong holding her close and keeping her wonderfully warm while a howling wind caused something to bang rhythmically against a wall outside.

Damn loose shutter, someone complained.

"At least it is not snowing, *mi amigo.*"

"Well, go tear the damn thing off. It's keeping her awake."

The next thing she remembered was sunshine. Someone lifted her onto a horse yet again.

"I'll find a place soon where you can truly rest, Ash." It was Nick's voice. "I'm sorry we have to ride again, but we don't have any choice if we're going to keep anyone from catching up to us."

Another long ride. Through all of it everything hurt, and she had a fever—so hot, yet so cold. Her throat hurt. Her head ached. She had trouble breathing. Was she dying?

"We've got to get her someplace warmer, or we'll lose her." Nick's voice again. "She could have pneumonia."

Isaac Stone had died from pneumonia. She kept blacking out from a fever that ravaged her in spite of seeing a little snow whenever she opened her eyes. She shouldn't be so hot. Not in this weather. The only comfort she found was recognizing Nick's scent and the sound of his voice. Both were becoming familiar now from his holding her so often. Sometimes her head and shoulders were wrapped right into his coat so that she rested against his solid chest, protected and warm, that familiar manly smell she knew now was Nick Calhoun. When she was held close to him, she knew Sergeant Oglethorpe and Corporal Brown couldn't get to her. Not as long as she was in Nick's arms. They couldn't keep her starved and thirsty and cold.

When was it that she was pulled from the horse again and carried inside a place far warmer than the first place they'd stayed? Was that a woman's voice? She thought she remembered screaming because someone bathed her in cool water. No! She had to be warm!

"It's okay, dear," the woman told her. "You and Nick are safe here. We just need to get you well, so you can keep going and live free someplace new. The cool water will help your fever."

Those were the last words she remembered until she stirred awake again with a much clearer head, far more aware of her surroundings. She opened her eyes to study a small, sparsely-furnished room. A wooden cross hung on one wall above a five-drawer bureau.

Why did I bother to count the drawers? She wondered silently.

She turned onto her back and realized she was snuggled into a thick, feather mattress and covered with quilts. She was wonderfully warm. Even the blankets were warm. A clock ticked somewhere. She thought she heard voices—even heard a baby cry.

She reached up to feel her hair. It felt flat and damp. Surely it needed washing. Was it damp from sweating out a fever? She moved her hands under the covers to realize she wore a flannel gown. She sensed she was very clean. It felt good to be clean. If she could just wash her hair, maybe she'd feel human again. She felt something else under the covers, something almost hot. She moved her hand over round objects and realized they were rocks—heated rocks —put there to keep her incredibly warm.

She lay still, enjoying the simple but wonderful feeling of heat and a clean gown and a soft bed. She slowly gathered her thoughts, remembered the awful jail cell, being sick and cold. Remembered Sergeant Oglethorpe grabbing her arms painfully, putting cuffs on her. She could see their faces—Oglethorpe and Brown—sneering at her, laughing at her, threatening her. Was that who was in the other room? Had they found her and kept her alive just so they could humiliate her in court? Watch her hang?

No. They were dead, weren't they? *The train!* Nick had come. He'd shot them. She remembered others had tried to shoot Nick, and he'd fired back. She remembered the gunshots exploding near her ears, remembered how much it hurt her ears to be so close to guns going off, especially inside the train. Someone big and strong got on a horse behind her and put an arm around her.

"I've got you, Ash."

Nick! She remembered his words. Maybe he was in the other room. She had to know. She had to be sure it wasn't soldiers.

"Nick!" Where was he? "Nick!" she called again.

The door to the room opened. There he stood—tall, handsome, strong—the picture of safety and protection.

"Ash, you're finally awake." He hurried over to her and sat down on the edge of the bed. "And you look more alert." He leaned closer and reached out to feel her face. "Your fever's gone! Thank God. I thought I was losing you. I never would've forgiven myself. I'm so damn sorry for all of this."

It was really Nick! She hadn't dreamed it all. She reached up for him. "Hold me, so I know you're real."

In the next moment she was wrapped in his arms. She wrapped hers around his neck. "Don't let go," she begged.

"You don't have to worry about that. I'm *never* letting go of you again."

"Where are we? What happened? I remember someone saying you were bleeding! Are you hurt? How did you find me? Are they after us? I remember a Mexican man's voice."

Nick pressed her closer. "Slow down. One thing at a time. We're safe, and I'm okay. A bullet took a piece of flesh off the top of my right shoulder. That's all it was. It's been cleaned up and bandaged." He kissed her eyes, her cheeks. "I love you, Ash. When I found out what'd happened to you, we all half killed our horses getting to you."

He tried to pry her arms away, but she clung to him tightly, breathing in his scent, relishing the feel of his powerful body. He was her safety. "I can't let go yet. I have to know this is real."

Nick pressed her closer again and spoke softly into her ear. "The Mexican man is a good friend of mine, Renaldo Cortez. He's in the kitchen, right in the next room. We're at a farmhouse several miles north of Junction City. We're heading for the main line of the Union Pacific in Nebraska so we can catch a train west to Wyoming."

Wyoming? "But if we get on a train, we'll get caught."

"I don't think so. The men and I made tracks straight west for a couple of hours. Then we all split up. They kept going west, but Renaldo and I came north. We rode for almost three days, but you were sick the whole time. I was so afraid the ride would kill you, but I had to get you far enough away that they couldn't track us. We left that train stranded because of those cattle. We figured that by the time those soldiers reached their destination and got word back to Fort Dodge, plus the time it would take for the law to get a posse together, we'd be far away—headed straight west as far as we can get by train as long as the winter stays mild. Soon we'll be in Outlaw Country. We'll hole up, and you'll be safe there. I promise my life on it." He pulled at her arms again. "Come on now. You need to lie back down."

Ashley reluctantly obliged, and Nick smoothed her hair back from her face.

"Let me stay with you from now on, Nick. At first I thought maybe you were right that we shouldn't be together, but I hated every minute away from you, and then bad things started happening, and I was so scared and wished you were there. I feel so safe with you. You used to always look out for me." Tears slipped from her eyes and into her hair.

Nick leaned close and kissed her forehead. "Ash, one of my men, Seth Cunningham, has been to Outlaw Country. He said there are towns and settlements there now, ranchers and farmers, just like anyplace else. I don't want you to worry about a thing. I'll never let anyone hurt you again, understand? You're safe with me. And when I almost lost you, I realized—" He hesitated, kissing her eyes. "I love you more than I even realized when I first came back. I'm so damned sorry for what happened to you. It never should have. I should've found a way to go with you and protect you. I've just never felt worthy to claim a woman like you."

Ashley studied his dark eyes. "Worthy?" she said weakly. "You were always worthy, Nick. Sometimes—" A coughing fit took over, and Nick hung on to her until she found her voice again. "Sometimes you're your own worst enemy. You try to...throw your life away because you think...it isn't worth anything."

She coughed again. Nick scooted to the edge of the bed and put an arm around her, holding tight until the coughing ended. Ashley rested her head on his shoulder.

"Nick, you risked prison to come and find me. You're brave and good. The whole thing with those soldiers was so...horrible. I just wanted to die. I didn't do *any* of the things those men said I did."

"Of course, you didn't. Why do you think I came after you? I didn't believe any of it for one minute. I tracked you down to check on you before we headed west. When I found out about the freighters and about Cliff—and you being alone with a bunch of worthless soldiers—I knew I'd better keep coming and make sure you were okay. We rode so damn hard. One of the horses collapsed and died, but I wasn't going to quit until I found you and got you out of that mess."

Ashley wiped at tears she couldn't control, tears that came from sheer relief and joy at being safe and warm and out of harm's way. She looked into Nick's eyes and saw only love there. He kissed her forehead again, and in the next moment his lips found hers. He'd said he loved her. If she was going with him to Outlaw Country, did he mean to marry her? She felt both nervous and on fire at the thought of Nick Calhoun making a woman of her. Why was she not afraid of that? Why was she not afraid of Nick himself?

Here they were, thrown back together by some strange twist of Fate, sitting in a room in a stranger's house somewhere in northern Kansas. Or were they in Nebraska now? What had happened to her wagon? Her draft horses? Her things? Her money? Had anyone back in Gainesville heard that Ashley Vale was now a murderess? What would Clay think? What would Clara think? Did they know she was with the notorious Nick Calhoun?

She felt herself drifting off. *So tired and worn out.* "I don't want to be scared any more, Nick." *Were those my words?*

"You don't need to be. I'll damn well make sure of it."

"Stay here with me. I don't want to be alone in here."

Someone helped her lie back down. She felt the bed move as that person took away the warm rocks and settled into bed behind her. Nick. She knew it was Nick. He pulled her close against him, and in the deep recesses of her mind, she knew he didn't mean her any harm or want anything she wasn't ready to give him. He was just Nick, the man she'd loved since she was ten years old. And because of him she was warm, safe, protected.

"Whose house is this? I ... heard a baby." Now more asleep than awake, Ashley wasn't sure she'd actually voiced the words.

"It's a nice little cabin."

Yes, that was Nick's voice.

"The owners are Anna and David Meeker. They agreed to let us stay here for a while. They have a new baby, a little girl. That's the baby you heard crying. Meeker is a preacher who came out here to start a new church. We're safe here, Ash. I won't let soldiers or the law get to you, ever. These are good people who agreed to hide us. And Meeker can marry us."

Marry us? She'd dreamed of such a thing, but not this way. Not for these reasons. Still, Nick could never go back to a normal life now. Rescuing her had sealed his fate.

"Nick," she said, trying to keep her thoughts focused.

He pressed her closer. "Go to sleep. You're okay. I'm not going anywhere."

"Am I ... a wanted woman now?" Was that Nick, kissing her hair?

"I don't know, but I expect you are."

Visions of the outlaw battle suddenly shot through her mind. "Nick, I've killed two men! Two!" The tears came. "I didn't want to kill either one of them. It just happened. I killed that soldier. And I killed one of the men who attacked the wagon train the night Cliff died." She cried harder. "I'm so sorry, Nick! I'm so sorry about Cliff. He was your friend."

"Calm down." He gently wiped at her tears with his fingers. "It's okay, Ash. You couldn't help any of it. You've done nothing wrong. Someday this will work out, and people will see killing that soldier was self-defense. And Cliff worked for Isaac. Without you he might've gone on that trip anyway and gotten killed. And you had a right to kill the man attacking that wagon train. Go back to sleep now. When you're well and more awake, we'll talk about all of it."

How good it felt to lie in his strong arms, knowing she was safe. Ashley grasped his forearm. "I love you." Why couldn't she open her eyes? Their entire conversation seemed more like a dream. "Tell me you love me."

"Of course, I love you. Why else would I have risked my neck to get you off that train?"

He'd saved her life. There was no other way to look at it. The thought of the horrid cell at Fort Larned made her curl as close as she could to Nick. She prayed this was all real.

Fate had led her into Nick Calhoun's world, and into his arms. And it had sealed their future together. There was no changing any of it now. She wouldn't *want* to change any of it, even if she could.

Chapter Twenty-Six

Ashley stirred awake and lay still, gathering her thoughts. She realized someone lay behind her, his arm around her. Was it some soldier, ready to hurt or abuse her? She gave out a little cry and sat up, looking around an unfamiliar room. She wasn't in a jail cell, and she wasn't cold anymore. Should she trust that this was real?

Someone grasped her arm, and she gasped and tried to jerk away.

"Ash, it's just me, Nick. You're okay."

She turned to look at him as he sat up. "You've been sick. A few hours ago, you asked me to lie beside you and hold you."

Close. He was so close. She looked him over more as she gathered her thoughts, realizing the poor man was too big for the homemade bed they were sitting on. It had a lumpy mattress, probably of straw.

Safe, remember? She reminded herself. *This man will keep you safe. You don't need to be afraid anymore.* "I—we shouldn't…" She said aloud.

"Just lay back down, Ash. We'll talk."

Nick. Yes. He'd risked his life to keep her from going to trial for murder. He'd been wounded and could have been killed. Now he was in even deeper trouble. After taking her off that train, he had no choice but to keep running from the law. And she was doomed to keep running, too.

She put a hand to her hair, thinking how awful she must look. "I...I thought at first that I was in that jail cell at Fort Larned."

Nick pulled her into his arms and gently forced her to lie back down. He leaned over her, bracing himself by one arm on her other side. "You are in the cabin I told you about, and you're safe. Your fever's gone. If you want, I can have Anna Meeker come in and help you clean up more, now that you're better. David Meeker is outside with Renaldo doing some shoveling and feeding the horses. His wife is in the outer room kneading bread, and their baby is sleeping. Something *you* need more of. I want you to rest a few days more so you can get your strength back." He gently stroked some of her hair away from her face.

"I must look terrible."

Nick smiled the handsome smile she'd grown to love more than ever. "You look beautiful. You're alive and safe and well, and that's all that counts. Renaldo and I had a hell of a time keeping you warm and getting you to eat. You were so damn sick you hardly knew where you were. As soon as you're ready, we'll get out of here and keep heading west."

Ashley watched his dark eyes. No demands. No orders. A simple statement. *We'll get out of here and keep heading west.* "To Outlaw Country?" she asked aloud.

Nick sighed. "I'm afraid so." He leaned down and kissed her forehead. "I'll always give you the choice of what you want to do, Ash, but after what happened, and me shooting those men who were abusing you, and the law believing those soldiers' lies...I'm afraid you don't have much choice but to go with us. I've heard enough about that area to be pretty sure we can settle there safely. A man can start a whole new life there. So can a woman."

Ashley studied the broad shoulders that hovered over her. This was Nick, her old friend, the man who'd once seemed part of the family, the man she'd secretly loved even at an age when she was too young for such things. He was alive, and he loved her. He'd ridden back into her life as though he'd never left. He could have his way with her any time he wanted, even now, but she felt only comfort and safety from his closeness.

"Did you mean what you said about marrying me?"

He studied her lovingly, grinning. "I'd sure rather take you as my wife. I love you, Ashley Vale, and it'd be damn hard to bring you along any other way, but it's your choice. I'll help you and keep you safe no matter what you decide. But marrying me sure would save a lot of gossip, and a lot of stress on my part, if you know what I mean."

Ashley couldn't help smiling at the teasing glitter in his eyes. "Nick, I was willing to go with you even when I *wasn't* in trouble. Why would I change my mind now? And when I said that, I didn't mean as a woman living in sin."

His smile widened. "Yeah?" He leaned even closer, resting with his elbows on either side of her shoulders. "Why would you be living in sin?"

Ashley covered her face. "You know why."

Nick pulled her hands away from her face. "Don't ever be scared of me, Ash. I love you. I've loved you much longer than you even know. You're beautiful and spirited and independent and brave. And you'll make a great mother. Best of all, we're already friends. We know everything about each other. If you still want to marry me after the things I told you about my past, then I couldn't love you more. But I still think you deserve so much more than what I can offer."

Ashley saw only truth and honesty in his gaze. "You couldn't help how life turned out for you, Nick. As far as I'm concerned, you haven't done one thing wrong. You have a good heart, and that's all that matters."

He kissed her lightly. "I thought I'd go crazy seeing the condition you were in on that train. I don't regret one bit killing Oglethorpe and that man called Brownie. How those other soldiers could sit there and see how you were being treated when it was obvious how sick you were, I can't even imagine. I think if I didn't know you at all, I still would've tried to help you."

"And that's what I love about you." She couldn't take her eyes from his, captivated by all that was man about him. "You had no idea, did you, that I had a crush on you when I was only ten. It never went away."

He chuckled. "When you were ten, I was an angry, fifteen-year-old Irishman who'd killed another man with my bare hands. All I saw in you was a cute little girl, nothing more. I just wanted to hide on your farm and try to go on with life. And then all of you became like family. When we grew older and I had more than brotherly feelings for you, I was afraid your father would get the wrong idea and chase me off. So, I never once let on. I guess we were *both* in love but never said a word."

Ashley reached up and ran her fingers into his thick, dark hair. "You were always so good to me, Nick. How could I not love you and want to marry you?"

He rolled to his side and took her hand. "I guess I could say that in some ways you saved my life, just by loving me when I don't deserve it. I don't want to keep throwing that life away, Ash. I want to settle once we reach a safe place. I'll build you a real house and make sure you have everything you need and deserve. My men and I are going to build a ranch and—"

"You don't have to explain. I trust you, Nick. I know you'll do everything in your power to make a good life for us. Just be patient with me as far as…I mean…marriage…going off to a place like Outlaw Country. It'll all take some getting used to.

You're all I have now. I have to trust everything you do. Every decision you make."

Nick squeezed her hand. "I'll be your husband, but I'll also be your friend. I'll never make demands of you that you aren't ready for, and I'll never hurt you or betray your trust."

Ashley turned to rest her head on his shoulder. "I believe you. We're going into wild, dangerous country, but I can't think of a better man to have with me. And our reasons for marrying might be a little out of the ordinary, but I know in my heart that it's right."

Nick kissed her hair. "David Meeker said that out here and beyond, people get married for lots of crazy reasons. Sometimes total strangers marry. A man needs a woman to give him purpose and give him sons. And a woman needs a man to help with all the hard work and to fight the elements—man and beast and weather. To put food on the table and put his life on the line for her. I'll do all those things. That's a promise."

Ashley threw an arm across his chest and clung to him. "I know you will." She closed her eyes and couldn't help the tears that came. "Nick, it was all so awful, and I wanted to die. I didn't think there was any chance you'd find me or know what had happened. I was so afraid you'd decide another good-bye would be too hard and you'd go on west without seeing me again."

Nick rolled to his side and pulled her into his arms. "I couldn't bring myself to do that. I had to know you were okay first. When I found out Cliff was killed and you were alone... My God, Ash, I was crazy with worry. I would have gone to the ends of the earth to find you." He hugged her close. "My men have gone on ahead, all except Renaldo. They're waiting for us in Cheyenne. And they have your wagon and your things."

Ashley drew in her breath and sat up. "How did you manage that?"

"Don't worry about that right now. We'll have lots of time to talk when you're better. Right now, I want you to rest. Sleep all you want." He rolled her onto her back and hovered over her again. "You need to eat and get stronger. I don't want you getting sick all over again. I'll go get Mrs. Meeker, and you can tend to whatever needs tending to. She can help you clean up and bring you something to eat, and in a few days we'll get married."

Ashley's eyes teared. "I'll never forget what you did for me, Nick. In that moment it was more like you were my big brother again, defending me like you did when you stopped Sid MacIntyre from hurting me."

Nick's smile faded a little at the mention of Sid MacIntyre. Ashley noticed a change in him. She wiped at her tears and searched his eyes. "Nick, what did I say wrong?"

He wrapped her into his arms. "Nothing. You didn't say a damn thing wrong. It's just something I didn't want to talk about until you were stronger."

"It's all right. As long as I'm with you like this, I'm strong enough for anything."

He kept holding her, and she could feel him tensing up. He said nothing for several long seconds.

"Ash," he finally spoke up, "it's about your mother. I know who killed her."

Mother! Ashley studied his dark eyes. "*Who?*" .

"It was Abel MacIntyre."

Ashley gasped and put a hand over her mouth. "*Abel!* But—he's dead!"

"That's what everybody thought, but he's alive." Nick explained what Seth Cunningham had told him. Ashley took several minutes to let it all sink in. "Then, he could be out there where we're going?"

"He could be. But as long as you're with me, you don't have to worry about it. Besides that, he doesn't know a thing about us. Whether I'm alive or dead, or that we're on our way to the mountains. He thinks you're still in Gainesville and probably married. And he doesn't dare go back there. People would figure it all out and he'd be hanged."

Ashley broke into tears again. "Poor mother. What an awful way to die!"

Nick kissed her hair. "I promise you that if I ever come across that man, he'll pay for what he did."

"Nick, he sounds so dangerous."

"I'm *more* dangerous when I'm angry, and what he did makes me *very* angry. Your mother's violent death was like losing my own mother all over again in almost the same way." He kissed her tears. "Please don't cry. What's done is done, and at least now we know who to watch for. We're going someplace where we don't need to run anymore, and that's what's important."

Nick reached for a towel that lay near the bed, letting Ashley use it to wipe at her nose and her tears.

"How cruel and sad that Abel didn't even try to see his son," Ashley said then.

"They never got along anyway. Abel used to beat him because of his mental condition. I saw him clobber him once and call him dumb and useless. And from the condition Seth says Abel was in when they met, Abel's mind is gone. He never was right in the head, but it sounds like he's worse now. He might not even remember he *had* a son."

Ashley touched his face. "Nick, if he finds out you killed Sid—"

"He won't. How could he? It won't matter anyway. I know what he did, and I know to watch for him now. We'll be okay, Ash." He gently pushed her back against the pillows, then sat up. "I'll get Mrs. Meeker to come in here and see what you need. Are you hungry?"

"I was until I heard about Abel MacIntyre." She turned to her side and wept. "Poor mama! I've hardly had a chance to mourn her, Nick. I suddenly miss her so much! I should've been there, but I wanted to pick those stupid berries."

"You couldn't have known." Nick tucked covers around her. "I'm sorry I had to tell you all that. I didn't want to yet, but when you mentioned Sid, I had to."

In the outer room the Meeker baby began crying. Ashley heard footsteps, followed by a woman talking softly. Mrs. Meeker came to the doorway then, a pleasant-looking young woman about Ashley's size and not much older than she. Ashley detected a light in the woman's eyes, a warmth, and the joy of a woman in love and holding a baby in her arms. She knew instantly that's what she wanted with Nick—a man to love and his baby to hold.

"Well, you're awake!" Anna Meeker glanced at Nick. "She's crying! Can I help?"

"I had to tell her about her mother. Things moved so fast after her mother's death that she's hardly had a chance to face the reality of it, let alone what she's been through since then."

"Oh, dear!" Anna walked to the edge of the bed and sat down, the baby still in her arms. "Ashley, I know what it's like to lose a mother. Whether violently or not, it's still hard, especially for a daughter. But you have this man here now, who loves you very much. You're free and you are safe. You'll be okay." She felt Ashley's face. "And your fever's gone. God has blessed you."

Ashley used the towel to wipe at her nose and eyes again. "I just need to let it all sink in." She looked at the kind and concerned Anna Meeker. "I'm sure Nick told you all that's happened. I'm not a killer, Anna."

"Goodness, I know that. Nick's talked about almost nothing but you since the two of you got here." Anna smiled. "And you're looking much better in spite of your tears. You have more color."

"I *feel* better. Nick and I've been talking. We're going to get married."

"I'm glad!" She rose and sat down in a rocking chair. "I'm afraid that right now I need to nurse my daughter. Her name's Shelly. As soon as she's fed, I'll help you clean up more, and get you something to eat. I have bread baking right now." She looked at Nick. "You can go outside and help my husband and Mr. Cortez."

"Sure," Nick rose and leaned closer to Ashley. "You rest some more." He smoothed back her hair once more before leaving the room.

Anna threw a light blanket over herself and opened her dress underneath it to let her baby nurse. She caught Ashley crying again.

"Don't be worried," Anna told her. "I know your story, and if anyone comes looking for you, my husband and I will never let on that you were here."

"Nick and I will never be able to thank you enough."

"Well, we all need to be good Samaritans, don't we?" Anna patted her baby's bottom. "God is with you, Ashley. That's how you ended up here. And although he doesn't know it yet, God is also with the man who just walked out of here. You two can stay as long as you need. I'm just sorry for all you've been through, but you're with a very able man who loves you. I see right through him. He has a good heart."

Ashley settled into the pillows. "I've always known that. He's going to be my husband, and I'll follow him wherever he goes."

"Of course, you will. Like Ruth in the Bible."

Ashley smiled, feeling sleepy again. "Yes. Like Ruth in the Bible."

Chapter Twenty-Seven

Wearing a white linen dress Anna Meeker loaned her, Ashley stood beside Nick in front of the cabin's fireplace, ready to take her vows. The dress was only slightly too big, and Anna gave her a pink silk sash to tie around her waist to pull it in a little more.

"A woman doesn't need much in the way of pretty things out here," Anna had told Ashley. "This is the only somewhat fancy garment I own, but you'd look beautiful in a potato sack, with that lovely red hair and your pretty smile. I know you'll be happy, Ashley. It's not an easy life out here, even harder where you're going, but you have a good man who is brave and able."

Ashley had caught the sadness in Anna's voice when she spoke the words. She liked the kind and helpful woman, who was only two years older than she. Ashley admired Anna's bravery for following her husband into a land hostile both in marauders and in the harsh, lonely land itself. She was a preacher's daughter who'd grown up in a nice home back East, but she'd given up a comfortable life to come west with her husband to help him build a church for settlers longing for such things.

There were no flowers to be found this time of year, so Ashley carried fragrant sprigs of pine that Nick and Renaldo had managed to cut from a tree nearly a half-mile from the lonely little sod and stone Meeker cabin, which sat in the middle of the relentlessly expansive Kansas prairie.

It was late-December, and Christmas was right around the corner. Pine branches decorated the fireplace hearth, and a rather sorry-looking tree strung with popcorn sat in a corner of the main room.

They had been here ten days while Ashley recovered. Outside the wind howled, but thankfully, it was not a blizzard of the nature that buried desolate farms for weeks at a time. Overall, the winter had been mild.

"For Kansas," as David Meeker had put it.

Renaldo and Anna looked on as witnesses while The Reverend Meeker stood before Nick and Ashley, reading scripture about a woman obeying her husband and a husband respecting his wife. He read scripture about Ruth following her love ... *"Whither thou goest,"* and Ashley remembered Anna comparing her to Ruth.

Yes, Ashley thought, *Whither thou goest—even if it means into Outlaw Country.* She said several "I do's," and Nick repeated the same vows. Their gazes held in a way that, six years before, Ashley never thought they would look at each other, let alone seeing each other again at all. They would not be able to consummate their marriage in this tiny cabin ... no room, no privacy. There would be the right time and place for that. All that mattered now was to make things legal before they continued their journey.

Love lit up Nick's handsome smile after he said his vows. He was a man who'd turned to the outlaw life out of circumstances he'd never asked for, and she'd been one of those circumstances. "I won't let you down."

"I know you won't. You never have, and I know you never will."

"In the name of the Father, the Son, and the Holy Ghost, I now pronounce you man and wife," David Meeker announced. "May God bless you both and keep you safe in the years to come."

Nick leaned down and kissed her. In the presence of a very Christian couple and their small baby and inside their tiny home, this was all there could be for now. Ashley reached up, and Nick fully embraced her, lifting her off her feet for a moment.

"Things will get better soon," he told her. "Right now, I'm just glad you're well." He set her on her feet. "By now Buck Davis should have made it to Wyoming, and the others will catch up with him there and go on to Cheyenne with your wagon. They'll wait for us there."

"What's to prevent them from just taking my things and selling them? And if the soldiers didn't find where I hid my money in that wagon, and your men *do* find it—"

"*I'm* what'll prevent them from taking your things. They're doing this for me, Ash, and I trust every one of them. You'll find out what good men they are and how safe you'll be when you meet them and they help us get settled. Just look at what Renaldo has put up with, staying in a barn most of the time while he waited for you to get better."

"Ah, *señor,* I was able to keep a fire going on the dirt floor and stay warm." Renaldo came closer, nodding to Ashley and shaking Nick's hand. "Now you are a married man, *señor!*" He smiled broadly. "You did not plan such a thing when we talked about coming to find the *señora.*" He winked. "Or maybe you *did* plan this, no?"

"I had my hopes," Nick answered with a wink.

Ashley wrapped her arms around Nick's middle and rested her head against his chest. "I didn't plan on anything like this either when I left Gainesville. We never know where God is going to lead us, Renaldo."

"I have told your husband that many times."

Husband. Nick is my husband now. Ashley felt a shiver of joy and anticipation. She was Mrs. Nicholas William Calhoun.

"We have cake to eat before I go into the bedroom and feed my little Shelly," Anna announced. "We only have four chairs, but there is one more in the bedroom. David, will you go and get it for Renaldo?"

The cabin came alive with smiles and joy as they all shared cake and coffee, while outside the snow-filled wind continued to howl past them. Ashley found it amazing how kind and accommodating the Meekers were toward them, in spite of knowing Nick's background, knowing Ashley's misfortunes, and being so put out by extra people in a cabin barely big enough for their own small family. The Meekers had felt it their Christian duty to help them, and because of the cold they had insisted Renaldo sleep inside the cabin near the hearth the last two nights, rather than outside in the barn.

"We'll be out of your hair soon enough," Nick told them now. "I was just waiting to be sure Ashley was well enough to travel. We've made things very inconvenient around here for you two long enough."

"All of us are warm and safe and well," David answered. "That's all that matters."

Ashley studied the kindness in Meeker's soft brown eyes. He was just an average man in size and looks, but she could tell he had a bigger than average heart. "I hope things stay that way for the two of you and your daughter," she told them. "There's so much danger in this country."

"Including outlaws?" David asked with a grin.

They all shared laughter. Ashley looked around the plain little cabin and realized how happy she could be with Nick in a cabin like this, as long as they were free and safe. If that meant living in Outlaw Country, that's where they'd live. Even there, human nature surely was not so different as far as desperate people helping other desperate people, and in a place where there were few to no neighbors, where towns were far apart, where there were hardly any doctors, and where danger lurked everywhere.

Still, people seemed to always find ways to survive. All that mattered was love, and she had that with Nick. Love and protection, a man who knew how to take care of himself even when the world was against him.

Anna picked up her baby daughter from the cradle and carried her into the bedroom to breast feed, while David picked up the dishes and refilled coffee cups. Nick reached over and grasped Ashley's hand. "You all right?"

"Yes. I mean, I'm a little bit in shock. My world's been turned upside-down." She clung tightly to his hand. "But the past is sitting right here in front of me. Not just the past, but also the future. Why do I feel so free even though I'm a married woman now, and a *wanted* woman?"

"Because you've followed your heart," David Meeker answered. "When the heart is unhappy, the most perfect life in the world can't mend it. But the two of you make each other happy. Nick needs someone to love him and help him deal with the anger that's plagued him since his mother was killed. You can help him, Ashley, through prayer and through your patient love. Trust in God as you follow your new husband into a new land. God will protect you both and bring you peace."

Nick looked from Meeker back to Ashley. "Well, I'm not so sure God cares what happens to me, but if He intends to take care of this woman here, that means He will keep me alive to do just that, so I guess that's my insurance."

Meeker smiled. "He *does* care about you, Nick, and Anna and I will be praying for both of you when you leave here."

"And I will also help keep your new wife safe," Renaldo added.

Nick grinned more when he looked across the table at his friend. "I know you will, Renaldo." He finished his coffee. "And

I think we'd better be on our way as soon as the weather takes a turn for the better."

Renaldo nodded. "I will be ready, *mi amigo*."

Nick turned his attention back to Ashley. "How about you?"

Ashley's heart beat faster at realizing a whole new life was about to begin for her. "I'm ready."

Nick looked her over. "Did I tell you how beautiful you look in that dress, your hair pulled up into curls the way it is?"

Ashley couldn't help the tears that formed in her eyes. "I think you did, but this day has gone by so fast and feels so unreal that I hardly remember *anything*. I think I spoke some wedding vows."

Nick gripped both her hands. "You did. Just don't hide any feelings from me, Ash. I want you to be happy. I don't want you to regret one bit of this."

"How could I regret it? I've loved you since I was just a girl."

Anna came out from the bedroom, holding her sleeping baby in her arms.

"Why don't you two go into the bedroom to talk?" David told them. "I'm sorry there's no privacy in this house, but at least you can talk alone in there."

"Thanks." Nick rose and took Ashley's arm, helping her up and leading her into the other room, where he urged her to sit down on the edge of the bed. He knelt in front of her. "Ash, what's bothering you?"

She felt the heat coming into her cheeks. "It's just...I love you, Nick. But suddenly here you are—my *husband*—not just sort of a big brother. I used to dream about you being my husband, but now it's real, and—" She looked away. "I don't know how to say this."

"And I have husbandly rights."

Ashley shrugged, still looking away. "Something like that. I mean, this just isn't the way I pictured all this happening when

I was younger. You were going to ride up to me on a white horse, and you'd wear a fancy suit and sweep me into your arms, and—"

"And David mentioned we had no privacy here," Nick interrupted, "which made you realize *why* we'd need some privacy." He grasped her arms gently as Ashley met his gaze.

"I *love* you, Ash, as the beautiful woman you've become, not just the little girl who became a good friend." He leaned up and kissed her cheek. "And I won't demand anything from you, not after what you went through with those soldiers, and being so sick. For now, I just want to keep you safe and find us a good place to live where we *can* be husband and wife. And I'll buy you a ring first chance I get." He rose and embraced her.

"I don't need a fancy ring." Ashley rested her head against his chest. "I just need you. I think I'm just more nervous than anything else. What if I don't please you as a wife? Everything is different now."

Nick squeezed her tighter and laughed lightly. "Mrs. Calhoun, that's the *last* thing I'm worried about. Right now, we just have to make it farther west and put a ring on your hand. Everything else will come naturally. And before you know it, we'll be settled somewhere and living like a real married couple."

Ashley looked up at him. "Can I have a garden?" Why on earth had she asked such a stupid question?

"A *what*?"

"A garden. A rose garden, like my mother had. Can we build a house and have a rose garden? I'd feel closer to her that way."

Nick smiled. "Is that all you want?"

"Well...I don't want to have to move around all the time because of the law. I want to be able to stay in one place."

Nick kissed her forehead. "I want the same thing. I promise we won't move around, and you can have a garden and raise roses. And babies."

Babies. Yes, she wanted babies — *Nick's* babies. She reached up and hugged him around the neck, breathing in the heady scent of man. Nick kissed her neck, her cheek, her eyes. His lips trailed down to her lips. He pressed her tight against him and searched her mouth in a kiss far deeper and more suggestive even than that night in her bedroom, a kiss that made her want him in embarrassing ways, one that brought out even more of a desire to be a real wife. She whimpered as she tasted his lips in return.

Yes, she'd loved him in a fanciful way when she was ten. She'd loved him more fully at sixteen. And she loved him completely now, as a whole woman. She was Mrs. Nicholas Calhoun, and she could face whatever was to come, as long as this man was by her side.

Part III

Chapter Twenty-Eight

"You ought not to be here."

Abel MacIntyre scowled at Joe Bloom, who sat across the card table studying the new cards he'd been dealt. "Who the hell are you talking to?"

Joe, a big man himself, kept his head bent but raised his eyes to look at Abel over the top of the cards in his hand. "You know damn well who I'm talking to, MacIntyre."

Abel held his gaze, gauging him to be a man he couldn't bully. "You got a reason?"

"Yeah. You're fucking ugly with that broken nose and that eye patch. As far as I'm concerned, that man called Moses Tucker shoulda' killed you insteada' just beaten you half to death."

Three other men at the table scooted back their chairs.

Abel didn't fold his hand. He laid his cards face-down and got up from his chair. "I haven't done anything to you, Mister. What's your beef? And how do you know about Moses Tucker?"

"Word travels in Outlaw Country." Joe also laid down his cards, but he remained seated. "My beef is that you talk too much, and you brag about things no man should brag about."

"You mean killing a woman?" Abel laughed nervously. "This is Brown's Park. Half the men in here have killed others, probably including women."

"Not innocent women who never wronged them. Most of the men out here wouldn't kill a woman for *any* reason. It sounds to me like the one you killed was a decent, Christian woman, a war widow minding her own business. And if she didn't want you touching her, I don't blame her. I wouldn't even want to shake hands with an ugly sonofabitch like you, and I don't want you at this table. Once this hand is over, you'd best leave."

Abel glanced around the room. Everybody in the Gold Digger Saloon was staring at him malevolently. He'd been talking again about killing Patricia Vale, a memory that brought him great satisfaction, and one, he thought, that would impress men like those out here. "You're all a bunch of thieves and killers. I figured most of you'd enjoy sharing stories like mine. I came out here to get away from the law. You telling me you think killing's wrong?" He put his hands on his hips. "You're a bunch of hypocrites!"

"Word is you already got thrown out of South Pass City for your bragging about the woman," one of the men shouted.

"Yeah," another spoke up. "And you've been making your way south. It might be a good idea if you *kept* heading south, Mister. All the way to Mexico!"

His comment was answered with a mixture of laughter and shouts of agreement.

Abel glanced at Joe, who still sat watching him. "There ain't any law in these parts," he told Joe, raising his voice for the others to hear. "This is *Outlaw Country*. Ain't one man in here can say he's better than me and who has any right to tell me to leave."

Joe folded his arms. "Sounds like you haven't paid any attention to *our* kind of law, MacIntyre. The law out here doesn't walk around with a badge on, but there's a code among men out here. If there wasn't, we'd all kill each other off and chase all the women, even the whores, clean out of Outlaw Country, and we sure as hell can't get along without women now, can we?"

Another round of laughter filled the room, but Joe wasn't smiling. He finally rose. "Look, MacIntyre, you're right that this part of the country's mostly lawless. It's a haven for wanted men. But even outlaws understand that you have to draw the line someplace, and one line we draw is you don't go around beating and killing women. No *real* man does that."

MacIntyre's hand moved toward his gun. "You saying I'm not a real man?"

"That's exactly what I'm saying. And if you think you're gonna' draw that gun and kill me, you remember there're a lot of other men in here, all wearing guns, and all fed up with you bragging about killing a good woman just because she didn't want your ugly dick in her. And by the way, what you wanted to do is called rape, and out here that's a real ugly word. I've seen men hanged for it, even if the woman was one of those who works upstairs over this saloon. So, we all suggest you move on, before you feel rough hemp gnawing at your neck."

"Yeah, mister, you've been braggin' about killin' that woman ever since you walked in here," one of the card players told Abel. "You've already ended up with a broken nose because of your big mouth. You want worse?"

"You're gonna have to leave," another told him.

Abel looked around the room at all of them. "You're actin' like a bunch of wolves around a wounded rabbit. I could kill any one of you with my bare hands."

"Like you killed that woman?" Joe asked. "Most of us figure it doesn't take much of a man to do that. Seems like that man who beat you near to death didn't teach you a damn thing."

"We're tellin' you to leave Brown's Park," another card player told him. "You can show those cards you were just dealt—bet or pass. It's your last hand."

Abel slowly eyed them all, realizing that if he drew his gun, he was a dead man. And if he landed into Joe, ten or more men would land into him and maybe even drag him off to be hanged. He reached down to pick up his cards. The ones he'd drawn hadn't brought him the hand he'd hoped for. He threw them onto the table. "Pass." He scooped his money into a pile and filled his pockets, then adjusted his hat. "I can't believe a bunch of no-good outlaws think they can throw a man out of a whore-run saloon in a lawless country."

"Think again," Joe told him. "You need to keep headin' south, Mister, *way* south."

"*I'll* decide which way I go." Abel looked around the room once more, thinking how he could take on each one of these men and beat them near to death, but all at once was another story. "I swear, I can't understand how men out here can get so upset about the death of one woman they never even knew. You're a bunch of weak-kneed, pussy-lovin' cowards!" He shoved a couple of them aside as he stomped out of the saloon and to the rooming house where his supplies were stashed.

The woman who owned the rooming house looked up from where she was knitting by the fireplace.

"I'm leavin'," Abel announced as he stormed past her.

He didn't notice the relieved smile on her face.

Chapter Twenty-Nine

They bought a horse from David Meeker, and, traveling under the names Robert and Mary Lacey, Nick and Ashley headed north with Renaldo. Because Ashley had arrived with only the clothes on her back, Anna Meeker washed everything for her, and Nick paid Anna for two extra dresses, even though they'd be a little big. At least Ashley would have a temporary change of clothes. In spite of Anna and David's protests, Nick also gave the Meekers money to buy more cloth so Anna could make herself some new dresses, and other supplies they'd need come spring to make up for extras used for their stay.

"You two have been more than generous to us," Ashley told Anna the day they left.

David gave Ashley a wide-brimmed farmer's hat. "To keep that red hair covered and the sun off that fair skin."

Renaldo loaned Ashley a sheepskin-lined plaid wool jacket for what would be at least a week-long horseback ride in still-cold weather. Though Renaldo was shorter and smaller than Nick, the jacket was still too big on her.

Nick decided it was best that the jacket didn't fit well anyway. "It hides the beautiful woman underneath," he'd teased. "It's like David said about that hat—the less you're noticed, the better."

Nick packed his gun belt away and wore an old wool jacket, ridding himself of anything that made him look more like a gunman than a farmer. He kept his six-gun tucked into his belt and extra bullets in his pants pockets. His jacket hid the butt of the gun.

They looked the role of the simple settlers they'd claim to be, and Renaldo would pose as a hired hand who'd help them once they claimed farmland in western Nebraska under the Homestead Act. That would be their story. Once they reached the Union Pacific and boarded a train, Renaldo would travel in a boxcar with the horses and supplies while Nick and Ashley would travel in a passenger car.

"But it will be so expensive," Ashley protested.

"I have money. I don't want you getting sick again," Nick insisted. "The trip there on horseback will be hard enough on you."

It hurt Ashley's heart to leave the Meekers and their baby girl, and she prayed God would protect them all from the elements and enemies and see that they thrived in this lonely, dangerous land.

There had been little in the way of conversation so far, their energy saved just for keeping warm and for making as many miles each day as possible. This was the third day of their journey, and they'd taken advantage of good weather. There would be time for talking and planning their lives once they were settled someplace safe. Just then, all three of them were concerned about how dark the skies had grown. The horses' hooves made soft thumping sounds into wet sod that was covered with two inches of old snow. Snow that could get much deeper if a storm was coming.

Ashley ached everywhere, but she refused to complain. Nick had promised it would take only about five or six days to reach the railroad, and he had, after all, saved her from a fate far worse than anything uncomfortable she might have to put up with for now. They'd slept the last two nights on blankets on the ground, wrapped individually into more blankets, with Ashley sheltered between Nick and Renaldo, her face buried into Nick's jacket to keep her breath warm. She was growing to love Renaldo as a loyal friend to Nick and as a man devoted to protecting her person and her health with as much determination as Nick.

Ashley had no idea where they were at this moment, and she hoped Nick was right that another day or two would bring them to a place where they could board a train. Her mare snorted and tossed her head, and Ashley patted its neck.

"Calm down, girl." She glanced at Nick. "I miss the Meekers. They were so good to us."

"People like that give me a lot of hope that we can be just as happy."

Ashley smiled. "Of course, we can be happy. We both agree this is what God wants for us, and the Meekers are praying for us. I have confidence in their prayers."

Nick slowed his horse to take a thin cigar from an inside jacket pocket. He cupped a hand over it as he lit it and inhaled deeply, then kept the cigar between his lips as he spoke. "I have confidence in their prayers, too, but only because it's *you* God needs to protect."

"You underestimate your worth, Nick Calhoun, and you underestimate God Himself and how much He cares about you."

"I really doubt that."

Ashley gave out a little yelp when a sudden gust of wind swept over them from the north. She ducked her head against it. "I think a storm's coming," she told Nick, raising her voice against the wind. "My horse senses it, too."

"I think you're right." Nick moved Satan closer to her horse so it was easier to hear each other. "It looks even darker in the west."

They rode for another mile or so, keeping an eye on Renaldo, who'd been riding at least a quarter mile ahead of them to watch for soldiers or hostiles. Nick reached out and grabbed the bridle of Ashley's horse, slowing both animals when he noticed Renaldo had turned and was riding back toward them, the horizon behind him ominously dark. The wind blew harder, and tiny crystals of sleet stung their faces. When Renaldo came closer, he pointed toward the crest of a low hill.

"Just over that hill, *señor*. It looks like a cabin and a barn. I think it is an abandoned farm. It is not in much shape—falling apart—but it could be shelter for tonight. It looks like this weather might get worse. That would be bad for the *señora*."

Nick nodded. "We should hole up there and see what this weather does."

"I saw a stone chimney on the cabin, so maybe we can make a fire," Renaldo yelled above the wind.

"It's a little early to stop, but we can't take chance of being caught in a blizzard out here," Nick told him. "That cabin could be our only shelter."

Renaldo looked at Ashley. "We will make sure you are warm, *señora*."

"Thank you, Renaldo." *What a strange new life this is. I hardly know this man, yet I slept right beside him our first two nights. Who ever heard of such a sweet man being an outlaw?*

Renaldo moved his horse beside Nick's as they headed up the hill, Nick pulling a pack horse behind them. "I think you and the *señora* can stay in the cabin, and I will put the horses up in the barn."

"That's not fair, Renaldo," Nick told him. "We'll have a fireplace, and you'll freeze."

"Oh, no, *mi amigo*. I will be out of the wind, and the barn most likely has a dirt floor, like with the Meekers. I can build a fire of my own, and you and your new wife can finally be alone. It is not right you have not been alone yet."

Renaldo wiggled his eyebrows and Nick laughed. "You're a better friend than I thought, Renaldo."

Ashley was glad to hunker down into the collar of her too-big coat so she could hide the red that came to her cheeks. She'd envisioned her first time with Nick being in a hotel room, bathed, her hair brushed out, a soft, clean bed awaiting them. Maybe Nick would understand and even want the same thing.

They made it up the hill and spotted the cabin, which in its run-down condition was more of a shack, but it did have a door and a sagging front stoop. They kicked the horses into a faster run as the wind picked up even more. All three were anxious to get out of the howling weather and stinging sleet. Nick ordered Ashley inside while he unloaded their most-needed supplies and some extra blankets, after which Renaldo took everything else to the barn, which was in worse condition than the cabin but still standing. It at least had a roof, and walls to buffer him from the wind.

Dusk still provided just enough light inside the cabin to show Ashley a room that had a few pans and dishes on a shelf along one wall, one table and one chair, and a stone fireplace. She gasped when some small creature made a squealing sound and skittered up the fireplace chimney. She put a hand to her chest and took a deep breath, looking around more to notice a broken board in the ceiling at one end of the room. She could see light through a crack in one wall board, but otherwise, it actually was a relief to be inside out of the wind. She spotted a few pieces of wood stacked near the fireplace.

So, this sad little cabin set in the vast Kansas-Nebraska prairie would be where she and her new husband would spend their first night alone. Fate continued to pull her in its own direction, oblivious to where she thought life would take her. She started stacking some of the wood into the fireplace, hoping it was dry enough to burn good and hot.

The door opened, and Nick walked inside and dropped an armload of supplies before closing the door. He shoved a lock board through the handle and a slot on the wall beside the door, then picked up blankets and the supplies and carried them over to the fireplace before looking around. He shook his head and met Ashley's gaze. "A bit drafty, but a good fire will help, and at least we are out of that wind."

Ashley did not miss the way his dark eyes moved over her. She was his wife, and for the first time since getting married they were totally alone. Whether this was where Nick would make her a full woman and his wife in every way depended on if they could even make things warm enough, how tired they were, and if she could shed this fear that she wouldn't please him at all.

Chapter Thirty

"Ashley." Nick spoke her name more like a command than to make a simple statement.

Ashley laid yet another piece of wood on the fireplace hearth. "We should have cleaned away some of these old ashes first," she told Nick, suddenly feeling the need to keep their conversation away from anything serious. "The fire would burn better without so many old ashes under it."

"Forget about that." Nick came closer and grasped her arm, forcing her to stand. "Look at me, Ash."

Ashley met his gaze.

"Don't pay any attention to what Renaldo was hinting at earlier. This sure as hell is no comfortable hotel room, so relax, all right? I don't expect anything tonight but a good night's sleep."

Ashley smiled bashfully. "I just feel so ... so ... I don't know." She put a hand to her hair. "I've been in these clothes so long. My hair is a mess, and I need a bath."

He pulled her close. "Well, so do I. And we've already talked about this, so relax. It's going to take time to adjust to this big change in your life." "Just getting warm will make both of us feel better. Let me finish building the fire." He knelt beside the hearth and began poking at the kindling under the bigger logs, then struck a match to light some straw under the kindling.

"Most of this is old wood, so it should burn good in spite of too many ashes."

Ashley felt like crying at learning Nick was much kinder and more understanding than she'd even expected. She watched him stoke the growing flames.

"All three of us need a hot meal and a good night's sleep. And you haven't been well long enough to trust that you won't get sick again, plus you need more meat on those bones."

Ashley smiled. "Be careful what you wish for. Once things are comfortable and I can cook real meals, I intend to eat like a pig, dear husband. And if —" She hesitated. "—if and when I'm carrying a baby, I might get as big as a house."

The fire finally began burning hotter, and Nick rose to face her. "It will be my kid, so I won't care *how* big you get, as long as you and the baby are healthy." He walked over to rummage through the supplies. "Let's see what we can cook for supper. We still have some of those potatoes the Meekers gave us, and a loaf of Anna's bread and even a hunk of ham."

The next several minutes were spent cooking their first decent meal since leaving the Meekers. They shared it with Renaldo, who then went back outside to make a fire for warmth in the barn and fix up a place to sleep.

"You lay closest to the fire," Nick insisted as he removed his gun from the waist of his pants and laid it on a barrel they'd used for a table.

Ashley kept Renaldo's wool jacket on and laid down on their makeshift bed. Nick pulled off his boots and jacket and settled in behind her. Sometime amid all the cooking and eating the wind had died down so that by the time they settled in and buried themselves under the blankets, the room actually felt comfortably warm. Ashley moved into Nick's arms, her back to him, and for several minutes they said nothing. They just watched the flames make the wood snap and pop. Glowing embers wafted up the chimney.

"Nick, I never asked you about other women. In all this time there was no one special?"

He kissed her hair. "I spent most of that time at war and then in a Union prison, don't forget. Once I escaped, the next several months were spent running and hiding and *finding* places to hide, and places where the men with me and I could rest and eat and get stronger. All we wanted was revenge for prison abuse and for the things we'd lost, so we robbed Union banks and sold guns and gave money to Southern rebels who didn't want the war to end and who kept fighting in other ways. Through it all, all I could think of was you, what had happened to you. There were a few of the kind of women who take money for a man's pleasure, but never anyone special. And all the while I meant to come and find you, explain what had happened. If I'd thought for one minute I'd have a chance at anything more, I wouldn't have visited those other women."

Ashley took hold of his wrist and kissed the palm of his hand. "I think I'm jealous of them." She felt Nick's smile.

"Don't be." He kissed her hair again. "Most men want a whole lot more than what women like that can give them." He kissed her ear. "And what about you? You're beautiful. Young men must have come calling. And what about that sheriff? What was his name?"

"Clay Matthews, and don't be silly. He's almost old enough to be my father. I never had that kind of feelings for him, although he wished that I did. Clay's a good man, a kind man. I think he really loved me. He tried his best to get me to marry him, but I don't recall that we ever even kissed."

"Not even once?"

"Well, maybe once, but it meant nothing to me."

"Well then, I think *I'm* jealous of *him*."

"There's nothing to be jealous of. And other than Clay, most of the younger men in Gainesville either marched off to war or were *killed* in the war. Those who returned had a lot of mental problems, and a lot of them were already married when they left. And there were always those rumors about…about you and me and what might have really been going on between us…about why you killed Sid MacIntyre."

Nick sighed. "I'm sorry, Ash. You didn't deserve those rumors." He kissed the back of her neck. The touch of his lips there made Ashley shiver with awakening desires. "I have to say that if I'd come back to find you married and settled with some other man, it would have broken my heart," Nick added. "But I'd have accepted it, after being away for six years."

Ashley frowned and turned. "Would it really have broken your heart?"

Nick raised his eyebrows and smiled sadly. "Does that surprise you?"

"Yes! I mean, I never would've guessed I could actually break your heart. When you rode in, I knew you were a wanted man, and you looked so big and mean and ornery, and you had that look of an outlaw—the kind of man whose feelings *can't* be hurt. At first I figured you as just an old friend come to say hello and good-bye before leaving forever."

Nick traced a finger over her lips. "I'm just a man, like any other. And men can love the same as women. They can be *afraid* to love, too, just like I was afraid to tell you the truth—that I'd loved you all that time."

Ashley studied his dark eyes, his full lips, the look of love in his eyes. "I guess I never thought of you as someone who'd be afraid of anything. I always just saw you as brave and daring because of what you did for me. And after getting me off that train and literally saving my life, I guess the least I can do is buck up and be a real wife for you."

"Buck up?" Nick smiled. "You make it sound like you need to grin and bear it. I kind of hoped you'd be more willing than that when the time came."

Ashley put a hand over her eyes. "I didn't' mean for it to come out that way."

Nick moved on top of her. "Then explain what you meant."

"I...I guess I meant...I mean...I guess I was trying to cover up the fact that I *want* to be your wife, Nick, in every way, but it embarrasses me to say it out."

He kissed her eyes. "There's nothing embarrassing about wanting your own husband, Ash. But it's like I told you, I'm not doing a thing you don't want me to do."

She saw nothing but love and promises in his dark eyes. "Nick, I'm cold and I'm scared and I'm nervous and I don't look the way I'd like to look, and I'm not in the best physical condition to do the things I'd like to do on our wedding night. But we can at least make it legal for once and for all. Nothing fancy, and it's too cold to, you know, undress and all that, for now anyway. But I'm not afraid to trust you. Now that we're more relaxed and warm, I guess I wouldn't mind...you know..."

He cut off her rambling with a kiss and moved more fully on top of her.

"You'd better be sure," he said then as his lips moved to her neck, "because a man can only go so far and still be able to stop, Mrs. Calhoun. Especially when the woman under him is his own wife."

Ashley closed her eyes. Nick's calling her 'Mrs. Calhoun' made her want him more. "I don't know what to do."

Nick frowned. "You don't have to know a damn thing." He kissed her throat. "It just kind of happens naturally, and I know what *I'm* doing, so you don't need to worry about any of it. All you need to do is relax." He moved to the side a little and slowly pushed up her dress under the blankets.

Ashley closed her eyes as she felt him tug at her pantaloons. She shifted her body to help him get them off. "I can't believe we're really doing this," she whispered.

"Just tell me again that you're sure, and that you don't' just want to get it over with. Do you want me, or not?"

She met his gaze again. "I want to give you sons. I want to be your wife in every way. I love you, and I'm so grateful—"

"Ashley Calhoun, do you *want* me, just for me. Not to make a baby. Not to fulfill a wifely duty. Do you want to enjoy the feel of a man inside you? It's okay, you know. There's nothing wrong with—"

Ashley leaned up and met his mouth in a passionate kiss that gave him the answer he needed. She felt him moving and fussing under the blankets, knew he was unbuttoning his pants and long johns. She sucked in her breath when she felt his fingers caress her in secret places, stirring an excitement she'd never known. Deep desires she'd sometimes had fantasies about in the night, after discovering that secret spot she'd wondered if it was sinful to touch. It brought such pleasure. She'd even envisioned Nick touching her there, and now he was.

She closed her eyes. "Nick." She whispered his name when he moved his fingers inside her and brought forth a silken wetness that he used to slide those same fingers over that sinful little nub that had always seemed so forbidden to a man's touch.

Their kisses grew hotter and deeper. Nick's caresses turned to more rapid, circular touches that made her open herself to him, made her want more, made her want to belong to him in every way. How did he do that? Yes, she was very, very jealous of any other woman who'd ever shared this with him.

"Hang on, Ash," he said softly in her ear. "You'll enjoy it more after the first time." Something hard yet silky soft pressed against her groin, and she tensed up, then sucked in her breath when Nick pushed himself inside her. The pain made her cry out with his first few thrusts, yet she found herself wanting more. She arched toward him with a desire to take in every bit of the penetrating, part of man that he could give her, wanting to please her husband, knowing without anyone having to tell her that once the pain was gone, she'd want him this way again and again. In moments, their rhythmic mating made them perspire in spite of the cold, both lost in the ecstasy of sharing each other's depths.

This was right. She had no doubts. Nick pushed himself deep and hard, all the while kissing her mouth, her neck, nuzzling her breasts through the dress she wore under the coat that had fallen open, feeling inside her camisole as best he could without her undressing.

"My God, Ash," he said between breaths. "I've wanted this for so long."

He moved his hands under her bottom and pushed deeper, moving in ways that made her feel wanton and wicked and aching to give him pleasure in return. His lips and tongue explored her mouth, tasting in ways that made it seem he was invading her there, too. He moved his lips down to kiss her breasts again through her dress and camisole.

She longed to be completely naked, longed to feel him touch her bare breasts, taste them. She wanted to see him naked in return, touch and kiss his powerful torso and arms, feel that nakedness against her own, see and touch all that was man about him.

Nick groaned her name again, took her with manly power, seemed to know every right move. By the time she felt his life surge into her, the blankets they'd cuddled under had fallen away. He pushed himself into her depths a few more times, more of his seed spilling into her, until finally he was finished. He moved off her just slightly and pulled the blankets back over them, and they just lay there quietly for a few minutes.

"You okay?" Nick finally asked her.

"Yes."

"That was beautiful, Ash. I love you more than ever."

He leaned over her and kissed her again, a deep, beautiful, gentle kiss that said it all.

Ashley ran her hands over the places where his muscles strained against his shirt sleeves. "And I love you."

Another kiss.

"I didn't plan on this," Nick told her. "That's the God's truth."

"Neither did I, but I'm glad. We're truly married now."

Nick smiled and pulled her close. "We'll do all this the right way when we get the chance."

"I know." Ashley kissed his damp neck. "But that doesn't mean we can't do at least this much again before the night is over."

Nick met her gaze and grinned. "Do you mean that?"

"You just made me feel things I've never felt before. Ever. And it's like you said. I wanted just you—just to enjoy my husband and give him joy in return. Everything hurts, but I know that the more often we do this the less it will hurt and the more wonderful it will feel."

Nick moved on top of her again. He unbuttoned the front of her dress and untied her camisole, pulling it open. "And this time I want more of you to touch. I want to taste these beautiful breasts."

"And I *want* you to touch them."

"You aren't just a wanted woman, Mrs. Calhoun. You're a *wanton* woman."

"Only when I'm lying underneath you."

"That had better be the only time."

Ashley kissed him and pushed a piece of dark hair behind his ear. "I'm happy, Nick. Happier than I've been since—I don't know—*ever*. I don't care that my life will never be the same, as long as I'm with you. I feel so safe here. Safe and loved."

"You *are* safe and loved."

Ashley studied the hard lines of his face, the square jawline, the full lips, the slight growth of beard, his dark eyes and the way they were accented by perfectly-shaped eyebrows and thick lashes. He frowned as he studied her in return.

"Your mother told me once that her grandparents came from northern Italy, but I think you must have some Irish in you, with that red hair, my lady."

Ashley smiled. "Mother said that a lot of northern Italians have red hair. My father's parents were from England. Did he ever tell you that?"

Nick kissed her throat. "Yes, so we really should be enemies," he teased. "I'll consider you my captive wench." He met her lips in another delicious kiss. "And I want to be inside you again."

"I can't think of anything I want more right now." Ashley welcomed more lovemaking, groaning with pure pleasure when he moved into her depths. She savored every inch of what he had to give, thinking how this part of him was just as commanding as the man himself, as gentle but as hard. She almost felt as though she couldn't give enough in return, but his moans of desire told her it *was* enough.

The fire continued to spit embers and crackle as pieces of wood split open from the heat. Occasional flakes of snow drifted down into one corner of the room through the hole in the roof, and a rabbit came out from its hiding place under a floorboard and made a dash for an opening in an end wall where wood had rotted away at the bottom.

None of it mattered. They became lost in each other again. As far as Ashley was concerned, this drafty little run-down cabin in the middle of nowhere was as beautiful as the fanciest room in the fanciest hotel in the most civilized town they might travel through. This was where they had become man and wife, and whatever lay ahead, she could face it with this man at her side.

Chapter Thirty-One

January 1869 ...

"Where's the best place to catch a train to California?"

The owner of Whiskey Hole glanced up from the bar, which was no more than a wooden plank set across three barrels. Abel could read the surprise on the bartender's face, the same shocked look others gave him at his size and his scarred face.

"I expect that would be Bitter Creek," the man answered.

"Where's that?" Abel asked gruffly. "And pour me a shot while you answer. Make it the good stuff. Not the watered-down shit I expect you serve most of the no-goods out here. I know good whiskey from bad."

The bartender set a shot glass on the wooden plank and uncorked a whiskey bottle. "This's the best I have." He set down the bottle. "And Bitter Creek is south of here. Folks come through there from Cheyenne, generally on their way to California. It's a good place for outlaws to rob the train—not a very big stop—no law there."

Abel slugged down the shot of whiskey. "You sayin' I'm an outlaw?"

"I ain't sayin' anything of the kind. I'm just warnin' you. That's all." The bartender poured him another shot. "This one's on the house. The first one will cost you two bits."

Abel pulled a dollar from his pocket and slapped it on the bar. "Thanks for the free one, but pour me a bigger glass. Name's Abel MacIntyre. You ever hear of me?"

The bar tender filled the glass. "Nope." He set down the bottle. "My name's Ed Potter, and I doubt anybody's heard of me either, except for the men who frequent this place." He folded his arms. "It's a big country, MacIntyre, and this place's nothin' but a little sod hut I put up for men who need to stop on their way someplace else, so not many of them stop here more than once. I have a smoke house out back and some beef and pork out there if you want a sandwich. I actually make my own bread. That's all I can offer if you're hungry. Fifty cents."

Abel frowned. "That's pretty expensive, but I'll have one. Make it ham." He squinted and leaned closer. "You sure you haven't heard of me?"

"Sure I'm sure. Why? You famous or something?"

Abel picked up the glass of whiskey, scowling. "Just wondered, that's all." He pushed up his eye patch. "See that?"

Potter squinted at the sight.

"Yeah. Ugly, ain't it?" Abel pulled the patch back over his eye. "A man gave me that in the war, and he wasn't the enemy. I, by God, paid him back for it."

Potter sniffed and wiped at his nose with his shirtsleeve. "You killed him?"

Abel decided not to mention he'd been kicked out of both South Pass City and Brown's Park for bragging about killing Patricia Vale. He'd like to kill every man who sent him packing because that snob of a woman deserved what she got for treating him like dirt. It was just too bad her daughter wasn't there that day. He would've enjoyed having a poke at Howard Vale's daughter. "Let's just say I found a way to pay him back."

"So, you're looking to head for California now?"

Abel walked over to a barrel that served as a table and sat down on a home-made wooden chair. "Figured I'd give it a try. Maybe I'll find gold there."

"Most mines are played out, but I hear there's lots of other opportunities there. Most folks say there's more gold in Colorado and Montana, but both places are having Indian trouble. There's some newspapers over in the corner there if you want to read somethin' while I get the meat. They're pretty old, but news is news out here. Maybe you'll see somethin' about a new gold discovery. I get the papers from men who come through here. Not often, mind you, especially in winter. Sometimes out here a man wonders if the rest of the world even exists anymore." Potter turned to the back door. "I'll go get some ham from the smokehouse."

Abel glanced at the stack of newspapers and decided it might be interesting to see what he'd been missing since leaving Patricia Vale lying dead in Gainesville. He walked over to rummage through the papers, noticing those at the bottom of the pile were chewed at the edges by mice. He took a couple from the top and carried them back to the table, sitting down and taking another drink of whiskey before opening one.

He scanned the main headline, which was something about Confederate President Jefferson Davis being tried for treason in Richmond, Virginia. A smaller headline mentioned amnesty for most of the Southerners involved in the rebellion, whether it was over secession or over slavery.

"Nobody knows *what* that goddamn war was over," Abel grumbled. "Far as I'm concerned, every Southern leader who kept that war goin' should be *hanged*. Texan or not, I wouldn't be sittin' here with this ugly face if not for that fuckin' war. And maybe by now I'd'a talked Pat Vale into leavin' that no-good husband of hers and goin' with me. It's the *war* that changed everything."

He scanned over a couple more of the bolder headlines, one of them catching his eye. GAINESVILLE WOMAN CHARGED WITH MURDER ESCAPES!

Abel sat up straighter. "*Gainesville?* What the hell?" He read on.

Ashley Vale, of Gainesville, Texas, was kidnapped from a Union Pacific train December 12, 1868. Accused of murdering a Union soldier, Miss Vale was on her way to Independence, Missouri for trial when a gang of outlaws attacked the train and stole her away, killing four soldiers and wounding three others in a shootout. Miss Vale has not been seen or heard from since. Some believe the kidnapping was an attempt to keep Miss Vale from standing trial for murder. Witness descriptions leave authorities to believe the woman was taken by Nicholas Calhoun, also from Gainesville. Calhoun is wanted on other charges of murder, robbery and mayhem. Authorities were unable to track Calhoun and his gang and believe they are headed for Outlaw Country farther west. Those close to Ashley Vale fear she will never be heard from again.

Abel read the article again, hardly able to believe any of it. "I'll be goddamned!" Ashley Vale could be out there somewhere! It didn't seem possible. And if he remembered right, Nick Calhoun had been more than friends with Ashley. "That wasn't no kidnapping," he exclaimed. "Somehow that big Irish sonofabitch found out what happened and got that woman off that train before she could go to jail! I don't know how in hell he could have done it, but it was fucking *deliberate*, and Ashley Vale's with him *willingly*. She's probably his *whore* by now."

"What's that?" Ed Potter had come back inside.

Abel re-read the article yet again. "Nothing you'd care about."

"I'm making you that sandwich," Potter told him. "I need the four bits it'll cost you."

"Sure. Sure." Abel leaned back, shaking his head. It was too damned bad he had to get out of this country. He shouldn't have bragged so much about killing Patricia Vale. He'd made enemies over it, never dreaming any man in country like this would care. Was he risking his neck if he didn't leave?

Damn! He thought. He'd love to stay and hunt down Nick Calhoun and see if Ashley was with him. Hell, maybe he could be a hero and make some bounty money, if he could find them and turn them in somehow, maybe get them to Cheyenne or someplace where the law could take over. He could kill Calhoun and turn in his body, and he could have his way with snobby Miss Ashley on the way. He couldn't imagine anything more satisfying than getting inside that bitch. She was likely a beautiful woman now.

Ed Potter set a sandwich in front of him, and he dug into his pockets to find two quarters for it. He'd killed a man camping alone on the way here, took his supplies and money, so he had plenty.

He bit into the sandwich, flashes of memory hitting him and reminding him he didn't used to be like this. He always was big and intimidating, but sometimes he remembered when he had good feelings and tried to fit in back in Gainesville ... when he joined a church and fell in love with Patricia Vale. When he thought maybe he could steal her away from that rich husband of hers who was so respected.

But then came the war, and the day Howard Vale shot him and slashed him with his sword. "Respected, my ass," he grumbled between bites. It seemed like he talked to himself a lot now, and hard as he tried, he couldn't get rid of urges to kill and rape and bully others. He blamed that, too, on Howard Vale. His injuries had caused these feelings he couldn't fight.

He supposed trying to find Nick Calhoun and Ashley Vale was almost impossible if they did come out there. This was the biggest damn country he'd ever seen. It would be like trying to find a needle in a haystack, and he'd be risking his own neck now if he revisited some of the main towns, where he was no longer welcome.

"Reckon I'll have to settle for knowing that uppity daughter of Howard Vale ended up a wanted woman living with a bunch of outlaws. That serves her right. And if her ma was alive, she'd be mortified at her daughter's fate."

"You say something?" Ed Potter asked again.

"None of your goddamn business. I like to talk to myself." *Look how the Vale family ended up,* Abel thought. *Howard Vale dying of horrible infection from a war wound, his wife beat to death, his daughter living with outlaws, never to live the good life again.* Just knowing all that was satisfaction enough, he supposed. "How far to that railroad pickup? What did you say it was called?"

"Bitter Creek. I'd say it's a good six more days from here by horseback, if this milder weather holds out. You never know in these mountains. You could be buried in ten feet of snow come morning."

"Well, then, I reckon' I'd best be leaving." Abel hawked down the rest of the sandwich, then rose and folded the newspaper, stuffing it into his belt. He turned then, the evil in his wounded brain taking over. He pulled his gun and shot Ed Potter in the forehead, then watched him stare at him with wide eyes.

"Why?" the man muttered before crumpling to the ground.

"Just because," Abel answered. "I'll take the rest of that whiskey now, and that meat you've got hanging in the smoke house. Just in case I do get caught in a snowstorm and can't go any farther." He walked out back and took down a hock of ham and stuffed it into a burlap bag he found there. He walked out to his stolen horse then and mounted up, hanging the burlap bag over his saddle horn. He headed south, hoping to make it to Bitter Creek without getting stranded.

Chapter Thirty-Two

Ashley sat next to a window in a rooming house called Ellen's Place, owned and run by a middle-aged widow woman whose husband had built the house next to a supply store he'd once owned. After his death, Ellen sold the store but kept the rooming house. It didn't take Ashley and Nick long to learn about Ellen's personal life, since she talked non-stop as they signed for the room under the names of Robert and Mary Lacey.

Ellen thought they were staying in Cheyenne long-term, and since it was very possible they truly would stay, at least for the winter, Ashley let her believe it. They hoped to head into the deeper mountains and Outlaw Country within two or three days but couldn't be sure about the weather. Nick left to find both a bath house and his men, asking Renaldo to sit outside their room and keep an eye out while he was gone. "I'm betting I'll find most of the men staying upstairs in the saloons," he joked before leaving.

Ashley wondered how often Nick himself had stayed in such places. She reminded herself it didn't matter now. He belonged to her, and she couldn't wait for him to come back, now that they had a room and a real bed. Nick had ordered a washtub so she could bathe and wash her hair while he was gone. It felt wonderful to be clean. She wore her hair pulled back with combs and wore the other dress Anna had given her, a plain, yellow flowered dress with white lace at the neck and around the cuffs. Nick had promised to take her shopping for more clothes the next day. She still had no slips to wear, and she needed new shoes. Most of all, she hoped to find a decent wool coat. There'd been little to offer in the way of women's clothing back at Willow Station in Nebraska, where they'd finally boarded a train for Cheyenne, and she wanted to feel like a woman again, which meant shedding Renaldo's too-big wool jacket.

She shivered at remembering what a cold, smokey trip they'd had getting here, but even so, traveling by train was still a big relief from horseback. If not for cold air that leaked through the train-car windows, and the smoke and soot that escaped the coal-fired heating stove in the passenger car, the trip would have been much more pleasant.

The bath she'd just taken had brought welcome relief from the rough trip. She leaned into a mirror and pinched her cheeks for color, wishing she had some earrings to wear. That was something else she might be able to buy. And perfume. She longed for some perfume to wear just for Nick. Once she got her belongings back with her wagon, if, indeed, everything was there, she would finally have everything she needed.

She was already beginning to feel strong and well enough to face her new life. Most of all she was anxious to share a real bed with Nick and be a wife in all the ways they still had not been able to enjoy. The thought made her nervous, but also full of passionate anticipation. They'd not had the opportunity to enjoy each other again as a married couple since leaving that abandoned cabin back in western Nebraska. She would treasure that night forever.

The window where she sat was dusted with snow. More snow drifted in tiny, light flakes that blew around as though spit into the air by the wind. She watched horses and buggies and wagons traverse the street below. So many people. So many secret lives, like her own.

Cheyenne was now the appointed capitol of the new Territory of Wyoming, another fact they'd learned from Ellen Anderson. It was a much bigger town than Ashley had expected, with stores of all kinds, liveries, a blacksmith, lawyers, land dealers, a church, and the ever-important saloons.

She waited nervously for Nick. She tucked a hair comb tighter, wanting to be as presentable as possible for formally meeting the men he rode with. Men who'd risked death and prison to help Nick get her off a train full of soldiers. She'd been such a mess when they first rescued her and, other than Renaldo, she couldn't even remember their faces.

Soon she'd be a lone woman traveling with six outlaws into the most dangerous country a woman could live in, filled with wanted men, hostiles, widowers, Army deserters, cattle rustlers and thieves, yet she was no longer afraid. Nick had promised never to leave her side, or to leave her alone.

So, here she was, in a strange town in a strange land—big, big country, from what she'd seen. The snow-capped mountains in the distance looked intimidating. They hid places like Brown's Park and Hole-In-The-Wall and Robber's Roost. They hid men who dared not go back home. And though she was a woman, even *she* dared not go home. Gainesville, Texas was a place she had to forget about, and she wondered if news of her killing a soldier and then being rescued from a train before her trial had made it to newspapers. Had Clay Matthews seen the story? What on earth must he be thinking now? Maybe she should write him and tell him the truth, if she could do it in a way that didn't give away her current location.

She heard footsteps then—the footsteps of several men on the stairway outside their room—men's voices, rich laughter. She heard Renaldo greet them.

"We were beginning to wonder if you were going to make it here, Nick," one of the men said.

"Yeah, we were worried the law or soldiers had caught up with you," another added.

"All of you remember that Ashley was pretty sick when we took her off that train," Nick answered. "We holed up for several days with a farm couple who were good enough to help us. Ash might have died if she hadn't gotten help. I wasn't sure good people like that existed anymore, but they do."

"Well, we're glad of that," another man spoke up.

"I have to tell you, it restored my faith in mankind," Ashley heard Nick tell them. "I was beginning to think there was no one left in this country but a bunch of no-goods like you men."

They all laughed. Ashley quickly got up and smoothed her dress nervously when someone knocked on the door.

"It's me."

Nick. Ashley rushed to the door and unlocked it, and he quickly stepped inside and swept her into his arms, closing the door with his foot. He swung her around.

"I missed you. We haven't been apart five minutes since I took you off that train."

They kissed, a deep, hungry kiss that spoke of much more to come.

"I missed you, too," Ashley answered. "Did you find all the men?"

"I sure did."

He set her on her feet and shed his sheepskin jacket, hanging it and his hat on a hook beside the door. Ashley thought he looked wonderful. It was obvious he'd found a bath house. His clean, black hair hung neatly just at his collar, and his several-day-old beard was gone. This was the most handsome Ashley had seen him since he'd first rescued her. He wore his familiar white shirt and black pants but still carried his gun in his belt rather than strapping on a gun belt.

He opened his arms. "Recognize me?"

"You're the most handsome man in all of Wyoming!"

Nick grinned as he looked her over with equal admiration. "I'm a little late, but I wanted to give you plenty of time to bathe and change and make sure you were ready for us. And from what I'm seeing, I'm glad I ordered up that tub for you. God, Ash, you look beautiful!" His gaze moved over her with the eyes of a man hungry for his woman. "But you've lost too much weight. We need to fatten you up."

Ashley smiled softly, smoothing the skirt of her dress again. "I wish I had something nicer to wear to meet your friends."

Nick grasped her face in his hands and leaned down to kiss her forehead. "You don't need anything fancy to be beautiful. That red hair and those big, green eyes of yours and your beautiful shape are all that's necessary, Mrs. Calhoun. I couldn't be prouder." He moved his arms around her, and Ashley breathed deeply of his scent.

"You smell good, too. But you took longer than I expected, so I was a little worried. You did, after all, have to visit some of the saloons to find your men." She smiled wryly. "I'm a little concerned about the women who *live* in those saloons."

"None of them could hold a candle to you. There is only one woman I want to be with. Speaking of which, let's get the introductions over, so you and I can be alone."

Ashley took a deep breath and stepped back. "All right. I'm ready to meet these men I have to learn to trust."

Nick frowned. "You nervous?"

"Yes."

He shook his head. "Don't be. I guarantee that every man out there except Renaldo, who already knows you, is ten times *more* nervous." He took the gun from his belt and laid it on a dressing table. "By the way, Buck found your wagon and draft horses and that paint you love back at Fort Dodge."

Ashley sucked in her breath, wanting to cry. "Patsy? He brought Patsy?"

Nick nodded. "And your money. Right where you said it'd be. Had to pry off some boards, but he found it, and he replaced the boards. Said to tell you that you're a clever woman when it comes to hiding things in plain sight. The soldiers had torn through the wagon floor, thinking there was a false bed underneath. They never thought to search the wagon gate."

Ashley nearly cried. "I wasn't sure it would work, but I'm so glad it did. I'll need all my things when we finally settle, Nick. And I had tools and dishes and blankets...so many things we can both use. Now I can thank your friends for recovering and saving it all. And you, for thinking to have someone go after my wagon in the first place."

"You've already thanked me a thousand times over by marrying me, Mrs. Calhoun. And once we're alone in here, I'll think of a lot of other ways you can thank me. So let's get that bunch of no-goods in here so we can be done with introductions."

Ashley put her hands to her blushing cheeks at the thought of Nick's remark. She took a deep breath as he went to the door and let in five men, including Renaldo. They shuffled inside with hats removed, and Renaldo stepped aside so Nick could present the other four to Ashley.

"Gentlemen, this is my wife, Ashley Irene Vale Calhoun," he announced proudly. "I would have had this meeting downstairs in the lobby or the dining room, but I didn't want to draw too much attention just yet in front of a lot of others."

"Well, hell, Nick, a woman pretty as this one is bound to draw attention *wherever* she goes," a rather stocky man with blond hair spoke up.

Ashley noticed the man who spoke was hardly any older than she was. He had blue eyes and an air of toughness about him that spoke of bold daring.

"You might be right," Nick answered him, "but meeting with a bunch of bums like you all at once might draw the wrong *kind* of attention. We aren't in Outlaw Country yet, so Ash and I need to look like common homesteaders, and not look like we're planning a bank robbery or something."

They all laughed, and the blond man nodded to Ashley. "I'm Trace Bell. I was in prison with Nick. I was seventeen when I first got throwed in there. Nick, he kind of watched out for me. I've got no folks, so I stuck with Nick after we escaped."

Always looking out for someone else. "I'm glad to meet you, Trace."

"You can call me Ringer. Everybody does. I got the name when I was only fourteen and was real good at horseshoes." His face reddened a little. "I'm the one who first put you on Nick's horse after he got you off that train, and I gotta' say, I can understand why Nick talked about you so much. You're right beautiful. Me and the others here, we're all ready to help you and Nick any way we can. That's a promise."

"Thank you, Ringer."

"I'm from Alabama, Ma'am," Ringer added. "And I actually fought in the war in spite of how young I was then. I'm real good with a rifle, and now I'm good with a pistol, so you're real safe with us. Ain't a man alive who wouldn't risk his life for a lovely woman like you. I'm real sorry for what happened to you with them soldiers—"

"Ringer," Nick interrupted. He stood next to Ashley with his arms folded. "Let the other three introduce themselves."

Ringer stepped back. "Sure, Nick."

Nick grinned, and the rest of the men chuckled.

"Ringer likes to talk—a *lot*," Nick told Ashley. "And sometimes he spouts a lot of bull, but we're used to it."

The others laughed harder, including Ringer.

"I sometimes cook for this bunch, by the way," Ringer told her.

"Yeah, and we're all hoping we might get some woman-cooked food once in a while, now that Nick has a wife." The joking words came from a pleasant-looking man about Nick's age, of average height and build, with soft blue eyes and brown hair. He stepped away from the others. "I'm Seth Cunningham, and I'm new to this bunch. I met Nick not long ago when he got into a scuffle back in Fort Worth. I liked how he handled himself, and I ... well ... I was going nowhere and don't have any responsibilities since I lost a wife in the war and others took my daughter to raise, so I asked Nick if I could ride with him, and here I am."

Ashley stepped closer to Seth. "You're the man who saw Abel MacIntyre at South Pass City."

He nodded. "Yes, Ma'am. He bragged about ... well ... what he did. He told me the woman's name, and after I met Nick I was telling him about it. He realized she was your mother. I'm real sorry about what happened, Ma'am. If I spot that man again, we'll damn well all deal with him and make sure he never hurts another human being." He shook his head. "Fact is, it'll likely take all of us to put down that big bear, but we'll damn well do it ... Pardon my language."

Ashley sobered. "It's hard for me to think about, but I'm glad you saw Abel, so we can be aware he might be out there, closer than we knew."

"Yes, Ma'am."

"When I left Gainesville, I had no thought that I might find a complete stranger who could tell me who killed my mother." Ashley reached out and took Seth's hand. "I'm sorry for whatever the war did to you and your family, Seth." She looked around at the others. "The war affected all of us in so many different and tragic ways. It changed the lives of so many." She squeezed Seth's hand before letting go.

"Yes, Ma'am." He nodded then looked up at Nick. "I might remind you I told the soldiers back in Kansas that this beautiful lady was my *fiancée*. I'm not real happy about you marrying her instead."

They all laughed, and Ashley looked at Nick curiously. "His *fiancée*?"

Nick put an arm around her shoulders. "Long story. I'll tell it to you sometime."

A black man stepped forward then. He looked older than Nick, with splashes of gray in his hair and short beard. "Ma'am, I'm Buck Davis. I grew up a slave, ran off to fight for the Rebels, believe it or not, on account of I liked the man who owned me. I ended up in prison with Nick. I helped nurse him back from a pretty ugly wound. Me and Ringer are the only men left in this bunch who escaped from prison with Nick. The other two were Bob Calloway, who got himself shot over a card game not long ago, and Cliff Albertson, who was killed in that wagon train attack, or so we learned at the Wichita Agency."

Ashley nodded. "Yes. I was with Cliff when he died. I feel so bad that he was killed. He was a good man."

Buck nodded. "Yes, he was. Now we're all just hoping we can start over and put all the bad things behind. I know Outlaw Country sounds dangerous to a woman like you, but we'll be around to help any way we can. And Nick, he's a take-charge kind of man, you know? He'll make sure you're always safe. Ain't many men who'll mess with Nick Calhoun, if you know what I mean."

Ashley smiled. "I certainly do. I've known Nick since I was ten, and he was fifteen. He was always looking out for me. Now I need to thank you, for looking out for Nick. He says you saved his life in that prison."

Buck grinned. "I don't know about that, Ma'am. I just did my best."

Ashley folded her arms and leaned closer to Nick. "Well, you were a God-send, to say the least."

Buck nodded and stepped back, and Ashley glanced at Renaldo. "Renaldo I already know well. He's become a very good friend," she stated. "I'm sorry I needed to be reintroduced to the rest of you, but I was so sick when you first got me off that train that I don't remember much." She glanced at a tall, thin man standing behind the others. "And what is your name?"

He hesitated before answering. "Sam Brady, Ma'am. I'm just a loner with an uninteresting past. I met Nick when I helped hide him and his men after they escaped prison. I'm glad to formally meet you."

"And I'm glad to meet you." Ashley brightened. "You lived in the Adirondacks, didn't you?"

Sam nodded. "Yes, Ma'am." He stepped back.

"Sam's the quiet one," Nick stated. "He's the one who saved our lives up in those mountains, and he's a good hunter as well as someone you can count on when you're in trouble."

Ashley scanned the group. "I can't tell you how happy I am that you found my wagon and horses, and my money. I take great joy in having my things back —familiar things that mean a lot to a woman."

Renaldo grinned ear to ear. "The *señora*, she is a good lady," he told the men. "She is brave and uncomplaining. Nick chose well." He faced Ashley. "We will all build you a fine home once Nick decides where to settle. And we will stay on and go after wild horses and buy cattle, and Nick will have a big ranch and life will be good, no?"

"Life will be good, yes," Nick answered for Ashley. "And all of you need to leave now. This is the first decent place Ashley and I've stayed since I took her off that train."

"Nick!" Ashley felt the color coming to her cheeks. "You don't need to chase them away so soon."

"Can't get rid of us fast enough, huh, Nick?" Ringer teased.

"Yeah, well we'll meet up tomorrow morning at the livery to discuss when to leave," Nick answered. "Be there at ten. No excuses of getting too drunk tonight to get up in time. There's still a lot of winter ahead of us, and winter in the mountains is nothing to take lightly. We need to figure out when it's best to keep going. First I want my wife to have a couple days' rest."

"Sure," Seth answered.

They made their way out the door, where Seth paused and looked back at Ashley. "If you have doubts about any of us, Mrs. Calhoun, you don't need to worry. We might have all done some bad things, but abusing a woman or stealing from her aren't on that list, so you rest easy. You're in good hands now, even if something should happen to Nick."

Ashley nodded. "Thank you, Seth."

Seth glanced at Nick, then left, closing the door softly. Ashley turned to Nick.

"Well?" he asked.

"I can tell they're good men. I wasn't sure what to expect, except that Renaldo was so good to me. I was hoping they were all like Renaldo, and they are."

"Don't underestimate their abilities with gun and fist, Ash, and they aren't angels, but you'll always be safe with them even if something happens to me. Understand?"

"But how would I go on without you?"

Nick stepped closer, unbuttoning the top button of her dress. "Let's hope you won't have to, Mrs. Calhoun. And right now, we *are* together. And for the first time since we became man and wife, we're in a nice room with a soft bed. You aren't sick, and we're both bathed and more relaxed." He opened more buttons and pushed her dress to her shoulders. "And there are a lot of ways to finish consummating this marriage that we haven't had a chance to enjoy yet."

Ashley closed her eyes as he pulled the dress open and began unlacing her camisole. "And what might those things be?"

Nick walked over to the door and locked it. "That's for me to know, and you to find out."

Chapter Thirty-Three

"I can't move my arms," Ashley told Nick, as he pulled the bodice of her dress only part way down.

Nick grinned. "Then you can't defend yourself." He unlaced her camisole even farther and leaned down to kiss her cleavage.

"Why would I want to defend myself?" Ashley closed her eyes and breathed deeply against the thrill of his touch. "I only want to free my arms so I can help you get your shirt off, Mr. Calhoun."

"In that case, I'll oblige you." Nick helped get her arms out of the sleeves of her dress, then pulled off her camisole and tossed it aside. He wrapped his arms around her naked waist, pressing her breasts against him and lifting her off her feet to nuzzle her neck. "Did I tell you how beautiful you look this morning? I'm sure all the men were impressed."

"You're the only man I want to impress."

Nick set her on her feet. "You did that when you were sixteen, so much so that I couldn't forget about you."

Ashley laughed as he swung her around and carried her in one arm to the door to make sure again that it was locked, then lifted her fully into his arms and carried her to the bed. He held her in one arm again as he yanked down the covers then set her on her feet and pulled her dress the rest of the way off, taking her pantaloons with it.

"Step out, lady."

Ashley's heartbeat quickened as she obeyed. Nick threw the dress aside and yanked down her stockings, pulling them off along with her shoes so that she finally stood naked before him. A hundred emotions ran through her as he ran his hands up over her calves and thighs. Self-consciousness, embarrassment, yet a longing to let this man see and touch everything he wanted to see and touch.

"My God, Ash, you're so beautiful." He kissed the crowns of her breasts. "This is the first chance we've had to see each other this way." He kissed her belly. "From now on there'll be no lovemaking under covers with half our clothes on." He kissed the red hairs that hid what belonged only to him.

Fire ripped through Ashley's blood when he kissed her belly again as he moved a thumb into her folds to toy with private places. She shivered with the erotic desires he stirred from the intimate touch. "Nick," she whispered.

He moved his lips upward to kiss her between her breasts, then licked and tasted each nipple, bringing forth wicked needs that had long simmered behind heartache and loss and loneliness. Making love with their clothes on back at the abandoned cabin could not compare to this.

Ashley ran her hands into his thick, dark hair as he tasted her breasts again, then stood up.

"Undress me," he told her.

Ashley looked up at him. "Everything?"

Nick laughed lightly. "Of course, everything."

She started unbuttoning his shirt, then paused. "You won't think I'm being too bold?"

"You're my wife. You're allowed to do whatever you want."

Ashley unbuttoned and opened his shirt, then rested her forehead against his chest. "Suddenly I feel so...I don't know…overwhelmed. I can't believe I'm standing here naked in front of you."

Nick went ahead and pulled off his shirt, then slung it to the floor. "And I can't believe Ashley Vale belongs to me in every way. So, we're even. Right now, all you need is to remember you're a grown woman, and we're in love. You're my wife, Ash, not just a friend, although I love the fact that you're both." He grasped her face in his hands and made her look up at him, then kissed her lightly. "It's legal, and if we don't do this, how in hell are we going to make a baby?" He grinned and let go of her, holding out his arms. "Now, get these pants off me."

His build was even more magnificent than she'd imagined. Hard, muscled arms, a broad chest with dark hairs that traveled down to a vee, as though pointing to all that was man about him.

Ashley noticed a deep, uneven scar on his left side. She touched it gently. "Oh, Nick! I've never seen you without your shirt on. Is this where you were wounded in the war?"

He sighed deeply, the sigh of a man remembering things he'd rather forget. "Yes. It's the reason your father thought I was dead."

Ashley kissed the scar. "Dear God, you could have been killed, and all because you were sent away because of me. I'm so sorry for how you must have suffered."

"Don't be sorry, Ash. None of it was your fault."

Ashley ran her hands over his arms and torso, kissing his chest. "You're a beautiful man."

Nick shook his head. "Men are supposed to be handsome, not beautiful."

"But you *are* beautiful, because of your compassion and your bravery." She met his gaze. "I just feel so bad about your wound, such a big scar on such a perfect body."

He grasped her shoulders. "That's in the past. This is now, and we've nothing left but to enjoy this chance to celebrate finally being together for good." He leaned down and kissed her eyes. "Now, forget about the wound and finish undressing me, Mrs. Calhoun. That's an order."

Ashley smiled bashfully and unbuckled his belt, then pulled his denim pants to the floor. Nick sat down on the edge of the bed, and she pulled off his boots and socks, then took his pants the rest of the way off. She just stood there a moment, noticing the bulge at the buttons of his long johns.

"I'm still wearing my underwear, woman," Nick teased.

Ashley covered her face again. "Nick, back at that cabin, I love what we did, but I never actually ... looked."

Nick pulled her onto the bed with him, rolling her over and moving on top of her. "Lady, before this day is out, you'll not only look, but you'll touch and maybe even taste."

Ashley drew in her breath. "Nicholas Calhoun!" She grabbed a pillow and put it over her face, then felt Nick fussing around. She knew he was removing his long johns. He moved between her legs and braced his arms on either side of her. "Look at me, Ash."

She pulled the pillow part way off her face.

"What did I tell you about how I'd treat you?"

She studied his shoulders and arms again. Power. All power.

"Just because we've already done this doesn't mean I'll start being forceful and demanding. You're my beautiful wife now, my Ashley. I want you in ways we haven't explored yet, but if you aren't ready—"

"I *am*. Really," she told him, voice muffled by the pillow. "It just seems sinful that I should enjoy this."

Nick chuckled. "That's what makes it more fun."

Ashley pulled the pillow farther down, sobering. "I can't help feeling like I'm going to wake up and find out this was all a dream and I'm sitting in prison."

"As long as we're together, I'll never let that happen. Understand?" Nick kissed her forehead. "I know how awful it was what Sid tried to do to you. And doubly awful how those soldiers treated you. I know that terrified you. But they're dead, and we're here, together. This is me, Nick, your husband and your friend. We've already made love, and it was beautiful and right." He kissed her mouth, a hungry, delicious kiss, then moved to her cheek, her neck. "This is no dream, Mrs. Calhoun. It's real." Another kiss. He ran a hand over her breast. "But I'll only do what you want me to do."

Ashley removed the pillow. "I want you to do everything."

He met her mouth again, his kisses melting away all doubts, and all fears from the past. "It's the same for me I want you to see me, touch me, taste me, if you want."

Ashley felt his hardened penis pressing against the crevice between her thigh and her most private part. "You won't think me wicked?"

Nick laughed amid more kisses. "The more wicked the better, Mrs. Calhoun." He planted a deep, invading kiss on her mouth as he moved a hand under her bottom and bent a leg up between her own legs, forcing hers farther apart. He kissed her ear, her neck, her throat, then trailed his lips down between her breasts to kiss her there before he gently tasted each nipple again, drawing forth an even more intense need in Ashley to have him inside her. She breathed deeply when he moved ever downward until his lips and tongue found that magic spot that made her want to be as wild and wicked as he'd like her to be. He touched and tasted and worked his way back up over her breasts to her mouth, while moving his fingers down between her legs and inside her, arousing the slick juices that only made his touch more heavenly.

Ashley groaned softly with every touch, every kiss, and with everything about him that was man and protector and provider. She wanted nothing more than to please him—her Nick—in every way. Remembering how men had dragged him away to send him to war only made her love and want him more, realizing that was all behind them and he was really here in her bed. He moved his fingers with an expertise that made her jealous of every other woman he might have done this with. She wanted him inside her so badly that she moaned his name, adding the word "please." She felt the back of his hand against her privates as he positioned himself.

Ashley gasped with ecstasy at finally feeling all that was man about him inside her. For the next several minutes she was lost in him, shrouded by powerful arms and shoulders, at his mercy. They moved in perfect rhythm, and she felt something wonderful building inside her as he raised up and grasped her thighs, changing his movements in a way that rubbed against that magic spot he seemed to enjoy toying with, until she felt muscles pulsating deep inside, drawing him to her depths. It was as though she had no control over her own body. She cried out his name, offering herself like a wanton woman of the night.

She relished the realization that this was real and right. They were free and safe. Nick Calhoun, the handsome young man she'd daydreamed about, was her husband now. He'd come back! He'd hunted for her and saved her from the horrid situation she was in with those soldiers. They couldn't touch her now. She had Nick to protect her. Nick to love her. Nick to provide for her and make a new home for her.

The erotic climax he brought forth from deep inside her soul lasted several minutes as he continued the thrusts that included rubbing himself over that magic spot that kept demanding more and more, until finally she felt his life pulse into her. Life that just might end up forming a baby inside her.

Nick grunted with the last thrust, then breathed a long sigh and nestled in beside her, both their bodies glistening with perspiration. He kissed her over and over. "I want to do this the rest of the day and all night. I want to taste every inch of you, invade you every way I can."

"And I want to give you anything you want," Ashley answered with a smile, pushing some of his hair back from his face. "It feels so wonderful to be lying in a real bed, with real privacy, in a civilized town where we can eat good food at a real restaurant and buy supplies and just, I don't know, be a real married couple."

Nick smiled softly. "We still need to be a little careful, but I didn't see any soldiers anywhere in town, and I even checked wanted posters outside the sheriff's office and at the train depot. I didn't see anything with our pictures on them. I didn't even see anything about a woman wanted for murder being stolen off a train and escaping."

"Wanted for murder?" Ashley put a hand to her mouth. "I *am*, aren't I? Things have been so good that I almost forgot."

Nick pulled her hand away. "Then I'm sorry I said it. And always remember that you didn't murder anyone. You shot a man in self-defense, and with all the trouble with hostiles out here and the government still involved in rebuilding the South, I've a feeling what happened will get swept under a rug and forgotten. It's my part in your rescue they won't forget, but before long we'll be in country so big and remote, no one who cares will find us, and no lawman will dare come looking."

Nick drew her closer and pulled the covers over them. "We'll leave after a couple more days here. The next stop is Bitter Creek, at the base of the Rocky Mountains. From there we find a guide and head to Brown's Park, weather permitting. We'll be far away from soldiers and the law, and around other people like us. Next spring I'll build you that house I promised you. The Green River runs through those parts, so we'll have grass and water and everything we need." He met her mouth again in a deep, delicious kiss, then pulled the covers closer as the room grew chillier. "And as soon as we make love again, I'll build up the fire in the stove."

Ashley glanced at the black, iron, pot-belly stove in one corner of the room. "They should've put the bed closer to that thing," she told him, snuggling against his chest.

"Well, right now having that stove too close would make us much too warm, what with all this exercise."

Ashley smiled. "I guess that's true."

"You feeling all right?" he asked. "Maybe this is too much for you."

"Not at all. Get all the exercise you want, Mr. Calhoun. I can take it."

He moved between her legs again. "Tomorrow we'll go shopping and look for a wedding ring. I want to make this as official as possible."

"I think what we're doing right now makes it very official, ring or not."

Nick moved inside her again with no foreplay. Ashley was still warm and on fire from the hard climax she'd experienced moments before. She welcomed him gladly, both still so full of desire they could hardly get enough of each other.

"Don't stop," Ashley groaned.

"I'll do my best." Nick moved his hands under her bottom and forced her upward as he invaded her again, taking, demanding, filling her, signaling that he owned and desired all of her, inside and out.

She no longer feared where they'd settle, because she'd be with a man who'd protect and defend her always. She was free from soldiers, free from fear and horror. In this man's arms she felt only love and warmth and safety.

Chapter Thirty-Four

Nick and his men waited out a two-day snowstorm in Cheyenne, then boarded a train for Bitter Creek, from where they intended to head for Brown's Park, weather permitting. Ashley couldn't stop watching the landscape as the Union Pacific made its way through Wyoming.

"Nick, look!" They weren't afraid now to use their real names.

She pointed out the window, and he leaned across her to see a herd of wild horses charging across a high, snow-covered plateau.

"Aren't they beautiful?"

Nick kissed her cheek. "Just like you. That dress and cape you're wearing are such a beautiful green. Brings out the green in your eyes. I'm glad you found some new dresses in Cheyenne."

Ashley shivered into the fur-lined cape as the conductor loaded more wood into the heating stove at the front of the passenger car. "Well, you can't see much of my dress under all this fur. I think that heating stove is in a tight battle with the cold air sneaking through these drafty windows."

She faced Nick, and they kissed again. Ashley decided she should feel worn out from all their lovemaking over the past few days—two people relegated to their hotel room while winter wind and snow battered everything outside. Instead, she felt invigorated, alive, free and happy. As far as she was concerned, they couldn't make love often enough to make up for the years they'd spent apart.

"Winter will end, and the boys and I'll go out chasing down horses like those outside your window once we get settled. We just have to get a cabin and barn and some corrals built. We'll sell horses and cattle and grow our own feed and sell that, too. One thing I know is farming, thanks to your father."

"Will you have to herd livestock to far-away places? I don't want you to ever have to be gone a long time, Nick."

"I don't what that either. Most of the time I'll send some of the other men and stay home with you. I might even have to hire more if I can build a ranch as big as I'd like. And believe me, there'll be plenty to do at first to keep me very busy—out-buildings to build, a garden to plant, cattle-buying, other stock to take care of, and you'll need protecting. If I do have to go with the others, I'll make sure men are left behind to guard you."

"How'll you know whom to trust if you hire more? Seth said there're more outlaws at Brown's Park than any other place along the trail. A lot of wanted men and deserters and..." She shivered. "And men like Abel MacIntyre and those awful soldiers. And there's no jail and no law of any kind."

"We'll make our own laws, and there's a code of honor among the men there, which is why that man named Moses Tucker beat Abel MacIntyre near to death. If I get hold of Able, he will die."

Ashley grabbed his arm. "The thought of running into Abel scares me."

"You doubting my abilities?"

"No. I just don't want something bad to happen to you. Even if you win some kind of fight with him, Nick, he's the type who might shoot you in the back or find some other underhanded way to get back at you."

"He won't be able to. He'll be dead."

"That would be fine with me, but I can't help worrying. I couldn't live without you. I won't care about anything if something happens to you. Renaldo and Seth and the others might not always be around, what with saloons and gambling and the kind of women in this country that men like to visit." Ashley straightened and faced him. "And women like that will love seeing a man like you ride into town, too."

Nick grinned and shook his head. "I'm married, remember?"

"Yes, well, for some men, being married doesn't matter."

He kissed her cheek again. "It matters to me." He frowned. "Where are all these doubts coming from?"

Ashley studied his gaze. "Probably from the fact that I could get quite fat in the next few months."

Nick watched her eyes, sobering. "My God, Ash. Are you saying—"

"I think I'm carrying, Nick. We weren't in Cheyenne very long, but I know I should have had—" She looked down. "You know. I think it's from that night at that abandoned cabin." She lowered her voice more and leaned in close. "I was afraid I'd have my time while we were in Cheyenne, and we wouldn't be able to make love. But now I'm past my time," she whispered. "I was close to it when we left the Meekers' place, and then we, we made things legal in that old cabin, and now I'm really late. And I've felt sick in the mornings. It's still a little early, but I'm pretty sure I'm going to have a baby."

Nick straightened and faced her more fully. He put a hand to the side of her face. "Do you feel all right? I mean, other than feeling sick in the mornings?"

"I feel fine. Are you happy?"

"Of course, I'm happy!" His dark eyes glittered with delight. "I'm a little worried, though. There might not be a doctor in

Brown's Park, and besides that, we'll be living well away from town. It's a big country, and I don't want you having a baby with nothing but a bunch of men around."

"You said there're other women in Brown's Park. Maybe we can find someone to come and stay when things get close. I'll be fine."

"But the country we're heading into—"

"I'll be with you, remember? That's all that matters. You and me. Your men have told me how good you are with that gun, and with your fists when necessary, especially when you're angry. I trust you, Nick Calhoun, with my life and with this baby's life."

Nick studied her lovingly. "I sure didn't expect this to happen so fast."

Ashley leaned closer and talked softly again. "Considering the fact that you took advantage of your husbandly rights in that old cabin, Mr. Calhoun, you should have expected this."

Nick took his arm away and leaned back in his seat. "We have a lot of planning to do. We'll have to buy what we can in Brown's Park to get through the rest of winter. We'll have to ask around town about where we can stay out the winter, and once we settle, some of the men will have to go back to Brown's Park and buy wagons and stock up on all kinds of things, including lumber so we can get that house built." He took hold of her hand. "These first couple of years will be really hard, Ash. And here you are carrying."

"I'm not worried." Ashley rested her head against his shoulder. "As long as I have you by my side, I'll be fine."

"I wish it was already spring so we could head out right away and look for a place to settle and start building. As it is, we might have to stay in Bitter Creek, or try to make it to Brown's Park at least. We'll have to hire a guide to get us there. I'm not sure how good the trails are to Brown's Park, and it's damn big country.

There are places where you can see for miles and miles—desolate and lonely."

"We'll have each other."

"Doesn't matter if you're carrying. I think we should stay in Brown's Park, at least until late spring when we're sure the worst winter weather's over."

"Nick, I don't want to hold things up."

He squeezed her hand. "In this case, Mrs. Calhoun, you'll have to obey my orders. The baby's more important than anything else."

Ashley turned her head to look out the window. She sucked in her breath. "Nick, look how high we are! Oh, dear Lord!"

The train's whistle let out another long wail that echoed against a rock wall to the left. Nick and Ashley both looked to the right, realizing they were on a very narrow cutout on the side of a mountain and looking down into a deep canyon. Ashley had to look away.

Nick pulled her closer. "I'm sorry, Ash. This country will take some getting used to."

"I can get used to anything if that's what it takes for us to stay together." Ashley kissed his cheek and breathed in his scent. "If I wasn't here, traveling with a husband, carrying his baby and looking forward to an exciting new life, I would be sitting in a horrid jail, or on trial, maybe hanged or sent to prison by now. You rescued me from a fate worse than death. The life we'll lead now will seem absolutely wonderful compared to how things could have turned out."

She clung to his hand as she dared to look out the window again. Nick leaned across for another look himself. The train was moving into flatter land already. They both watched the amazing landscape that seemed to change by the yard rather than the mile, as the train moved away from the mountains they'd just traveled through to reveal what lay beyond—wide open spaces with an endless horizon.

"It's so beautiful, Nick, yet so frightening in how big and lonely and intimidating it is. I've never seen the landscape change so violently and so fast. I heard someone talking about grizzly bears before we boarded the train, and mountain lions."

Already the wide expanse of nothingness was gone as the train again moved into snow-covered mountain foothills. Nick watched the maze of buttes and mesas, vast chasms that snaked among the flat peaks, where just a few miles earlier wild horses charged over flat plains dotted with snow-covered bunch grass and sage. He'd seen wild, changing land before, but nothing like this. Boulders were scattered in places where they shouldn't be, and huge rocks sat balanced on smaller ones in ways that made it seem they should tumble any moment. The train car darkened then as it headed through a tunnel under a mountain.

"You'll have to teach me how to properly use a rifle," Ashley told him. "I might need to know." She faced him as the train moved into daylight again. "This is God's country. For some reason, deep in my heart I feel I was always meant to come here. My God, life in Gainesville seems like years ago now, doesn't it? That life doesn't even seem real anymore."

The train emerged from the tunnel, and Nick glanced out the window again. "I sure can see why outlaws live out here. What lawman would bother coming to such a dangerous place? And even if one tried, he'd have to search through thousands of square miles of mountains and canyons to find whoever he was looking for."

It started snowing harder again, the wind picking up to the point where the snow outside the window slashed sideways. Ashley snuggled against Nick's shoulder as the train again moved into open country. He kept an arm around her, ignoring the stares of a couple men who sat across from them in a facing seat.

"You two lovebirds fresh married?" one finally asked. He sported long hair and a beard that made its way clear to his gun belt. "Or—uh—might the woman there be somebody a man could strike a bargain with?"

Nick frowned and urged Ashley fully back into her own seat. "She might be my wife. And you should apologize for that remark, Mister."

The bearded man put up his hands in a defensive manner. "Just admirin' a beautiful woman. In country where women are rare, you can't blame a man for that. I'm right sorry for askin'. Didn't mean no insult."

"This country is all new to her," Nick told him, "and she doesn't care to be stared at. I don't like it either."

Ashley put a hand on Nick's arm, worried about the fact that the bearded man looked like the kind who knew how to use the gun he was wearing. "Nick, it's okay. I think he means well."

The man nodded. "The lady is right, Mister. I mean no offense." He rose and removed his hat, bowing to Ashley. "Beggin' your pardon, Ma'am. Not many beautiful women of proper behavior come to this country."

"What's proper behavior, Mister?"

Everyone turned to glance at the woman who'd made the remark. She sat toward the back of the train car, her coat open just enough to reveal a daringly low-cut dress under it. She wore a lovely flowered hat, her dark hair done up in curls that hung from under the hat brim. Her face was heavily painted, and she smiled through red lips. "Leave the lady alone and come on back here, honey. I'll show you some *im*proper behavior!"

The few other passengers in the car were men, and they all guffawed at the remark. A few whistled.

The bearded man grinned and nodded to her. "I'll be there shortly."

More laughter filled the rumbling train car as the stranger turned back to Nick. "Mister, when women as lovely as that one beside you come to these parts, they get stared at, so you ought to get used to it." He grinned and nodded to Ashley again. "Be assured that out here any man who don't follow the code for treatin' a woman right and proper generally don't last long, if you know what I mean."

Ashley suppressed a smile. "Yes, I think I do. And I accept your apology."

The man put his hand out to Nick. "Hank Truelove. I know that's a strange name, but it's my folks's name, so it's mine, too. I usually do a good job of quickly wipin' the smiles off the faces of them that makes fun of it."

Nick rose and created a barrier between Hank and Ashley. He shook Hank's hand. "Nick. I'm not giving you my last name yet, or my wife's name, not until I know you better. Suffice it to say that she belongs to me, and we're hoping to get to Brown's Park before severe winter snows stop us."

Hank looked him over, giving Nick a knowing nod. "I expect you've got your reasons for holdin' back on your full name, but I assure you, Nick, that it's okay to use it now, although a lot of men who come here never do use their real moniker. Ain't nobody cares what your name really is, or if there's a reason you don't use it." He turned to the man who'd been seated beside him. "That there's my friend, Sven Eaton. We've both done buffalo huntin' and worked as guides for wagon trains and such. I've been livin' out here on and off ever since before the war, but Sven—he showed up afterward. We're headed for Brown's Park, too. Maybe we can help you get there. Where might you be from?"

"I'd rather not say that right now. And just so you know, I have several men with me. They're back in one of the box cars watching our horses and supplies. Together we're from all over the country, and some of my men were in a Union prison with me."

Hank scratched at his beard. "Well, now, maybe eventually you can tell me more about yourself, Nick. Either way, it's nice meetin' ya'—and the lovely wife there."

Nick glanced at the others in the train car. Ashley knew he was worried about revealing anything more about himself, or drawing too much attention. She glanced at the painted woman in the fancy hat, who grinned and nodded acknowledgement.

One of those saloon women, Ashley thought. Yes, this was a brand new life she'd have to get used to. She nodded to the woman in return.

Hank folded his arms. "You and the wife there are new to this country, ain't ya'?"

"Might be."

"Well, now, I know an Outlaw Country greenhorn when I see one, but you, Mister, look like a man who can damn well take care of himself no matter where he is. You'll get along just fine. Just keep in mind that out here, all that matters is honesty and how good you are with a gun." He shrugged. "And with fists. Somethin' tells me you do okay with both."

Sven stood up and walked a couple of seats farther back. He glanced at Ashley and nodded, then sat down again, facing forward.

"My friend there, Sven, he can't talk on account of a Union soldier's bullet caught him sideways right in the throat," Owen said. "Blew out his vocal cords. So, if you fought for the Confederacy, we're both glad to help you out if you need it."

Nick studied the gritty old scout a moment longer, then sat down and motioned for him to take a seat across from him. "If you really know your way around out here, I guess I could use you to get us to Brown's Park. And if you're looking for a job, I'm looking for men who'll help me round up wild horses and maybe some stray cattle and help me build my ranch come spring. First thing I want to do is build a decent house for my wife."

"Sure. Sven and me're always lookin' for work." Hank gave him a mostly-toothless smile. "We can do pretty much anything. How many more men do you have?"

"Five. For safety's sake, I'll need more until we settle and I get the lay of the land, so to speak. We're getting off this train at Bitter Creek."

"Hell, I've been there plenty of times—Brown's Park, I mean. I can help you get there. I hope all your men are good with guns and don't take no guff from nobody."

"They're seasoned."

Hank nodded. "I gotta' tell ya', with a woman like yours along, you'll need to be a man who stands his ground. I can see by your eyes and how you conduct yourself that you're that kind of man. One who sets his own rules. That's important out here. There's gangs—the Tip Gault Gang, the Herrera Gang, Diamond Mountain Gang, the Brush Creek Gang—all of 'em have marked out their own territories. Long as each one leaves the other alone, ain't no trouble. Sometimes they even help each other out when they're in a fix." He grinned and winked. "Now there will be *your* boys. Whatever you end up callin' yourselves, somethin' tells me you'll show everybody that you ain't about to take no nonsense."

"That I can guarantee. And you and your friend there can join us if you choose. Just so you know, we'll be keeping an eye on you for a while."

"That's fine with us. I don't blame you at all, but you'll find out you can trust us just as much as them men you already ride with." Hank glanced at Sven, who smiled and nodded. "We just come here from Cheyenne. Needed to stock up while there was a break in the weather. Been livin' out the winter there tryin' to decide what to do next. Now we have a purpose—buildin' a nice place for your wife, maybe rustlin' up some cattle and horses to get you started, buildin' a barn for the horses."

"Just don't be taking cattle from the property of any of those other gangs you mentioned," Nick warned.

Hank let out a hardy laugh. "No, sir. You don't want that kind of trouble. Oh, plenty of rustlin' goes on out here, but that's what will lead to shoot-outs and murders. You build a reputation as an honest man, and you'll be okay." He stood up. "I'll let you two be for now. I know this country real good. I can guide you any place you want to go."

"I appreciate that." Nick shook the man's hand again, and Hank left them, walking back to talk to the painted woman in the big hat.

Ashley watched him, then leaned close. "Is that one of those women who live in the saloons?"

Nick grinned. "Should I go ask her?"

Ashley's eyes widened. "Don't you dare!"

He shook his head and smiled as he settled into his seat, taking her hand again. "Hank seems like a man who knows his way around. He could end up being a big help." He squeezed her hand. "We'll be okay, Ash. We have a baby on the way, and now I've hired two more men."

"Do you really think you can trust them?"

"The kind of men I've been around the last few years, you learn to read a man's eyes. I can trust those two."

Ashley leaned back, breathing a sigh of relief over what could have been a dangerous situation. She looked out the window again. "This is some of the most beautiful country I've ever seen. And the biggest, in spite of how big Texas is. But it must also be dangerous—wild weather and wild animals. And wild men. When we got on the train, I had to hang on to my hat because of the wind. I heard a man say that the wind never stops blowing in Wyoming."

"Brown's Park is closer to Utah and Colorado, but right below the Wyoming border. I expect it's just as windy, though, especially with all the canyons in country like this. If we're lucky, we'll find some land along the Green River, so we'll always have plenty of water."

Ashley breathed deeply, picturing a green valley, the river, spring wildflowers, a cozy cabin that she'd share just with Nick and their baby. She squeezed his hand tighter. "Stay close until I get used to all of this."

"I'm right here, where I always should've been since you were sixteen."

The train whistle blew again, a lonely sound in a lonely land filled with lonely people. Ashley thought how lonely she would be right now, too, without Nick Calhoun at her side. She held his hand even tighter as the man called Hank and the painted woman laughed over something.

What a strange new life this is. I'll have to get used to people like that woman, and like Hank Truelove.

Chapter Thirty-Five

"Bitter Creek ahead!" the conductor called, startling Ashley awake.

She'd fallen into a half sleep against Nick's shoulder. The "great black beast," which was what Ashley called the steam engine that had powered them through the steep mountains, chugged its way into Bitter Creek, blowing its whistle while steam burst from its belly. Between the clouds of steam and the blowing snow, it was impossible to see the people standing on the station platform as the engine chugged and puffed into the poorest excuse for a town they'd had seen so far in this desolate land.

"Folks, Bitter Creek is just a place to take on wood and water and use the privies behind the ticket station," the conductor called to the passengers. "There's a place to eat, mostly just biscuits and coffee, one saloon and one rooming house. There are stables down a steep slope just south of the rooming house where the stable man keeps a few supplies. Them that's getting off should do so now, and them that's going on have only about a half hour to get something to eat and take care of personals. Bear River City is our next stop, and the last one till the U. P. gets finished next year."

"Stay here 'til I see to the men and horses," Nick told Ashley. "I'm also going to get you a room, even if I have to kick some man out of it. I don't like this weather, and I don't want you in it any more than you need to be."

"Hurry back." Ashley squeezed his hand tightly.

"Don't worry." Nick got up and gave her a quick kiss before exiting the passenger car along with all the other men on board, including Owen and Sven.

Ashley looked out the window, watching the men hold on to their hats and duck their heads against the wind-whipped snow.

"Don't worry, lady," the painted woman spoke up. "The weather in these parts can change in a matter of minutes. The sun will be shining any time now."

Ashley looked back at her. "I hope so. Do you live out here?"

"I move around, go where the money is. Mostly gold towns. The only thing more inviting to a man than a woman is gold. Out here the shiny stuff's more of a mistress than any woman could possibly be."

Ashley looked away, embarrassed by the remark and wondering if Nick ever thought about going after gold. He'd never mentioned it. She watched for him out the window again.

"I have to say, that man with you is damn easy on the eyes. I'm sitting here wishing he wasn't married. Not that it'd matter to me, but I think he's one of those who takes marriage pretty serious."

Ashley thought about the three days they'd spent in Cheyenne. Three passionate, erotic, romantic, promise-filled days.

"Yes, he does," she answered absently, while straining to see Nick. She feared the train would leave while she was still on it, but she had orders to stay put. She could hear horses whinnying, and men's raised voices as they tried to shout above the wind. She wasn't sure it was proper to talk to the painted woman, but the fact remained she *was* a female, and it felt good to be able to talk to one. "What's your name?" she asked.

"Bella James. What's yours?"

"Ashley Calhoun." She quickly turned to look wide-eyed at Bella. "I'm not sure I should have said it. Don't tell anyone."

Bella laughed lightly. "Don't worry. You're far enough into Outlaw Country that it doesn't matter if someone learns your real name. But it's just us here, so nobody else heard you."

"We've been using different names on our way out here."

"Well, you shouldn't need to anymore." Bella shifted in her seat. "So, Calhoun, huh? Doesn't ring a bell with me, but apparently your man is wanted for something. Is he good with that gun of his?"

"Yes." Ashley decided not to go into details about why they'd come west, or to mention *she* was wanted, too. "I hope he never has to use it or his fists again."

"Out here?" Bella chuckled. "He'll use them, all right. But I have a feeling that others will learn real quick not to give him trouble."

"I hope so. Trouble just seems to come his way without his asking for it. He's really a reasonable man who's trying to stay away from trouble." *Hurry, Nick.* Ashley still hated being apart from him for more than two minutes. She turned and looked out the window again, searching the station platform, but Nick was still out of sight, and those who'd disembarked the passenger car had disappeared into a building that simply showed a sign saying "Eat 'N Go." She could make out the forms of two people who did stand on the platform, one an average-sized man, the other quite tall and broad. Both were shrouded in the blinding snow.

"Aren't you getting off to eat?" she asked Bella, still not turning around.

"Not hungry, and I have just enough money to get where I'm going. I'm fine."

Ashley faced her again. "We have food along if you're hungry. I'm sure Nick's men would share it for free if you really *are* hungry."

The woman smiled. "Oh, they'd share it, all right, but not likely for free. It just wouldn't be money they'd ask for."

Ashley felt her face redden. "Oh!" She looked away. "Well, if Nick or I told them to leave you alone, they would."

"Well, now, aren't you sweet? I appreciate that, but I can take care of myself. And I'm really not hungry. I have my own place in Bear River City, and that's the next stop. I'll be fine."

Ashley watched out the window again. "If you say so." Still no sign of Nick. She heard clunking sounds and knew it was wood being thrown into the wood box behind the engine. She heard more steam being let out, heard the whistle blow. She grew anxious, still unable to see Nick.

Someone climbed the steps into the passenger car, and Ashley figured him to be just another drifter like all the others. The snow was blowing so hard as he came inside that he still had his hat pulled down so that she couldn't see his face. He was a large man who wore a heavy, animal-skin coat, probably one made of buffalo shag. She'd seen a lot of those in Cheyenne. She looked away when he came closer, his body literally blocking the light from the windows across the way because of his brawny size. Ashley felt a chill when he stopped near where she sat. She could smell him ... the foul smell of a man who'd gone too long without a bath.

"Well now," he said in a deep voice, "this is just what I like—climbin' aboard a train car with a couple of whores on it."

Ashley shivered and refused to look at him.

"Don't be calling her a whore, mister," Bella told him. "*I'm* the whore. That's a married woman you're standing beside. Leave her alone."

Nick is nearby, Ashley reminded herself, her heart pounding over the sheer size of the man. She turned her head just enough to notice he wore a gun. *Stay calm,* she told herself. *Nick will come back any minute.*

"That red hair looks familiar. Look up here, Missy."

Ashley refused. "You'd better leave. My husband will be back any minute, and he won't like that you're talking to me."

"I ain't scared of no man, lady. I don't give a shit *where* your husband is, and I don't like no woman bein' snooty to me."

His voice sounded vaguely familiar.

"Come pick on me, you big galoot," Belle told him.

"I'll fuck you later, bitch."

Ashley cried out when he reached out and grasped hold of her chin, squeezing her jaw painfully and forcing her to look up at him.

Ashley recognized him immediately. *Abel MacIntyre!* She was so dumbfounded she couldn't find her voice.

Abel apparently recognized her in return. He leaned closer, gripping her jaw even tighter and leering at her. "What the fuck? Are you Ashley *Vale?*"

Ashley's eyes widened in total shock and terror. She was looking at a very big, intimidating man whose face was badly scarred. A black patch covered one eye. She screamed when Abel yanked her out of her seat by literally pulling on her hair and knocking off her hat.

"Hey! Let go of her!" Bella got out of her seat and ran down the aisle to pull at Abel's arm. In one quick movement he backhanded Bella and sent her flying half-way down the aisle, then jerked Ashley around in front of him, holding her against him by an arm tight around her waist.

"I read about you and Nick Calhoun in a newspaper," he told her. With his other hand he felt her breasts. "You turned into a whore—murdered some soldier you was messin' with.

Folks figured you were on your way out here with that big, worthless Irishman, but I sure never dreamed I'd actually run into you. Is he fuckin' you, little girl?"

Ashley struggled to get away, but it was impossible. He leaned down and nuzzled her neck, laughing. "Is it true? Is Calhoun the one who kidnapped you off a train that was takin' you to trial?"

"Let go of me! If Nick finds you, he'll kill you! He knows you're the one who killed my *mother*!"

"Really? And how would he know that?"

"Because one of his men heard you bragging about it a while back, you filthy coward!" Ashley continued struggling to get away as she spoke, but Abel kept her tight against him with one arm and squeezed her jaw again with his other hand.

"Why'd you kill my mother!" Ashley managed to yell through her half-closed jaw.

"Because I wanted to *fuck* her and she wouldn't have me!" Abel grinned through yellowed teeth. His breath was unbelievably foul. "And because your pa gave me this ugly face!" He yanked off his eye patch, and his hat went flying with it.

Ashley thought she might vomit at the sight. Abel had released her jaw to pull off the eye patch, and Ashley took the opportunity to kick him between the legs, but because of the thick layer of slips she wore, combind with his heavy buffalo-skin coat that hung long, he hardly felt a thing. He just jerked her close again. Ashley screamed Nick's name as loud as she could.

"Go ahead and call for that no-good," Abel growled. "I'll enjoy killin' him and takin' you off with me. We'll have a right good time. You *owe* me, Missy! I never got the chance to kill your pa or have at your ma. Now they're both gone, and it's your turn!"

Just then the conductor climbed aboard. "Hey! What's going on here?"

Abel pulled his gun and shot the man without warning. Ashley screamed Nick's name again, afraid he'd never hear her above the wind outside. Maybe he heard the gunshot. And those still waiting outside on the platform would have seen the poor conductor fall out of the train. That would get Nick's attention. She closed her eyes and turned her face away from Abel's own hideous face. He was unshaven, with tobacco stains in his beard, a horribly crooked nose, some missing teeth, and that ugly hole where his eye had been. A deep red scar streaked across his eye and cheek and was shaped almost like a bolt of lightning.

"What's wrong?" Abel asked her. "Can't look at me?" He jerked her face up again by another painful grip of her jaw. "Well, you just take a good look! I remember you were just as uppity as your ma back in Gainesville. I *wanted* that woman, but she wouldn't give me the time of day! And after what your pa did to me, she deserved what she got." He pressed her so tightly against him she thought he might break her ribs. "You'll die like your ma did, but not before I get between them pretty little legs of yours and show you what it's like to get fucked by a *real* man."

Abel tried to kiss her, putting his slovenly lips on her mouth, but Ashley pressed her own lips tight together. Abel nuzzled at her neck again while running his free hand over her breasts.

"Let her go!" Ashley heard Bella scream. The woman must have come around from the awful blow she'd taken.

"Shut up, bitch!"

Ashley heard a gunshot, and Bella screamed. No! Had he shot the poor woman? Bella was innocent of all of this. So was the conductor. She remembered Abel MacIntyre being a bully, but she'd never dreamed he could be this cruel and ruthless. She screamed Nick's name again, hoping he could hear her above the blowing wind outside.

"You think I'm crazy, don't you? Maybe I *am*, but it's because of this injury your *pa* gave me." He lightened up slightly with his grip, then grabbed Ashley's hair and gripped it tightly. "Damned if you didn't turn into a beautiful woman." His foul breath turned her stomach.

"Let me go!" she begged again, pushing at him. "I'm carrying!"

Abel jerked her tighter against him. "Pregnant, huh? By that big Irishman?"

"He's my husband!"

"The hell he is." Abel grinned. "He's a no-good, just like he was back in Gainesville. He just wanted to *fuck* you back then, and now he finally got his wish, but he ain't got the balls to come after somebody like me."

"Let me go or he'll *kill* you."

Abel tried to kiss her again, then suddenly stopped, sobering. He jerked Ashley around, pinning her back against him and resting his free hand on the gun at his side. Ashley stared wide-eyed at Nick, who stood there with a gun pointed against Abel's forehead. The look in his eyes was unlike anything she'd seen there before. Except for the day he beat Sid MacIntyre near to death.

"Nick!" Ashley managed to choke out his name.

"Let go of her, or I'll put a hole through your head so big people will be able to see out the other side," Nick sneered, keeping his gaze only on Abel.

"Well, now, if it isn't the Irish potato farmer," Abel growled. "I'll be Goddamned! I remember you. And I know all about you and this bitch. You're both wanted. I heard you were both headed this way, and I can hardly believe we actually ran into each other."

Nick cocked his gun. "You have only a couple of seconds left, MacIntyre. I remember your ugly ass, too, and your *son's!* I killed Sid for attacking Ashley the way you're attacking her now."

Abel's eyes widened.

"You didn't know that, did you?" Nick snarled. "Because when you went back to Gainesville to murder Ashley's mother, you didn't even bother looking for Sid. Your brain's so fucked up, maybe you forgot you even had a son, you murdering bastard! Now, let go of my wife, or you can join your son in hell." Nick's eyes were so dark that even Ashley was afraid of him.

Ashley felt Abel hesitating. His grip relaxed a little, and she used the opportunity to quickly duck down and wiggle out of the startled man's grip. She scrambled away on her hands and knees, moving past Nick's feet and staying down as Nick shoved the end of his gun harder against Abel's forehead.

"Don't be reaching for your gun," Nick warned. "The minute you do, I'll blow your brains out."

An animal-like look of the hunt for prey moved into Abel's good eye. "Go ahead, Irishman. That's the only way you'll be able to get the better of me."

Nick shook his head. "Blowing your head off right now'd be too easy. I mean to kill you, MacIntyre, but not this way. You need to die from a beating. The way Ashley's *mother* died."

"Nick, no," Ashley whimpered.

"Get to the back of the car and stay there," Nick ordered her. "And *you,*" he told Abel, "get off this car!"

"Please don't do this, Nick!" Ashley warned.

"Well, well. So, you intend to fight it out with *fists?*" Abel laughed in more of a growl than genuine laughter. "That's fine with me, Calhoun. If that's how you want it, I'll beat you bloody and throw you over a cliff and have at your woman. You should listen to her when she asks you not to try me that way." He backed away slightly. "Go ahead. Take my gun, and we'll go outside where there's plenty of room for me to kick in your balls and gouge out your eyes."

Ashley put an arm to her stomach, feeling like vomiting. "Nick, just *shoot* him!" She could hardly believe she'd said it, but the alternative...

"Not good enough for the likes of this trash," Nick answered, his dark, nearly evil gaze boring into the man. "You stay here, Ashley. That's an order!"

Ashley knew he'd gone beyond reason. He never called her Ashley. The way he'd said her name told her there was no arguing.

"Let's go." Nick backed Abel down the steps. Both men left the car, and Ashley rushed to a window seat to watch in terror as they handed over their weapons and removed their coats, then began circling each other.

Chapter Thirty-Six

Ashley frantically glanced at Bella, torn between helping the poor woman and keeping an eye on her husband, who could be killed at any moment. She was glad to see a man had come aboard from the back end of the train car and was helping Bella. Against Nick's orders, Ashley hurried to the front steps of the car to watch Nick, wishing there was something she could do to help. A crowd had gathered, most of them cheering for Nick. She saw Buck, Sam, Seth and Ringer in front of the crowd, all ready to step in if Abel pulled something dirty.

Renaldo made his way through the crowd to the train and pulled the conductor's dead body farther away from the platform. He climbed up the steps to stand near Ashley. "Are you all right, *Señora*?"

"Yes. Oh, Renaldo, Abel will kill Nick in a fistfight!"

"I do not think you know Nick's true temper." Renaldo took her arm. "You should move back inside in case there is shooting," he warned. "You can watch through a window, *Señora*."

"I don't know if I can stand to watch at all."

Abel landed the first blow, and Ashley grasped her stomach.

"Come," Renadlo said. "Come inside. I will stay with you."

"Renaldo, Abel MacIntyre is incredibly strong! He broke my mother's neck. And he won't fight fair."

"Nick, he is strong, too, and very good with his fists." Renaldo urged her inside and to a window seat. "I have seen him fight. Some say his Irish temper makes him stronger than the normal man."

"But Abel is, too, and he's not normal as far as being fair." Ashley winced as the two men slammed fists into each other, falling, rolling, kicking. Nick landed a hard blow that sent Abel stumbling into a stack of flour barrels. One of them broke over his head. Abel got back up, his hair and shirt covered in flour.

The weather cleared, and the sun only made the blood on both men's faces seem more gruesome.

"*Señora*, you should not watch," Renaldo suggested. "Go and sit on the other side of the car."

"No. I don't want to watch, but it's Nick. I have to watch, just to assure myself that Abel isn't killing him." Ashley huddled into her cape, pulling it closer under her chin, as though doing so would somehow protect Nick, too. She winced and fought tears as the fight grew even more vicious.

Men cheered and shouted with raised fists as Abel charged into Nick's mid-section, shoving him hard against a hitching post. Ashley could see the pain on Nick's face when his back hit the post hard. Abel reared back and made ready to kick Nick between the legs, but Nick turned to his side just as Abel's foot landed into nothingness, causing the man to fall backward onto his rear end.

Nick grabbed Abel by the waist of his pants and the front of his shirt and literally threw him into a pile of wood. Some of the wood tumbled onto Abel, and before Abel could recover, Nick grabbed him again, this time by the back of his shirt, yanking him up and spinning him around before slamming a fist into his already-broken nose. He began hitting Abel over and over again, while the men watching roared with supportive yells of "That's it!" and "Hit him again!" and "Kill the bastard!"

Abel's face was so covered in blood that it was hard to tell where his eyes and nose and lips were. But Nick's face wasn't all that much better. Ashley could see his hands were covered in blood.

"Oh, Nick," she lamented, looking away.

Renaldo put an arm around her. "It is better you do not look any more, yes? It is not good for you to watch."

Ashley could hear the blows, and with every crunch she winced harder and buried her head into Renaldo's shoulder. "Tell me Nick is winning."

"Oh, mostly he is winning. You are right about how strong that other man is, but he killed your sweet mother. Nick will not let that go, *Señora*."

Ashley finally turned back to the window to see both men rolling on the platform in front of the ticket office. The snow there had long been swept away by the vicious fight. Horses skittered sideways. Barrels and wood and stacked crates and luggage went flying every which way as each man fell against them. Finally, Nick landed three hard blows in a row to Abel's face and sent him flying into some of the men who'd been watching. Abel grabbed a gun from one of them, ripping it out of the man's holster.

"Oh, my God!" Ashley yelled. "Renaldo, Abel has a gun!"

The crowd quieted and backed up more as Abel stood there, panting and waving the gun. "I killed Patricia Vale," he snarled. "But you say you killed my *son*. That makes us even!"

"No, it doesn't," Nick shouted back. "Pat Vale was a decent, innocent woman who couldn't defend herself and who never did you any harm. Your son was a fucking bully, just like you. He was attacking Ashley in the barn, and I stopped him. And what difference does it make to you? You never even tried to see him when you went back to Gainesville."

Abel spit blood and stumbled a little, looking confused. "I...can't remember..." His words were slurred. "There's some things...I can't remember...on account of what...what Howard Vale did to me. But I...remember *you*! You probably killed my son...because you wanted to fuck that girl yourself."

Ashley felt sick at the remark.

"Do not listen to his talk, *Señora*. He is a crazy man," Renaldo told her.

"You're scum, Abel MacIntyre," Nick shouted. "You don't deserve to be alive."

"Here, Nick!" Ringer tossed his six-gun to Nick. It landed on the ground in front of him.

Abel grinned. "Go ahead. Pick it up, you bastard. I'll shoot your fuckin' ass."

The crowd seemed to freeze for a moment, as did Ashley and Renaldo.

"You can do it, *mi amigo*," Renaldo said softly, gently pressing his hands on Ashley's shoulders. "That man is stumbling and confused."

Ashley noticed the rest of Nick's men had their hands on their guns. Then Nick moved so fast she hardly realized what happened. She didn't even see him pick up Ringer's gun, but she heard him fire it. She thought she heard three shots, but she wasn't sure if Abel had fired his own gun or not. Abel just stood there, staring at Nick. The crowd quieted and waited. Smoke drifted from the ends of both guns, and Nick still held his straight out, pointed at Abel.

Ashley noticed blood dripping off his left hand. "Nick!" She started to get up.

"Wait!" Renaldo told her, gripping her shoulders tighter. "That big man has not dropped his gun yet."

Abel stood there so long that Ashley wondered if he'd been shot at all. He finally dropped his gun, then went to his knees and stayed in that position for a few more seconds before falling on his face. Nick stood there a while longer, still panting from the fight, his face bloody and bruised, more blood dripping from his left hand.

Seth ran over to Abel and rolled him over, feeling for a pulse. He looked at Nick then. "He's dead!"

The crowd quieted, and Owen Truelove walked up to Nick, nodding and smiling rather sadly. "Well now, I reckon' you'll fit in just fine out here," he told Nick.

Nick just stood there a moment looking at Abel, then turned to see Ashley watching from the train window. He stumbled toward the train, and Seth and Buck hurried to help him climb inside. Renaldo moved out of his seat and let Ashley go to him.

"No!" Nick backed away. "I'm filthy, and bloody."

Renaldo quickly removed his wool jacket and put it around Ashley. "Cover yourself with this, *Señora*," he told her. "I don't care if blood gets on the jacket."

Ashley quickly removed her cape and pulled on Renaldo's jacket, then ran up to Nick. "Nick, you've been shot. Sit down and let us help you."

He jerked away from Seth and Buck. He reached out and touched Ashley's face. "Tell me you're okay first." He ran a thumb over her lips. "Did he hurt you?"

"He didn't have a chance," Ashley answered, refusing to tell him Abel had indeed hurt her jaw and touched her breasts and had put his foul mouth over hers. "I'm all right."

"The baby—"

"I'm just fine," Ashley repeated.

"*Baby*?" Seth exclaimed. "You two having a baby?"

"Nick, let's take care of your arm," Seth told him, urging him to sit down in one of the passenger seats. "It's just a crease, but we'd better wrap it up."

"I'm sorry, Ash. I promised you'd be safe. That I'd protect you."

"You *did* protect me. Look at me. I'm all right. Please sit down and let someone look at your arm."

Nick finally obliged, but more because his wounds from the fight and the gunshot were beginning to set in and weaken him. For the next few minutes, all was bedlam as some of the men went for supplies and returned with bandages and whiskey, while others clamored around Bella James, who was awake and flirting with the men helping her. Someone came in with a bucket of snow and dug some out to hold against the cuts and bruises on Nick's face.

It all seemed so unreal to Ashley. One minute she'd been talking to Bella. The next she was jerked to her feet by the one man she'd dreaded ever seeing again, her mother's killer, a man she never imagined could end up right in front of her in such big country. She sat stunned, aching to hold her husband, to kiss his cuts and bruises. He kept watching her in return, deep concern in his eyes. Eyes that moments before burned with a need to kill, but now were full of love. He kept asking if she was okay, and she kept reassuring him she was fine.

"Ash!" The next thing she knew, Nick had pulled her up from her seat and into his arms. "My God, Ash! I said no harm would come to you out here and look what just happened! I'm so sorry, baby. I saw you in his grip, and I was so afraid he'd break your neck like he did your mother."

He rocked her in his arms for several minutes while people moved about in the car.

"Nick, I was so scared I'd watch you die!" Ashley wrapped her arms around his middle and hugged him tight, the tears coming then.

"It's okay now. I told you I'd find that sonofabitch and kill him. Now it's done. We'll get you someplace where you can rest, and I can clean up and get rid of these filthy clothes. My God, I was going to keep hunting for that man. I never dreamed we'd run into him this way."

Ashley breathed deeply of his familiar scent. Moments before, he'd been hardly recognizable because of the murderous look in his eyes, yet now he held her so lovingly, saying he was sorry over and over. He'd come at Abel like a grizzly bear protecting her young, but now his touch was gentle and loving.

"What would I have done if he'd killed you!" Ashley lamented.

"He never would have gotten away with you," Nick answered. "My men would never have let that happen."

She leaned back and looked up at him. "Oh, darling, your face!"

He managed a light smile, but Ashley could tell it hurt to do so. "That bad, huh?"

She reached up and touched his face gently. "It doesn't matter. You're alive." She quickly wiped at her tears. "Nick, Abel shot the conductor for no good reason, and he hit Bella so hard, and then he shot her, all because she tried to help me, and she doesn't even know me."

They both looked toward the back of the car to see Ringer and the mountain man helping Bella now. Buck and Seth joined them, the four of them half falling over each other in their efforts to impress her.

"Bella and I talked a little before Abel came into the car." Ashley met his gaze again, and saw his eyes were just beginning to soften from their terrible darkness minutes earlier. "I can't believe she risked her life the way she did."

"It's like men have been telling us. Out here everybody, helps everybody. You can't judge people as all bad in places like this." He gently stroked her cheeks. "Every man over there would've stood up to Abel to defend you. I guarantee it."

The train engineer came aboard. "We have to leave pretty quick, folks. I have a schedule to keep. We'll be taking the conductor's body to the next stop."

"I'm okay, boys," Ashley heard Bella telling the men. "I've been beat on before, and this gunshot is just a flesh wound. It's all wrapped up, and I can go on without any more help."

They all fussed over her, and in spite of the horror of what had just happened, Ashley couldn't help smiling inwardly at how the men all did their best to make an impression on Miss Bella James. Asking if she needed any water, finding out where she was headed, checking the bandages on her arm and if there was any more they could do for her. In spite of her injuries, Bella laughed and flirted with them.

The engineer came inside yet again and told everyone the train had to get under way.

"All who are going on, have a seat. The rest of you *must* get off now. The Union Pacific prides itself on being on time!"

The men still stumbled over each other tending to Bella. She insisted she was all right in spite of a purple welt growing on her right cheekbone and bloody bandages around her arm. "I'm a survivor, boys, and I'm headed for the last stop—Bear River City. I have my own saloon there, if any of you would like to come visit." She patted each one on the cheek. "All of you need to get off and go wherever you're going and let me do the same. I'm grateful for your help."

Nick got up from where he sat and kept an arm around Ashley for support as he led her back to where the men stood around Bella. "Time to get off, boys. We have a lot to do to get on our way to Brown's Park. Seth, you and Buck go get Ashley's bags from where she was sitting."

The two men did as he asked while the others grumbled about having to leave Bella.

"Hell, Nick, we'd all like to take this lady with us," Ringer told him.

"I'm sure you would," Nick answered.

The said their good-byes to Bella and Nick put out his hand. "Thank you for trying to help my wife. I'm sorry you got hurt over it."

Bella squeezed his hand. "Oh, I've been handled rough before. Your wife seems like a real fine lady. She didn't deserve what that man did. And, I might add, it's too bad what he did to your handsome face."

"I'll heal. A good brawl is nothing new to me."

"Apparently." Bella glanced at Ashley. "Take good care of that man." Her blue eyes sparkled teasingly. "He's a gem." She moved her gaze to Nick. "And you do the same with this pretty wife of yours."

"No worries there."

"Thank you, Bella," Ashley told her. "You shouldn't have risked your life like that. Abel MacIntyre has no respect for women, no matter what their walk of life. That man killed my mother back in Texas."

"Oh, you poor thing!" Bella reached out and took her hand. "I always say things work out for a reason. God led you clear out here to make sure the matter about your mother was settled. I say that means you belong in Outlaw Country. Don't be worried about this crazy, wild plce, young lady. There really are some good people here."

"This train will get under way in thirty seconds," the engineer shouted from outside. "All aboard!"

"You can come with us if you'd like," Ashley told Bella, hardly able to believe she'd just invited a lady of the night to join them. "I'd like to find some way to thank you, and I hate to see you go off alone, injured like you are." She noticed the sudden lonely look in Bella's eyes.

"You really don't have to worry about me, honey. I hope you two find what you're looking for and don't have any more trouble." She glanced through a window across the aisle. "See? It's just like I told you. The sun is out already. Get going, and have a good life."

The train whistle blew again, and Ashley thought how strange it was that a fight and a shootout were apparently as common here as having lunch. Back home there would have been a huge crowd around Abel's dead body, but these people had returned to whatever they were doing before the fight began. She said a last good-bye to Bella as Nick urged her off the train. When they stepped outside, Ashley noticed someone had dragged Abel's body off to the side of the station platform, and the body of the dead conductor was gone. Apparently, he'd been loaded onto the train.

One more blast of the train whistle told people there would be no more waiting. Ashley wondered how Bella had ended up living the life of a prostitute. Was Bella even her real name? She felt a deep loneliness at realizing she'd likely never again see the woman who might've saved her life by buying her a little time.

The train engineer pulled a chain and blasted one more long whistle, and black smoke billowed from the smokestack. Steam hissed and shot into the cold air in white clouds that again hid people on the platform, including Abel MacIntyre's bloody, dead body. The locomotive began its rhythmic chug as the wheels spun on freezing cold rails before grabbing hold and carrying the train and its supplies and passengers out of Bitter Creek.

"What should we do with the woman-killer?" Buck asked Nick. He nodded toward Abel.

Ashley noticed the cuts on Nick's face were already scabbing over, and his cheeks and chin were bruised and swelling. He looked east along the tracks that had brought them this far.

"We came around the side of a mountain only about a quarter of a mile back, if that far," he told Buck. "I remember how steep it was—at least a couple hundred feet down on one side—all jagged rocks. Tie his body to the back of a horse and take it there. Throw his body over that cliff and let the buzzards and cougars have it. The man has enough meat and fat on him to provide the animals a good meal for a month."

Ashley turned away from the sight. Part of her wondered how Nick and the others could be so cold about what to do with Abel's body, but she knew that out here she'd have to get used to such attitudes. Men like Nick could be gentle and loving, while out of pure survival they also had to sometimes be ruthless, and often had to take the law into their own hands. She had to admit that Abel MacIntyre deserved no better than to be left to the elements and the animals.

Buck left, and she heard him explaining to Renaldo and the others what they should do with Abel's body. "A couple of you help me out," she heard him tell them.

In the distance the train whistle cried out somewhere in the mountains. It had already disappeared, and Ashley couldn't help feeling sorry for Bella James and how lonely she must be. She felt lucky to be safe and loved. The sun warmed her shoulders. Yes, just like Bella had told her, the weather here could change in minutes.

She glanced up at Nick, who was giving more orders to the men. He was the man she knew again. And now no one seemed concerned that Nick's men were dragging Abel's body away to be dumped without ceremony.

Nick pulled her aside and looked her over. "Are you really all right?"

"I should ask you the same thing."

"And I'd have to say no. I'm dizzy and I hurt like a sonofabitch, but I'm more concerned about you. Did that man do anything that could have harmed your insides? The baby?"

Ashley wilted against him. "No. Oh, Nick, I can't believe any of this. I can't believe we ran into Abel MacIntyre, and now he's dead. After all the horror of that day I found my mother...all we've been through since then...it's like it's all finally ended with Abel's death. Now we can move on. That awful day they almost hanged you back in Gainesville...that trip I made...It all seems like years and years ago. I feel like something or someone was leading me out here, to live my life with the man I've loved for so long."

Nick put his arms around her. "Owen says the weather is decent enough that we can head for Brown's Park come morning."

She looked up at him. "And home?"

"And home." Nick winced as he leaned down to kiss her cheek. "Welcome to Outlaw Country, Mrs. Calhoun. Much as I hurt, I'd sure like to find a way to make love to you tonight."

Ashley wanted to both laugh and cry. Here she was, getting ready to live among a lawless breed of men in lawless country, yet she'd never been happier, or felt more free. She was with the man she'd loved since she was ten years old, and Nick Calhoun would never let anything happen to her.

Somewhere in the mountains the train whistle echoed its lonely wail. Buck and Seth rode by with Abel's body tied over the back of Buck's horse, while other men began hitching horses to Ashley's wagon. She remembered the day she'd packed it, so sad, so scared, never dreaming her trip north would lead her back to Nick Calhoun and into an entirely new life in the grand western mountains.

So, this was Outlaw Country, and this would be home.

From the Author...

I hope you have enjoyed JOURNEY TO HIGH LONESOME, the third book in my series about men of the Outlaw Trail. I plan to write more books for this series, which I will announce on Facebook and on my web site at www.rosannebittner.com, where you can "one-click" order my books, and where you can find information on all the other 70 (+) books I have written.

If you want to read more about Moses Tucker, the bearded man who gave Abel MacIntyre a good beating early in this book, look for my story LAWLESS LOVE, published many years ago and recently reissued with a new cover. The book is available from Amazon in print and for Kindle. Books #1 and #2 of this series – RIDE THE HIGH LONESOME and LAWMAN IN THE HIGH LONESOME are also available from Amazon.

I love to hear from my readers, so visit my Facebook Author Page and join my Street Team, where you can leave comments and also learn about contests and giveaways.

Happy reading!

About the Author:

USA TODAY best-seller Rosanne Bittner has written and published 72 novels for various publishers over the past 40 years. Her first love is American history, the Old West and Native Americans. Her well-researched books cover real events and locations involving the birth and growth of America. She has won numerous writing awards, including a RITA nomination from Romance Writers of America for SONG OF THE WOLF and a WILLA award from Women Writing the West for WHERE HEAVEN BEGINS. She was named "Queen of Western Romance" by Romantic Times Reviews, who nominated her second "Outlaw" book, DO NOT FORSAKE ME, as best Western romance for 2015. Most of Rosanne's novels have garnered over 95% five-star reviews from Amazon readers and great reviews from Publisher's Weekly and USA TODAY. Rosanne belongs to several historical societies and is an active volunteer in a home-town charity organization. She and her husband of 55 years live in southwest Michigan.

www.rosannebittner.com – www.rosannebittner.blogspot.com –

Twitter – Facebook – Goodreads – Instagram – Amazon – Sourcebooks and more!